Mistaken Identity Crisis

Mistaken Identity Crisis

Braxton Campus Mystery Book 4

James J. Cudney

Acknowledgments

Writing a book is not an achievement an individual person can accomplish on his or her own. There are always people who contribute in a multitude of ways, sometimes unwittingly, throughout the journey from discovering the idea to drafting the last word. *Mistaken Identity Crisis: A Braxton Campus Mystery* has had many supporters since its inception in February 2019, but before the concept even sparked in my mind, my passion for writing was nurtured by others.

First thanks go to my parents, Jim and Pat, for always believing in me as a writer as well as teaching me how to become the person I am today. Their unconditional love and support have been the primary reason I'm accomplishing my goals. Through the guidance of my extended family and friends, who consistently encouraged me to pursue my passion, I found the confidence to take chances in life. With Winston and Baxter by my side, I was granted the opportunity to make my dreams of publishing this novel come true. I'm grateful to everyone for pushing me each day to complete this sixth book.

Mistaken Identity Crisis was cultivated through the interaction, feedback, and input of several talented beta readers. I'd like to thank Laura Albert, Mary Deal, Misty Swafford, Anne Jacobs, Nina D. Silva, Carla @ CarlaLovesToRead, Tyler Colins, Anne Foster, Lisa M. Berman, and Valerie for supplying insight and perspective during the development of the story, setting, and character arcs. I am indebted to them for finding all the proofreading misses, grammar mistakes, and awkward phrases. A major thanks to Tyler for encouraging me to be stronger in my word choice and providing several pages of suggestions to convert good language into fantastic language! A special call-out goes to Shalini for countless conversations helping me to fine-tune every aspect of the setting, characters, and plot. She read every version and offered a tremendous amount of her time to advise me on this book over several weeks. I am beyond grateful for her help. Any mistakes are my own from misunderstanding our discussions.

Much gratitude to all my friends and mentors at Moravian College. Although no murders have ever taken place there, the setting of this series is loosely based on my former multi-campus school set in Pennsylvania. Most of the locations are completely fabricated, but the concept of Millionaire's Mile exists. I only made up the name, grand estates, and cable car system.

Thank you to Creativia / Next Chapter for publishing *Mistaken Identity Crisis* and paving the road for more books to come. I look forward to our continued partnership.

Welcome to Braxton, Wharton County
(Map drawn by Timothy J. R. Rains, Cartographer)

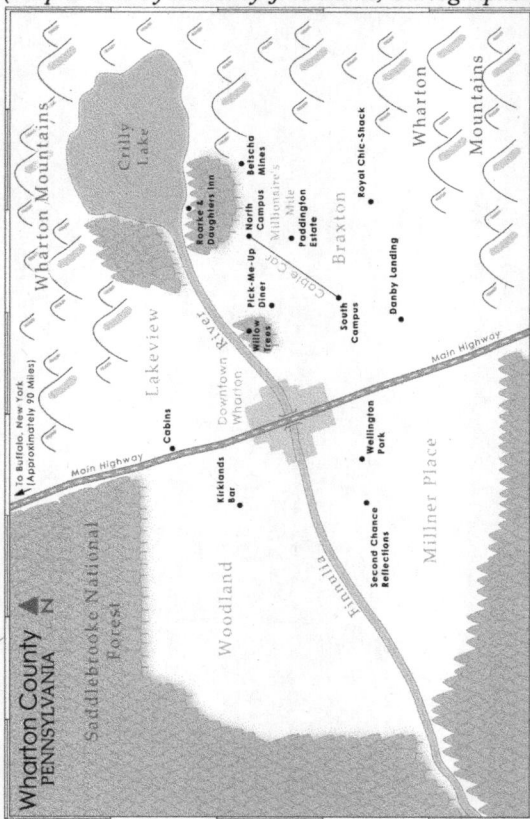

Who's Who in the Braxton Campus Mysteries?

Ayrwick Family

- *Kellan:* Main Character, Braxton professor, amateur sleuth

- *Wesley:* Kellan's father, Braxton's retired President

- *Violet:* Kellan's mother, Braxton's Admissions Director

- *Emma:* Kellan's daughter with Francesca

- *Eleanor:* Kellan's younger sister, owns Pick-Me-Up Diner

- *Gabriel:* Kellan's younger brother, dating Sam

- *Nana D:* Kellan's grandmother, also known as Seraphina Danby

- *Deirdre Danby:* Kellan's aunt, Nana D's daughter, Timothy's fiancée

- *Francesca Castigliano:* Kellan's estranged wife

- *Vincenzo & Cecilia Castigliano:* Francesca's parents, run the mob

Braxton Campus

- *Ursula Power:* President, Myriam's wife

- *Myriam Castle:* Chair of Communications Dept., Ursula's wife

- *Fern Terry:* Dean of Student Affairs, Arthur's mom

- *Arthur Terry:* Engaged to Jennifer, Fern's son

- *Maggie Roarke:* Head Librarian, dating Connor, Helena's sister

- *Quint Crawford:* Electrician, Bertha's son

- *Raquel Salvado:* Current student

- *Imogene Grey:* Lara's daughter, Paul's fiancée, former college sorority girl

- *Siobhan Walsh:* Office Manager, current student

- *Krissy Stanton:* Marcus's daughter, former college sorority girl

Wharton County Residents

- *Cristiano Vargas:* Runs the mob, kidnapped Francesca

- *Bertha Crawford:* Quint's mother, Silas's brother-in-law

- *Tiffany Nutberry:* Lydia's daughter, former college sorority girl

- *Lydia Nutberry:* Tiffany's mother, runs Whispering Pines Funeral Home

- *Helena Roarke:* Maggie's sister, former college sorority girl

- *Nicholas Endicott:* Construction company owner, former college student

- *Karen Stoddard:* Restaurant owner

- *Cheney Stoddard:* Karen's son, was dating Helena

- *Timothy Paddington:* Deirdre's fiancé, Jennifer's brother

- *Eustacia Paddington:* Head of Paddington family, aunt to Jennifer and Tim

- *Jennifer Paddington:* Engaged to Arthur, Timothy's sister

- *Sam Taft:* Dating Gabriel, nephew to Jennifer and Timothy

- *Chef Manny:* Cook at Eleanor's diner

Wharton County Administration

- *Silas Crawford:* Former Sheriff, Bertha's brother-in-law

- *April Montague:* Current Sheriff

- *Connor Hawkins:* Detective, Kellan's best friend, dating Maggie

- *Paul Dodd:* New Braxton Town Councilman, Imogene's fiancé

- *Marcus Stanton:* Former Braxton Town Councilman, Krissy's father

- *Judge Grey:* Wharton County Magistrate, Imogene's grandfather

- *Lara Bouvier:* Reporter, Imogene's mother

Chapter 1

"The first time we met, I knew you'd cause me to gray prematurely," April griped while clawing at clumps of her brassy blonde hair and squeezing her golden badge until a star-shaped imprint marked her left palm. "But I honestly thought I'd have a better chance at predicting the Pennsylvania state lottery numbers before guessing you'd paint a bullseye on your own forehead for the Castigliano mob family. Seriously, Kellan, you've made a royal mess of this situation. Are they gonna take potshots at me next?"

We bantered steadfastly in her downtown office at the Wharton County administrative building with the door glued shut. Very few people knew what'd happened to my supposedly dead wife, Francesca. I shrugged and offered my best apology face, which unintentionally resembled a confused puppy in search of a warm place to sleep, rather than a truly sorrowful man who'd never intended to wreak such havoc. "We've covered this several times in the last three weeks. I should've immediately informed you that Francesca's family faked her death. I didn't know what to do until that last note from Cristiano Vargas confirmed they'd kidnapped her as a revenge tactic to punish the Castiglianos." I rested both hands and my chin on the heavily papered desk, grinned widely as if my jaw were about to unhinge, and blinked twice through stylish glasses to endear myself to the sheriff.

At least she'd stopped calling me *Little Ayrwick*. Of all the nicknames I'd heard during my thirty-two years, that was the most insulting. There was nothing *little* about me anymore. Upon graduating from Braxton a decade ago, I'd transformed from an awkward middle child in a complex, overachieving family into what many women eagerly deemed a devilishly handsome and well-built guy blessed with clever wit and a charming personality. Don't get me wrong, I'm not an egomaniac. I've merely settled into myself and accepted the positive and the negative. Lately, there were tons more negative than I cared to tolerate. At least Nana D still called me *brilliant one*, which melted my heart every time.

"That's your apology?" April vigorously shook her head and slammed a *Tweety Bird* coffee mug on the desk's smooth metal surface. Drops of cold, muddy brown liquid splashed across it and landed on my upper lip. "*I'm sorry*, I didn't mean to do that," she whined repentantly while handing me a napkin from a squeaky drawer. "Oh, and in case you forgot, that's how you ask for forgiveness."

Had it not been for the tiniest of curls at the sides of her sarcastic mouth, I wouldn't have known April was teasing me. We'd spent an inordinate amount of time joined at the hip, organizing everything that'd happened in the last two-and-a-half years since *the accident*. Okay, backstory time—Francesca and I had arrived separately at a Thanksgiving party because I'd been working out of town earlier in the week. Our daughter, Emma, begged to ride home with me—a monumental blessing in disguise—rather than her mother. Little did I know at the time, Francesca's parents, Vincenzo and Cecilia Castigliano, had orchestrated the entire façade. When I received the call that my wife had been struck and killed by a drunk driver, I did my best to rally with the help of Nana D, my five-foot-tall spitfire grandmother. Meanwhile, Francesca lived covertly in the Castigliano mansion until her parents could divine a way to resolve the turf war with Las Vargas, the rival mafia family controlling much of the West Coast. Two years had zipped by without a viable solution or anyone learning their secret.

A few months ago, Emma and I moved back home to Braxton, the small town in north-central Pennsylvania where I'd been raised and now worked as an assistant professor specializing in communications and film studies. Francesca chose that moment to materialize from hiding, jealous and angry about the sudden inability to watch her daughter grow up in LA. After I refused to *hibernate in captivity*, she took off, letting her parents and me think she was visiting all the places we'd once vacationed in—a blissful trip down memory lane. At some point, Cristiano Vargas had discovered Francesca was alive, captured my not-so-dead wife, and forced her to mail postcards from every location to dangle us in a state of confusion. Now, we pondered their next move.

"I'm sorry, April. I know you intended to leave this spectacle of intense drama when you relocated from Buffalo, but I'm confident we'll find a solution." I wiped the coffee from my lip and internally chuckled over her persnickety comments. "I should teach you to brew a better cup of joe. I guess it's true that cops will drink any sludge someone—"

"Don't continue with that stereotypical, inflammatory insult unless you want me to handcuff you to my desk and head out for the day!" April released a long pent-up sigh and shuffled through stained papers in a worn manila folder. "Let's focus on our next steps. The Castiglianos will soon arrive in Braxton, and they better have answers. I agreed not to *formally* include the FBI until we received an official ransom request. We also need proof Francesca is alive before they'll get further involved."

April and I hadn't been friends previously, especially because I'd unexpectedly solved four murders sooner than she had—not a helpful icebreaker for our relationship. She mostly viewed me as a prickly thorn that irritated every nerve in her body. We'd brokered a tepid alliance in the last three weeks, and I convinced myself that the intense display of awe-inducing fireworks in her office, when our fingers had accidentally brushed against one another, was only a freakish blip on the radar. Then, a visceral flash of lightning surged inside my body and a sensual, steamy dream left me quite flushed and bewildered. I was technically still married and shouldn't have welcomed those types of thoughts about other women, right?

Once the war ended between the two families, Francesca could reveal herself to the rest of the world, and we'd deal with the repercussions. I only cared about the impact on our seven-year-old daughter. Emma didn't deserve this level of pain and confusion. Neither did I, but in the few encounters I'd already had with Francesca upon her triumphant reincarnation, it'd grown clear we were both different people. As a good Catholic—my family attended church on Sundays—divorce was a tricky solution. I knew I loved Francesca, but I was no longer in love with her. After all the lies and deception, how could I forgive her? Yes, her life had been in danger from Las Vargas, but she could've told me the truth years ago. I'd only discovered the reality of her shady family business by accident after she 'died.'

"Cristiano's latest update said he'd contact me soon with next steps. Maybe he'll offer easily attainable ransom terms for the Castiglianos. Then, this whole mess will blow over." All remaining confidence drained from my body with each reticent word. "Ugh! Why am I in the middle of this quandary? Las Vargas should work directly with Francesca's parents for her safe release."

"Excellent point. Perhaps your uniquely innate charm just begs for more attention? Regardless, I'm collecting evidence on the Castigliano drug-trafficking exploits to put them away for good. Someone will go to prison over this entire ordeal. I won't be able to protect her, you know," April said convincingly with a pointed stare. "I get she's your wife, but the mafia princess committed several crimes. I'm glad you never collected any insurance payments upon her death."

"I was a fool not to ask more questions about her background when we'd met." Although my immediate family members were a fantastic crew, the Ayrwicks also liked to pry into each other's business much too often. When I'd moved to Los Angeles to escape their clutches, an all-encompassing, powerful first love had blinded me from recognizing the truth. Francesca and I married way too quickly, and before long, I'd obtained my PhD, gotten a job as an assistant director at a Hollywood television show, and become a father upon Emma's arrival in this world. We lived a good life, but I'd always known something important was missing between Francesca and me.

"We'll sort it out, Kellan. You're going through a lot, but you can't tell anyone else until we dismantle Las Vargas. Anyway, I have to follow up on another jewelry heist that happened last week."

"I've been meaning to ask Nana D about those pesky robberies. Anything you can share?"

April swallowed heavily. "Jewelry was stolen. Victims are unhappy. Is that what you need to know, oh holy meddlesome one? Don't even think about inserting yourself into another one of my—"

"Blah, blah, blah. I read the papers and have some clue, April. I'll just ask Nana D. She tends to dig up the latest facts. I vaguely recall something about an unusual calling card being left behind, right?"

"I'd rather not discuss it. The ineptitude of the former sheriff still infuriates me. My predecessor had a penchant for burying facts from his townspeople." April grunted and shook her head.

"Nana D claims he took bribes to hide petty crimes," I said, hoping to keep her talking about it. "Maybe you and I should compare notes about the case. I *have* been helpful in the past."

"And we're officially done here," April muttered as she advanced toward me with alarming concentration in her eyes. "Let's talk tomorrow about your wife's kidnapping." Moist, hot breath from her lips passed over mine, and her skin smelled like black peppercorns and coriander—spicy yet fresh.

Although tempting comfort swayed between us like a pendulum jam-packed with uncertainty over its destination, I retreated before April and I approached a line we weren't prepared to cross. Too many intimate moments had encircled us lately, and I couldn't fathom how to properly interpret them. "Sure, I'll update you as soon as I hear from Cristiano."

Leaving her office, I noticed my reflection in the shiny glass pane of the door. Several days of dirty-blond stubble peppered my cheeks and chin, and dark circles occupied the sunken spaces below my disconcerted blue eyes. At least I'd managed to comb my frequently untamable hair, so I didn't look horribly disheveled. Nana D would slap my bottom silly—her words, not mine—for drawing shame to her, especially now that she'd won the election to become the new mayor of Wharton County.

* * *

Later that Saturday afternoon, I drove to Wellington Park in Millner Place to celebrate Nana D's seventy-fifth birthday in style with the party of the century. Millner Place and Braxton made up two of the four towns in Wharton County—the others, Woodland in the northwest and Lakeview in the northeast. Ninety miles south of Buffalo, New York, our county was one of the earliest settlements in Pennsylvania and had been founded by my ancestors.

"Is today the double wedding, Daddy?" Emma asked as I steered the SUV into a narrow spot.

Aunt Deirdre, a famous novelist and one of my mother's siblings, had returned from England and coordinated Nana D's party while simultaneously planning her own upcoming nuptials to Timothy Paddington, an international business mogul.

"Nope, that's in two weeks on Independence Day," I reminded my precocious daughter. Timothy's sister was also engaged, prompting their family to suggest a double wedding to make it easy on all the guests. Both couples had only recently met one another, and it made more sense as a way to reunite the

Paddington family who'd experienced several traumatic events earlier in the year. "Do you know what Independence Day is about, honey?"

When Emma nodded with enthusiasm, mahogany-brown pigtails bounced feverishly against her slightly chubby, olive-tinted cheeks. My mother had located a picture of seven-year-old Nana D and designed a matching outfit for my daughter since Emma looked so much like her at that age. "We talked about it on the last day of school. It's when we shoot firecrackers into the sky!"

"Yes, that's part of it, but it's also when we became our own country. Aunt Deirdre thought it would be amusing to shed her independence on the same day America officially separated from England two-and-a-half centuries ago," I explained. Having lived there for half her life, Aunt Deirdre deemed herself British for all intents and purposes. She also lived *inside her head* where she dreamed up Victorian romances all day. Ply my aunt with more than two glasses of wine and her American roots were more obvious than the henna rinse in Nana D's wild, three-foot-long braids.

"That sounds like an adult joke. I don't get it." Emma gave a thumbs-down symbol. "When will Nonna and Nonno be here?" My daughter referred to Francesca's parents by the Italian words for a grandparent. Her hazelnut-brown eyes were darkening this summer, highlighting how much she also resembled her mother before my wife had adopted various disguises. Emma was being kept far away from any conversation about her not-so-dead mother, something even the Castiglianos had easily agreed to with everything exploding around us.

"Monday evening." I grabbed her hand and rambled toward Wellington Park. Nana D had chosen the cherished location across the Finnulia River, touting it as a critical place to rebuild. She'd also promised *free ice cream every weekend* in her campaign speeches during the mayoral election. "Look, here's Uncle Gabriel," I added when my brother caught up with us at the tree-lined entranceway.

At a complicated and sentimental family dinner earlier in the month, Gabriel had announced his unexpected homecoming and the not-so-earth-shattering news that he was gay. Not surprisingly, the Ayrwicks openly welcomed him back into their fold with minimal concern. My mother cried the entire time at her youngest son returning to the roost. Our older siblings couldn't visit for that dinner or for Nana D's birthday party, but I hadn't expected them to travel. When both had mentioned they would come back for the birthday party *or* the double wedding, Nana D vehemently insisted on the wedding.

"Emma? It can't be! She's grown two feet in the last few days," Gabriel teased while picking up my best girl and swinging her from side to side. In observance of the warm late June weather, Gabriel donned a pair of dressy long shorts and a collared, black polo shirt. One of his many tattoos peeked out from the shirt's sleeve as his taut, muscular arms carried Emma in near-perfect circles.

"It's too fuzzy! Does it hurt?" Emma giggled as she touched his lip piercing and trim, dark-blond beard. He was four glorious years younger than me, as he always reminded me, but our semblance remained uncannily similar. Although he projected a mysterious and rugged appearance, I erred toward the clean-cut side—except for days like today when I hadn't shaved. I secretly clung to the worthy excuse of dealing with a back-from-the-dead wife. Also, Gabriel had been accepted by the family and was currently the favored, treasured sibling whom our parents and Nana D couldn't stop fawning over. Even our father, the resolute Wesley Ayrwick, seemed overjoyed at his prodigal son's return.

"Nope! But you can't get a tattoo either, I already asked your daddy. He's a party pooper," Gabriel responded, smiling as his boyfriend, Sam Taft, meandered to his side. After releasing Emma, who excitedly jumped to the ground, Gabriel shrugged and narrowed his eyes at me. "Isn't that so, brother?"

I shot a spectacular warning look at him. He earned only one of those before I'd tackle him for saying such nonsensical and controversial things to Emma. I'd already mandated she wasn't allowed to wear makeup or jewelry, go on a date, or talk to a boy—or a girl, if that's what she decided—until she turned eighteen. I wasn't overprotective. I was cautiously aware and attentive. At least that's how I justified my helicopter parenting. "Why don't you and Sam find Auntie Eleanor? I need to remind

Uncle Gabriel about the many afternoons he spent sprawled on the dirty ground as a dumb teenager."

Sam, the essence of compassion, cocked his head and groaned. "Will you two ever grow up? I'm younger than you both yet more mature than the combination." To Emma, he said, "Let's go, bean sprout. Grow some legs and race me to the deejay. I bet I can do a better Chicken Dance than you!"

During my distraction while watching them take off, clucking and flapping their arms at their sides, Gabriel tackled me and jumped on my back and shoulders. "Like this, you mean?" he shouted before hooking his legs around my waist, pressuring me to fall, and torturing me with a noogie.

We tossed each other back and forth for fifteen seconds, each of us trying to gain and maintain the upper hand. We only stopped when Nana D intervened and chastised us.

"What is wrong with the two of you? Can't you act like civilized men instead of delinquents who don't know any better?" As we separated, she grabbed each of us by an ear with nimble hands, lowered our heads until they were closer to her own height, and held us side by side. For a moment, we expected a harangue over our behavior, even though we were completely goofing off and not at all fighting. Then, she released our ears and gave us both noogies. "Ha, got you both!"

"Not cool, Nana D," Gabriel shouted, rubbing his head after escaping her bizarrely strong grip.

"That's not very becoming of a new county mayor. You should be ashamed of yourself," I added.

"Pish! I'm glad to have two of my grandsons back home. You have no idea what it means to this middle-aged lady to spend quality time with you before I—"

"Move into the Willow Trees retirement complex?" Gabriel interrupted saucily.

The sly smile plastered across his face was more than I could handle. I burst out laughing, grateful he'd said something sarcastic instead of me. Middle-aged at seventy-five? Nana D had not only pushed the envelope, but she sent it reeling over the edge of a cliff to its ultimate death on arrival.

"Gabriel, if you want to keep on living at Danby Landing, you better shut your pie hole. I'll kick you out as quickly as I offered you a temporary place to crash," Nana D reprimanded, hugging him and kissing his cheek. "I've got big-time control now that I run this county."

After squashing Town Councilman Marcus Stanton in a landslide victory, Nana D wouldn't stop reminding everyone about the power she'd gained. Of course, she only planned to use it for good, but there was something unnerving and dubious about a woman with a Napoleon complex wielding control over us. "Everyone here already?" I inquired as we marched into the park like wooden soldiers.

"Yes, I'm sorry my other grandchildren couldn't attend. I also wish my two sons could make time for their mother, but I'm glad to have *some* of my family here to celebrate with," Nana D said, fighting back

13

a small whimper. She wasn't sentimental very often, but on a grand occasion like a seventy-fifth birthday, the well-hidden side of my nana's personality snuck out for a brief respite.

For the remainder of the afternoon, we shared stories of Nana D's past and presented her with a custom-made drawing of our family tree dating back to the 1600s, the earliest records she'd been able to trace of her ancestors. A local artist specialized in transferring computer-generated genealogical family trees to a 3D-like graphical print format. Everyone had chipped in to make Nana D's birthday as extraordinary as she was to us. Even my father made a brief announcement about how, despite their fervent and frequent disagreements, she was a remarkable woman and a treasure to the family and the county. She frowned when he said *ancient* treasure, and I knew she'd engineer a way to implement revenge. There'd be a summons from the mayor's office in his mailbox when she officially took charge the following week. As I said, her Napoleon complex was going to have an infinite impact on our lives.

After a delicious picnic spread and tons of games, we watched brilliant colors cascade across the sky as the sun set. Sam exited to join a dinner party with his mother, and Gabriel indicated an urgency to check on something at the lab where he worked. His questionable timing prompted me to suspect he suffered from a hangover and needed to sleep it off. Emma requested a sleepover at my parents' house, the Royal Chic-Shack, and departed with them. Although Aunt

14

Deirdre had driven Nana D to Wellington Park, she'd wandered away an hour earlier with Timothy to discuss wedding preparations. I was graciously assigned responsibility for getting my nana home safely.

Other guests exited too, lamenting the few remaining hours before ushering in a new workweek. While many of my colleagues from Braxton College had attended the celebration, I hardly had time to socialize with them. Nana D had insisted Emma and I stick close to her side most of the afternoon. Did she want me nearby to prevent another small breakdown, or had she known I was distracted thinking about Francesca's disappearance?

"Penny for your thoughts, brilliant one?" she asked while we loaded her gifts in the trunk.

Nana D had been present when the final postcard and new puppy, a gift notifying me that Las Vargas had kidnapped my wife, had arrived. She supported me while I'd contacted April, in her official role as the sheriff of Wharton County, to ask for help. "It feels like this was my last moment with Emma before I rip off the Band-Aid. How do you tell a little girl her mother isn't dead, and that the woman *chose* to leave her?" I sighed with exasperation and leaned my head against the side of the SUV.

"You tell her the truth, Kellan. She's your daughter, which makes her brilliant, remember? Francesca caused this debacle, and you'll need to wait for her to resurface. When she does, I plan to give that little harpy a piece of my mind!" Nana D smiled at me and stepped into the SUV's passenger seat, unfazed by the entire kidnapping tribulation. "I have faith you'll determine the best approach—"

Nana D was interrupted when Connor Hawkins, a good friend who'd recently changed jobs from Braxton College's security director to a Wharton County Sheriff's Office detective, approached us. "Happy Birthday, Nana D! What are you now, a half-century?" he said with an infectious beam of excitement gushing on his chiseled face. While I was usually a pasty and pale-skinned kinda guy who couldn't ever find the proper length of time for a good suntan, Connor inherited the perfect balance of skin color from his South African father and Caribbean mother. It even *offset his brooding, stormy eyes,* as he selflessly and frequently pointed out. Called an Adonis by some, to me he was the mere mortal who managed my workouts so that someday, I might look more like him. Don't tell him I admitted that!

I stepped to the side to let him embrace my grandmother. They'd known each other for a long time since Connor and I had grown up together. While we'd lost touch when I moved to LA, we'd bonded again in the last few months. "I'm glad you stopped by. I worried we'd missed you."

"Sorry about that, Kellan. I'm still pulling double duty until the college finds my replacement. Just finished organizing the team for the upcoming week, and now I'm headed out on a call. There's been another jewelry heist," Connor explained as he elbowed the passenger door shut.

"That's awful. Who was it this time?" Nana D settled into her seat and pulled out her phone to make notes. Through the open window, she said, "I was alarmed before, but this is the third one, right?"

Connor replied, "Fourth, ma'am. I suppose I can fill you in on the little I know from today, especially since you're soon to be our new mayor. The Grey family was hit hard this time."

The Greys, a prominent and wealthy clan, controlled a sizable portion of the county. Judge Hiram Grey, a few years younger than Nana D, sat on the bench for over thirty years. I'd taught his granddaughter the previous semester before she'd graduated from Braxton. "What did the perp steal?"

"I'm not sure. A uniformed officer was called to the scene, but once he realized who it was and what'd really happened, the sergeant contacted me. I'm on my way now." Connor responded on one of his many technical communication devices that he'd be onsite in ten minutes.

"Was anyone hurt?" Nana D asked as I shook Connor's hand to say goodbye.

"Yes, Imogene Grey is being treated by the paramedics for a head injury. She caught the assailant trying to abscond with a piece of her jewelry and endeavored to stop him before he escaped. I'll let you know later tonight if I find out anything more, Your Honor."

Once Connor took off, I boarded the SUV and buckled my seatbelt. "It's getting out of control, huh?

Imogene is one of the students in my summer session starting Monday."

"You don't know the half of it, Kellan. This seems inexplicably analogous to the last time we had those unruly jewelry thefts in Braxton. Imogene's mother, Lara, was here recording some video of the party for a news segment. She was one of the victims during the previous round," Nana D harrumphed.

"That's right, I forgot. You never did tell me what happened." Lara Bouvier, a reporter for the local news outlet, WCLN, had been married to one of Judge Grey's sons years ago. Their daughter, Imogene, had lived in France for a big part of her life. Imogene was the cousin of my former student, Carla, who'd just graduated and become an art dealer. "I don't think I've ever met Imogene."

"Sure, you did. She used to run around with Gabriel when they attended Braxton together. Come to think of it, that's the last time those jewelry heists occurred. They stopped right before Gabriel vanished during that nasty thunderstorm." Nana D cracked her knuckles, lost in a pensive reflection. "Oh, you weren't around then, my mistake. Let's head home, brilliant one. It's been a long day."

"Are you hinting at something with that comment?" Gabriel had been secretive since his return, and he'd grown darker and more evasive, but he was a good guy at heart. That I was positive about.

"I'm not really up for talking about it this weekend, Kellan. Why don't you drop me off and come for brunch on Monday when I'm more relaxed? My schedule is slammed with meetings all day tomorrow for the upcoming inauguration."

I had no choice but to grudgingly consent to Nana D's wishes. It was her birthday. She made it acutely clear she wasn't up for discussing it tonight, and I could only handle one melodrama at a time. As we left Wellington Park, a couple dashed across the street and into the park, neglecting to check for any oncoming traffic. I slammed on my horn to warn them, and they briefly looked up with shocked expressions before blocking their faces from my headlights. Given their rush and my focus on the larger surroundings, I hadn't gotten a solid glance at them.

"What's he doing with her?" Nana D mumbled, scrabbling the side of her head.

"Who?" I watched them disappear on a walkway heading south once they crossed the street.

"That was Paul Dodd, Imogene's fiancé. Shouldn't he be home attending to her after the robbery? Not running around with some other woman!" Nana D reproved before reminding me Paul had been elected the new town councilman of Braxton, assuming the role from Marcus Stanton.

"Maybe he was rushing to get home to Imogene?"

"Heading *into* the park? Nah… and he's supposed to be a stand-up guy. I can't be certain, but the woman he left with looked like Krissy Stanton, Marcus's troublesome daughter."

Krissy was another student in my upcoming class, which made their sneaky behavior sound as suspicious as that persistent *deer* invading Nana D's orchard and stealing heaps of ripening fruit. Marcus had threatened to cause a rumpus and wouldn't acknowledge Nana D had officially won the race. He lived next door to us, hence why I also suspected him of being that *deer*! "Want to follow them?"

"No, I've got ways to elicit the truth from Paul Dodd, Braxton's supposedly perfect politician and model citizen. Leave it to me." Nana D tapped the dashboard and directed me which way to drive home. "Something's fishy in the state of Pennsylvania. And it ain't your father's feet this time, Kellan."

Chapter 2

I spent the following morning preparing for my new class, speeding through the lesson plans and syllabus to ensure maximum quality time with my daughter when I visited my parents. Gabriel and Eleanor played various board games with us that afternoon. Even my folks joined in for several rounds of cards and dominoes. Knowing I still had a few hours of work to complete before classes began the next day, I accepted my mother's offer to watch Emma for another night. My daughter reveled in glory, which was all that mattered to me in the insufferable situation with the Castiglianos and Las Vargas.

The evening and my work passed by expeditiously, enabling me to suggest meeting for a beer to Connor. I secretly wanted to find out what'd happened at the Grey estate, but he was too wrapped up in the case to take a break. All I'd learned was that Imogene hadn't been able to identify the jewel thief, despite being at home when the crook had broken in. Connor proposed a new time for our workout later that week, and I fell asleep early in preparation for the start of a new class schedule.

After a fierce battle deciding what to wear on Monday morning, I dressed in my finest professorial duds. The summer term had made its illustrious debut, and I wanted to appear mature enough to command respect yet modern and casual in a way that befitted the television and film industry. The end result: slim cut, well-tailored trousers in traditional checks and stripes; a heather-gray, open-collared dress shirt; a thin cashmere, V-neck sweater the saleslady called the color of eggplant; and sophisticated dark loafers sans socks. Despite Nana D's effusive insistence, I wasn't morphing into a popinjay!

I hurried to The Big Beanery, a student gathering house providing some of the richest and most flavorful coffee and the craziest and most unfortunate hookups in the entire county. Thankfully, I avoided the latter, except when Nana D had set me up on a blind date those few times. I ordered a couple of coffees and apple tarts sprinkled with powdered sugar and cinnamon glaze to go. I needed something to tide me over until brunch at Nana D's. My body craved desserts just as much as it felt energized by my daily workout, which had been fulfilled by a six-mile run earlier that morning. I assumed the two ends of the spectrum balanced each other out and refused to question the greater authority of a god who permitted me to have free will.

Braxton College was comprised of two campuses, North and South, separated by a one-mile tree-lined esplanade of cozy storefronts, student housing, and charming historical points of interest. One campus perched atop a semi-steep incline of the Wharton Mountains, the other sat near the base of a lower hill leading directly into the downtown district. Traditional Victorian and Queen Anne homes, painted in vivid colors and adorned with massive stone turrets and white scalloped shingles, reminded visitors of a smaller and quieter version of San Francisco. Without the Pacific Ocean nearby, Crilly Lake and the Finnulia River generously provided our daily water supply, a source of relaxation, and stunning views. Locals referred to the large estates set atop the hill as Millionaire's Mile, and that's where you'd find folks like the Greys, the Paddingtons, and the Stantons.

North Campus was the college's main site, but I worked on South Campus which catered to scholars in the humanities, communications, and music departments. An electric cable car system, currently under maintenance, transported students back and forth between the two academic spaces. For two weeks each summer, usually when the weather reached a scorching one-hundred-degree temperature, a local company would repair the mechanics and reconfigure the inside panels based on whatever the most recent graduating class had gifted the college. This year, as a dedication to the valiant efforts of a few folks—primarily me, who'd played amateur sleuth to locate a couple of murderers—the theme was a Hercule Poirot and Miss Marple, 1930s-style mystery car. Construction had begun ten days ago, and the final ribbon-cutting ceremony would occur at the end of this week.

I climbed the steps to the sturdy but chaotic platform and scanned the sweeping uptown view of mesmerizing foliage-covered hills. My latest routine included a visit to the cable car each morning to inspect its progress with the local contractor leading the effort. Quint Crawford was in his late twenties, had shaggy blond hair, and proudly boasted a full beard. Years of working construction sites had tanned his skin a golden color and transformed his lithe body into a solid machine capable of frequent hard labor. When I called out his name, the suave and shrewd craftsman poked his head out the car doors and saluted. While I dressed up for my first day of summer classes, Quint had chosen a white fitted t-shirt and a well-worn pair of jeans slung low on his hips from all the tools weighing down the thinning denim. Although he only stood an inch below me, a slight slouch made him appear shorter.

When I'd first encountered Quint two weeks earlier, the enigmatic electrician puzzled me. Quint fancied himself quite the ladies' man, evident by his wandering eye whenever an attractive girl would meander near the cable car station. Quint was a tad too full of himself, easily enchanting the women around him by posturing a rakish allure and approach to life. But he'd privately mentioned recent heartbreak over lost love and a desire to convince the ex to proffer him a second chance. Unfortunately, Quint hadn't shared specific details on what had gone wrong the first time between him and his beloved. Nonetheless, I'd been impressed by his mercurial attitude and ability to quickly dust himself off and get in the ring again, despite his painfully obvious attempt to conceal several wounds stemming from the end of the relationship.

Once he'd formally introduced himself, I'd realized his mother and I had met a few times earlier in the year. Knowing Bertha Crawford was such a kind and gentle soul, I settled on believing Quint was a sophisticated yet opportunistic version of his mother who didn't like to hear the word *no*. "Morning, Quint. How're things looking for your mother this weekend?" I asked, passing a steaming cup of coffee and a warm pastry to him.

"I appreciate you dropping by with breakfast again. You're a good man, Kellan." His eyes darted to the panel he'd been installing and instantly looked apprehensive about my arrival. "Momma's doing better ever since she retired from the Paddington estate. Being on her feet all day as their housekeeper, slaving away at their every outlandish whim, has taken its toll on her over the years."

"Does that mean the radiation treatments are going well?" She'd discovered a lump in her breast shortly after I'd met her months ago, then learned she had an advanced form of cancer. The Paddington family also confirmed she'd quit to focus on her deteriorating health. That's when Quint had made it a priority to take extra care of his mother, a widow for the last two decades. His father had perished years ago in an explosion at the Betscha mines.

"So far, the doctors aren't positive," he mumbled, unscrewing an interior panel near the door.

"That's not good to hear." From what I could see, the winning design was close to being installed. I noticed a few wires creeping out at the bottom and wondered how the repair portion of the work was going. "The new panels look fantastic. Is the electrical upgrade on schedule?"

"Got two cables to replace, but I'll be done tomorrow afternoon. Then we can run some tests to see how the old girl's working. Should be right smooth!" Quint tapped his knuckles on the side of his head as a sign of luck. As he bent downward, he gingerly flinched and moaned before rubbing his back.

"Did you hurt yourself on the job?" I asked, uncertain what company had been awarded the contract for the redesign project. Hopefully, he'd reported any injuries to the school's administration.

"Nothing to grumble about. A man in my line of work deals with rough spots." He gently kneeled to the floor and turned away to finish removing the lower panel. "How's that daughter of yours?"

I'd brought Emma to campus with me the previous time because she had reduced hours during her last week of school. Since she'd stayed at my parents' place last night, tagging along today wasn't an option. I'd also scheduled summer camp for her to attend while I'd be teaching my classes over the subsequent seven weeks. Orientation was scheduled for tomorrow. "Emma will visit again soon. I'll be sure to bring her by, so you can say hello. She had fun watching you work last time."

"That'd be cool of you, Kellan. Don't mean to rush you off, but I've got to finish this today. Fern Terry plans to stop by to check out my progress," Quint advised with an equal mix of hesitancy and substantial irritation, then winked. "Not that she's too knowledgeable about men's work."

Fern was the dean of student affairs as well as a good friend of mine. I needed to schedule lunch with her to catch up on the wedding plans. Her son was marrying Timothy Paddington's sister, hence the double wedding on Independence Day. I ignored Quint's shallow and ludicrous comments about Fern, keenly aware we'd already discussed his opinions in the past. He regarded women more as beautiful objects or conquests rather than equals, yet he easily disguised such views when he needed to appear polished enough to charm one into offering her affections.

"I understand. Do you own the company that won the project bid?" I paused and waited for a response, but an unusually long time went by without his trademark riposte. "Quint, did you hear me?"

"Sure did. My apologies, I was thinking about the best answer," he replied, unlatching a tool from the hook on his belt. "I'm working for someone else who promised me a cheap buy-in. I'll earn a stake in the company once this project is complete. Not to be rude, buddy, but I did mention I was busy. Gotta finish tinkering with this beauty until she's sparkling like a diamond again. Chat another time?"

Quint powered up a drill on full throttle. I waved goodbye to his back—he'd already moved on to his next priority without another word—and walked toward my office in Diamond Hall. My curious nature wanted to ask more questions about whom he worked for, but Fern could supply the answer just as easily. It'd also require less impudence than dealing with my edgy new acquaintance, Quint.

Diamond Hall had previously been a grand colonial home, a mansion by modern-day standards, before its transformation into the communications department's offices. The architecturally stunning building stood three stories high and was covered with a limestone façade mined from quarries owned by the Betscha side of my family. On the top floor were a large open working area and departmental library, and on the second resided offices for academic staff. The ground floor held four classrooms, and for the next seven weeks, I'd occupy the northwest one overlooking Stanton Hall.

As I stepped through the front door, my boss glared at me with a sour expression. It wouldn't be a typical day unless I experienced at least ten minutes of Dr. Myriam Castle's uncalled-for-but-amusing wrath. Even after I'd investigated her wife's stalker the previous month, Myriam still brushed me off with a chilly disposition and delivered ruthless Shakespearean quotes that made little to no sense.

"There's a man here to see you," she stated curtly, her hands locked on her hips. Adorned in her traditional exquisite couture, her trim frame sported a cream-colored suit and slate-gray blouse assuredly flown in from some European designer's latest collection. It was the spiky, more-gray-than-black, short, no-fuss, no-muss hairstyle that initially captured a person's attention. "He doesn't have a visitor pass, and I don't recognize him. You should tell your ne'er-do-well associates to follow the rules, and if I might remind you, we should be working, not socializing."

Well, this was a perfect start to a day at the office. "I don't have any scheduled meetings. Perhaps he's a student in my summer course." I tried to dart past her, but she swiftly grabbed my arm.

"See to it this doesn't happen again. I run a clean and tight ship, and strangers are usually up to no good. I don't like his swarthy looks." She paused as if she had more to say but thought better of it.

"I'll address it right now." Swarthy? I didn't know anyone fitting that description.

"Have you considered my recommendation from last week's meeting? *'God has given you one face, and you make yourself another.'* I'm thinking only of you." Myriam frowned as if she'd bit into an acidulous piece of candy, then dug her heels into the floor like a cat in heat.

She'd been harping about instructing students to refer to me as *Dr. Ayrwick,* not *Professor* or *Kellan,* beginning with this summer's courses. I wasn't excessively opposed to it, but my Ph.D. was in film studies. I didn't feel like a bona fide medical professional, and I was still considered a temporary assistant professor. "I'm not the type to be caught up over labels. I understand your opinion that we as doctorates have earned the respect and title, but if it's all the same to you, I'd—"

"It's not my decision, this is college policy. Your father was instrumental in choosing that outcome. Take it up with him if you care to debate it. As an employee in my department, you will follow the guidelines. Are we clear?" She nodded at the puzzled expression on my face and exited the building.

Lacking any and all desire to speak with my father, the result of our discussion was a done deal. He'd been the president up until he retired the previous semester. Lucky for me, the new president was Myriam's wife, Ursula. *Fate* and *Irony* were two of my least favorite divas! "Dr. Ayrwick it will be," I shouted as I mounted the steps, wondering who skulked outside my door.

When I reached the second floor and peered down the hallway, it looked empty. The door to my office was unlocked and ajar, and the light from my desk lamp was on—not the way I'd left it the previous Friday. I cautiously stepped inside to find the *swarthy* male sitting at my desk, except I wouldn't have considered him swarthy. Knowing Myriam often chose odd ways to describe people, I ignored her comment and focused on why this man sat in my chair. He looked familiar from the side angle, but I couldn't easily place him. "May I help you?"

Once he stood, a six-foot-three solid frame coated with a bronzed skin tone proclaimed his stature as larger-than-life. Piercing golden-brown eyes stared directly at me, and floppy espresso-colored hair cascaded down his forehead in multiple layers, reminding me of genetically engineered male supermodels gracing the covers of fashion magazines. In an instant, I knew it was Cristiano Vargas. He'd finally decided to bestow his unblemished presence upon me.

"I'm confident there's no need for proper introductions, but if you feel that's necessary, I'm happy to oblige." He exuded confidence and spoke in a smooth, distinguished voice with a cultured accent containing slight hints of his Latino heritage. From everything I'd read about the man, he functioned like a finely tuned, expensive automobile, charmed all the women he'd met, and inspired fear in all the men he'd chucked down. A Harvard pedigree also made him a wizard in the business world, no doubt ensuring his success as *numero dos* in the Las Vargas syndicate.

"Not necessary. Just a brief explanation of what you need from me, then we can both proceed with our priorities." Wishing April could be present for the conversation, I discreetly reached for the phone in my pocket, trying to recall where I'd previously placed her on speed dial. After surmising he could've taken me out at any point in the last few weeks, I considered how fearful I should be of Cristiano Vargas.

"There's no need to call the authorities or make any sudden movements. I've no intention to kill you *today*, but if necessary, I will disarm you." He lifted a panel of his suit jacket to reveal a Beretta 92.

I wasn't sure of the specific caliber, but it was a lethal one. I'd been researching handguns with the aim of procuring one to protect Emma from anyone involved in this unfortunate and over-the-top situation, yet I hadn't executed the purchase. I abhorred the thought of brandishing a weapon in the house around a child or anywhere near Nana D, who'd undoubtedly want to target shoot with me. I fought the urge to chuckle upon remembering when Rose shot Blanche's favorite vase in the apropos *Golden Girls* sitcom. Nana D had forced me to stay up late watching it with her every night when I lived in Danby Landing's main farmhouse. "Fair enough. I can put a little trust on the table, Cristiano."

"Shut the door. Sit tight. Spend a minute with me." Cristiano effortlessly walked to the guest chair on the other side of my undersized desk and pointed to his original seat. "I'm not the enemy. As a show of good faith, I'll authorize you taking the more powerful position for this conversation, yes?"

Authorize? Why did I get the impression I already hated this man? I stepped cautiously inside, scanned for any makeshift weapons, and assumed the use of my regular chair. "I'm not sure I agree with that statement. You broke into my office and scared the bejesus out of my boss."

Cristiano laughed, boasting two winning dimples balanced below his perfectly structured cheekbones. "Women are never scared of me. They want to be with me. It can be a curse, but such is my lot in life. We all have, how do you say, an albatross around our necks?" When Cristiano crossed his legs, his sleek, burgundy Ferragamo shoes tapped the corner of my desk. "Based on my research, Myriam Castle does not frighten easily. Please do not start our cozy little meeting with a preposterous lie."

"You might have researched Myriam, but suffering through her brand of crazy is an utterly inimitable experience." She was certainly an albatross. I'd give him credit for that snarky comment. I sat with my hands folded on the top of the desk, willing my confidence not to falter in the slightest.

He snickered menacingly again. "Francesca said you were an amusing guy."

"So, you're the one holding her captive. Is there a reason you're not dealing directly with the Castigliano family? I have no power in this convoluted predicament." I'd watched enough mob movies and read countless crime novels. I needed to relax and approach the meeting as if we were negotiating a common business deal. I couldn't reveal my desperate fear or complete inexperience in this lifestyle.

"Francesca also said you were very smart and would cut to the chase. I think I'm going to like working with you." Cristiano matched my position, our foreheads barely six inches apart.

I squished my knee against the side of the narrow desk to stop my leg from quivering. "I'm hopeful we only need this one meeting to discuss resolving the dispute between our two families."

As I attempted to back away, Cristiano's hand pressed down on my right shoulder. "Don't move until I permit you to do so. I want to be certain you understand what I'm about to tell you. Is this clear?"

Why was no one else in the building at this hour? I'd even accept Myriam as my bodyguard for this brief moment. In his silence, I heard the clock ticking in the hallway and the air conditioner vent blowing from the corner of the room. What had Francesca gotten me into? "Yes, like a cloudless sky."

Cristiano's other hand landed on my left shoulder, applying enough pressure to be uncomfortably intimate and dangerous. It resembled a powwow or a huddle before a championship game, except in reality, this was a duel where one of us had a broken and bullet-less pistol. "It is excruciatingly important you fear what I am capable of doing. My wrath is boundless. Las Vargas doesn't play games we cannot win... one way or another. Nothing is as it appears. Your wife is a fascinating, resourceful woman who understands the art of a mutually beneficial deal." Cristiano gripped the back of my head with his hands, then thumped the top of my scalp repeatedly with both index fingers.

Being this close, I had an in-depth look at the immaculate skin adorning his face. Cristiano had no pores—it was as if he'd been blessed with a flawless complexion. Perfection frightened me because it meant someone would fight until death to retain every aspect of it. If he hadn't told me he wouldn't kill me today, I would've expected the next move to be a swift twist of my neck until it hung limply at the side of my lifeless body. "Leave me out of this mess. Just deal with Vincenzo and Cecilia who are used to this craziness. It'll be a lot simpler that way."

Cristiano released me, walked casually around the desk, and whacked my cheek with the back of his hand—powerfully enough that my eyes saw stars and my mouth tasted blood. When I stood and attempted to punch his perturbed face, he effortlessly grabbed my forearm and twisted it around my back. I couldn't move without intense pain shooting into my shoulder blade. "Do not ever tell me what to do, Kellan. Such consequences have been known to kill stronger men than you."

I stood still, unwilling to accept but forced to listen to his words. "Why am I involved?"

"Surprisingly, Francesca offered to sacrifice her own life to end the war. Yet, as much as she cooperated with me and as anxious as she was to get out from under the watchful scorn of her devious parents, I didn't completely trust your wife. Although an eye for an eye would make up for a lot, it wouldn't have made my family content." Cristiano released me and stepped backward, crossing his arms and casting a look that made it clear I shouldn't attack him again. "My family wants more than equivalent payback. Reparations for the Castiglianos' past indiscretions have become necessary."

"You didn't answer my question. Why are you looping me into this negotiation?"

"Patience, I'm telling you a story. I thought hard and long about why Francesca was willing to die. I wanted to locate any hidden motives that might harm the Vargas family. I tried a few different methods to break her, but after I threatened to hurt Emma, Francesca finally cringed, begged for mercy, and revealed all the plans her parents had made to destroy us. Don't try anything funny. I'd hate for anything bad to happen to that precious little girl," Cristiano said, a sinister shadow cast across his face from the glow of the desk lamp. "Once locating the right incentive, with Francesca on board, forcing the Castiglianos to agree to whatever I asked became simple. Using you as a middleman, Francesca and her parents are unable to talk to one another or pass any clues to play tricks on me. People are willing to cooperate when they're unable to hear or see what's happening to someone they love. Now, I'll have everyone's full collaboration and obedience. Fear can be a highly encouraging factor."

"The Castiglianos won't share anything with me. They've hated me for years," I explained, unclear how that would gain him any leverage or control over my in-laws. I only understood how Francesca would listen, knowing she wanted to be with Emma again—that was obvious.

"The Castiglianos don't want to sacrifice their daughter, but they're also frightened I'll harm Emma. No one wants to lose their entire family, do they?" The sneer on his face manifested all too easily when he handed me a phone from his jacket pocket. "Your monstrous in-laws have zero choice but to trust you if they want to see their daughter and granddaughter survive this ordeal."

"I get it now. Emma and I are your leverage. You want me to broker the deal between you and the Castiglianos because it motivates everyone to behave. If I don't or if any of the Castiglianos try to escape or retaliate, Emma, Francesca, and I end up dead. Then, everyone loses."

"You catch on quickly, Kellan. That phone is how we'll communicate in the future. Do not use it for anything else but our conversations. I will be in touch in forty-eight hours with instructions. My diligent staff is organizing stimulating bedtime reading that Francesca has generously shared with us."

"Do we have the same goal in mind? Are we expecting an outcome we'll both be happy about?"

"That depends. If you imagine moving forward with your life minus any future worries, we have similar desires. If you anticipate the Castiglianos retaining control of their business investments and interests, we do not." Cristiano removed a handkerchief from his pocket and rubbed a spot on his shoe.

"Will Francesca be safe until then?"

"This has never been about her. It was about revenge against her parents and accepting the consequences of their past actions. When I met Francesca two months ago, something fortuitous happened. She's not the woman I thought she would be. Based on her cooperation thus far, no harm should fall her way. If anything feels suspicious, harm will fall your and Emma's way. Agreed?"

"Not until I speak with Francesca." I ignored the bitter metallic taste overwhelming my mouth.

"In time. Do not contact me. I'll call you when I have the details you need." He stepped a few feet closer and faced me directly. "Emma certainly loves her new puppy. Baxter is the perfect name."

"How did you know we named him—"

Cristiano looked at me as if I'd spoken a foreign language or said the most ridiculous series of childish words, then furiously smacked my abdominals with the palm of his hand. His unexpected physical aggression was taking its toll on me, but I wouldn't let him see me retreat in pain. "I know everything, Kellan. Even how you skipped the last half-mile on your morning run near Crilly Lake. Imagine how much better shape you'd be in, if you challenged yourself and stopped devouring those insidious apple tarts. I'd be more worried those desserts are what'll kill you one day, *Little Ayrwick.*"

Five seconds later, Cristiano was gone, and I rushed to the men's room. Either the coffee had cycled through me more quickly than usual or I was more scared than I thought. Once I felt normal again, I swiped my mobile's screen and began to dial April before realizing Cristiano might've tapped my phone line. I wasn't sure if one could tap a mobile phone or if the scheming mastermind had hidden a voice-activated recording device in the office to listen to my every move. I wanted to check with Connor, but

April had warned me not to reveal anything to him unnecessarily.

I briefly searched the office but found nothing obvious. I abandoned the mission and instead downloaded student profiles for my summer course. I walked to Paddington's Play House, the campus theater next door, and commandeered their office phone. April and I made plans to discuss our next steps the following day, and she promised to locate someone to scour my office for any recording devices while I taught *Documentary Filmmaking* that afternoon. Shortly before noon, I left the Play House and called Nana D from my cell phone to let her know I was driving to Danby Landing for brunch and to solicit background on the jewelry burglaries. Knowing I only had a couple of hours before class started, she'd promised earlier that our meal would be ready when I walked through the door.

"On your way home yet, brilliant one? You better hurry up," she said in a muffled voice.

"Yes, I'll be on time. Why are you acting like I'm already late?" Punctuality was at the high end of Nana D's expectations, and I was certain to avoid punishment for something easily obtainable.

"You've got some early visitors. We're having a cocktail in your guest cottage—*Whiskey Sour* for me, *Death in the Afternoon* for them. It seemed appropriate for your in-laws. I hope you don't mind, but I saw the Castiglianos pull up and didn't want to leave them unattended," Nana D explained.

I slammed on the brakes and jolted forward. The last time Nana D had seen my in-laws was when she'd visited LA after Francesca had supposedly died. For the last two-and-a-half years, they'd managed to avoid one another like the plague. "Please behave, I've had enough drama for today!"

"Gotta run, don't want to leave them sitting by themselves. I need to find Grandpop's shotgun. Better to be armed than defenseless, eh? Toodle-oo, Kellan." Nana D hung up, snickering wickedly.

I drove twice the speed limit to get home before one of the three flamboyant caricatures in my life committed murder. If I were a betting man, Nana D would garner the best odds, but what was her aim like these days?

Chapter 3

Ten minutes later, I opened my front door to the sound of three distinct laughs. Nana D's garrulous and all-encompassing guffaw, Cecilia's pompous and high-pitched chortle, and Vincenzo's single grunt resembling a snorting pig searching for food in his empty trough. "You're extremely early," I said, tossing my keys on a nearby table. "What's so funny?"

Vincenzo's shiny bald head seemed to grow exponentially as he aged, and the salt-and-pepper goatee that insisted upon clinging to his chin in despair left me embarrassed for him. Nonetheless, his eerily calm tone and menacing, stocky body shape frightened most people to no end, including me. "I've missed this face. Hopefully, we can keep it this way. You need to visit more often, especially once everything is back to normal." He immediately greeted me with a big hug, then kissed both my cheeks.

Hmmm... had I entered *The Twilight Zone*? When he pulled away, I felt his fingerprints still etched into

my back and shoulders. "I trust you had a safe flight."
I directed my gaze at him, then turned to Cecilia. She
stared at me coldly and offered no embrace, which
was a relief after Vincenzo's salutation. Cecilia, wil-
lowy and gaunt, though pretty in the right light with
her striking blonde coiffure, matched her husband in
height. Neither had ever needed a stepstool to change
a lightbulb in a ceiling fixture, not that they'd deign
to do that kind of chore themselves.

She unclenched her teeth. "Let's skate past the
small stuff, Kellan. We're not here to partake in afternoon tea. If Seraphina hadn't won her recent mayoral election, I would've suspected she poisoned our
cocktails. Alas, she can't afford a scandal right now.
I trust you are following our orders?"

Orders! Everyone wanted me to follow their orders. I was fed up with it all and felt like a pup-
pet whose strings were mismanaged frantically by
maniacs. Cecilia and Vincenzo instructed me not to
speak with the police or the Vargas family, encouraging me to leave the negotiations in their capable
hands. What kind of convoluted scheme were they
kicking off this time? I couldn't tell them that Cristiano had visited me earlier that day. I also wouldn't
reveal April's involvement in a secret investigation.
"I'm aware of your directives. I intend to follow them
to the best of my ability. Please cut me some slack; the
world of ominous crime families is new to me."

Nana D cleared her throat. "For your information,
Don Castigliano, or whatever you ridiculous mafia
types call yourselves... I wouldn't poison you. I'd ar-

range for my sons to take you on a little trip into the Saddlebrooke National Forest to monitor our famous grizzly bears coming out of hibernation. Though I'm not sure they'd relish the taste of rancid meat." She downed the remainder of her cocktail.

Cecilia pranced forward until she stood face to face with Nana D, albeit an entire foot taller. "I thought we were getting along so well before Kellan arrived home. I suggest you be careful with the words you choose, Seraphina. You wouldn't want to get caught in the crossfire, right?"

"That's enough threats from the lot of you. Why are you here?" I asked my pugnacious in-laws.

Vincenzo explained that he and Cecilia had been spying on the Vargas family, looking for information they could use to prevent them from keeping Francesca. "I uncovered a few possibilities last weekend, but I need to set something in motion that will force Las Vargas to return my daughter safely. I cannot go into the details, but it seems Cristiano might not be as clean as he claims to be."

I grabbed the bottle of whiskey from the coffee table and poured myself a shot. I swallowed it immediately. Then I poured another and stared at the smooth golden liquid like it were the elixir of life. I downed it just like Nana D had. I debated pouring a third, but two were enough for the afternoon. There was a class to teach. "For years, you've caused nothing but grief for me and my family. Emma knows little about this, and I intend to keep it that way. Push me too much, I will shove back. Do what you want to rescue

Francesca, but don't play games with me. Like you, my daughter will always come first."

"I assure you; we are just as much victims in this catastrophe as you are, Kellan," Cecilia tactfully tried to reason with me. "If you'd stayed in Los Angeles, this wouldn't have become a problem."

"If he'd stayed in Los Angeles, he might've been fish food," Nana D whined in a mocking voice, looking as if she was gearing up for a sucker-punch. "What a bunch of stupid—"

I moved near Nana D to assert control over her actions, which were problematic based on prior experience. "Look, you two plan whatever scheme it takes to find a solution," I directed at Cecilia and Vincenzo, "and I'll keep Emma sheltered from the truth. She's all I care about right now."

Cecilia blasted, "When offered a choice between saving you or my daughter, you'll always lose."

"And if there's a choice between saving Francesca or Emma, as I said earlier, I'll choose my daughter every time." How dare my psycho mother-in-law go down that path!

"Don't you love Francesca anymore? Don't you want her to return safely?" Vincenzo pleaded with me in a way I knew was meant to frighten and warn me.

"Yes, of course, but it's been a long time, and I have no idea how this will turn out. Francesca and I need to make that decision together when it's appropriate to do so." I'd already decided I couldn't recommit to my wife after everything that'd happened, but this wasn't the time or place to discuss it.

"You haven't heard from Las Vargas since the kidnapping, right?" Cecilia barked conspiratorially.

I shook my head. I didn't want to lie, but my best course of action was to trust neither side and to bide my time until April found something useful. "How long will you be in Braxton?"

"A few days," Vincenzo replied, grabbing Cecilia's arm and shepherding her out the door. "We will call you tomorrow for an update. Our agenda is quite full this afternoon with... other discussions."

After they left, Nana D said, "I'm proud you stood your ground. You're doing the right thing."

I prayed that she was correct, or that she had a direct line to someone who could protect us all. My mind and body were a wreck. The lies and fear were taking their toll on me, and the thought of what would still play out once Emma learned her mother was alive reminded me of someone who waited for a derailed train to pummel them. "I love you, Nana D. You're my rock throughout this entire fiasco."

"Of course, I am. Now, do you want to hear about those jewelry thefts from eight years ago, or did you already forget the purpose of brunch?" Nana D shuffled out of the cottage toward her house to prepare our meal, sighing the entire way about how long it took me to follow her.

"You're gonna drive me to an early grave. I don't believe anyone can keep up with you." When we reached her kitchen, she slowed down, enabling me to regain her attention. "What are we having?"

"Chicken salad with walnuts and cranberries. I know you love them." Nana D ripped the plastic cover off an oversized bowl. "Whole grain bread, avocado mash, and a small slice of lemon meringue pie on the side. Can't have your sugar dip too low in front of the students, but you need to watch what you eat at your age," she added, reaching over the table and poking the top of my already tender stomach.

Was she coordinating today's insults with Cristiano? "My metabolism hasn't stopped. Don't jinx me." I poured us each a glass of sun tea and selected the two largest sandwiches as my own crude way of fighting back. We sat side by side at the banquette in her farmhouse kitchen staring at the corner of the orchard, where many of the trees dangled and released blossoming fruit. We were experiencing the June Drop, a natural process where trees self-pruned and shed some of their gifts. "Have you heard anything further about the jewelry theft at the Grey estate? Or caught up with Paul about his park dalliances? Imogene is supposed to attend this afternoon's class. I wonder if she'll show up."

"I'm meeting Paul on Wednesday. All I know is that the crime happened at Imogene's mother's place, not the family estate. Marcus Stanton is monopolizing all the sheriff's time. He has a few days before leaving office, but he's trying his best to keep information from me." Nana D made an odd gesture with two curled fingers cursing the vitriolic man. Eleanor must have taught her—not that the women in my family believed in witchcraft, but several claimed to have psychic abilities and receive well-intentioned premonitions. Eleanor had once fastidiously learned to read Tarot Cards and tea leaves.

"So, that weird gnarly finger move means it's a *no*?" I asked, gobbling the avocado mash. I'd wanted to interrogate Connor at our workout, but he'd canceled again due to his caseload. Although the jewelry thefts had zilch to do with me, the curious devil inside me wouldn't let it go. Nana D crossed her arms as if my insurgence had insulted her—the epitome of a sullen child when it suited her needs.

"You really are the best cook in town," I patronized, hoping to appease her sudden disdain. Nana D shot me a staggering warning glance. "I mean county." Her added ruffled gaze gave me the willies. "Definitely the whole state. Indubitably." When she leaned closer, I finished expediently, saying, "Okay, maybe I'll just stuff my mouth full of pie."

"You've finally said something that makes sense!" she grumbled and handed her plate to me, indicating she wanted a large slice. Nana D shared what she knew of the jewelry thefts from eight years ago. Between May and June, five homes had been burglarized. The first item was an *en tremblant* brooch, an iridescent French floral spray with a striking trembling effect, owned by Gwendolyn Paddington. She'd been attending a theater performance at the Paddington Play House on campus when it had been purportedly lost. Her family couldn't remember seeing

47

it clipped to her gown, but several witnesses had recalled noticing its glow from the candlelight of the wall sconces at the theater. "The following day, when it didn't turn up in the lost and found or at the Paddington estate, Gwennie contacted the sheriff who sent an officer to check both places. It was a useless exercise."

"No leads on who stole it?" I pondered the confusion about where it'd been lost and wondered whether it'd anything to do with the bribes April once mentioned in association with the former sheriff.

"No, Gwennie insisted the investigation be kept quiet. She was embarrassed at the uncertainty of when and where it had been stolen. Nine days later, Agnes Nutberry lost a choker while listening to her granddaughter, Tiffany's, concert in Stanton Hall." Tiffany was the daughter of Agnes's son, a pharmacist, and his wife, Lydia, the director of their family mortuary. I'd known the Nutberrys for years and had unfortunately stumbled upon one of their clan's roles in a murder the prior month.

"Did they publicize the loss?" Something didn't make sense if it had also been silenced.

"Yes, but no one connected the two crimes initially. Sheriff Crawford wouldn't broadcast the investigation's core facts until much later when he couldn't unearth the criminal." The former sheriff being Quint Crawford's uncle, who'd passed away a few years ago shortly after his retirement.

"Okay, what about the rest?" I wanted to ask if there were any suspects, but she was on a roll.

"In the third robbery, a pair of ruby earrings were pilfered while on display at an historical society event on campus. Lucy Roarke had donated them to the exhibition because they'd been one of the earliest documented gems in Braxton's history."

After Nana D noted that the third robbery occurred exactly nine days after the second one, I asked the obvious, "What's the significance of nine days?"

Nana D had no insight but thought it peculiar. She revealed that the fourth stolen item had also gone missing nine days later—a pearl necklace Lara Bouvier had been gifted at her wedding to one of the Grey boys. They'd married on her eighteenth birthday after she'd graduated from high school, but it wasn't for love. Lara had gotten pregnant while still in school, and Judge Hiram Grey forced his son to marry her to prevent Imogene from being born out of wedlock. Even though this had only happened twenty-eight years ago, his family had gone through enough scandals, and he'd been up for his first reelection to the bench that year. After the divorce, Lara had retained the necklace as part of her generous settlement. "When the Grey family offered to pay Imogene's college expenses, Lara was thrilled; however, they demanded the necklace be returned as part of the arrangement. To get even with them, Lara decided to sell the necklace at an auction, but it was stolen the night before she could present it for bidding."

"If Lara couldn't figure out what happened, the thief must've been highly intelligent and savvy," I suggested while sampling the smoothest and tangiest lemon curd filling I'd ever tasted. Nothing about the nine-day gap between each heist made sense, unless the timing was only a coincidence.

Nana D explained that fifty-thousand dollars had been pinched from the Stanton family in the fifth robbery, but she couldn't remember the entire episode's details. "A massive thunderstorm caused a power outage for twenty-fours during some big shi-shi party with hobnobbers clippity-clopping about all night. Marcus caused such a ruckus, everyone panicked, and no one knew what was going on."

While Nana D cleared the table, I perused the local newspaper but found nothing about the recent burglary at Lara's place. "And no one was ever caught eight years ago?"

"Nah, all those wealthy families were hesitant to go public and look foolish for being tricked. Silas Crawford, my friend's brother-in-law, was the former sheriff. Bertha knew of a few shady things going on back then but tried to dissociate herself once the rumors about him taking bribes increased." Nana D handed me a Tupperware dish with another slice of pie. "The thefts stopped after the fifth one, and then the whole affair quieted down. That's also when Gabriel disappeared."

"When did it all start up again?" I visualized a calendar to piece together the timing. "Just the basics, I've got to get back to campus for class soon."

"Last week of May, right before we had our big family dinner to welcome Gabriel home." Nana D pursed her lips and closed her eyes. "Talk to your brother to find out if he's concealing useful information from the police. I can't start my term as mayor with a black cloud hanging over this family."

"I understand." After a goodbye hug, I chatted with Emma to verify her visit with my father was going well. They'd just finished lunch at the country club and were delivering coffee to my mother, who was working in Admissions Hall for the afternoon. Emma begged to crash at the Royal Chic-Shack again, and once my father blessed the idea, I agreed to it. She needed to be far away from the Castiglianos.

On the drive to Braxton, I called Gabriel to propose meeting up for a beer, where I could also find out what he knew about the burglaries. He didn't answer, and his voicemail was full. I couldn't leave a message. What had he gotten himself into this time, and how did his former friendship with the latest victim, Imogene Grey, fit into the puzzle? Nana D had said they'd been close before he left town.

Documentary Filmmaking was my seven-week summer class meeting Mondays, Wednesdays, and Fridays for two-and-a-half hours in the afternoon. It was an elective course for any students majoring in communications, but it was also open that summer to any Braxton citizens interested in the film industry. As a result, much of the crowd were locals in their late twenties or early thirties who didn't work full-time. After taking attendance, reviewing the syllabus, and answering questions, I divided the class into three groups consisting of four students each. They were tasked with selecting and agreeing on topics for future group and individual documentaries. I spent the final hour walking around to provide clarification and input, then met with each team, who shared their proposed projects for my approval. The first two presentations went effortlessly, and I encouraged them to utilize their remaining time to get better acquainted.

I dragged a student desk across the linoleum floor and joined the third and final group, who'd gathered in a circle near the open bay window. Initially, all four women were silent. Disgruntled expressions occupied most faces. I recognized one of them, Siobhan Walsh, as she'd held the role of office manager in our department last semester. She'd gone on maternity leave two months before I'd begun working on campus. Upon her return, she'd quickly transferred to another department, something which had displeased my boss, Myriam.

I'd never met the other three women in the circle, but during a preliminary review of the course roster, I'd recognized two of their names. Imogene Grey showed up for class in spite of the prior weekend's burglary, and Krissy Stanton was the daughter of our outgoing, monosyllabic town councilman, Marcus Stanton. I worried about the possibility of tension in the classroom resulting from my nana defeating her father in the mayoral election but hoped we could handle the situation as mature adults. I wasn't certain

Krissy was the same girl I'd seen running in the park with Paul Dodd, despite their similar body type. The fourth woman, Raquel Salvado, was unfamiliar to me and new to Braxton.

"How's this group working out so far?" I asked, eager to encourage their discussion.

Siobhan smiled and attempted to speak first. Her garish makeup and bright-red hair made her seem like an over-the-top exaggeration of herself, but she was actually a sweet, down-to-earth mother caring for newborn twins. The only concern I remembered from our interactions, besides thinking she might've killed a friend of mine, was that she could be impetuous and confrontational if you crossed her the wrong way. "We haven't made a lot of progress. Imogene and Krissy are unable to agree on a group topic. Raquel and I are flexible, and we're happy to—"

"All I said was that her proposal wouldn't capture an audience's attention," Krissy interjected while tossing her hand in Imogene's direction. "She's just too sensitive sometimes."

I'd forgotten how thick Siobhan's Irish accent was, despite her relocation from Dublin to the United States over five years ago. I looked at Raquel, who nodded in agreement with Siobhan, and smiled confidently. "Perhaps I can help. Have we had proper introductions from every member in the group? We should understand the reason each of you has enrolled in this course."

"I'll go first. My father taught me how to be a leader," Krissy said, then hesitated to continue as she realized to whom she was talking. Krissy, in her late twenties, looked overly pouty for this early in the summer session and had pulled her wavy dirty-blonde hair into a ponytail. She wore chic dark-colored jeans, four-inch crimson-red heels, and a flowery silk blouse that covered a few extra pounds she didn't want anyone to know about. I only knew because my sister, Eleanor, had shared her own tricks with me. "Anyway, my name is Krissy Stanton. I'm thinking of moving to California, and I've always loved the movies. I thought… why not take a class… maybe when I get to Hollywood, I'll be ahead of the curve. With this experience and my family's name and fame, I'm a shoo-in for a big-time director role."

"Great to meet you, Krissy," I began, pondering how to best temper her excitement and confusion over the way things worked in the film industry. "Not to alarm you, but sometimes it can be difficult to break into the business without any formal experience. I'll do my best to educate everyone on the different paths filmmakers might take, especially in terms of documentary-style movies."

"Thanks, Dr. Ayrwick." Krissy scrolled on her cell phone and grinned scornfully at Imogene.

"Excellent. How about you, Imogene? Please share a little about yourself." I turned my focus to a woman in her late twenties with expressive eyes and short, curly dark-brown hair. She appeared timid, but I couldn't be certain if it was the aftereffect of her encounter with the thief, her discord with Krissy, or simply her normal personality having been raised in the Grey family.

"It's a pleasure to meet everyone. I'm Imogene Grey, and you might know my mother, Lara Bouvier. She's a reporter at WCLN and covers all the major exclusives in Wharton County. I'm excited to be here," she said with a brief giggle, prompting her to cover her mouth and glance downward. "I grew up in Braxton before attending boarding school in Paris. I graduated from Braxton College six years ago and moved back to Paris to get an advanced degree, but I recently returned home to be with my fiancé. When I wanted to learn more about my mother's work, she suggested I take a course in communications."

Imogene spoke with traces of a French accent, and her wardrobe must've been inspired by her experiences in Paris. She wore a lace-trimmed designer black dress and a playful red beret, reminding me of the actress who starred in the movie *Amelie*. I noticed Imogene's strong resemblance to Lara as well as how lucky she'd been to avoid inheriting the protuberant jaw of the Grey family.

"I've met your mother a few times. She's a gifted newscaster. I won't be able to offer you every detail on the life of an investigative reporter in this particular class, but many of the skills required to create a documentary, such as in-depth interview techniques and summarizing events of the past, will be covered," I replied, finding no obvious sign of injury to her upper body. Knowing news of her attack had been semi-public, I questioned it. "I understand you found a spot of trouble this weekend. Are you well enough to attend class today? I'd love for you to stay engaged if you're feeling up to it."

When Krissy snorted in the background, Raquel shot her a disapproving look. Imogene and Krissy must've known one another previously from their ladee-da social circles. If something were going on between Paul and Krissy, maybe Imogene had become aware of it. I could see resentment in the women's eyes. Raquel and Siobhan would hopefully function as the calming forces in the group.

"Oh, I'm much better today. The creep didn't hit me too hard, and as soon as I realized what was going on, I shoved him away and ran from the room. I'm lucky he didn't follow me," Imogene responded as she clasped her hands in her lap and rubbed her fingers together. "I am still shaken up but don't want to miss anything you're planning to teach us."

In a tone bubbling with excitement and energy, Siobhan said, "Good for you. I've had a few encounters with less-than-stellar jerks too. I always hit back. Did you get a chance to knock him out?"

Imogene looked downward. "I think... maybe... I cut his arm with my fingernail."

"How unlike you! I guess Paul, Mommy, and Daddy weren't there to help, huh?" Krissy scolded.

"I'm glad you're well enough to be here," I interrupted, "but I don't want to keep everyone too late. Siobhan, tell the group about your background and why you're taking this class."

"I previously worked in this building but needed to earn more money. Single mothers have it so hard. I accepted an offer in the admissions office last month. I've always been interested in documentaries, and this was the best way I could stay connected to all my former colleagues. I miss working with them." She beamed widely and sat back in her chair, waiting for me to respond.

"We miss you too, but to ensure everyone is clear, I plan to treat you equally in this classroom. It doesn't matter if you know someone in my family," I said, looking at Imogene and recalling she and Gabriel had once been well acquainted. I couldn't bring myself to look at Krissy. "Or if we've worked together in the past. So, let's hear from our final team member before discussing the presentations."

An exotically attractive brunette in her mid-twenties cleared her throat and introduced herself. "I'm Raquel Salvado, and this is my first class at Braxton. I recently moved to Wharton County, and I haven't been able to find a job. My husband told me about these summer classes. I thought it might be a productive way to meet new people and learn something fun." Her voice was soft but strong, and she spoke eloquently as if she'd attended elite schools and came from a well-to-do family.

"We're thrilled to have you here," I replied while analyzing the dynamics in the group. Krissy and Siobhan would be the two to vie for control. Imogene and Krissy's pasts might result in disagreements. Should I consider changing groups now before the projects began? I decided not to make any switches. If they couldn't act mature and find a way to partner together, I'd reassign their team at the end of the week. I owed it to the entire class to allow the situation a chance to work itself out. "Now that we know each other better, who wants to explain the two options you've come up with for the project?"

After back-and-forth negotiations, we settled on a new theme for their group effort, and all four women appeared content with the solution. I reminded them what to do for Wednesday's class, ushered them out of Diamond Hall, and drove home to finish my day sans all the crazy people in my life. Nana D was meeting friends for dinner, and Gabriel was probably working again. I wouldn't be interrupted by anyone and could get to sleep early. Once I returned a few emails and ate dinner, I called my mother to check on Emma. After a quick catch up, she passed the phone to my daughter.

"Daddy! I'm super excited to visit the summer camp tomorrow. What time do we go?" Emma's voice was so incredibly sweet and enthusiastic, it almost turned my evening around.

"We attend orientation at noon. Grandpa and Grandma will take you somewhere special for an early lunch. I'll be at work for a few hours, but I'll use my magic lamp to find you." Being a single parent was not easy, Siobhan was right. At least I had the benefit of a partially flexible teaching schedule to ensure I could be there for all the notable events in Emma's life. Without my parents, Nana D, and

Eleanor, I would be a royal mess, to quote the sheriff as she once described our current situation. Still, it was better than the alternative in LA where the Castiglianos had frequently cared for Emma.

"I love surprises. I bet it's the science lab. Last time, I got to eat lunch next to a giant tarantula!" She chuckled and continued dazzling me with the story I heard every single time she'd visit campus.

"I love you more than desserts, ice cream, and anyone else," I said, feeling my heartstrings twang over the disastrous war between Las Vargas and the Castiglianos. "Baxter misses you very much, but it's your bedtime, honey. We'll see each other tomorrow."

After hanging up and walking her new puppy, I began to feel better, or at least strong enough to get through another day. Pets and kids; they always made life brighter!

* * *

Tuesday morning came so fast, it was as if I blinked and the night had passed. In reality, I'd spent every waking moment staring at the ceiling and attempting to concoct a non-existent solution for my dilemma with Cristiano Vargas. After yielding to the lack of clarity on our next steps, I drove to The Big Beanery to buy morning pastries and coffee for Quint, choosing a French-vanilla blend on this occasion. Thinking about something other than the mafia or jewelry thefts had ensured my good mood. On the five-minute walk to the cable car station, chirping birds soared through the trees and someone's heavy foot-steps jogged on a nearby pathway. When a pungent sandalwood scent wafted by, I gazed around and saw through the branches as the jogger picked up a pair of gloves from the path and took off in the oppo-site direction. Mornings on campus, especially in the summer, were often incredibly quiet. I ascended the steps to the platform and tossed out Quint's name, wondering whether he might recall anything his un-cle, the former sheriff, had said about the past jew-elry thefts. "Chocolate-glazed donuts, buddy. How's progress?" I rounded the corner and stepped through the entrance into the cable car.

Unfortunately, it was not the scene I expected to encounter or one I needed to encounter. Quint was there, but the sounds of his tools humming along as they finished the repairs and redesign weren't present. Quint quietly lay on the floor without a care in the world, except I knew it wasn't a brief morn-ing nap between tasks. I'd seen the look of an ex-tinguished life many times before. Quint was perma-nently sleeping, as in deceased for all eternity.

Chapter 4

After verifying Quint was unquestionably dead, I debated whether to call the sheriff or Connor. Grateful that my relationship with April had swung to the positive side, I notified Connor, hopeful it might unfold less painfully with him. While he rushed over, I surveyed the scene to determine what had transpired.

Quint laid supine on the floor of the cable car with his eyes wide open, staring at various pictures of Agatha Christie on the finished ceiling. He wore his usual jeans, white t-shirt, and construction boots, and his hands were slightly clenched. On closer inspection, I noticed red and dark brownish-black spots on his fingers as though he'd recently been burned by something. Two exposed wires from the panel across the cramped space carelessly drooped to the floor but produced no sparks. It was the only remaining panel disconnected from the body of the cable car. Had he accidentally electrocuted himself while doing repairs? My heart went out to the man who'd lost his life too early.

It appeared Quint had touched the exposed wires. I would be safe, assuming I avoided those. I'd need to advise Connor to confirm whether the main electrical power supply to the cable car was currently switched on or off. While searching the remainder of the car, a bouquet of black calla lilies resting beside Quint's immobile body seemed out of place. Had someone discovered the accident and put a remembrance token near him? Or was it a revenge message, a call of death? It raised curiosity about what'd occurred in the darkest hours of the night inside Braxton's beloved transportation system.

When a car pulled into the lot, I checked my watch and noticed it was barely eight in the morning. Connor exited his unmarked vehicle and trudged up the steps. "Kellan, are you inside?"

I called back to him and waited for him to reach me. "He's definitely gone. I'm not sure if he electrocuted himself or something else happened. Look," I said, pointing to the calla lilies once he arrived. "That's unusual, don't you think?"

Connor climbed under the platform and confirmed the power was off at the external supply box, which made little sense based on the burns on Quint's hands. Had he still been alive after the first jolt, enabling him to turn off the power, and died from a secondary issue? While Connor notified the sheriff and coroner, I continued looking around the cable car. Quint's open toolbox sat on a blanket on a newly cushioned seat. At least he took caution not to scratch or tear anything in the car while working. I inspected the floor and saw a shiny red object underneath the bench nearest Quint's feet.

I bent down to catch a better view without disturbing any potential evidence, in case this was a crime scene. My mind was inclined to enter overdrive, but I wouldn't let myself get too concerned this early in the game about Quint's death being unnatural. I pointed to the shiny red object as Connor walked back in the car. "Is that a piece of jewelry?"

To my chagrin, Connor asked me to step outside while he inspected it. "Wait on the platform, please."

I thought back to my conversation with Quint the prior morning. He'd been quick to dismiss me, noting he had work to do. Could Quint have discovered the thief coming back from another heist last night? Then again, Nana D told me they'd happened every nine days. The last one had occurred only three days ago. I gulped a large mouthful of coffee with a hope it'd alleviate my confusion. It didn't.

Connor stepped back on the platform and accepted the coffee I'd intended to give Quint. "I believe it's a ruby, but I don't want to touch anything until the forensics team arrives onsite. Did you notice anyone hanging around the cable car when you showed up? And what time was that exactly?"

I paused to mentally walk myself through every step I'd made after setting foot on campus, then grabbed The Big Beanery receipt from my pocket. "I paid for coffee at seven twenty-five. Takes less than five minutes to walk here, so I guess about seven thirty. Now that you mention it, I briefly noticed someone. At the time, I assumed it was a jogger out for a morning run. I never saw the person's face, just the silhouette of someone picking up a pair of gloves and continuing on his or her way."

"Okay. His body is cool to the touch. Rigor has set in. The coroner will confirm, but he's been dead maybe six or eight hours." Connor scratched his chin and shook his head. Something about the situation perturbed him too. "I took multiple photos of the crime scene before the team arrives."

"What do you think happened?" Based on Connor's math, Quint had died around midnight.

Connor peered at Quint's body with speculation, focusing closely at the collar of his shirt. "I assumed he was electrocuted, but there are red marks on his neck which look suspicious."

"I suppose they couldn't have been from the power of the voltage," I said, hearing the sheriff's voice calling Connor's name from the platform steps. "Could he have been strangled?"

"Possibly; they do resemble distinct finger impressions. To be honest, the calla lilies and the ruby suggest this wasn't an accidental electrocution." Connor nodded at April, who dipped her head before walking by us to enter the car.

"Gentlemen, not the best circumstances to be meeting one another this morning," April began, raising her voice from inside the center section. "Kellan, I hoped we wouldn't have to do this again. Do you go on walkabout quests searching for dead bodies as one of your cherished hobbies? If you're that bored, maybe you could consider needlepoint or ballroom dancing."

From the quick glance I'd stolen as she glided by, I'd originally surmised a calmer and more open-minded sheriff would be making an appearance today. I was wrong. "Your sarcasm knows no bounds. I purposely contacted Connor this time, hoping to avoid exactly this conversation—"

As she stepped out of the car, April covered my mouth with a gloved hand and guided me toward the end of the platform. "You finally did the right thing. It's bugged me for months why you insisted on contacting me instead of the detective I'd assigned to a case," April interrupted and glanced down at her car.

Someone sat in the passenger seat, but I couldn't sneak a fully unobstructed look at him. Other than recognizing he was on the younger and taller side, I was perplexed. She didn't wear a wedding ring, yet I'd never seen her on a date before. Had April Montague been on a clandestine overnight jaunt with a boyfriend?

"Perhaps I just enjoy your company," I said, shrugging and mentally slapping myself. Why did my mouth utter things I had no control over whenever April was around? "Or, I guess, I didn't know any of your other detectives before Connor joined the force."

"Now that you know one, I think it's best if you consider him your primary contact in the future.

We're already working together enough on your personal situation. Let's keep it that way." April caught
me gawking at the man in her car, but she didn't acknowledge him or offer any explanation.

"Sure, I'm hopeful I can walk away from this one
after giving a formal statement." I hardly knew Quint.
Why would I need to stay involved in this investigation?

"Good. I assume that means you unintentionally
found the body this morning and don't know who
it is. I'll verify Connor has this under control, then
I need to take my...." April looked back at her car.
"Then, I have an errand to run. Try not to get into
any more trouble this week, okay?"

Hmmm... I didn't want to lie to her. "You should
know that I've been chatting with the victim almost every morning for the last ten days. I purposely
stopped by to see him today."

April's right hand slowly clenched. "I see. I'm
confident Connor will take that into consideration.
You're unfamiliar with his family or next of kin,
right? Nothing to keep you here longer?"

"Oh, well... about that...."

"Little Ayrwick!" April's eyes burst open like a
spring flower witnessing an unexpected flurry of
snow and curling its frustrated petals.

"Hey, you said you'd stop calling me that!" I threw
my hands in the air in pseudo-shock. "You also know
someone in his family." I mentioned that Quint was
the son of Bertha Crawford, a witness she'd inter-

viewed in the Paddington murder case. I also noted the woman's current bout with cancer.

"That poor soul. First, she gets sick. Then, her son is murdered." April's lime-green eyes revealed a genuine sadness for Bertha. "That also makes the victim the nephew of the former sheriff."

"Definitely murdered." My ears tingled with curiosity about the calla lilies. What did they mean?

"Yes, I trust you'll keep that quiet. I'll wait for the coroner's report, but he was obviously strangled and electrocuted. Someone desperately wanted Quint Crawford out of the picture."

The sheriff exchanged a few words with Connor and the team who'd begun cordoning off the area. After she left saying she'd call about our other case soon, Connor escorted me down the steps. "Other than Quint's mother, do you know whom we should notify of his death?"

"No, I hardly learned much about him. I hadn't even known Bertha was his mother until he told me a few days after construction started." I'd volunteered to talk to the bid winner with Fern to flesh out the redesign timeline and details. We'd quickly learned that Quint was the type of guy who responded better to a male boss, despite Fern's stern warning and direct instructions. Rather than make a huge issue out of it, she asked me to monitor his progress. I found the whole redesign process fascinating and enjoyed my daily touch-base with Quint. "I don't know what company he's working for. Fern handled that part and just told me Quint was the primary point of contact."

"Endicott Construction," Connor replied, scrabbling his chin again. "I've seen the truck around, and there was a jacket with the name and company logo at the other end of the cable car."

I must've missed that on my initial scope of the space. "I could talk to Lindsey Endicott to find out if he owns the company." Lindsey, a retired attorney who'd opened a brewery in the downtown district, was one of Nana D's closest friends. I assumed he had family in the area but wasn't certain.

"You wouldn't be trying to take over my job, buddy, would ya?" Connor cautioned and walked me to the bottom of the steps. "I'll handle it from here. Come by the sheriff's office tomorrow to review a formal statement with me. You might've seen someone else talking to him recently."

Connor returned to the cable car, and I headed to my office to complete as much work as I could before picking up Emma for orientation at day camp. I updated Nana D, knowing she'd want to check on her friend, Bertha. My grandmother had taken the woman to chemotherapy in the early part of her diagnosis before Quint had gotten involved. Nana D planned to call on her friend later that afternoon, once she was certain someone had informed the woman of her son's death. I also called Gabriel, but he didn't pick up again, and his voicemail was still full. Something didn't feel right about his isolation.

* * *

"As much as I'll miss Nana D while I'm at camp, she's way too famous to worry about being a babysitter, right?" Emma asked as we entered the Woodland Warriors summer program for noon orientation.

I would've preferred to enroll her in Braxton's camp facility, but they were renovating the building this summer. Woodland College had an early childhood center for their students majoring in education, and during summers, they offered a local student teaching program for children from kindergarten through third grade. Emma had only just finished second grade and was eligible for this final year. It also helped that the bus would pick her up every morning at eight and drop her off every evening at five or seven on the Braxton College campus.

"You could say that. As mayor, she'll be busy babysitting an entire staff of county workers hoping to improve citizens' lives. You'll still see her at night." I dropped Emma's hand to let her buzz the entrance bell, which suggested the facility had dependable security. The structure was a typical two-story, red-brick school building with blue-tinted windows and an enclosed playground area containing a basketball court, resurfaced blacktop, and grassy field. Old and slightly chipped ceramic tiles covered the floor, and children's art projects and posters festooned the off-white-beige walls. It was in decent shape but in need of a makeover. Luckily, the technology, talent, and curriculum were top notch.

"I want to be like Nana D when I grow up," Emma declared while we walked to the main reception office. "She's more awesome than Wonder Woman!"

Francesca had forced Emma to watch all sorts of superhero shows with positive female role models. I supported the decision but sometimes thought it'd gone a little too far. My daughter had even higher expectations for herself than I'd developed at her age, and that scared me. Managing through the disappointment a harsh reality could deliver was never easy, but she'd taken it in stride thus far.

When we entered the head office, Helena Roarke, drenched in an overly sweet perfume, greeted us. Helena was the younger sister of Maggie Roarke, my former college girlfriend, and had gotten herself into some trouble the previous month when she was found standing over a dead body and holding a knife. What was she doing at Woodland Warriors?

"It's going to be a fantastic summer," Helena exclaimed, stretching her agile yet voluptuous body on the walk toward us. Blessed with huge thick hair, she often teased it to the point she couldn't fit through narrow doorways without brushing against the molding. Nonetheless, her feminine facial features and sultry disposition always made her the girl people wanted to know and converse with. "I'm one of two assistant teachers in Emma's classroom."

I rolled my eyes hoping they'd shoot lasers for once. Don't get me wrong; she was a fun girl and smarter than most people had acknowledged, but she was also inconsistent and flighty. Helena explained that she'd studied early childhood education during her years at Braxton but hadn't finished her student teaching. She was taking a final class this summer and would obtain her degree in the fall.

"How are you going to handle classes, teaching students, cleaning rooms in your parents' bed and breakfast, and working at the catering facility?" I asked, recalling she'd been all over the place trying to get her life in order the last time we chatted.

"Ugh! The Stoddards fired me when I broke up with their son, Cheney. He wanted to get serious, and I wasn't ready for that. Gosh, I'm only twenty-eight. I have ten years before I want to get married." Helena grabbed Emma's hand and mine, then led us to the classroom. "Walk with me. I'll introduce you to the head teacher."

After we arrived, I covered the basics with Emma's instructor, Jane O'Malley, granddaughter of the previous Braxton librarian whom Maggie had succeeded. Miss O'Malley wanted to chat with Emma for a few minutes to get to know one another. Helena and I sat at an art table in the corner of the room while Emma explained all about Danby Landing to her new favorite person. At least my daughter was open-minded and friendly when trying new things. She didn't inherit that from me.

"I take it Cheney wasn't happy. Did he push his parents to fire you?" I asked. Helena and Cheney weren't a proper fit, especially since he had a less-than-perfect background and spent time in prison.

"They never liked me. I doubt Cheney asked. He still sends flirty messages and pictures of his—"

I cut her off not wanting to know where that lurid statement was going. Knowing Helena, it was going exactly where I expected it to go. "That's great. It's nice to remain special friends with someone when you break up. So, they axed you, and you needed a new job?"

"Pretty much." She shamelessly grabbed my wrist. "After that whole ordeal of discovering the body and spending a weekend in jail, I kinda had a wake-up call. I decided to focus on getting my teaching degree and educating the kids in Wharton County."

Why hadn't Maggie told me her sister was working at Woodland Warriors? We'd just shared lunch the previous week and talked about Emma spending her summer here. Maggie must not have known; she and her sister weren't the closest—although, their relationship had seemed to improve lately. "Congratulations. It's wonderful to hear some positive news about the future. It's been a rough morning." I disentangled my hand from her unrelenting clasp and sat on it to prevent another attempt.

"Poor Quint. I can't believe he electrocuted himself to death." Helena fluffed her blonde hair and stretched her neck from side to side. "I'm gonna miss him."

How did they know each other? "Who told you he was dead? I just found him this morning."

"Seriously? This is Wharton County. Jane O'Malley, Emma's teacher, heard it from Calliope

Nickels. Calliope works as a waitress at the Pick-Me-Up Diner for your sister. She overheard two cops mention it as they were gobbling down Chef Manny's fresh apple-cinnamon waffles at breakfast. They call you *The Unlikely Death Locator*." Helena's hands gestured like two gossipy sock puppets divulging secrets about small town citizens.

That was *not* a name to be known by! I'd have to inform Connor his colleagues were talking too freely in the diner. Just as Helena ceased chatting, my mobile phone vibrated. It was my sister.

Eleanor: *Did you really find Quint Crawford's body this morning? Calliope Nickels said he was naked.*
Me: *No. You've got your information messed up as usual.*
Eleanor: *Umm, so he is alive? But his body was painted like the American flag for the 4th of July?*

How did shocking news travel and change so quickly? This was worse than a child's game of telephone. The whole town had forgotten how to be respectful. A man had died, and while we didn't know the cause, freak accident or murder, this wasn't the time to start fabricating rumors.

Me: *Ugh! I'll call you later. He IS dead. He was NOT naked. There was NO body paint. You ARE ridiculous.*
Eleanor: *Apparently, you're a divining rod for locating dead bodies. Makes sense, I'm psychic.*
Me: *Crazy does run in our family. Did you coin my new nickname as* The Unlikely Death Locator?

Eleanor: *Don't shoot the messenger. At least you got to see April, right? Hugs and kisses, Romeo.*
Me: *Mind your own business. Search your broken crystal ball for answers next time. Goodbye.*

And that was lucky reason number thirteen why I never should've come back home to *Hooterville.* I hid my phone away and focused on Helena. "Did you know Quint well?"

"Yep, we went to school together. There was a core group of eight of us who used to hang out all the time. He was the athlete in our group, always showing off how agile he was." Helena fastened a button that had popped open on her blouse as she shifted in her seat. She'd soon realize her wardrobe wasn't suited to working in a summer camp. "Quint and I were going to grab a drink this week, but we never picked a time." Helena's smile faded as she accepted her friend was truly gone forever.

"I'm sorry for your loss. I met Quint about seven or eight times in the last ten days. He was working on the cable car redesign." I patted her hand, hoping she didn't take it the wrong way.

"Oh, right. I forgot Nicky had hired him on that project."

"Nicky?" My eyebrows arched like a pyramid, highlighting my confusion.

"Nicholas Endicott. Lindsey's son, you know, the kid he had kinda late in life." Helena explained that Nicky was one of the four guys in their core group. When Nicky had graduated from college, his father had just turned seventy and retired from his law practice. Lindsey had sold it to Finnigan Masters and gone into the brewery business. "Nicky helped him choose the beers, but he always wanted to run his own company separate from his dad. That's when he opened Endicott Construction."

Quint had mentioned he hoped to get a piece of ownership in the construction business, but based on what Helena had said, Nicky wanted to run his own company. "Were they still friends?"

Helena wasn't sure, offering little explanation whether Quint and Nicky had communicated recently. "A lot of people from our little group have been coming and going lately. Like your brother."

I'd hoped she wouldn't reveal Gabriel was part of the illustrious octet. I knew he and Helena had attended Braxton together during their freshman and sophomore years, but while Gabriel had left town, Helena had remained here to torture me upon my triumphant return. Knowing Connor wasn't going to publicize any news indicating Quint might've been murdered, I'd have to be careful when posing any questions to determine potential or viable suspects. Perhaps I was jumping the gun and declaring it a murder too soon, but it wouldn't hurt to ask a few innocent ones. "Who else was involved in the—"

As two shadows approached us, Helena said, "Looks like Emma is done with Miss O'Malley."

Emma had a productive meeting with her new teacher and was excited to hang around for the remainder of the afternoon. I spent a few minutes digesting the various activities and subjects Miss O'Malley would be teaching, then headed back to Braxton to get some work done. Learning Helena would be with Emma was both a comfort and a worry, but I trusted her to take care of my daughter. Without a way to find out what else Helena knew about Quint, I gave up and left Woodland Warriors. I'd call Helena later to ascertain more details about their group of college friends, once I engineered an opportunity to pressure Connor into throwing me a few scraps of information about Quint's death.

While I didn't believe Gabriel had anything to do with the jewelry thefts, something suspicious had been encapsulating his recent return. Between the repeating robberies aligning with his absences from Braxton, the strange calla lilies and ruby on the floor of the car, and Quint's likely murder, the intertwining mysteries had become exceedingly fascinating and yanked me into their clutches. Truthfully, I wasn't yet certain the ruby in the cable car had a connection to the jewelry thefts. It might've just loosened from a ring Quint had been wearing when he fell to the floor.

Remembering how victims often knew their murderers, I considered whether the jogger wearing the sandalwood cologne who'd retrieved the gloves was associated with Quint's death. It would depend upon confirming the presence of fingerprints. If Quint had been dead for six hours, the jogger was more likely a random passerby. Just who was in the group of eight, and why did I have a tough time avoiding trouble? I couldn't help myself lately. I'd found the dead bodies and was inclined to punish the ruthless monster who'd cut someone's life too short. Some naysayers around me called it a sickness. I preferred to categorize it as generously doing my civic duty.

After arriving back at my office on the Braxton campus, I attempted to reach Gabriel who'd been ignoring me for two days now. I still couldn't leave a voicemail and had to assume he was up to no good. I decided to text one more time, knowing if he didn't respond, I'd sic Nana D on him.

Me: *Are you dead? Have you left town again? Talk to me, or I'll break out the big guns.*
Gabriel: *Get a life. I've just been busy working. I'll check in over the weekend. Promise.*
Me: *Need to talk to you about several things, including Quint Crawford. Don't play games with me.*
Gabriel: *I'm not, seriously. I heard about his death. Life is too short. Maybe I'll see you on campus.*

Several messages later, Gabriel still refused to respond. If he wanted to be evasive, I'd confront him when he wasn't expecting it. He'd be working at Cambridge Hall of Science for tomorrow's next public flower show. I could surprise him before my afternoon class. Get ready, brother. I'm on the trail, and you are being hunted down by an ultra-determined, intelligent wolf in sheep's clothing.

The rest of the afternoon focused on planning my upcoming classes and reading as many news articles as I could on previous and current jewelry thefts. I'd learned several interesting facts to review with Nana D, Connor, and April, but I wasn't certain they'd be able to answer my open questions. If they couldn't, or wouldn't, I'd consider going directly to the main sources. Lara Bouvier had been intimately involved in tracing the commonalities between all the robberies, but even she'd never postulated on potential suspects in her public news segments. Perhaps I'd convince her to share her private theories with me. At first, I just wanted to prove Gabriel wasn't involved, but now, with Quint's murder conceivably linked to them, I worried for a variety of additional reasons.

After Emma arrived at the bus stop, I carted her to gymnastics practice where she impressed me with her agility and strength. I demonstrated my excessive dose of pride to the other parents of less athletically inclined children, then we met Eleanor at the Pick-Me-Up Diner for dinner. While we shared a luscious dessert—Emma wasn't a huge fan of sweets, so I suppose I should confess to having eaten a majority of it—an unlikely pair discretely snuck into the eatery and hunkered down in a corner booth.

I racked my brain to conjure a legitimate reason for interrupting their meal, but nothing came to mind. I also didn't relish the idea of dealing with the wrath of a man who'd lost the election to Nana D. Marcus Stanton and Imogene Grey might not benefit from my wickedly delightful presence this evening, but I'd certainly ask Nana D what she thought of that duo when I visited her the following morning. As far as

I understood, Krissy and Imogene disliked one another, and Imogene's fiancé, Paul, was taking over the role of town councilman from Marcus. There was something nefarious going on, and if it had anything to do with the jewelry thefts or Quint Crawford's death, April needed to know post haste.

Chapter 5

When I woke up the next morning, my body demanded exercise. I'd consumed too many desserts the previous week, and it always came back to haunt me. Once Emma was safely on the bus to camp, I changed into my running clothes and swung by Nana D's for a brief catch up. A few days remained before her official start as the new mayor of Wharton County. We'd been working on her speech whenever we found free time, but it wasn't complete. Nana D wanted to lay out a three-month plan on what citizens could expect, and she insisted on providing target metrics and deliverables that would be impossible even for an experienced politician. My gentle warning hadn't dissuaded her, suggesting I'd need to try harder. It wasn't that I didn't believe in her ability to get the job done, but without having a deeper background in county government, she might set herself up for a tumble way too soon.

Nana D was sitting at the dining table when I popped by and opened the front door. She waved me in and pointed to a chair. "Have you heard from Gabriel? That nincompoop won't return my calls."

"At least I'm not the only one he's ghosting." I took a seat across from her at Grandpop's custom-made table, tracing my fingers along the burnt scalloped edges he'd spent hours perfecting. I missed him more than I'd realized the last few years.

"What kinda cockamamie word is *ghosting*?" Nana D suspiciously looked up from whatever she'd been scribbling on a notepad.

"It usually refers to when someone stops returning messages after giving you some sort of indication that they were interested in—" I began to say, but Nana D twirled her finger in the air a few times to let me know I was taking too long to explain its meaning. "Basically, ignoring you."

"Why say something in thirty words when you can say it in two, brilliant one? Wasn't that part of your bachelor's degree? Master's? Doctorate? You've been in school so long, you must know everything by now." Nana D pushed a steno pad across the table. "Please weigh in. I think I've nailed it."

I knew better than to defend myself or take her bait. Yes, brevity was important, but sometimes an elaborate way of saying something provided context and tone. *Some people* struggled to understand that approach and preferred to be exceedingly direct in their feedback. "Sure, give me a minute." When I finished, I gave her a high-five. "Perfect. Looks like you came around to my way of thinking with—"

"Can it. We're done. You don't need to analyze who contributed which parts. Now, what about Gabriel?" she said, pouring herself another cup of tea.

"Well, he finally responded to me last night. I told him I needed to talk about Quint Crawford, but he ignored me and said he'd see me on campus. I might show up at his lab this afternoon." Gabriel had only been back for a couple of months, but he must've known by now that no one in our family walked away without paying the price. When an escapee finally returned to the zoo, the inmate was subjected to scrutiny until every last precious metal bar was soldered back onto the cage.

"Poor Bertha, she's beside herself with grief over her boy's death. She asked me to stick around after the funeral service to talk. She specifically requested you to be there too." Nana D sipped her tea and placed her speech in a folder on the table. She was all jazzed up in a navy-blue pantsuit with a white silk blouse that had a fluffy bow tied across her chest. Her hair was braided and wrapped around the top of her head, and she sported a pair of old-fashioned spectacles strategically placed on the bridge of her nose. She rarely donned them in public, but her eyesight had gotten worse lately, and even she couldn't deny it. Oh, the anguish that would be thrust upon me if I mentioned anything about the cheaters.

"I hardly knew Quint. We only met ten days ago on campus." What did she need from me? I was still trying to understand why Quint had never told me he'd been friends with my brother years ago.

"I guess we'll find out. My bones have been aching whenever I think about that ruby you saw in the cable car near Quint's body. I fear there's a connection between his death and the missing jewelry. Maybe he discovered the thief's identity and confronted him in the cable car. Or perhaps—"

"Or perhaps it's just arthritis?" After she flicked my ear, I conceded to her way of thinking and told her about the dinner between Imogene and Marcus. "I agree with you. Helena and Gabriel should be able to tell us whom Quint had been closest to. They might shed some light on his activities throughout the last few weeks. That's where I'll dig for clues about the contractor's untimely death."

"Maybe Marcus was supposed to meet both Paul and Imogene. Could Paul have shown up after you left, to discuss the transition of the town councilman role?"

"I suppose. Add that to your list when you talk to Paul later," I jokingly directed.

"Yes, master. Did you find out from Imogene if the bandit left another calla lily again this time?"

I considered Nana D's old-fashioned expression carefully, but nothing sparked other than reminding her no one had said the word *bandit* post last century. Then, I remembered the black calla lilies in the cable car next to Quint. "Wanna explain what you meant about the flower being at Imogene's place? Is the calla lily some sort of ironic calling card among thieves that I'm unaware of?"

"How would I know? All I'm saying is that in each place where he'd absconded with the goods, the perp left a single black calla lily. Didn't I tell you that the other day?"

"No, you conveniently left out that part in our rush to discuss all the jewelry thefts before my class began. I didn't know flowers came in black." I should've paid more attention at the flower show's debut last month but catching a murderer was ultimately the proper priority back then. Wait! Given there were calla lilies next to the body along with the ruby, it generated two definitive links between the jewelry thefts and Quint's shocking murder. I needed confirmation on whom the gem belonged to.

"It's a heavily debated topic in the botany world. Millard and I have often discussed it. What most people think of as black petals are dark purple," Nana D clarified as she tapped several bony fingers against the table in quick fashion.

"Do they spray-paint them for certain holidays, like Halloween or Valentine's Day?"

"Wash your mouth with soap, Kellan. That's just nonsense. I never agreed with altering nature's beauty in an artificial manner. Splicing various species is one thing, but spraying a flower with paint seems excessive." Nana D was adamant about organic farming and not messing with Mother Earth.

"Got it, black calla lilies are deep purple. I'll ingrain it in my memory next time. Are they rare?"

"Used to be. Nowadays, you can get anything off the Internet. It's rare to actually see a black one but not difficult to cultivate and grow them." Nana D fetched a gardening catalog from the shelf and flipped to an article on the flower. "While you peruse the magazine, I've got a few calls to make. If you don't talk to your brother today, let me know. I'll order him to the mayor's office to find out what he knows about the jewelry thefts."

"It says calla lilies represent elegance and mystery and are used at funerals. How creepy!"

"Grow up." Nana D crossed into the kitchen to retrieve her old-fashioned, daffodil-yellow wall phone and dialed a number. "Skedaddle. I've got to be downtown in two hours to find out why Paul Dodd was sneaking around with Krissy Stantor, and why his fiancée was sneaking around with Krissy's father. I feel like we've been tossed in the middle of one of your mother's kitschy soap operas. You still gonna drop me off after your little exercise routine to lose the flab you've been packing on?"

"Oh, right, I almost forgot. Wait… what did you say?" She was already talking to someone, so I checked my watch, set an alarm, and took off for my run. Normally I'd drive to Braxton, race the indoor track, and shower at the campus gym, then head to my office in Diamond Hall. With Nana D's new job and hesitancy to drive on her own, she'd become reliant on me until her chauffeur started the following week. A driver was part of the many perks she'd garnered by winning the election, but the current mayor wouldn't give up the town jockey until his final day.

I jogged across the orchard to where I could pick up a narrow trail running toward the eastern range of the Wharton Mountains. It was a four-mile distance to reach them and guaranteed me one uninterrupted hour of exercise. Along the path, I blocked out everything weighing me down and focused on keeping my adrenaline high and my running form solid. I reached the midpoint and took a brief water break to admire the cloudless sky and colorful trees and bushes. It was still early enough that the sun's heat hadn't peaked, and the air near the mountains was always a little cooler. My moment of complete relaxation was intruded upon by a ringing cell phone, except it was an unfamiliar tone. I'd also remembered turning mine off, ensuring only calls from Emma's camp would make any noise. I needed to escape from any distraction but couldn't be unreachable for my daughter.

When I retrieved the phone from my pocket, I gulped. Instead of taking my personal cell phone earlier, I'd mistakenly grabbed the one Cristiano Vargas had bestowed upon me as his personal lackey. I pressed accept and uttered a weak "hello," knowing the purpose of my run was now forever ruined.

"Good morning, Kellan. Four miles in thirty minutes, not too shabby," a cheery yet alarming voice greeted.

"You're certainly a man of your word, Cristiano. It's been exactly two days." Another reason to dislike the man, his impeccable timing and incredible accuracy. Of course, he was watching me right now. I looked around for a professional goon hiding around the edges of the mountainous terrain, but there was too much territory to cover in this brief amount of time.

"It brings me immense pleasure to know I can deliver on any promise I make. Perhaps under different circumstances, you and I would be good friends. Let's table that thought for now. I need your assistance." Cristiano was listening to the Hamilton soundtrack. I recognized one of the songs. Francesca and I had attended an early preview of the show several months before she'd faked her death. Her father had gifted us the tickets, which had shocked me at the time—it had been impossible to buy them! Now, I knew why he'd been so successful; running a mob family had its advantages.

"Are you finally ready to deliver Francesca to us?" I was feeling more direct than usual.

"Not exactly. I'm enjoying her company. She's introducing me to music and culture I know little about. The favor I need won't be too complicated." Cristiano cleared his throat to let me know he was finished speaking.

"Hit me with it," I replied. What could he possibly ask me to do that I'd be willing to entertain?

"You need to tell *Signor e Signora* Castigliano that I've learned what they're up to, and it will not fly. Be exponentially clear with them. If they do not retreat, I will be forced to punish those insolent fools." Cristiano informed me that his team was aware Cecilia and Vincenzo had recently sent a spy into the Vargas camp. "Tell them the friendly face who showed up to offer me a deal isn't looking particularly friendly anymore. I'm sure his battle wounds will heal in time. War can be brutal on someone who is as delicate as a soufflé. Remember that if you ever try to cross me, Kellan."

I'd never understood the idiom *felt my blood boil* until now. How was I stuck in the middle of this sick, twisted vendetta? "What did you do? For that matter, what did the bickering caterwaulers do?"

"Your only role is to be the messenger. It's better when you don't know any details. If the Castiglianos follow my orders, Francesca will be returned to you within the week. I must go now."

"Wait, I don't know what they did—"

"Goodbye, Kellan. We shall speak no further until I get a sign from them that they understand." Cristiano hung up on me. How would they give him a sign? Shoot up a Harry Potter *Dark Mark* in the sky? I had to be missing information that would clarify what was combusting into flames around me.

My energy level soared after the phone call, and I ran back to Danby Landing more quickly than it'd taken me to get to the mountains. Arriving home, I showered and changed, dropped Nana D off at the administrative building in downtown Wharton County, and zoomed to Braxton where I spent three hours preparing for my afternoon class.

I also suffered through a departmental staff meeting where Myriam notified everyone of changes in the fall schedule. An adjunct professor had backed out of a job because she'd been awarded an assistant professorship role at Woodland College. "I need a volunteer to interview a potential new candidate next week."

I had no time to take on anything additional, prompting me to keep my head down reading the remainder of the bullet points on her tedious agenda. I'd gotten distracted when the meeting ended and hadn't realized everyone else except Myriam exited.

"Thank you, Kellan. I appreciate your generosity," she said, thrusting a resume at me.

"Wait, what did I do?"

"You volunteered to help me with the interview process. Did you not stick around after the meeting as I informed everyone to do if they were interested?" Myriam adjusted her glasses and pursed her irksome lips while waiting for my response.

She had me there. If I confessed my failure to pay attention, it would hurt me eventually. No one else had stuck around. If I didn't accept the task, she'd just assign it to me anyway. "Happy to help save the day," I contritely replied and began to leave the room.

"*Let none presume to wear an undeserved dignity.*" Myriam cited a well-known line from *Merchant of Venice,* then waited for me to redirect my attention to her. "One more item. A student in your class visited me yesterday." A puzzling grimace danced eagerly on my boss's face.

"Another satisfied customer?" I pushed my glasses higher, above the small bump on my nose.

"That would make you quite pleased, wouldn't it? Unfortunately, no, that is not the case. While she didn't request any changes, the student wanted me to know that she was unhappy about the group she'd been assigned to work with." Myriam recited her personal opinion on how to handle the issue, then asked me what I planned to do about it.

"Will you at least tell me who it was?" I wouldn't confront the student, but I'd know to tread carefully in the future. I was convinced it had to be Imogene or Krissy. Both were frustrated when class had ended on Monday, even though they'd claimed to be okay with the compromise for the group's topic selection.

"It's best that I do not. If she returns, we'll have a deeper discussion about the problem. For now, please be certain you are more attentive to student issues and preferences. We can't always kowtow to their every single need, but we also shouldn't alienate them," Myriam warned as she collected her belongings. "You must be careful about this situation. It could become a problem for your future at Braxton. I'll be putting a note in your file with Human Resources."

Once *Barracuda Boss* left, I bought lunch in the cafeteria and chatted with a colleague about his summer lectures. I finished early enough to swing by Cambridge Hall to surprise Gabriel before my class. On the walk across campus, I noticed him entering the building's front doors. I picked up enough speed to almost catch up, but before I could arrive, the elevator door closed. Inside, he held an animated conversation with one of my students, Krissy Stanton.

Gabriel worked on the second floor in the science labs. Rather than wait for the elevator, I ascended the stairs at the end of the hallway. Upon arriving, I realized I didn't know exactly in which lab he'd spend his afternoon. I'd been in the building a handful of times but never to meet him. I asked a distracted lab assistant if she knew where Gabriel's office resided. With her hands flapping and bobbing about, she whined, "He doesn't have his own place, kinda hangs out in different labs and keeps things in order. He got off the elevator, but like, I don't know where he went. I'm not his keeper!"

"Got it, thanks." Was everyone nuts today? I walked around the entire floor but couldn't locate him anywhere. Ten minutes later, I exited the building and headed to class. Where had he disappeared?

I stopped at my office to collect my lecture notes, then strode to the classroom on the first floor. A few students were already assembled in their seats. Siobhan approached me at the desk. I didn't think she was the student who'd complained to Myriam, but I'd poke around to discover whether she knew anything. "How're the twins doing?"

"They're flying it... doing well, I mean. I sometimes forget you're not Irish. I'm knackered, I'll tell ya," Siobhan responded, collapsing into a chair across from my desk. "With Mrs. Crawford needing some time off this week, my schedule has been quite hectic."

"Come again?" I didn't understand her news. "Was Bertha Crawford working for you?"

"Aye. After she left the Paddington estate on account of the cancer, she needed more income. Mrs. Crawford watched the twins while I attended work or class. It's easy pay for a few hours when I couldn't bring them to daycare." Siobhan covered her mouth as she yawned. "After what happened to her son, Quint, she couldn't handle it anymore. I don't blame her. Just left me a bit stuck, ya know? I had to find a new sitter. Today is the new girl's first time watching my babies."

I hadn't realized Siobhan knew the Crawfords. "It's an awful shock for Bertha. How's she doing?"

"Haven't seen her since it happened. When the police contacted her, she was watching the twins. I left work and went to get them. Your mother was very understanding about me needing to take the afternoon off after I was already late that....." Siobhan paused as a few more students walked into the room, including her groupmate, Raquel.

"I guess you must've known Quint?" It wasn't my business, but I didn't want to jump directly into my question about any potential complaints with the groups.

"Oh, he was a clever bloke. I... uh... didn't know him all that well. I'm sorry that he died, but... well... I don't have much to say about that topic. Anyway, I'm a little worried what it's gonna be like in this group with those other two," she said hesitantly, then breathed deeply and waved to Raquel. "Not her,

Raquel's a doll. I mean Krissy and Imogene. Krissy gave me quite an earful after our last class."

"Really? About concerns with the course? Were you happy with the last session?" I asked, finding my opening but also curious about the relationship between the other two women. Also, had I imagined it or did Siobhan clam up when I asked whether she'd known Quint well?

"This class? Aye, it'll be fun. I might just have to keep the others under control. Krissy and Imogene used to be best friends, but after—" Siobhan stopped speaking when someone rushed into the classroom, creating an uproar worthy of a bad referee call on a football field.

"Sorry. I'm late. Got held up talking. I'm here now. Class can start." A frowzy and somber Krissy squirmed through the desks, knocking over books and a chair, then plopped down in a frenzy.

While several students sighed profusely and picked up their belongings, I checked my watch. We were one minute shy of the lecture's start time. I really wanted to know what Siobhan had almost revealed, but I'd have to confront her afterward. I also sought an explanation for why Krissy and Gabriel had been together. "It's okay, we're just about to begin." I looked around the room, confirming all but one person was in attendance. "Let's give Imogene another minute before we dive in."

"She's not gonna be here today, you can proceed." Krissy huffed, grabbed a pen, and fixed her hair as she settled into the seat. "Everyone else has finally quieted down."

I wasn't fond of Krissy's overly direct and bossy way of speaking to others, but if she'd been the student who'd complained, it wouldn't help to provoke her in front of everyone. "Sure, I'll call Imogene tonight to let her know what she missed. Let's talk about Grierson's *Nanook of the North*, the first original American documentary produced in...."

I taught for ninety minutes, then took a ten-minute break. I motioned to Siobhan, but she frantically rushed out of the room, one ear glued to her cell phone. I assumed she wanted to check on her kids and didn't interrupt. Instead, I approached Raquel and Krissy, who were engaged in a lively discussion. "Pardon me, I thought I'd take an impromptu poll to see how you both felt about the class so far. We're still early enough if you had anything to share, I could make some adjustments."

Raquel was quiet, but Krissy speedily responded. "You're a great lecturer. I was very connected with today's lesson. I knew you'd be a good professor, just as a friend of mine told me," she said with a quick but obvious wink. I assumed she'd meant my brother, Gabriel.

Raquel nodded, "I agree. I'm really excited about the next chapter, but we only have a few minutes remaining, and I need to use the restroom."

When Raquel left, I refocused my gaze on Krissy. "May I ask how you knew Imogene wouldn't be attending this afternoon? I am only curious because I need to make a note of her absence. I'm allowing two for this summer's course without any grade penalizations."

"Did you hear about that guy who died working on the cable car, Quint Crawford?"

"Yes, I did. I was the one who—"

"Quint was Imogene's ex-boyfriend. They used to date back in college before she dumped him for Paul Dodd, the new councilman. Now, she's engaged and hardly ever sees her friends anymore," Krissy said with a defiant and palpable aggravation. "Except suddenly she's all broken up about Quint's death and couldn't bring herself to attend today. Ugh, I'm upset about it too, but...." Krissy paused and began to sob in front of me. A few students in the room looked over awkwardly.

"Are you okay? Did you know him well?" I asked, unsure whether to pat Krissy's shoulder or give her a moment of privacy. The relationship between her and Imogene was beyond odd. I handed a tissue from my pocket to her, wondering why she'd been with Paul the night of Nana D's birthday party.

"We were all friends years ago. I cared about Quint too, but I forced myself to show up today." Krissy hurriedly cleared her tears and fixed her makeup.

"When you say *all*, does it include my brother, Gabriel?" I figured it was the most apt time to confirm the names in their convoluted octet—my *innocent* questions re his death required answers.

"Yep, there was a whole bunch of us who hung out during our freshman and sophomore years. Then, the group sorta broke up, and everyone went their separate ways. I tried to reunite the rest of them, but not everyone stuck around Braxton. I guess you knew that already, huh?"

"Yes, I did. I just saw you with Gabriel, didn't I?" I lifted my eyes to match hers and held my ground. I wanted to see how she'd respond to my question before inquiring who else had left town.

"Oh, yeah, he saw you as we went up the elevator. I ran into him on the way to class. We were catching up, but he was in a rush to check on an experiment," she explained, as the door opened with a flurry of students rushing in. Raquel and Siobhan were included in the group who sat closest to Krissy.

"Looks like we need to get started. Maybe we could finish our discussion after class?"

After Krissy cautiously confirmed, I returned to the front of the classroom and finished the lecture. By the time it ended, she was packed and ready to leave. I had little chance to stop her before she exited Diamond Hall and tore off for the parking lot.

Raquel, tossing her long dark locks to the side, approached me. "She's a little scatterbrained. I wouldn't take it personally." She deftly applied pink gloss on her plump lips and smacked them together with a snappy pop. The color added a fresh glow to match her naturally smooth and silky skin.

"She's just lost a friend she'd known for a long time. I understand what that's like. What can I do for you?" I said, shutting off a display screen and laptop.

"I wonder if I could talk to you about the courses you'll be teaching next fall. I want to enroll in something else, but I'm not sure which would be best for me," she added, rearranging her books and pulling out her phone. "I'm free tomorrow morning. Could we get coffee at The Big Beanery? Isn't that where all the students and teachers hang out?"

"It is," I said guardedly. Her tone was more suggestive than I expected. I might have misread the situation, but it never hurt to be too careful, especially if she was the girl who'd complained. "I'll have office hours on Friday. How about we block thirty minutes at five o'clock after class ends?"

"Oh, sure. I guess I can wait until then. It will give me enough time to read up on a few things." Raquel batted her suspiciously thick eyelashes while entering the details of our appointment into her phone, thanked me, and withdrew from the room.

Siobhan was also out of pocket, so we couldn't finish our conversation. I headed directly to North Campus where Emma's bus would arrive momentarily. While walking, I considered everything I'd learned that afternoon. It unearthed more questions than answers, and I still didn't know which student had expressed concerns about my last class. Could Myriam have exaggerated what'd been said, to make me feel nervous or uncomfortable? Or had one of the students lied to me tonight about how she felt?

Emma and I spent the evening cooking dinner together and training Baxter how to sit and let us know when he needed to go potty. At sixteen weeks old, he was learning basic tricks, which made Emma as excited as a proud parent. After we read a short story, she nodded off to sleep. As I poured myself a glass of wine, the phone rang. When the caller ID indicated it was the Castiglianos, I chugged every remaining drop of liquid courage, poured myself another to guarantee an enjoyable time, and pressed accept. "What will it take to be rid of your constant barrage of complaints and intrusions?"

Chapter 6

After I explained Cristiano's instructions, Cecilia blasted me. "I warned Vincenzo his plan wouldn't work. Now, I must assume control. Do not be alarmed, Kellan, I have the solution."

I tried to elicit basic details or an explanation from my mother-in-law, but she told me there wasn't any room for children in the games she currently played. "I still don't understand why Las Vargas is involving you, but apparently they think it will make things more successful. If only they knew weak men like you weren't cut out for this life. I always told Francesca you'd be her downfall. Now, my proclamation has come to fruition."

"I don't like being the mediator either, but since Cristiano threatened Emma's life and informed me that I'd be his primary point of contact, we're stuck. Aren't we, *Mommie Dearest*?" My anger and frustration had reached its limit. I was being played on both sides, and there was little way I could ever assume control or gain the upper hand in this war. I had to sit back and wait for two devious players to move their pawns on an unstable board until someone dared to attempt the final gnashing kill.

After we disconnected, I needed a distraction from everything that was slowly eroding my sanity. I caught a couple of minutes of my favorite television series and watched a rerun of the episode of *Dark Reality* that I'd directed in Los Angeles the previous year. I'd been anxiously awaiting the executive producer's decision on whether he'd consider letting me direct my own true crime show, rather than the reality series I'd been stuck working on before my boss had been fired. I wasn't due to find out until the beginning of next year, which timed out well with the end of my one-year teaching contract in Braxton's communications department. I wasn't sure what I'd do if neither place offered me a permanent role, but that wouldn't occur for at least another six months.

Just as I changed into a pair of comfy shorts and a t-shirt, my cell phone rang again. I put the ringer on mute in case I forgot to do so after talking to Nana D. I was desperate for no further interruptions and a full night's sleep. "Hi. What's going on?"

In the background, a television blasted Lara Bouvier's local news segment covering the upcoming inauguration ceremony.

"Paul Dodd claims Krissy Stanton was harassing him at the park. He'd been at home working on his campaign speech and decided to go for a walk. She found him there and followed him around until he got a call from Imogene about the break-in at Lara's place."

"Do you believe him?" I heard voices talking on top of the news report. "Wait, where are you?"

"Kirklands. I'm having a drink with Eustacia. She heard it's a happening place. We came to check out my constituency. Let me guess, you're in bed already?" Nana D teased.

"Whether I'm in bed or not isn't the point. It's been a long day. You didn't answer my quest—"

"Can it, brilliant one. I don't want to keep you from your precious beauty sleep. I believe Paul, but he also said something interesting." I waited for her to continue speaking, but all I could hear was Eustacia debating what drink to order with their waitress. "Earth to the eccentric woman bugging me?"

"You're getting belligerent like your cranky old father, Kellan. Come meet us for a drink?"

"Emma is sleeping, and it won't help my social life to be seen hanging out at local bars with my grandmother, the mayor," I explained, hoping it would keep her from delaying the conversation any further. "What did Paul say?"

"I'll pretend I didn't hear that part about your social life. And you can pretend I didn't say your social life is equivalent to the existence of the Loch Ness monster," Nana D replied with a chortle and a burp. Then, Eustacia cackled and screamed through the phone at me, "Meaning you ain't got one, boy."

"I'm hanging up."

"Ugh, fine, you wet blanket. Paul told me Krissy tried to convince him that Imogene was cheating on him. He claimed he didn't believe her, but I saw the anger flare up in those dreamy eyes of his. He was mad as a hatter, especially when I told him Imogene was hanging out at the Pick-Me-Up Diner with Marcus. He offered no explanation, mind you."

Nana D and Eustacia continued to share their opinions on how attractive Paul was, then shifted to how crass Marcus Stanton and his daughter, Krissy, were. I could barely understand them once they began shouting over one another and the screechy television.

"Thanks for finding out. How is it you persuade everyone to talk to you, Nana D?"

"A girl's gotta have some secrets, brilliant one. Go drink your hot cocoa and tuck yourself into beddy-bye. Let the Sandman bring the baby a dream! Can't have you getting ill-tempered because I kept you up past the witching hour. To think, the sun just finished setting and you're conking out already."

"Who's the designated driver tonight?" I really couldn't take her anymore tonight.

"Uber, unless you want to be a good grandson and come get us?"

I hung up. I'd hit my limit of dealing with semi-inebriated grandmothers and their ridiculous frenemies. Sufficiently placated with a third glass of wine and Baxter curled up in the crook of my knees, I opened the latest mystery from my favorite author and began to read. Then, my phone buzzed again, leading me to mumble a few not-so-nice words. I'd turned the ringer off but accidentally left on the vibration mode. This time it was a text message from April, and as usual, I had no idea what to make of it. It wasn't a question or a suggestion. It was another order and the final nail in my coffin this evening.

April: *My office at nine tomorrow morning. Need to discuss your 'role' in* Quint's murder inquiry.

* * *

"Listen, I know I said to work directly with Connor on the cable car incident, but he's been pulled into another angle on this investigation and has gone out of town." If April's furrowed brows weren't enough warning, her harried countenance indicated it'd already been a rough Thursday morning.

"I had to chat with you anyway. A few things came up regarding Las Vargas yesterday," I confessed, checking what else I had to accomplish on this bright and sunny morning. I craved more coffee but wouldn't dare endure the nasty torture of the discarded remnants in April's office pot.

"By the way, your office is clear. We found no bugs," April casually notified me before asking what had happened the day before with my missing wife drama.

It felt good to be able to speak freely inside my office without worrying about who snooped on my conversations. I let April know what Cristiano had told me and how Cecilia had reacted to his threats.

"I'm not sure how much more I can take of this disruptive seesaw."

"It's not easy, I understand. For what it's worth, you've handled this lunacy well. I've always admired how adept you are at keeping your cool and holding your own. Not many men could stand up to the mob, worm their way into a police investigation where they're almost killed, and push back on an amazing sheriff who threatens to arrest him for obstruction of justice nearly every day. You're a brave man, Kellan." April laughed at her attempt to assuage my concerns and boost my ego.

"Those might be the nicest and strangest words you've ever said to me. I don't feel very brave but thank you for that compliment."

April briefly dipped her head in my direction. "We've released Quint's body to the funeral home, and I'm under the impression it will be a quick service tomorrow evening."

"Although Quint's mother has been sick, she'll be present. A group of us from the college will attend to pay our respects," I declared. I'd never been fond of attending wakes, but they'd been prevalent in my life the last few months. Nana D and I had recently commiserated over watching some of her friends pass away. The sudden and wasted loss of life was both depressing and alarming, especially surrounding the current situation with Francesca's kidnapping. "Any leads on Quint's killer?"

"I'm the one asking the questions here, buddy. Tell me everything you remember about the time you spent with Quint Crawford," she countered with an obsequious grin.

I updated April with every tidbit I could remember from my previous conversations with Quint between the moment I'd initially met him and when I'd found him dead in the cable car. "He was often aloof, and while he hadn't kicked me out every time I visited him, I'd never felt fully welcomed. He seemed to have a knack for reading people and situations easily. At first, I'd only intended to verify his progress, but there were flashes when he got rather chatty. Or should I say, he asked a lot of questions."

"About you or the college? Was he particularly angry toward anyone?" April asked, hoping I had more information than I knew I had.

"Not really. I didn't know much about him. He asked about my teaching schedule and my daughter. When he told me how sick his mother was, I mentioned how difficult it had been to lose my grandpop. Quint brought up Francesca's death once, but I couldn't say much about it."

"Why did he ask about that?" April leaned in closer to focus on my response, a peculiar expression commandeering her face.

"Just said he'd heard about it from his mother, and he wanted to tell me how sorry he was that I'd lost a wife so young." I barely recalled the specifics of the conversation that day as it had been shortly after I'd pieced together Francesca's kidnapping and could barely keep my own thoughts straight. "What have you learned about the ruby I found in the cable car? Is it from the jewelry thefts?"

"I'm not sure why that's anything you and I should be discussing, Kellan. I'm grateful you noticed it, and Connor is investigating that angle in San Francisco right now. I asked you here in case you knew anything else important enough to share with me about Quint. Not the other way around." April was hesitant in her response, suggesting she'd learned something she didn't want to tell me.

"I'm only trying to help. I know some of the people involved. Maybe I'll discover a valuable connection, April." Gabriel had lived in San Francisco when he'd left town eight years ago after the first set of burglaries had occurred; that was certainly a connection. "What's Connor in California for?"

"Fine, I'll share a bit. One of the originally stolen jewels was recovered there years ago. It'd been sold at a pawn shop on Mission Street. Of all the lost items, the Roarke ruby earrings were the only ones returned or found. Connor is seeking a better description of the person who sold them to the pawn shop." April shifted in her seat and looked uncomfortable with our conversation's focal point.

"If they'd been recouped, wouldn't that information already be in the Wharton County police reports?" I knew I was pushing too deeply for answers, but I'd been willingly drawn into the enigma.

"It should have been, but my predecessor's files leave a lot to be desired," April groused with obvious contempt for the man. "The former sheriff never put out an alert on the missing jewelry beyond Wharton County. All he'd documented about the recovered ruby was that a *random* caller had notified the pawn shop in San Francisco of the owner's identity." After the pawn shop subsequently called Sheriff Crawford, he requested a picture and showed it to the Roarke family. Eventually, Lucy had been able to retrieve her family's precious gems. No other details had been included in the records.

"What happened to the rest of the jewelry and the money from eight years ago?"

"Why do you want to know?" April asked, narrowing her gaze as she stood to remove her blazer. *Old Betsy*, her prized threatening revolver, was strapped to her hip.

I didn't want to implicate my brother, but I couldn't lie to April any longer. I explained what I knew about Gabriel's disappearance and how there might be a link between him and the jewelry thefts. "Can you tell me anything about the past robberies and how they line up with the current ones?" I was focused on the missing jewelry because I now believed for certain the string of break-ins had something to do with Quint's death. There was little chance a bouquet of black calla lilies and a stolen ruby next to Quint's dead body were unrelated to the reason he'd been brutally murdered.

April considered my request, and by the pensive look in her eyes and the frequent crack of her knuckles, she wanted to alleviate my concerns yet also protect herself from revealing too much. "Most of this is public knowledge. I'll share the basics of what the newspapers had printed at the time. If I say something is confidential, please keep it that way."

Once I agreed, April filled in the blanks Nana D hadn't remembered or been aware of. "In the first robbery, only four students confirmed seeing the stolen brooch at the Paddington Play House. There was a black calla lily left in Gwendolyn Paddington's bedroom, similar to the ones found by Quint's body and all the other robberies. The brooch has never been recovered, and Sheriff Crawford's details were erratic at best."

"Bertha Crawford worked for the Paddingtons. Was she interviewed afterward?" There had to be an association if one of the filched gems was found near Quint and other jewelry had been stolen from the family who'd employed his mother.

"Not according to the files. Gwendolyn insisted she lost it at the estate and not the Play House. The report containing her input affirmed she'd personally interrogated her entire staff, but no one knew anything." April resumed explaining the previous occurrences, eyeing me dubiously the whole time. While I doubted the ability to learn anything new from the previous jewelry thefts, some obscure minutiae might surprise us.

"What did the Nutberry family do after their diamond choker was stolen?"

"Agnes died a few weeks afterward, and the whole affair was relegated to the backstage. Everyone in her family had rock-solid alibis, thus proving they weren't responsible for stealing the jewelry." The sheriff flipped to the next report in the file.

"I'm most familiar with the third victim, Lucy Roarke." I planned to visit Maggie and Helena's mother to find out all I could in the next few days. I didn't want April to know I was separately investigating on the side, so I navigated the conversation along a different angle. "How did the thief get access to all the houses and jewelry without getting caught?"

"Unfortunately, in three of those cases, there was little security protecting the jewelry. I see how it could've been stolen without the thief being trapped on camera. Back then, people were more trusting. Even Braxton's administrative department admitted they were too lax. The key for the exhibit room where the Roarke rubies were on display had been sitting in a tray on the secretary's desk. Anyone could've walked in and taken it," April complained. We agreed that the thief had to be clever enough to ensure never getting captured, but that he or she must've been someone whose presence people wouldn't have questioned for hanging out in all those places.

"You mentioned there was other jewelry on display, but only the Roarke rubies were stolen, right?" In the nine days between the burglaries and the specific targets who'd been chosen, there must've been a pattern we failed to distinguish—one that could lead to identifying Quint's killer.

April confirmed her agreement on my theory. "None of it makes sense. Could Gabriel have stolen the rubies, then tried to innocently return them to the Roarkes after a change of heart?"

"I suppose it's possible, but we'll have to ask him. San Francisco was one of the first places he'd visited and ultimately lived for two years." I remembered Nana D wanted to know if I'd gotten my brother to talk, but I never updated her that he and I hadn't connected the previous day. While April rooted around for the next police report, I texted Nana D to fulfill my commitment.

"After the original fourth robbery, Lara Bouvier searched for the thief herself, which is what ultimately led her to convince WCLN to hire her as an investigative reporter for their news segments. She wasn't able to find the responsible party, and the rift between her and the Grey family widened immensely," April explained, citing she'd already questioned Lara to obtain all the historical details.

"I met Imogene recently. She's spent a lot of time outside the country in France over the years. I can't imagine she had anything to do with it. Could the Greys have stolen back the jewelry and taken other things to avoid suspicion?" I worried that my brother had also known Imogene quite well back in the day. Had he been trying to help her get money for tuition since the Grey family wouldn't support her unless Lara returned the family necklace? Perhaps he was simply a modern-day '*Robin Hood*.'

"The Greys have been out of town for weeks on business trips, so it's unlikely. Connor will interview everyone involved eight years ago to compile a list of suspects. Your brother will need to provide an alibi for each instance where jewelry was stolen, and possibly Quint's murder should it come to that," April declared before mentioning we needed to tread carefully in that part of the investigation.

"What about the fifth and final burglary from eight years ago?"

"Wendy Stanton, Marcus's late wife. Same timing except it was a bag of cash instead of jewelry. Her story is an interesting one. She'd been married to Marcus for five years, but there was a rumor she'd been looking for a divorce. During his reelection campaign, she suspected he'd skimmed money from alumni donors," April revealed. His opponent had been a no-name from the rural parts of town who'd little chance of winning, which meant Marcus didn't need to use the donations for marketing and advertising. Wendy confirmed Marcus had kept fifty-thousand dollars in cash from a recent fundraiser in the Braxton alumni office that weekend.

"I read that newspaper article. Marcus indicated he planned to bring the money to the bank the following Monday, but then it disappeared when the power went out during the thunderstorm. Wendy claimed her husband had stolen the cash and ratted him out to the erstwhile sheriff," I replied.

"Of course, that deadbeat didn't do anything to investigate if Marcus had been skimming money from the alumni event for personal gain. Our soon-to-be-former town councilman must've paid off the sheriff to focus only on finding the money." April closed the report and slammed her fist on the desk.

Wendy and Marcus reconciled after his subsequent reelection win eight years ago. Wendy also revealed that Marcus had found a calla lily when he went to retrieve the money. I asked, "Does anyone know if she was covering up her husband's dirty laundry or whether there really was a calla lily?"

April grunted. "Surprisingly, the one thing Sheriff Crawford did correctly was not immediately divulge to the public that a calla lily had been left at every theft. Wendy and Marcus had no way of knowing there was one present at the other crimes unless they'd spoken to those victims. Nobody publicly acknowledged that they'd been robbed at first." Silas Crawford had been smart enough to keep that calling card close to the vest until the burglaries ceased. He wanted to find the responsible thief, but when it looked to be an impossible feat, he slipped details to the public to trigger the memory of anyone who might've seen someone walking around with calla lilies.

"No one offered up anything?"

"Not according to the original reports. Based on the new interviews we've conducted thus far, either everyone's memory is a bit hazy or they throw out so many names that we'd have to haul in the entire town for questioning." While shaking her head in disgust, April indicated she'd only focus on the current round of thefts, hoping those would be more effective in determining the identity of the thief and Quint's murderer. "There's nothing worse than solving a crime someone covered up years ago."

"I agree, it's probably the same thief. You should be able to crack the current robberies and discover how they tie to Quint's murder. We're probably missing something simple and obvious," I said, worrying that it only made things look worse for my brother if his exit and reentry into Braxton coincided with the time frames of all the missing jewelry.

"It's possible. So far, there have been four thefts with nine days between each one." April opened a cabinet on her wall to reveal a whiteboard listing the dates, locations, and items stolen during the last month.

"Any theories on why nine days?"

"Not yet. It gets weirder with the way these crimes have now been repeated," April said before explaining the basic facts associated with the current robberies. "Could be an accomplice or a copycat."

The first victim had been Jennifer Paddington, who indicated a watch made of crystal and diamonds was stolen from the family estate the weekend of the costume extravaganza. Nine days later, Lydia Nutberry lost a pair of sapphire earrings while attending her sister-in-law's funeral. Eight-thousand dollars in the mortuary safe was also pilfered that evening. Another nine days passed before the matching ruby necklace and the same original pair of ruby earrings were stolen from Maggie Roarke's home. After they'd been returned to Lucy, she'd gifted them to her eldest daughter rather than leave them locked away in a safe, never to be used by anyone. Then, just a few days ago, Imogene Grey was attacked when she caught the thief robbing her mother's home. While she'd been sleeping, a diamond tiara, a present from her grandfather that'd been handed down from an ancestor who'd married into royalty, went missing.

"Let me guess. In all four instances, a black calla lily was left behind?" I knew the truth already but wanted indisputable confirmation.

April replied, "Yes. If the pattern continues, the Stanton household will be the next one hit in four days. Therefore, I need to speak with your brother to find out what he knows."

"It doesn't explain why one of the Roarke rubies was found in the cable car near Quint Crawford's dead body with a bouquet of spray-painted black calla lilies."

"I shouldn't tell you, but perhaps you'll have an explanation. The bouquet of calla lilies left near Quint's body wasn't spray-painted. Those were actual black calla lilies. Only the individual flowers left at the locations where jewelry was stolen were white ones that had been spray-painted."

"That's unusual," I remarked, not sure what the distinction meant. "Hopefully, Connor will find a lead while he's in San Francisco. Maybe he'll get a description or name from the pawn shop owner, indicating who'd sold them the ruby and who'd told them that it belonged to the Roarke family. Perhaps something will explain the calla lily connections. Can you tell me anything about those red marks around Quint's neck?"

April closed the whiteboard and glanced back at me. "That's one of those confidential things, Kellan. I've said enough for today, especially if your brother is somehow mixed up in this situation. He has a knack for getting close to criminals."

"I know my brother. He's acting strange, and I admit, he might've had something to do with the jewelry thefts. But he's not a murderer. He wouldn't hurt anyone, April. You have to believe me."

"That's why it's best for you to work with Connor on anything related to this case. You guys are close, and he knows your brother. I'm already involved deeply in your wife's kidnapping."

"My family must look pretty messed up, huh?" I wasn't being cavalier in sharing my thoughts, but a dark cloud shrouded the Ayrwicks, and I needed all the help I could obtain to disperse it.

"For the sake of our developing friendship, I won't respond to that question." April looked past me as the coroner arrived at her office. She waved him in and indicated it was time for me to leave.

I walked a few steps down the hall but kept my ears attuned to their conversation. The coroner said, "Based on the autopsy, I can confirm Quint Crawford's cause of death as strangulation. My analysis showed major damage. Bruising to his larynx and windpipe with a shattered hyoid bone, and petechiae, also known as blood spots, in his eyes. No DNA obtained from the killer, as far as I can tell right now. I have a few more tests to run later today."

April grunted. "Can you tell me anything about his killer to help the case?"

"Given the size of the individual marks on the victim's neck, the killer had medium-sized hands. Not too small, not too big. Based on past experience and research, males most often choose strangulation as a murder method. You should look for a man with average-sized hands."

I heard footsteps shuffling in April's office before she said, "You're being presumptuous about the gender. We've had our fair share of unusual female killers around here lately. Any fingerprints?"

I recently had a conversation with Connor about forensics being able to trace the killer's identity by picking up impressions on the victim's skin. Oils left behind had allowed for the unique qualities of a person's fingerprints to be more easily obtained. Had we gotten lucky this time?

"No fingerprints. My guess is the killer wore gloves or some sort of protection on his hands. However, let me tell you about the order of events the night Quint Crawford was murdered. A few things might surprise you. At roughly midnight, he was—" the coroner said as the door slammed shut.

Chapter 7

Later that Thursday morning, after working out at the Grey Sports Complex and drafting an article for a mystery journal about Alfred Hitchcock's early career, I texted Connor to find out when he'd return from San Francisco. I assumed he was still in the Pacific Time Zone, but his lack of a response meant he was either in flight or busily attending to the case. I desperately wanted to find out what else the coroner had shared with April, and I was certain Connor might be slightly more open to telling me. My brother and I had similar-sized hands, and they were unquestionably larger than average. If what the coroner had told the sheriff was accurate, Gabriel couldn't have been responsible for strangling Quint Crawford.

I strolled across North Campus and headed toward Memorial Library, hoping Maggie might know Connor's current location. During summer sessions, Braxton always held a mini four-week May-June term where students spent a majority of their day focused on one specialized class. From late June through early August, each department also offered two regular classes for those students continuing their studies in between terms who would work twice as hard in half the normal amount of time. It provided an option for transfer students, or those who might've failed a previous course, to catch up before the beginning of the next semester. Locals often used the summers to squeeze in extra classes to graduate sooner than the normal four years.

As I approached the last meandering walkway, I ran into Fern Terry, the dean of student affairs, exiting the main administrative building. Most of the college's non-academic departments had offices in the large colonial-style structure built in the early twentieth century, each with an identical single window peering across campus. Several chimneys poked out of the medium-pitched, dark-colored roof, and a giant circular clock in its center upper peak served to report the official campus time.

"We're overdue for lunch," I said, stopping at a nearby pink dogwood tree where the two paths crossed. "I'm probably free any day next week. How about you?"

"I've got an out-of-town conference, then I'll be in panic mode trying to get ahead of the curve. Any chance you have time this weekend? I'd love to pick your brain about this upcoming family wedding." Fern towered over me. Her wide frame often reminded students of a football player fully dressed in all his gear and padding. She'd been trying to lose a few pounds lately and had hired a trainer to focus on the problem areas, a suggestion Dr. Betscha posed while reminding Fern she wasn't getting any younger. I believe she body-checked my poor cousin when he'd cavalierly delivered that news.

Although Fern's son and my aunt marrying into the Paddington family wouldn't make us related, we enjoyed thinking somehow it meant we were suddenly some sort of step-cousins eighteen times removed from one another. "Let's do dinner on Saturday. Emma has a sleepover with a friend, and I'll have the evening to myself." One of her schoolmates would be celebrating a birthday and had invited her four best pals to spend an afternoon at the local gymnastics facility followed by dinner at a Chuck E. Cheese's restaurant and an animated cartoon movie night.

"Perfect. Want to check out Simply Stoddard?" Fern explained that they'd be catering the wedding, and she wanted to sample a few of their dishes again before making the final decision on what would be served. The Paddingtons were paying for everything else at the wedding but had agreed to let Fern fund the food. I'd met the owners of the new downtown restaurant the month prior and recently tried to repair the remnants of our awkward relationship, especially after previously pushing them hard for answers during a murder investigation about their relocation to Braxton.

We agreed on a time, and Fern offered to make the reservation. "What's the status of the cable car redesign project?" I knew the area had been released by the police, but I wasn't sure if Fern had found a replacement crew.

"Endicott Construction is sending over a new guy to finish the last few items. I met with Nicholas myself, and he hired Cheney Stoddard to finish it," Fern added, complaining that Nicholas had gotten black paint all over her new blouse that day. While she excused herself to attend a meeting on time, I wondered whether the same black paint had been used to change the color of a few calla lilies. What motive could Nicky be hiding for stealing jewelry or murdering Quint? There seemed to be some confusion or discrepancies over future ownership of the company. I added it to my mental follow-up list.

I was glad to hear Cheney had found a job after losing out on the last opportunity when my brother had been hired to fix several cabins near the Saddlebrook National Forest. I rambled down the rest of the walkway and navigated my way toward the library to visit Maggie. On display in the lobby were the plans for the renovation they'd undertake in the fall semester. I was extremely excited to see the boring old structure being razed in favor of a newer, more modern facility.

Once I reached her office, Maggie said, "What brings you by, Kellan?" Maggie had immaculate alabaster skin, and her luscious brown hair had recently been cut shoulder length. She easily charmed others with her girl-next-door personality, a pleasant change of pace from her former ultra-reserved self.

"A few things. I heard the new library plans were released and wanted to see what the place would look like. That's gonna be one fantastic building when it's finished," I said, noticing her sister, Helena, standing in the corner. Wasn't she supposed to be at Woodland Warriors with my daughter?

"Hey, gorgeous. Looking sexy as always," Helena teased, following with a serenade of '*Super Bass*' by Nicki Minaj, complete with a brief booty dance that caused her sister to scowl.

"Helena, that's enough, we're in the library!" Maggie's face flushed bright red.

Helena repented by crossing her hands against her chest and bowing. "*Miss Innocent* over there says it's only going to take one year to pull off the whole re-model. Fancy that!"

"We'll be able to use part of the existing building while the new structure is built, but in the spring semester, we'll have a temporary library setup else-where. I'm still working through the final details," Maggie explained, before offering me a bottle of wa-ter and ignoring Helena. "What else can I do for you? Sorry, but I have a staff meeting to lead in a couple of minutes."

"I won't keep you. Have you heard from Connor? I need to talk to him about something."

"He should be landing at the Philadelphia airport around this time tomorrow, then he's driving back to Wharton County. Everything okay?" Maggie asked with a slight squint.

"Yes, just wanted to find out about his trip. I left him a message. He'll probably reply when he has time." I didn't want to say too much in front of Helena, but I also wasn't sure how close Connor and Maggie were these days. He'd been dating both Maggie and my sister, Eleanor, which wasn't something I could ever be comfortable with. I've always been a one-woman kind of guy, but if he was able to keep the peace until deciding which girl was better for him, I could easily keep my mouth shut about the situation. I was currently under the impression Eleanor's feelings for him had begun waning over time.

"I'll escort you. I need to get to work," Helena said, as Maggie led us back to the lobby of the library. While Maggie kept walking down the hall to her meeting, Helena locked onto my arm as we exited the building. "So, what's shaking, studly?"

"I heard Cheney is finishing the cable car repairs. A good move for him," I said while rolling my eyes, even though she'd previously told me things weren't going well since their break-up.

"He mentioned it this morning. Cheney's excited, but I'm not letting him get the wrong idea. I don't want to be in a relationship," Helena explained once we reached the main campus entrance.

"Are you attending the funeral for Quint tomorrow?" I asked when we stopped near the gate.

Helena repeated that she needed to get to Woodland Warriors for her afternoon shift. She and the assistant teacher split the day, guaranteeing there was someone onsite for early morning drop-offs as well as someone for late evening pick-ups. "Yes, but I'll be there late. I won't be done at the camp until seven o'clock. It's sad, but I'm looking forward to seeing the rest of the Alpha Iota Omega sisters," Helena replied while digging in her pocketbook for her car keys.

"I didn't know you'd been part of a sorority," I exclaimed. Helena, like Gabriel, was four years younger than Maggie and me, which meant we'd never attended high school or college at the same time. "Is that the group of friends you mentioned the other day?"

Helena nodded. "Imogene Grey, Krissy Stanton, Tiffany Nutberry, and I pledged together in the spring of our sophomore year. We had such an amazing time back then, but I was a lot pluckier femme fatale when I was younger, I guess."

From everything I knew and what Maggie had told me, Helena was still a wild child. "You were all in a pledge class together? Was Gabriel a part of this group of friends?"

"Sure was. Quint Crawford, Paul Dodd, and Nicky Endicott were the other guys we hung out with. The eight of us spent our free time together before eventually parting ways," she explained.

"Did Gabriel talk to you about why he left town that summer?"

"Nah. He and I weren't all that close. It was a little awkward because we knew you and Maggie had once dated... we kinda kept a little distance between us." Helena declared again that she had to leave to ensure on-time arrival at Woodland Warriors.

I hadn't realized Helena knew everyone involved. Could she have unexpected information about who might've stolen the jewelry or killed Quint? I planned to tread carefully. Most people believed Quint had died of natural causes, despite my inclination that electrocution didn't qualify as *natural*. I'd have to navigate the conversation gently from the jewelry burglaries toward motives for wanting Quint dead. "A couple of questions. It shouldn't take too long. Your family had some jewelry stolen lately, right?" I knew the rubies belonged to her mother and her sister, but what did she know about them?

"Yeah, it was kinda creepy. Maggie freaked out when she realized someone had stolen them while she was at work, but that calla lily was the strangest thing. I overheard Connor tell Maggie there was a flower left at all the places where something had been stolen. You can't tell anyone else, though." Helena looked at her watch and motioned for me to hurry up. "Sorry, can't lose this job, babe. Plus, Emma prefers me to the other assistant teacher."

I'm sure Emma did. She'd raved about Miss Roarke's lessons the prior evening. "It's a little strange that four of the girls in your sorority's pledge class had something stolen last time, and it appears to be happening again to the same crew of families. Anything you might know about that?"

Helena's face flushed, and she averted her gaze. "I really need to go, Kellan."

"Wait. This is important. If you know something, please tell me so I can... never mind why." I gently grabbed her arm to prevent her from walking away. "I don't mean this how it sounds, but I helped find George Braun's real killer last time, so you weren't stuck in jail. It's payback time." Helena owed me for everything I'd done to protect her when she'd been accused of knifing the professor.

"Ugh, okay. You can't tell anyone else." Helena made me swear on Francesca's grave, which made no sense, but she didn't know the reason. "It's about something we did to join the sisterhood."

My fraternity had done some questionable things back in the day, but there were lines we'd never crossed. It seemed like that wasn't the case for other Greek societies, but not everyone operated the same. Generally, each new semester, sororities and fraternities would hold social functions to search for new members during the *rush period*. It allowed everyone to decide which organization best matched their interests before officially moving forward with a decision. Some Greek societies requested formal applications for a board review; others accepted any new members. At Braxton, it had been more of an exclusive membership. The sorority or fraternity employed clandestine notification procedures when notifying potential members about entering their probationary period. During the subsequent weeks, the candidates became official pledges and would have to learn detailed facts about each official member. They'd also perform semi-shady actions before being inducted as a full sister or brother, hence the appropriate fear of hazing and bullying practices. As part of the pledging process to become a member of the Alpha Iota Omega sorority, each new pledge class had been burdened with a trifecta: something complex, dangerous, and unethical. It was considered a test to see how far each girl would go to become a full-fledged sister, but it'd also been designed to create a bond and a secret between the girls, ensuring they'd protect one another no matter what the cost.

"What exactly were the four of you tasked with doing when you pledged?" I pushed, worried about what she might reveal and how it connected to suspects responsible for Quint's strangulation.

"Look, it was foolish, but we only stole that first piece of jewelry. We were going to give it back, except then...." Helena revealed the entire sordid story.

The Alpha Iota Omega sorority had been founded by a group of women from five major families who'd lived in Braxton in the early 1900s—Paddington, Nutberry, Grey, Roarke, and Stanton. The year Helena pledged had been the one-hundredth anniversary, and the sorority's leadership had requested something preposterously massive to prove to all the alumni that they were the strongest members. The assignment dropped on the newest pledge class—steal a piece of jewelry from one of the original founding families, then present it on the night they'd be formally inducted into the sisterhood. There were only four members in Helena's class representing the Nutberry, Grey, Roarke, and Stanton families. None of the Paddington girls had been in college at the time, enabling the four of them to easily agree to steal the jewelry from the Paddington family.

"We were attending a performance at the Paddington Play House when Krissy saw the brooch on the floor. We decided to take it that night and agreed to keep our actions secret. The plan was to give it back to the Paddingtons at the induction ceremony, but then something went off-track," Helena added with noticeable discomfort over revealing her sisterhood's reprehensible secrets. "Krissy gave the brooch to the president of the sorority after the show. We all saw her put it in the safe, but when we went to retrieve it for the induction ceremony the following week with the alumni, it was missing."

Helena explained that they'd been too scared to go to the police, especially when more thefts kept happening over the next month. Once the burglaries had stopped, the girls vowed never to speak about them again. Helena and her pledge sisters had become full members of the sorority, the police never learned it'd been meant as a joke, and the girls had moved on with their lives. I assumed that one of the girls in the sorority must've removed the brooch from the safe, which meant she was potentially the same person who'd committed the crimes years ago. It didn't explain how Quint's death aligned with the burglaries unless one of the girls had started stealing again and had lost the ruby while killing him in the cable car for some other reason. Had Quint caught the thief and been punished? It also didn't explain Gabriel's involvement, but the timing of his departure from Braxton could've been an abject coincidence. It was imperative I found out what records the pawn shop had kept eight years ago.

* * *

I spent the rest of the evening researching a work project, training Baxter, and watching a few cartoons before tucking Emma in bed and nodding off on the couch. When I woke up on Friday, Connor still hadn't returned my text message which worried me that he'd unearthed troubling news about my brother. I dropped off Emma at the bus stop, watched her leave for camp, and spent the morning dealing with some administrative responsibilities at Braxton. Since I would attend the wake for Quint Crawford at the Whispering Pines funeral parlor after class, my mother agreed to meet Emma when the bus dropped her off after camp. I planned to pick up my daughter from the Royal Chic-Shack once my evening finished.

In need of a break, I escaped to run a few errands and order a sandwich at a local deli for lunch. By the time I ate and returned a few phone calls in my office, my afternoon lecture was ready to begin. I used the back staircase to access the first floor and walked toward the classroom. As I approached it, I heard two women chatting. I recognized the voices as Imogene and Krissy and remained in the hallway to snoop on their conversation. I usually wouldn't eavesdrop on someone else's private discussion, but if they knew something about the current burglaries or Quint's death, it would be beneficial for me to listen in and share any news with April and Connor. I just hoped it wasn't a conversation about shoes!

"Seriously, you've always wanted him. You tried to steal Quint from me years ago too," Imogene said to Krissy in a demure voice.

Krissy shouted, "I would've had him except you kept stringing him along with promises. You broke his heart when you chose Paul. And you probably broke his heart again this time, you fool."

"That's just silly. You've got it backward. Quint was acting strangely while we were together, and that's when I decided to get serious with Paul," Imogene countered with a curt, supercilious tone. "None of it matters anymore. He's gone, and I'm engaged to Paul. And I know things about *you*."

"You've been dating Paul for almost eight years now. I doubt our new town councilman will actually marry you. He'll want a wife he can be proud of, not a disingenuous French tart," Krissy yelled.

I heard the sound of a harsh slap and assumed Imogene must have attacked Krissy. The door opened down the hall and Siobhan called out to me. "Hi, Dr. Ayrwick. How're you today?"

Imogene responded, "You're jealous because none of the guys in our group desired you."

"That's not true. You don't know anything about—"

I interrupted by walking into the room. I couldn't stand there playing the role of slobbering spectator while Siobhan watched me, so I waved her over and attempted to calm the other girls. "Whatever is going on between the two of you needs to stop right now. Students are beginning to arrive, and it's obvious you're both terribly upset. Let's take a quick break." I asked Siobhan to accompany Krissy to the restroom while she splashed cool water on her face since she'd just been smacked.

Imogene stepped outside with me, and I said, "Do you want to talk about what just happened?"

"That's not necessary. Krissy is, and has always been, a bully. We were best friends a long time ago, but she's grown far worse over the years. We'll work it out. I promise it won't interfere with class," Imogene said, looking nervously at the ground and rubbing the hand she'd used to whack Krissy's cheek.

Something about Imogene's reaction felt insincere or forced. Given the sudden violent outburst I'd witnessed, her newly calm exterior wouldn't have been my initial expectation. If she were capable of such a quick transition, what else might she be hiding? Could Imogene have been the one to steal the Paddington brooch from the sorority's safe eight years ago, then gone on a rampage thieving all the rest of the jewelry? If that were true, she would've had to fake the robbery at her mother's place the prior weekend.

Then, I remembered that Quint had been distraught over a break-up. Krissy had mentioned Quint and Imogene had been in love years ago, and she'd ended it for some reason. The only motivation I could understand for Imogene killing Quint would be if he'd discovered the truth about the robberies and confronted her. Was Imogene truly capable of murdering someone she'd once been seriously involved with? Sometimes people surprised you with the secrets they kept. It was a long shot, but I needed to consider all theories and suspects while collecting more information about Quint's life and current relationships. "I'm glad your issues with Krissy won't cause further incidents in class. You're overwhelmed by your friend's death. Emotions run high during painful times."

"Quint and I were friends long ago, but we lost touch. I'd overlooked how much I missed him until recently," Imogene said as she perched modestly on a nearby bench.

A few students walked by, including Raquel. I'd forgotten she wanted to talk after class today. As Imogene's head hung low, Raquel checked if everything was okay. I nodded and told her we'd be inside momentarily. "Imogene, maybe the funeral will help provide a way to say a proper goodbye."

"You're right, thank you. I appreciate your kindness, but we should get back to class." Imogene jumped up and walked toward Diamond Hall with determined steps.

After she trotted away, I struggled to understand the exchange that had occurred between her and Krissy. It was clear Krissy had been jealous of Imogene, but what was Krissy's relationship with Quint before he had been killed? Neither girl seemed capable of strangling Quint under normal conditions, yet during an intense argument, it might be possible, especially if Quint had threatened to call the cops. Both women had average-sized hands, though

Krissy's were slightly larger than Imogene's. What I struggled to understand was *why someone would electrocute Quint after they'd already strangled him.* It was unfortunate I couldn't listen to the coroner's explanation about the order of the events when Quint had been murdered. Was the electrocution simply to cover up evidence, or had it occurred first? Still, someone had turned off the power source before I'd arrived, making things even murkier. Could the jogger I'd witnessed have been the killer coming back to retrieve the gloves and turn off the power? Sandalwood was a strong scent, and I might stumble upon someone wearing it again. I wanted to ask more direct questions, but people believed Quint had died of an accidental electrocution. I couldn't even hint about murder, not without the repercussions of idle gossip. Ugh, so frustrating!

The remainder of my lecture completed smoothly. I made a last-minute change to limit the amount of time students would work in groups, theorizing it'd be best to keep the two girls from interacting with one another immediately after they'd had a fight. After everyone left, Raquel and I spent thirty minutes reviewing her background and discussing her interest in the film industry. "What was your undergraduate degree in?"

"Political science and economics, but I went to graduate school and earned an MBA with a focus on management and leadership. I worked for a few years before getting married. I'm still figuring out what's next," she responded and crossed her legs. Only a few inches of skin could be seen below the hem of her skirt and the top of her knee-high leather boots.

"Do you see yourself working in the entertainment business, or is this class just something to keep from being bored until you find the right job?" I asked, curious whether she planned to remain in Braxton or move elsewhere. There would be little opportunity to make movies or films in this part of the country, at least not as a full-time job. While a few production companies and studios had opened in New York City and the southern part of the country, I wasn't familiar with anything major in Pennsylvania that would attract her attention.

"Mostly to keep busy while my husband focuses on his career. We might move to the West Coast if his current job doesn't pan out. What's Los Angeles like?" Raquel flashed her colorful eyes at me and leaned in closer. "Did you work with any celebrities or important people? Were you on camera?"

"A few stars crossed my path. My expertise is in investigative reporting, historical crimes, and behind-the-scenes coordination. I'm not interested in acting or dealing with fans. I like my privacy." In the past, several colleagues had pushed me to audition for roles on the popular crime shows, but I didn't want to worry about always looking perfect, interacting with followers, and playing distinct roles. My skills were in getting things done, not projecting an image I couldn't possibly maintain twenty-four-seven.

"You're a handsome man. You've built a following, even if you don't want to admit it. I did some research when I saw you'd be teaching this class. How come you're back in Pennsylvania? Based on what you want to do, you'd be better off in LA." Raquel licked her lips and tilted her head to the side.

For a hot second, I wondered if she were flirting with me. While she was attractive, we were both married even if I intended to terminate my relationship as soon as Las Vargas released Francesca. "I'm not comfortable having that conversation. Let's focus on you and what I can do to help."

"Just trying to comprehend how you made your decisions. I thought it might help me understand if I'd be better off moving to Hollywood." She leaned back again, reining in her lingering glances and coquettish smile. "I've heard the rumors about you solving a lot of murders around here. You must be fantastic at your job. You should've gone into the FBI instead of directing and teaching."

"I considered it when I was younger. I've always had a knack for solving puzzles and figuring out people's secrets. It's easy to see through the walls people put up when you listen to the words they use, especially if I feel like someone's not being truthful with me." Once I'd moved to the West Coast and been granted a few lucky breaks, I'd grown too enamored with Hollywood and decided not to leave it until recently. But I was happier with my life these days, especially being closer to my family again.

"As long as you're careful. I overheard Krissy and Imogene talking about the jewelry thefts during break. It sounds dangerous. Hopefully, you're not getting involved in solving that crime!" Raquel handed me a print-out of next semester's courses. "This is what I hope to take. What do you think?"

"First off, I think the sheriff is capable of solving the burglaries. Second, my plate is full these days. Now, let's peruse your proposal." I glanced at her suggestions and agreed with her enrollment plans. Perhaps she was simply bored and nosy and wanted to get to know me better. I shared some background on how she could study the film industry outside of Braxton. After Raquel left, my phone vibrated with a text that accentuated the already disastrous aura surrounding the upcoming evening.

Connor: *Just landed. We need to talk about your brother. It's important.*

Me: *What did Gabriel do now? We can meet at the wake tonight.*

Connor: *Okay. For starters, it seems like he's involved in some or all the jewelry thefts.*

Me: *Perhaps it just looks that way? Give me some hope here, man.*

Connor: *Gabriel has also quickly risen on my list of suspects potentially connected with Quint's murder.*

Me: *That's not helping me! He's NOT a murderer.*

Connor: *I wish I had better news, but I might be forced to get a warrant issued for his arrest tomorrow.*

Chapter 8

Post Connor's last text message, my body yearned for positive distraction. When I checked on Emma, my mother had just arrived home and was heating dinner for all of them. The housekeeper had stored a meal in the refrigerator when she'd finished cooking earlier that day; my mother was not the most domestic person I knew. After our chat, I stopped at the Pick-Me-Up Diner for a quick bite to eat with Eleanor. With one hour before Quint's service, it would be beneficial to hold a sibling catch up.

"Look what the cat dragged in," she teased as I walked inside the recently renovated eatery a few blocks from campus. A turquoise and slate-gray sundress adorned my sister's solid and compact body, features she'd struggled to accept until realizing their value during her field hockey days. Wide hips and thick, muscular arms came from the Danby side of the family, and they weren't something she could change. Eleanor handed a receipt to a customer who dashed past me and into the parking lot.

"Good evening to you too. Do you greet all your best customers that way?" I asked as she kissed my cheek and handed two menus to a waitress who was seating someone ahead of me.

"Only the ones I love. Follow me to the office. I need to call back a supplier. You can stop in the kitchen to pick up our meals from Chef Manny. He should be done by now," Eleanor said while walking to the far corner of the diner. When she said Manny's name, I could swear her eyes brightened.

While she made a right toward her office, I stopped in front of the kitchen and gently pushed open the swinging door. Before I could lean my head inside to let Manny know we were ready, his voice echoed in the hall. It would either be an insurance issue or a health code violation for me to wander into the kitchen. I didn't work there and had no training; therefore, I wouldn't step all the way inside.

"Nah, she doesn't know. I'm afraid to tell her. What if it doesn't come through?" Manny said with an excess of hesitation in his voice. I couldn't see him because he stood behind the door cooking on the grill. He must not have been talking to me, given I hadn't a clue what he'd meant.

Another muffled voice responded, "She's the boss. You gotta tell her today if you're gonna leave town. It's an amazing opportunity. Does Eleanor know you got married on that Vegas trip?"

Manny replied, "Nope. I couldn't bring myself to disappoint her. We've worked together for years and gotten very close. I'd feel like a jerk to up and leave just when she took over the joint."

As far as I could tell, Manny was happy working at the diner. I'd always suspected he had the whisper of an attraction to Eleanor, but nothing had ever come of it. He'd gone on vacation after she'd bought the place that spring, but once he'd returned, Eleanor thought he'd begun acting strangely. She assumed he was solicitous because they used to be peers, yet as the owner, she was officially his boss instead of just the serving staff manager. It hadn't been an easy road for my sister, especially when the contractor she'd hired for the repairs absconded with some of her money and she later failed the initial electrical inspection. It would be a disaster if her chef resigned in the first few months.

Manny must have noticed the door was slightly ajar. "Who's there?"

I poked my head inside and smiled. "*Hola, amigo.* Eleanor says she's ready for our dinner."

"Hey, Kellan, I'll bring it to her office in a minute. Is Emma here?" Manny loved visiting with my daughter. She would suggest ideas for meals whenever Eleanor watched Emma for me.

"Not today. She's with my parents, but we'll be back again soon, I'm sure. How's everything with you?" I asked, wondering if he'd say anything to me about the news I'd just overheard.

"*Bueno.* Tell her I said hi," he replied without looking up from the grill.

As a waitress picked up a hot dish, I scooted out of her way and headed toward Eleanor's office. When I arrived, my sister hung up the phone and said, "All good?"

"That depends. Have you figured out why Manny was acting weird the last two months?" I didn't want to be the one to tell Eleanor but also wasn't sure I knew the whole story. What amazing opportunity had the other kitchen worker been talking about?

"We chatted a few weeks ago. I got the impression he was doing okay, but I know he's holding back. I'm not sure if he's upset that I bought the diner and he wanted to try to swing it himself, or if there's something else going on." Eleanor absentmindedly cleared her desk, so we had a place to eat. "I didn't think he wanted to buy his own place. He likes operating behind the scenes, kind of like you."

I told Eleanor what I'd overheard and offered a minor concession to make her feel better. "Maybe I misunderstood the conversation. I can be easily confused."

"Him quitting would be awful news. I'm gonna confront Manny." She marched past me in a fury.

I grabbed her arm. "Hold up, Attila. Maybe now isn't the best time. Wait until things slow down when you can talk to him alone."

Eleanor couldn't respond when Manny walked in with two plates and set them on the desk. "It's today's special. Chicken cordon bleu with scalloped potatoes."

"It smells amazing. You're the best chef around. I'm really glad we're working together. I should probably give you a raise, huh?" Eleanor said, patting him on the back. She was laying it on a little thick, in my humble opinion, but at least she didn't confront him.

Manny blushed and waved his hands at her as he stepped backward out of the office. "No, no. Everything is good. I need to get back to the kitchen." He glanced back at her longer than I'd expected.

Eleanor scowled at me. "He's got that same look on his face that you get whenever you feel guilty about something. Is it a man thing? Why can't you just tell us the truth?" She sliced into her chicken with a little too much energy and precision and grunted at me like an angry troll.

"Don't take your frustrations out on me, little sister. I do not keep things from people."

"One word," she said, looking at me with a devious smirk.

"Awesome?"

"Francesca."

She had a point. I was keeping my wife's reincarnation from our parents. "That's different."

"I know." Eleanor's entire demeanor had changed since I'd shown up fifteen minutes earlier. "I just wanted to bring up her name, so you could tell me the latest."

I updated Eleanor on my partnership with April, the calls from Cristiano, and the meeting with the

Castiglianos. I expected something new to happen over the weekend but feared the outcome of it would be another unwelcome surprise. She helped me stay as calm as possible under the circumstances. "I should head to the funeral home for Quint's service soon."

"Poor guy. He used to flirt with me all the time when he'd come in for lunch or a late dinner. I liked him a lot, and he could be awfully persuasive and assertive, but Quint just wasn't my type. Although, I almost yielded to his seduction once. He knew how to make you feel special, but he'd also pined away for Imogene way too long and couldn't commit to another girl," Eleanor explained with a rueful sigh.

"I've heard that about him. Do you think he'd ever hurt a woman?" I'd experienced mixed responses from different people in Quint's life regarding his behavior. He'd worshipped all the ladies he'd dated but struggled to view others, like Fern, as an authority figure. I could only conclude that he was a bit of a chameleon, depending on the situation and balance of power in the relationship. I theorized someone had resented his quicksilver ability to dazzle a woman and then disappoint her when he snatched back his charms. Or had someone like Paul begrudged Quint's past with Imogene? It wouldn't be the first time a jealous man killed to protect the woman he loved.

"Nah, I think Quint pushed too hard, but he would stop when a woman said *no*. He always did with me. He was very smart, despite having an ego even bigger than yours." Eleanor mindlessly massaged the scar on her elbow she'd gotten from a grease fire years ago.

"Touché, Attila." I didn't want to gossip about Gabriel's potential role in the jewelry thefts until he and I talked through it, even though she was our sister. When we finished eating and I noticed it was time for Quint's service, I warned Eleanor to go easy on Manny and suggested he was only *thinking* about moving to Las Vegas with his new wife. Sometimes people mulled over their options before making a final decision—she shouldn't jump to conclusions. As the words spilled from my lips, I realized I should take my own banal advice. I'd already deemed Gabriel guilty of a string of crimes, regardless of discovering adequate proof or having a discussion with him about what'd happened in the past.

* * *

I stepped through the front door of Whispering Pines, shivering at the thought of having to attend another wake. The funeral home smelled like lilacs even when they weren't in season. It was the Nutberry's attempt to disguise the smell of embalming fluids and force people to forget what happened to dead bodies before they were put on display for grieving relatives and friends.

Lydia Nutberry chatted with Nana D and Bertha Crawford in the far corner. Unwilling to interrupt, I circulated the room to verify who else had attended. I stopped at the casket to pay my respects and say goodbye to Quint Crawford. I'd only known him for less than two weeks, but I'd never seen him dressed in anything other than jeans and a t-shirt. Today, he wore a dark-brown suit, off-white dress shirt, and a muted beige tie. He looked like a completely different man, one who was uncomfortable in his current attire.

"I told you I'd be here, Kellan. You didn't need to sic Nana D on me. She was all over me earlier, like a lion on a fresh carcass," Gabriel blasted once I stood from kneeling at the coffin.

I turned and stared at my brother. He wore a dark-colored suit and light-blue dress shirt and matching tie, looking just as uncomfortable as Quint and me. "I didn't force her to do or say anything. You know Nana D. She grabs the bull by its horns with her own hands."

Gabriel led me by the jacket sleeve to the side of the room. "Let's not do this tonight. I got all your messages. I know you have questions, but this isn't the appropriate place. Are you available tomorrow? We could grab a drink at Kirklands like last time, where I spilled my secrets."

"Sure, tomorrow's fine, but come by in the morning for breakfast. Emma would love to see you," I replied as Connor ambled nearby and jerked his head to the side to indicate where we should meet. "What I know doesn't make much sense, and you're foolishly hiding something from everyone."

"Tomorrow at nine. I'll be there," Gabriel said before walking away. I followed to remind him I was on his side, but he joined two guys sitting a few rows away near the front window. One of them was the new town councilman and Imogene's fiancé, Paul Dodd. Based on the resemblance, I assumed the other was Nicholas Endicott, the son Lindsey had procreated with a former girlfriend he'd met at his forty-ninth birthday party. It'd had been quite a shock to his friends and family when he'd become a father again at such a late time in life.

In another row just beyond, Imogene, Krissy, Tiffany, and Helena were deep in conversation. All eight members of the former close-knit group were present, except one would soon be buried six feet underground. What did each know about Quint's death and the jewelry thefts? As I strolled away, that familiar sandalwood scent I'd smelled near the cable car filled the air. I couldn't exactly walk up to each of them and sniff their necks like a pig searching for truffles; that would look bizarre. Which one had been the jogger I'd seen collecting the gloves the day Quint had died? It could've been a coincidence, but I no longer believed in them when it came to the murder investigations I'd become embroiled in.

"I'm glad you waited for Gabriel to step away before we talked," Connor began as soon as I reached the corner. "April told me she informed you why I was in San Francisco."

"I'm not going to like your news very much, am I?" Briefly abandoning my quest for the person wearing the cologne, I planned to sniff out the trail after Connor and I conversed.

"It's not all bad. I managed to track down the employee who was working the night the Roarke rubies had been pawned," Connor said, demonstrating why he'd been the perfect addition to the Wharton County Sheriff's Office. "Two people had initially come into the shop, but they both left after an argument in the main entranceway. Only one person returned afterward to fill out the forms to sell the rubies. The store still had the record."

"Why didn't they offer it to Sheriff Crawford? April indicated the information wasn't in her files."

"The shop owner swears he faxed over the record when the former sheriff requested it. What happened after that, I have no clue. I have my suspicions but can't be certain." Connor might do his best to protect my brother, but he wouldn't skirt the law. "This wasn't the shadiest shop I've seen. I think they tried to do the right thing, and they were cooperative with me. I'm quite sure they broke a few rules last time." Connor put his hand on my back and squeezed my shoulder. "The name on the record is Gabriel Ayrwick. Sorry, buddy."

A minute passed as the news digested. I looked at my baby brother as sadness crept inside my body like I hadn't experienced in a long time. "Does that mean he's the thief you're looking for?"

Connor explained that there was no record of the other person's name, nor were there any video recordings from eight years ago. "The worker handed the money to your brother. Do you know how pawn shops function?" After I shook my head, as I hadn't been one-hundred percent familiar, Connor shared the store's policy for loaning cash to a customer who pawned an item. If the hawker brought back the cash within one month, plus any additional amount for store fees, the item would be returned. If nobody showed up within one month, the item could be sold to someone else for any price. "There is an interesting fact about how this one turned out."

"Gabriel went back to try to retrieve the item, right?" I wanted to believe my brother was innocent, but the details Connor had learned on his trip were incontrovertible.

"He couldn't have. Just before the one month was up, an anonymous caller notified the shop that the rubies belonged to someone in Braxton. The shop eventually contacted Sheriff Crawford who requested photos. Formal paperwork was filed, and the rubies were returned to the Roarke family." The pawn shop dealt with their insurance agency, and the sheriff followed up on the report of who'd pawned them. But we don't know what Crawford did because the report wasn't included in his files. Something happened to stop him from searching for Gabriel.

"Do you have any idea whom Gabriel was with at the pawn shop?"

"The worker at the pawn shop couldn't remember if it was a woman or a man who'd initially walked in with your brother. Gabriel's tattoos and piercings had made too big of an impression on him that day," Connor replied, shaking his head and smirking. "I'll ask Lucy Roarke what Sheriff Crawford said when he returned the stolen rubies. He might have been covering for your brother."

"Do you think the Roarkes opted not to file charges because Gabriel was involved, and they didn't want to hurt my family?"

Connor nodded. "I'm afraid that might have transpired. It doesn't explain why no one tried to locate all the other stolen items, nor why similar thefts are happening all over again."

When we looked up to see what Gabriel was doing, my brother had already left the funeral parlor. So had Nicholas Endicott, Paul Dodd, and most of the girls from the sorority. I considered telling Connor what Helena had revealed about the hazing ritual to steal the original brooch from the Paddingtons, but I wanted to speak with Gabriel first. If he and Quint had gotten into a volatile argument together, could Gabriel have taken it too far? A man can go through a lot in eight years to change his personality; however, the size of my brother's hands and fingers couldn't have matched the marks around Quint's neck. Was there an accomplice, an unknown person who could be responsible?

Nana D interrupted me before I could ask Connor about his next steps. "Bertha would like to speak with you. Do you have a minute?"

Connor excused himself, indicating he'd follow up with me over the weekend. I didn't know whether he was going to arrest my brother or wait until he had more information. As far as I was concerned, Gabriel's role in the current round of robberies was circumstantial. It was likely Gabriel would only be a person of interest until they found something to tie him to the new crimes. Could they arrest him for the ones eight years ago? I assumed there wasn't any statute of limitations on robbery if you eventually found the guilty party. I followed Nana D to the small sitting area in the other corner where a worn-down Bertha Crawford leaned against the arm of the chair. The sandalwood smell had already been replaced by lilacs. I'd lost my chance to locate the potential culprit or accomplice.

"Thank you, Kellan. I'm glad you could spare some time." Bertha's shaky hand reached toward me, and her Georgian accent was still strong, despite the cancer's persistent grip on her life. The once plump and matronly woman, blessed with a head of thick gray curls, had deteriorated into a bony and sallow-skinned shell. She'd done her best to hide the painful changes in her body, but nothing concealed the effects of the rampant disease on her face and hair. A black scarf was elegantly wrapped around the top of her head, yet it was obvious she had little desire or strength to combat the truth.

"I'm truly sorry for your loss, Bertha," I said, remembering she'd yelled whenever I'd called her Mrs. Crawford in the past. "Quint and I had a few laughs the last couple of weeks while he was working on the cable car redesign project. I know how proud you were of him."

"I can't believe he's gone. I should've been the one to die first. I don't understand how an old lady like me can linger around with cancer, but a strong young man like him can be murdered by a crazy person." Her face was stoic, and she refused to cry in public.

"What do you mean murdered by a crazy person?" Had April or Connor told her more than me?

"That new sheriff promised me she's going to find his killer, but I saw how you tracked down what happened to Gwendolyn Paddington. I need your help, Kellan. I'm begging you to investigate who killed my boy." Bertha closed her eyes and buried her forehead in her hands.

I looked at Nana D with confusion and hesitancy over Gabriel's potential involvement in the situation. "I'm not sure that's the best idea. What did the sheriff indicate was the cause of death?"

Bertha mumbled a mostly incoherent response. All I could understand was that Quint had been electrocuted, but someone had also choked him to death with their hands. There were no fingerprints found on his body or inside the cable car. "I can't speak too much about Quinton's life outside of the little he'd told me. For the last month, all he'd done was work for Nicky Endicott and take care of me."

I'd investigate Nicky as a priority, but if I had any chance of finding Quint's killer, I needed to know everything he'd been up to and whom he'd socialized with recently. Bertha confirmed there were no other family members in the area, and they'd mostly kept to themselves since her diagnosis. "Was Quint dating anyone? He told me he'd fallen in love, but it'd ended poorly."

Bertha considered my question, then shook her head. "Not that he shared. He dated a few women in Braxton, but he'd never gotten over Imogene. Isn't she engaged to another man, though?"

Paul Dodd was on my list, but I knew little about him. Had he been wearing the cologne? When I pushed Bertha for more information, she lost most of her energy. I squeezed her hand and told her I'd do my best to look into it. "Imogene told me they were once friends. I'll see what she knows. She might be our only other real lead right now."

"Is there anyone Quint fought with who might have tried to hurt him?" Nana D asked.

"I can't imagine who would've been that angry. The only person he had an argument with was that Irish girl, and she was just upset because my boy changed his mind about her." Bertha closed her eyes and rested her head against a pillow Nana D had placed on the back of the chair.

Irish girl? Who was she talking about? It took me a minute to piece together everything she'd said. "Do you mean Siobhan Walsh? The young woman whose twins you'd been babysitting?"

"Yes, that's her. Quinton and Siobhan went on a few dates, but it didn't work out. She was irate with him when it ended." Bertha's pleading eyes were cast in my direction. "Please find out who did this to Quinton. I must know soon... it's doubtful... I'll recuperate from this invasive disease."

Nana D suggested I search Quint's bedroom at Bertha's house to locate any potential clues. It was a solid idea, and I agreed to visit as soon as possible. We agreed that someone needed to chat with Siobhan to understand what'd taken place between her and Quint, even if it had nothing to do with his death. On the flip side, if Siobhan had a motive for hurting him, and they had a fight in the cable car, maybe she was somehow involved in his murder. She also mentioned not earning enough money before taking the new job with my mother in the admission's office. I vividly recalled Siobhan's response to Imogene on the first day of class about how she had to take care of a man who'd once hurt her. Had she been referring to Quint? It couldn't be, I convinced myself. This was merely another case of circumstantial evidence.

Bertha asked Nana D if she could accompany her to the casket for a last goodbye before the graveside service the following morning. As they shuffled away, I felt someone fiercely jab at my shoulder. Upon turning around, an awkward-looking Lydia Nutberry thrust one hand on her hip and waggled an index finger with the other. The last time I'd spoken with Lydia occurred before I'd provoked her sister-in-law into confessing to murder the prior month. What was I about to get myself into?

Chapter 9

"I'm very angry with you," Lydia scowled. Unfortunately blessed with an austere countenance, she also kept her dark-gray hair shellacked tightly in a bun on the crown of her head. Lydia wore an oversized suit jacket that hung on her body like last threads gripping a broken hanger in fear of eternal loss. Delicately balanced tiny glasses connected to a stringy beaded chain and chunky black orthopedic sneakers completed the peculiar outfit. Her pointy nose and chin, not all that different from a stereotypical cartoon witch, usually warned people not to mess with her.

Convinced she wouldn't make a scene in the middle of a funeral service, I let her quietly vent rather than defend my actions. "I'm terribly sorry for how everything exploded at the Mendel flower show opening. I had no intention of harming your family when my speech compelled your sister-in-law to admit what she'd done to Judy's husband." While it wasn't exactly a true statement, the Wharton County Sheriff's Office preferred that my involvement appeared unintentional to the general public. They feared Lissette's lawyer would claim she'd been coerced into a false confession, but the proof of her crime was irrefutable.

"At least you know well enough to begin with an apology." Lydia led me down the hall to her office. Our feet trod softly on a plush, emerald-green carpet as we passed endless walls covered on the top half with a floral print and the bottom half with burgundy wainscoting. "But you've got it all wrong. I'm not angry with you for discovering what my sister-in-law did."

Had I heard her correctly? "What do you mean? I thought you'd never speak with me again."

"Just like my husband thinks. The whole lot of you needs to be reeducated," Lydia pointed out as she took a seat behind her desk. "I'm ticked off because you didn't visit me after that incident happened. How long have our families known one another, Kellan?"

"Well, it's at least... oh, I'd say close to... um—" I began tracing our history and had just remembered attending camp with one of her sons when she interrupted me.

"Decades. That's long enough to expect a better reaction." Lydia explained that while she was saddened one sister-in-law had passed away and another had gone to the psychiatric ward for evaluation prior to a prison term, she passionately believed that people should be punished for their crimes and should seek mental help to recover whenever possible. Lydia was disgruntled with me for not checking on her or showing solidarity and support for her after all the bad publicity and rumors circulating around town about the Nutberry family.

"I should've known better. It's been a rough year for you." I recalled some of the reactions from the community. Sales had been down for her family's mortuary when customers went to neighboring villages to purchase funeral services. Nana D had also mentioned that the pharmacy was a ghost town since people worried about the unstable Nutberry family filling prescription drugs for patrons. After we repaired our relationship, Lydia flabbergasted me with her next topic.

"My daughter, Tiffany, is distraught over losing her friend at such an early age. You really ought to visit her this weekend; she could use some cheering up. But truthfully, there's another reason I wanted to talk to you." Lydia handed me a cup of tea from the Keurig machine on the credenza behind her. "With you being such a clever detective, I expect you are putting those skills to use and trying to find out what happened to Quint. Bertha is counting on you to solve this before she passes away. Quint didn't die from electrocution. He was murdered!"

I hadn't realized Bertha and Lydia were friends, but it made sense if their children had known one another. "Bertha asked me to help, but what if I discover something neither of you would want people to know?" Someone in that group of eight had stolen the jewelry, and my guess was that one of them had either killed Quint as revenge for something yet to be discovered or to cover up a role in the robberies. Quint couldn't have strangled himself, and I swore my brother wasn't capable of murder. It left six other options, despite nothing obvious connecting Tiffany, Lydia's daughter, to the crimes.

"The truth always has a funny way of clawing its way to the surface. I trust you will handle it with proper caution and respect," she counseled. Lydia was a strong woman who'd married into the Nutberry family and struggled to find her own place among a very stubborn crowd. She was direct but fair when listening to what other people had to tell her. "How can I help?"

"Since you've asked, perhaps you could tell me what you know about the jewelry thefts. Your family lost two things, right?" When she nodded in slight confusion, I added, "Not that Quint's death is necessarily connected to them, but it's important for me to understand everything. There was a stolen ruby found near Quint's body. Tell me what happened to your mother-in-law's choker eight years ago."

"I'm not sure what that has to do with the price of beans, but I'll share anything I can remember." Lydia removed her bifocals and pinched the bridge of her nose. "Agnes had taken it out of the safe that morning because she planned to wear it to Tiffany's concert. I know everyone thinks she bribed the director, but Tiffany was a wonderful musician. Maybe she wasn't the best flutist that season, but she was in the top three. What no one else ever admits is the girl who was the best had been suspected of a little powdered candy," she said, tapping the side of her nose and smiling ruefully at me.

Lydia finished sharing her story. Agnes had changed her outfit at the last minute and decided not to wear the choker. They were running late, prompting her not to take the time to lock it in the safe before leaving for the concert. When they'd returned home, it was missing. Agnes called the police, and the former sheriff personally visited the family the next morning. It had been the second theft at that point, but no one had made any connection to the first one until much later because of the confusion with where the Paddington brooch had been stolen and the revelation about the calla lilies consistently appearing at all the locations. Eventually, Agnes reported it to her insurance company and had been compensated for the loss. The choker was still missing to this day.

"How did Tiffany feel about the whole event? Quint was her friend, and his uncle couldn't help much," I said, wondering what Lydia might have surmised.

"Tiffany was barely twenty years old. She was acting a little strange, but all kids do at that age."

"Was she living in the Braxton dorms?"

"Yes, but she'd come home that weekend for a family party. I think she had friends over the day of the concert and was wrapped up in her social life. Come to think of it, Agnes showed everyone the choker that night while they were having dinner." Lydia confirmed all eight kids from the group, including Quint and my brother, had been at that meal before they'd left for the concert. All of Tiffany's friends had attended the concert, but they'd returned to the dorms once it finished. Lydia and Agnes had gone out for drinks. When they'd arrived home, the house was empty, and Agnes had discovered the choker was stolen. Tiffany confirmed she hadn't gone back to the house after the concert, so she wasn't sure either. She couldn't remember anyone disappearing, but it could've been possible.

"What about your earrings? Weren't they stolen a few weeks ago while you were at your sister-in-law's memorial service at the church?"

"Yes, Tiffany had worn them to an engagement party the night before, and she dropped them off at Whispering Pines. I also had eight-thousand dollars in cash in our safe that day." Lydia explained that she'd kept enough money in her office for incidentals and payments to vendors who offered discounts if she'd paid cash for certain services. She'd been the last one in the funeral parlor that evening and had thought she'd locked the safe but couldn't be certain. She was going directly to the church, so she left the earrings at the funeral parlor overnight. When she arrived the next morning, the safe had been emptied and a black calla lily left behind. She'd never needed cameras at the facility before, especially in her office, and there were no resultant fingerprints other than those of regular employees. "We've installed a new surveillance system already."

"Do you have any idea who might be responsible?" I asked, wondering if Tiffany had inadvertently revealed to anyone that she'd dropped the earrings off at the funeral home.

"Sheriff Montague mentioned there'd been a string of burglaries happening again. I just assumed it was random, but then she asked me this morning if I'd seen your brother lately. Surely, she doesn't think he's involved somehow, does she?" Lydia pulled back and gasped a little as if she'd just remembered something important.

"Are you okay?"

"Gabriel was driving Tiffany the day she dropped off the earrings. I forgot about it until just now. It was very quick, but she said he was waiting in the car as he had to make a call before they went to lunch." Lydia didn't know of other potential suspects who might've killed Quint, so I decided to hold off on any further questions. I needed to speak with Tiffany to find out what she was hiding from everyone.

Once Lydia and I finished chatting, we returned to the main room. I said goodbye to Nana D and Bertha, promising to call her soon with some questions and any updates on what'd happened to Quint. The room was mostly empty, and there was no one else I could follow up with about the situation. I'd had a long enough day and needed to pick up Emma from my parents. We were overdue to take the puppy out for his evening walk and read a bedtime story before Emma went to sleep.

* * *

Once Gabriel texted he was on his way over on Saturday morning, Emma and I prepared breakfast. It was less than a ten-minute walk from Nana D's place to the guest cottage, so I scrambled a half-dozen eggs and popped several slices of whole wheat bread in the toaster. I didn't have time for a full spread like Nana D would've, but mine would suffice for this morning.

Gabriel knocked twice and opened the front door. The bags under his eyes were heavy and as dark as mud. "Nana D sends her regards. She has an early meeting with Paul Dodd to prepare for their first year working together and sent over a coffee cake she made yesterday morning."

Emma and Gabriel set the table while I finished cooking. When everything was ready, we ate breakfast together, keeping the conversation civil and focused on lighthearted topics. Once we were done, Emma took Baxter outside to practice his tricks. I watched them through the window as they played in the small fenced-in area just outside the back door. I could hear Emma sternly warning the puppy that he wouldn't get any treats if he didn't properly listen to her. She was gonna turn into another Nana D if I wasn't careful!

"We have a lot to discuss, and you better be truthful," I firmly warned Gabriel, realizing my daughter was more like me than I'd previously acknowledged.

"Yeah, your non-stop messages and cruddy attitude has made that clear." He poured himself a glass of orange juice, kicked off his shoes as he sat across from me, and plunked his feet on the couch next to me. "There are two sides to every story. All I ask is that you don't judge me until I'm finished."

Gabriel and I had always been close as young kids, even though we were four years apart. I'd never shared that kind of relationship with our older brother, Hampton, who'd tortured me and treated me like his servant. By the time Hampton had moved out, I was tired of being the middle child in our family and went off to college to build a new life. I blamed myself for abandoning Gabriel when he'd needed me most. Accepting the truth about his homosexuality must have been difficult if he'd felt he had no one to talk to about his emotions and his fears.

"I promise. It might be a little too late, but I'll do whatever I can to help fix what you've done," I said, playfully slapping his thigh as a show of support. "Talk to me."

"That's just the thing. I already tried to fix it years ago and look what's happened." Gabriel grunted, jumped up from the couch, and walked toward the front door. "I didn't steal the jewelry eight years ago. I know people suspect me, but I'm innocent."

"I'm glad to hear it. Why do you think they suspect you?"

"Because I know who did. And that person forced me to get more involved than I needed to be." Brow furrowed and eyes focused, he paced the living-room floor.

"I know what happened in San Francisco at the pawn shop." I should have waited for my brother to share when he was ready, but I wanted answers.

"What? You've got to be kidding me. No one was supposed to know about that. He promised me he'd keep it hidden." Gabriel punched the front door to let out his frustrations.

"Who promised you that? Connor?" My head felt too cloudy to interpret his explanation.

"Connor? What does he have to do with the pawn shop? I'm talking about Dad. He took care of everything. That's part of why I left town." Gabriel had thrown out a curveball with that reveal as he leaned against the opposite wall and groaned loudly enough for Emma to check on us.

I ushered her back out the door and assured her everything was fine. "You've completely lost me, Gabriel. Connor and I found one of the Roarke rubies near Quint's body in the cable car. He realized it was from the original pieces of jewelry someone had stolen and that had eventually been hocked at a pawn shop in California." I shook my head, trying to make sense of the situation. "Connor thinks whoever killed Quint is the person stealing all the jewelry and lost control—"

"Are you saying the police suspect me of killing Quint? That's absurd; he was my friend. Quint might've done some stupid things and tried to take advantage of me, but I'd never physically hurt him." Gabriel looked as wounded as he was shocked by the thought of someone accusing him of murder again.

"I gotta get out of here. It was foolish of me to return to Braxton. Nothing's changed."

"Wait! You said something about Dad. What does he have to do with this mess?"

"Ask him yourself. I need to talk to someone else before this gets out of hand again," Gabriel shouted and raced out the front door toward the main house.

Who was he going to speak with? I couldn't follow him since Emma was outside with Baxter and too young to be on her own. My discussion with Gabriel only confused the matter further. I called my mother and verified we were still on for lunch at Nana D's the following day once church finished. My father would try to avoid the conversation, but I intended to drag out of him whatever secret he and Gabriel had been keeping.

* * *

After Tiffany agreed to meet me for a drink at Kirklands, the rest of the early afternoon revolved around Emma. We straightened up her room, packed her overnight bag, and drove to the gymnastics facility near the Betscha mines. I watched her twist her body on the parallel bars and hang upside down on the rings. At one point, I had been fairly adept at it myself, but the thought of hanging upside down only made me nauseous these days. Emma hugged me goodbye and went back to her friends, worrying me that I only had a few more years left with her as my baby girl.

Tiffany was sitting, and slightly swaying, at the bar when I arrived. Considered a dive by most, the usual patrons at Kirklands were more than satisfied with two-dollar beers and five-dollar cocktails during happy hour. Its most appealing feature, besides the dark and gloomy corners where drinkers could easily hide, was a flair for playing eclectic music and showcasing local talent on weekends.

"Mom reveled over the chat you two had last night. I kind of expected you'd call soon." Tiffany partially hugged me and slid over a pint of beer. The light hit her in just the right way to highlight her mousy-brown hair, freckles, and petite waist. Her hands were not at all petite, which meant she might be the person who'd killed Quint. When she spoke, a trail of Cosmo breath fluttered by.

"First, let me say how sorry I am about Quint. I understand you two were very close." I offered to pay for the beer, but she waved my arm away and sprayed a flowery perfume on her wrists.

"What a pretty scent," I said, lifting her hand to my nose. "I've been smelling sandalwood cologne lately but can't figure out the name."

"You should ask Nicky Endicott. He's a cologne fanatic. I'm quite sure the woodsy ones are his latest obsession too. Everything is woodsy right down to his boxers, and don't ask me how I know that! That lumberjack of a hottie even prefers to jog through the wood-chipped trails at Braxton all the time." After sipping a mouthful from the mug and turning a little green, she seemed disinterested in her beer. "What can I do for you? It sounded urgent on the phone. I only showed up because I happened to be in need of an excuse to escape a brunch that wasn't going well."

That was a tip I hadn't expected to get today. Could Nicky have been the person I'd seen at the cable car the morning I'd found Quint's body? I'd have to track him down soon to find out as well as relay the news that Tiffany had a secret crush on him. "I've learned something I'd rather not share straightaway, but it's connected to the jewelry thefts that started up again. Can you share anything you know about them?" Was she drunk enough to tell me the truth, or would she be evasive on the topic?

"What do they have to do with me?" She pulled her bottom lip into her mouth and gently bit it.

"I'm hoping you'll reveal everything you know, starting with the sorority prank eight years ago and ending with what you and Gabriel talked about the day you returned the earrings to your mother at Whispering Pines." I picked up my pint, clinked hers, and said, "Drink up. We've got a lot to cover."

Tiffany was not thrilled to learn I knew about the sorority's hazing practices. "It was supposed to be confidential. I don't know who told you, but she's definitely going to be in big trouble for it."

"Forget how I know. Just help me connect the dots. Do you know who stole the jewelry?"

"It was just a harmless prank we played on Gwendolyn Paddington, but then the brooch really disappeared. When a second item was stolen, this time from my family, I wondered if it was a coincidence or connected in a warped way."

"Why didn't anyone say something to the cops? Or you could've told your parents. It might've stopped the thief from stealing more jewelry and cash from the Roarkes, Greys, and Stantons."

"We were scared. I couldn't tell my parents we'd stolen the original brooch. No one wanted to be accused of all the other burglaries or go to prison." Tiffany began slurring more frequently.

"Okay, I can buy that. Did you suspect one another of being the real thief?"

"Not really. I mean, I thought only the four of us girls in the pledge class knew about the prank. One of them must have told someone else," she snarled.

"Don't get snippy with me. I'm just asking questions." I wasn't the enemy, but it wouldn't help to push back. "Did you leave a calla lily at the Paddington estate after you stole the brooch?"

"No, are you kidding me? We took the brooch from the Play House, locked it in the safe at the sorority house, and moved on. Someone must have decided to keep stealing items and tried to make it look like it was connected to Alpha Iota Omega, but the culprit was never caught."

"How do Quint, Paul, Nicholas, and Gabriel fit in? Did they know about the sorority prank?

"I already answered that. No one was supposed to know what we did, but I can't tell you what anyone else was privy to." She slapped a ten-dollar bill on the bar and waved to the bartender.

"We're not done. Is there anything else you can tell me? I'm worried Quint confronted someone about the jewelry thefts in the cable car." I paused to let the news sink in. "If you know something, you might be able to determine what really happened to the poor guy the day he died."

"I'm devastated my friend passed away, but it wasn't anything more than an accident. I don't see how his death has anything to do with the jewelry robberies." Frustrated, Tiffany exhaled loudly.

"Where were you the night Quint died? I'm just curious how and when you found out," I said nonchalantly.

"Um, I don't remember. Didn't he electrocute himself in the middle of the night? I guess I was sleeping probably. My mother told me the next morning. Ugh, I need to get out of here." Tiffany jumped up from the barstool and faltered more than expected. She was partially drunk and couldn't look me in the face, yet she'd been reading something on her phone. It seemed like an act. Why?

"You're hiding something from me. If you're worried about Gabriel, you're in good company."

Tiffany closed her eyes and breathed deeply. "Gabriel is the one who disappeared after all that cash was stolen from the Stantons during the first round of robberies. I also saw him shove something shiny in a duffel bag when I stopped by his dorm room to surprise him the night he left town."

"Are you certain it was Gabriel?" I asked, wondering if it had been a case of mistaken identity.

"Unless I was confused about whom I saw through the crack in the door, your brother is involved. I guess I didn't see the guy's face, but it was your brother's room. I assumed based on a few coincidences and the timing that Gabriel might've been the thief, but I couldn't turn in a friend, so I kept quiet. Then, he mentioned leaving my concert early the night my mother's house had been robbed to—"

"Wait! Your mother said you didn't remember anyone disappearing that night. Which is the truth?" I wasn't thrilled to hear that change of news, as it made my brother look guiltier.

"I'd been too excited by the concert back then. When Gabriel told me recently that he'd left the concert to meet his secret boyfriend, it triggered my memory that he'd been missing."

"Do you believe he's guilty, or do you think he really met his boyfriend that night?"

"I'm not sure. No one else had enough knowledge and access to details about everyone's comings and goings both in the past and now. If Gabriel isn't the thief, then I don't understand who's robbing people again." Tiffany settled the bill with the bartender and stepped away from the bar.

"What about when you dropped off the earrings with your mother at the funeral home a few weeks ago? Did anyone else know you were doing that?"

"Gabriel and I had lunch with Quint, Krissy, and Nicky that day. I might've mentioned returning the earrings, I can't be sure." She dropped a few singles on the bar and hastily rushed out of Kirklands toward a taxi. Thankfully, she wasn't planning to drive.

I felt like my wheels were spinning—even my brother's friends thought he was guilty. I'd have to follow up on Krissy and Nicky's alibis at the time Lydia's earrings had been stolen. At this point, I could only hint about Quint's death being unusual, which meant asking people for alibis wouldn't be easy. Could I prove my brother's innocence that way? If not, perhaps when Fern and I had dinner, she'd have insight about the girls in the Alpha Iota Omega sorority. It was also time to check in with Connor to find out what he'd learned from the coroner about the exact circumstances surrounding Quint's death.

Chapter 10

"Connor is at an offsite meeting presently. Anything I may assist with?" April asked as I bumped into her in the lobby of the Wharton County Sheriff's Office. Her stereotypical tweed blazer and bootcut jeans were nowhere in sight this afternoon. In their place, she wore a pair of high-waisted gray dress pants, a canary-yellow blouse with a brown silk scarf draped across her left shoulder, and a pair of shiny pumps. She looked positively radiant and ready for an evening out on the town.

"It can wait. I don't want to interrupt anything," I said, watching her look past me as if she was waiting for someone to walk down the hall. "I had peculiar conversations with Gabriel and a few folks in the Nutberry family. Just wanted to compare notes."

"It's almost like you think you've got a sleuthing partner now that one of my detectives is your former best friend, huh?" She smirked and punched me lightly in the shoulder. "I'm only teasing, don't get too testy on me now. Did you need to talk about it?"

I did, but the timing didn't seem ideal upon running into her. "You're about to head out. I'll wait for Connor. Do you think he'll be back soon?" I checked my watch to confirm I had a couple of hours before meeting Fern for dinner.

"Doubtful. He's with the coroner reviewing the final report on Quint Crawford's death." April nodded at someone behind me, then waved at the person to join us. "I'm attending a sort of cocktail party this evening, but I can spare a few minutes for you."

Those were words I didn't expect to hear together—April and a cocktail party. Based on everything she'd ever shared with me in the past, she loathed that type of gathering. I turned my head to discover who approached us and instantly recalled having seen the guy in her car the other day. Was I about to meet the potential boyfriend she'd kept ensconced from everyone?

"I hope you two have a wonderful evening." I extended my hand toward the guy once he reached us, attempting to contain my shock at his babyface and wide-eyed, innocent expression. If her date were a day over eighteen, I'd cash in my 401K retirement plan and donate it to the least worthy cause I could find. "You will certainly get some looks wherever you're going tonight." Was April a secret cougar? Who could have guessed that she liked younger guys!

"August, this is Kellan Ayrwick, a..." April said while pointing at me and pausing momentarily, "friend of mine whom I'm working with on a case."

"Good to meet you, Mr. Ayrwick," he replied and stretched a confident hand toward me. His platinum blond hair was buzzed short on the sides but had several inches of length slicked straight back with gel on the top of his head. "Call me Augie. She refuses to listen to someone else's preferences, yet I'm in trouble when I don't do whatever she asks of me at home. Such a drag sometimes."

I liked him already. Anyone who gave April a tough time was golden in my book. "Have you two known each other long? You've got witty banter going on here." Wait! Did he say they lived together?

"You could say that," April replied, checking her watch.

Augie glanced at her, rolling his green eyes in grand fashion. "Way longer than I like to think about."

The guy jumped up another notch for performing my signature move. "You must know a few secrets about her." I slanted my eyes in April's direction. "In my experience, she can be a real handful."

"Dude, she's off the charts sometimes. It's like she was born to be a mother hen, ya know?" Augie wrapped a thin, long arm around April and kissed her cheek. "You ready to roll, Momma Dukes?"

That last comment felt like a sucker-punch. Was Augie her son? Who knew she had a kid? She'd never said anything before. Doing the math—we were roughly the same age—April must have been fourteen or fifteen when she'd given birth. I found it amusing they both had first names that matched months of the year beginning with the letter 'A.'

"Is that how you're gonna talk when you meet everyone on campus tonight?" April grabbed Augie by the back of his neck and squeezed hard. "How did I get stuck dealing with the likes of you?"

I feverishly needed to know what was going on more than I could stand. "For the clueless and those ready to vomit, is he your son or your date?"

Augie dropped to his knees and tugged on April's blouse. "Please, Mom, I mean, wifey, don't make me go tonight," he whined, then cackled so loudly, the police officer manning the front desk shushed him. "Can't you try to be a better sugar momma, love? I'll be a good boy at the party."

"Kellan… August is… not… my son." April turned and handed him her keys. "Get the car started, you tool. I'll be out in a few minutes."

"Thanks for the laughs, man. You made my night." Augie slapped my back, tossed two buds in his ears, and kicked off some music on his mobile phone before strolling out the front door. They shared identical high, prominent cheekbones that framed their well-structured faces, but he exited with a bit of awkwardness while April had a more confident and determined walk.

"He's my brother. August has been living with me the last five years since everything happened back in Buffalo." April sat on a nearby wooden bench and waited for me to join her. "My parents were older when August was born. It'd been a surprise, as my mother was in her late forties, and I had just started high school. She had a tough pregnancy but managed to live for another ten years. Unfortunately, when she passed away, my father wasn't capable of taking care of August by himself."

April shared that her father was an alcoholic who'd started abusing her brother that first year after his wife had lost her battle with a painful illness. He'd blamed August for his wife's death and taken it out on the poor kid who'd been too young to defend himself. April fought their father for two years before the courts finally awarded her custody on her twenty-seventh birthday.

"I'm so sorry. You never said anything," I replied. April had always been silent regarding her background until I'd learned about her fiancé's death in a drive-by shooting several years ago. "He seems like a strong kid. I like that he pushes back on you."

"He is a strong kid, but it took time to get him there. He'll be a senior this fall, and we're going to check out local colleges this summer." April sighed and showed me a picture of him and her from when she'd been granted guardianship. "Tonight is Braxton's meet and greet for prospective students. We're on our way there in a few minutes."

"You've got this entire life that I know nothing about, April. I feel like I've confessed everything about myself, yet I'm in the dark when it comes to you." I admired April's ability to protect her privacy.

Learning about her relationship with Augie clarified a tremendous amount for me regarding who she was as a human being. "What you've done for him speaks volumes to me."

"Sometimes I forget I need to be a parent. He's always been smart for his age, especially having to grow up so quickly when our mother died. Our father took advantage of the situation." April put the picture away and grabbed one of my hands. "We're not all that different, you and me. It's hard to accept that as a fact, but when I saw you with Emma for the first time, I knew I'd been too rigid those early months."

The surrounding air seemed to contain a magic that desperately pined to pull us closer together. Part of me suppressed a desire to gently caress April's cheek and experience a physical connection like we had when our fingers brushed against one another last month. Could something be developing between us? April smiled when I cupped her slender fingers inside mine and looked directly at her. I was considering whether to lean in to kiss her, but a phone rang somewhere nearby.

"I think that's you." She separated from me and pointed to my leather satchel.

I jerked out of my temporary trance and reached for the device. It was the phone Cristiano had bestowed upon me earlier that week. "It's Las Vargas."

"Answer it. Hurry up, maybe we're closer to solving one of our dilemmas," April encouraged.

I clicked accept. "This is Kellan."

"It's Francesca. I'm glad to hear your voice."

My eyes opened wide and filled with excitement and fear. I was happy to know she was alive, but the reality of the situation had become fully apparent at that moment. "Are you okay?" I asked Francesca, before turning to April to whisper the name of who was on the phone.

"Yes, Cristiano has only permitted me a minute to talk to you. He's standing here too and wants you to know he's aware of your current location." Francesca's voice was calm and collected, as though she weren't afraid of what was happening to her. "Don't do anything foolish."

"Is he going to let you come home soon? What can you tell me?" I asked, looking from April to the floor when I couldn't settle on the most comfortable place to stare.

There was a moment of silence followed by a muted conversation before Cristiano hopped on the line. "I've fulfilled my promise to let you speak with Francesca. Now that you know she's alive, I must ask... have you fulfilled your promise to notify the Castiglianos with my instructions?"

"I told them, Cristiano. I can't force them to respond, but they understood your message." I switched seats so April could listen to the conversation with me. Our ears were pressed together in another unexpected intimate moment as we waited for his response.

"Excellent. Francesca convinced me that I could count on you. You shouldn't need to wait much longer. I'm arranging for a discussion early next week. The Castiglianos have something I want, and if they deliver it to you, we can put an end to this inconvenient situation."

April pulled out her phone and typed the word *where* on the screen.

"Will you be coming back to Braxton for this discussion? Do I need to meet you somewhere?" I asked, trying to ignore the pleasing tickle of April's fragrant hair against my cheek.

"For such a clever man, you certainly miss the obvious, Kellan. I never left Braxton after our last conversation in your office." He then whispered something I couldn't hear. "Francesca asked me to tell you that Emma looks happy at Chuck E. Cheese and that she misses seeing her daughter every day."

I closed my eyes and dropped my head to my lap. I knew Cristiano was spying on my every move, but did he bring Francesca with him to monitor me too? "Where are you? Why can't we just meet immediately and solve this?" A fire crept inside my body, threatening to incinerate everything around us. Why couldn't they just leave Emma alone? While April sent a text message on her phone to someone on her team to get to Chuck E. Cheese immediately, I felt her rubbing my upper back to calm me down. I turned my head and mumbled a thank you.

"A few more days, and this should all be over, Kellan. I'm sorry that kidnapping Francesca had to be my insurance policy, but if her parents do the right

thing, we will all get what we want. I'll be in touch."
Cristiano abruptly disconnected the phone call.

"Wait!" I shouted, despite knowing he'd already hung up. "This is a nightmare. Every time I think we can get back to normal, that guy scares the crap out of me by following Emma around."

"I've got an unmarked vehicle pulling into the restaurant parking lot. Have faith, Kellan. Your daughter will be fine, and we'll catch the people responsible for causing the war." April grabbed my shoulders and forced me to face her directly. "Trust me. I've got your back."

We waited in silence for five minutes before one of her officers confirmed he'd just missed two people walking out the side door of the restaurant. They'd gotten into a limousine and pulled away in a hurry, but Emma had been unharmed and completely unaware of their presence. April said, "Emma's happily playing with her friends as if she had no cares in the world. Do you want to visit her? I can drop you off on my way to Braxton."

I shook my head. Francesca would never let Cristiano harm Emma. "It's okay. I'm just frustrated. I might swing by before dinner with a friend of mine. You should go to Braxton and help Augie decide if it's where he wants to attend college in another year."

April nodded. "I'll have my cell phone in case you need anything. Are you sure you don't want to talk about your brother or what happened with the Nutberry family?"

I briefly filled in April on my conversations with Lydia, Tiffany, and Gabriel, excluding the part about my father knowing something important. I needed to speak with him before revealing that piece of news. "Is Connor going to arrest Gabriel for the jewelry thefts or Quint's murder?"

"Not yet. We don't have sufficient evidence, and I probably shouldn't be telling you what I'm about to tell you, but you could use a bit of good news," April replied as she stood to leave. "We lifted a set of prints from the main power source to the cable car. We don't know to whom they belong, but they weren't a match to your brother's. We had his on file from the George Braun case last month."

I breathed a small sigh of relief. "That's helpful. I'm sure the prints could belong to any number of electricians, right?"

"Actually, there were only two sets—Quint's and the unknown person's. We're strategizing how to check everyone involved. I can't tell you everything, but a few of the folks in this group of friends aren't being totally honest." April indicated she would check on me later that evening.

As she left the building, I reflected on the changes beginning to develop in our relationship. When we'd first met, we were like two barnyard cats vying for territory. During the last three months, I'd helped her solve several cases and gotten on her bad side more times than I cared to remember. In the last few weeks, ever since she'd begun assisting with Francesca's kidnapping, things had been pleasant. I considered her a friend; someone I could trust to look out for my welfare. After the moment we shared today, I knew something stronger was percolating between us. I couldn't let myself process it until things calmed down. Wild gale-force storms tossed us about, and until this tornado dropped us on safe ground, it would be best to keep anything more serious from blossoming.

* * *

An hour later, after verifying for myself that Emma was okay, I drove back downtown to meet Fern at Simply Stoddard for dinner. The new eatery had a prime central location on *Restaurant Row* overlooking the Finnulia River, where a gorgeous octagonal cedar-shake windmill and cleverly arranged outdoor teak furniture welcomed guests in the summer and early fall.

I arrived before Fern and informed the hostess of the reservation. After learning our table wasn't ready, I sat at the cherrywood bar and ordered a Jack Daniels and ginger ale, minus the ice. It only diluted the drink, and I always quivered when ice banged my teeth. As the bartender handed me the cocktail, one of the owners, Karen Stoddard, approached from the opposite side of the room where a newly renovated, top-of-the-line kitchen with a traditional brick oven and delectable pastry counter teased customers. Karen's bright neon blouse and pencil skirt glimmered as she shimmied through the narrow spaces between two tables.

"It's nice to see you again, Kellan. I'm glad to see we can put our past differences aside and coexist in the same town," she quipped. Newly frosted tips accentuated her stylish shag hairstyle, an odd yet bold statement on a woman whose snub nose was all too prominent of a feature.

"I couldn't agree more. Your husband is a talented chef, and I always prefer to find common ground with someone rather than bicker over the petty things. How're Cheney and Sierra doing?"

"My kids are well. Sierra's back in London, and Cheney is happy to be finishing the cable car project. I'm hopeful he's capitulated on wooing Helena. She's a fine girl, but Cheney needs to focus on getting his life in order," Karen cautioned me, then told the bartender my drink was on the house.

"I appreciate it. I happen to agree. Helena should focus on herself. She's got a rambunctious side that needs to simmer down before she gets involved in a committed relationship," I consented.

"Exactly. She was in here earlier today with a few women. There was a shouting match and drinks being thrown across the table. I had to kick them all out," Karen explained, shaking her head and groaning. "For four women quickly approaching thirty, it was very immature."

"Really? Do you happen to know whom she was with?" I assumed it was her sorority class who'd been discussing the jewelry thefts and Quint's death. Tiffany had mentioned needing to escape a brunch that wasn't going too well.

"I knew two of the girls, Imogene Grey and Krissy Stanton. I overheard them arguing about calla lilies and who stole whose boyfriend over the years. Trivial stuff," Karen said, as if she couldn't understand what it was like to get catty with a girlfriend.

I described Tiffany Nutberry, and Karen confirmed she was the fourth girl. "I appreciate the update. It explains a lot." The girls had undoubtedly gotten together to compare information and agree on a story in case anyone else asked more questions. Tiffany had been extremely angry that one of them had fessed up about the sorority ritual.

As Karen left, Fern waved to me from the hostess desk. I dropped a few singles on the bar, met her at our table, and ordered another drink. We chatted about her day and the upcoming wedding. Her son Arthur was marrying my Aunt Deirdre's fiancé's sister, Jennifer Paddington. They'd begun dating earlier that year and when Jennifer had learned she was pregnant, Arthur proposed to her. It was an unusual match for their clan. Arthur was my age and a tad on the nerdy side while Jennifer was in her mid-forties and from a wealthy family. I needed to speak with Jennifer to find out the circumstances of the jewelry theft at the estate. She'd lost an expensive family watch in the current round of burglaries.

Once we covered all the major topics and finished our meal, I asked Fern about the Alpha Iota Omega sorority. Fern had worked at Braxton for over twenty years and advised all the Greek societies on campus. If there were any secrets to discover about the sorority's connection to the jewelry thefts, she'd know them. "What can you tell me about the current state of the Alpha Iota Omegas?"

Fern laughed. "Oh, that's easy. I shut down that sorority years ago. They were one of the infamous ones who liked to push my boundaries way too many times. I used to challenge you about some of your fraternity's initiation practices, but these girls were monsters."

"What do you mean? Did they do something illegal?"

"Hazing itself wasn't illegal then, but I've always believed it was highly unethical and hazardous. I was at the forefront of Pennsylvania's commitment to institute anti-bullying and hazing laws. Although I couldn't prove it all, there were rumors about excessive drinking, violence, and dangerous pranks with those girls." Fern asked the server for a cup of coffee when he passed by.

"How about jewelry theft? Did that ever come up?" I shared a little with Fern about what Helena had told me, knowing it wouldn't go any further, especially with the dismantling of the sorority.

Fern shook her head. "Not that I'm aware of. Most of my information came from witnesses who saw things happening on campus or girls who complained when they were treated unfairly. If you're referring to all those burglaries from years ago, no, I don't know anything."

"That's disappointing," I said, feeling disheartened that I hadn't learned anything new from my discussion with Fern. "I hoped you might offer some missing clue. Between those calla lilies showing up and the repetition of the original crimes happening this year, I'm baffled."

"Calla lilies? You know that's the official flower of the Alpha Iota Omega sorority, right? It's tradition for the house mother and big sister to present a white calla lily to each new inductee when she becomes a full member." Fern leaned in closer to me and whispered, "It was designed to mimic something special that the original founding families used to do when a daughter revealed which boy she was sweet on. A mother would send a white calla lily from her daughter to the boy for nine days in a row. It was a sign that he was welcome to ask her daughter on a date. If he was interested, he'd show up with a bouquet of white calla lilies on the tenth evening. If he was not, he'd send back a single black calla lily to the mother as his notice of rejection." Fern explained that in the *Book of Revelations*, Alpha and Omega meant the beginning and the end of life. Iota was also the ninth letter in the Greek alphabet, and it had a special meaning to the sisterhood in terms of the calla lily presentation.

"You've got to be joking me!" Fern had just filled in an important piece of the riddle. If the thief was leaving a black calla lily every nine days, was he or she trying to show his rejection for something? The puzzle was starting to fit together, but I needed more information. Unfortunately, Fern couldn't share anything else of value. Somebody in that sorority knew what was going on, or at the very least had shared

the history of the calla lily being used to tell someone that you were or weren't interested in dating
them. Now, I just needed to figure out exactly what
the thief's symbols meant and whether we could prevent the next robbery from happening in a few days.
It might also reveal Quint's probable killer.

Chapter 11

"Gabriel won't be here for lunch today. He took off late last night to do some soul-searching. He left a note indicating he'd gone camping with Sam up in the mountains," Nana D said as we fed the horses on Sunday morning while waiting for my parents to arrive from church. Although she was prepared to turn over the entire farm to her right-hand man, my nana wanted to cherish the last few days before getting bogged down with all the mayoral responsibilities she was about to absorb.

"He left because I confronted him yesterday. I didn't get a clear answer either." I never expected him to confess everything he'd done while he was away from Braxton, but his explanations left more open holes than Nana D's favorite pair of worn overalls—and that was saying a lot, not to mention scarier than all get-out! "Did he tell you anything else?"

Emma held the bucket while her favorite horse gobbled his morning oats. One of her friends' mothers had picked them up this morning from the sleep-over and dropped Emma off at Danby Landing for me. "Uncle Gabriel isn't gone for good, is he?"

"No, honey. He just needed to cool his jets," Nana D said, comforting my daughter and looking at me. "He's clearing his head before talking to some important people." Nana D grabbed Emma's hand and began walking back to the farmhouse.

By important people, Nana D had meant the sheriff's office. Although the police did not officially want Gabriel, he would need to discuss everything he'd known about the jewelry thefts now that Connor had found his name on the San Francisco pawn shop's reports. "Has Marcus finally conceded to you? Or is he just ignoring your inauguration?"

"He called yesterday to acknowledge I beat him. I also forced Marcus to explain why he'd been meeting with Imogene at the diner last week. Apparently, she requested the discussion to warn him that if his daughter continued to cause trouble for her fiancé as he was beginning his new role in Braxton, she'd sue Krissy for slander. Paul must've told her what Krissy had said in the park the night of my birthday party about Imogene cheating on him with Quint."

Nana D tickled Emma as we crossed through a flower garden, then chased her for several feet before finally throwing her arms in the air announcing defeat. The flowers reminded me of the news Fern had shared the previous night about the calla lily's role in the historical courting processes of the Alpha Iota Omega sorority. I still couldn't figure out the connection between the flowers and the jewelry thefts or with Quint's death. If Imogene had cheated on Paul with Quint, maybe Paul was angry about being cuckolded and killed Quint in retaliation. Had Paul left behind a bouquet of calla lilies to get even with his friend for backstabbing him? Nonetheless, I still wasn't certain Imogene had cheated on Paul.

Nana D explained that Marcus had only told her because he'd gotten drunk in order to find the where-withal to admit defeat. "Marcus did blame the election loss on someone else, of course."

On the return path, Eleanor joined us. She was only able to visit for an hour before needing to attend to the lunch crowd at the Pick-Me-Up Diner, but she wanted to spend some time with the rest of the family. "Let me guess, he blamed Kellan?"

Go Eleanor! I assumed that man was going to cause trouble at some point. "Probably."

"Nope, Quint Crawford. Apparently, Quint had done some work on Marcus's house next door, and Marcus never paid him. I heard from a couple of folks that Quint was starting to tell people about it," Nana D indicated, then suggested I should find out if there was any truth to the rumor. As we meandered up the path by the orchard, Aunt Deirdre and Timothy Paddington pulled into the driveway.

A few minutes later, we sat in the living room and caught up on everything going on between them. Once Timothy had finished his three-month program at Second Chance Reflections, he'd moved back into the Paddington family estate. Aunt Deirdre had been staying with Nana D at Danby Landing, but she'd relocated to Timothy's after a separate room was prepared for her. An old-fashioned gal, she didn't want to share his bedroom until their wedding night, but she also acknowledged that it would be beneficial for them to spend as much time together as possible. Most of their relationship had developed via electronic communications while she'd lived in England and he'd been in recovery.

"*Facebook* brought us back together. We dated years ago, but a lot happened in the eighties that we both care to forget," Aunt Deirdre explained with a narrowed gaze at Timothy. My lovely aunt's shoulder-length, dark-blonde hair was tied back with a pink ribbon, highlighting the sleek curve of her neckline. It'd also been adorned with a silver and diamond necklace, courtesy of her wealthy fiancé.

"Exactly, pumpkin. Second Chance Reflections offered me a new lease on life, and now we need to take advantage of it." Timothy squeezed her hand and kissed her nose. His time in recovery had reversed many of the physical impacts of his addiction to alcohol, drugs, and gambling, but his hair continued to gray further at his temples and above his ears. He was a prime example of why people said men were *distinguished* as they aged. "I just adore this magnificent peach of a woman."

Nana D walked behind the couch, where only Emma and I could see her. She pretended to stick two fingers down her throat and expel whatever thoughts had gotten trapped inside her body. By the time she came into everyone else's view, she said, "Oh, aren't you two precious! Tell us about your *simply divine* post-wedding plans." It was such a blessing not to be on the receiving end of her sarcasm, yet I knew my time would come soon enough.

"Thank you, Mother," Aunt Deirdre said with a slight but noticeable twitch in a vein at the side of her neck. Evidence of her British accent slipping away as she drank, or grew frustrated and angry, was becoming clearer as she spoke. "Timothy is taking me to the Maldives for nine days, and then we're going to stop in England for a celebration with all my friends back home."

"Where are you planning to live after the wedding? Are you leaving Braxton that quickly?"

Timothy wrapped his arm around my aunt's shoulder. "We'll only be gone for a few weeks while I get up to speed on what's been happening at Paddington Enterprises. We'll return at the end of July when I can assume control and let Uncle Millard go back into retirement."

"Timothy and I plan to split where we reside. My London flat is large enough to accommodate a remote office for him as well as an extra bedroom or two for when we have little ones," Aunt Deirdre explained, resulting in an uncontrollable gasp from my grandmother. Seconds later, Nana D kicked the coffee table leg and casually blamed her outburst on an unexpected, painful leg cramp.

Out of the corner of my eye, I saw the strangest glare form when Eleanor realized Aunt Deirdre was hoping to get pregnant with Timothy's baby. My sister had been considering artificial insemination the last few months because she hadn't found her own husband. Aunt Deirdre was every bit of fifty, and while modern science had made gigantic advances, this was quite a leap for the family to accept.

"While we're here in Braxton, we'll run the Paddington estate. Aunt Eustacia is moving back to Willow Trees to resume her own life, but my sisters will remain in the mansion with us. There are plenty of wings to give us all the privacy we need," Timothy added.

"Do you really think you two need to have a child at your ages when—" Nana D was interrupted when the front door opened, and my parents walked in carrying a box from a local bakery and a small gift for Emma. My mother spoiled my daughter, and there was little I could do to stop it.

As Aunt Deirdre sneered and whispered something to Timothy, Emma jumped up from her seat and ran toward my father. After we all exchanged greetings, I grabbed the box from my mother and walked with her into the kitchen. My father chatted with Emma about Baxter's latest trick. I'd find time to corner him later about his and Gabriel's dirty little secret.

"You look wonderful today, Mom. I miss seeing you all the time. We should arrange a weekly lunch. We both work on the same campus, right?" She'd been the director of admissions as long as I could remember, yet we rarely made the effort to meet around my teaching schedule.

"I'd love that, Kellan. At church this morning, Father O'Malley talked about the importance of family. I'm so grateful you and Gabriel are back in Braxton, and Hampton will be here at the end of the summer. Even my sister's come home again." She hugged me like I was a small child and gleefully flitted around the kitchen. "I convinced Nana D not to make dessert today. I wanted to bring those éclairs you love from that cute little bakery on Main Street. They are *simply divine!*"

"Thanks, Mom. I'll check my schedule and suggest a few days for lunch. Is Siobhan managing your calendar now that she's working in the admissions office?" I asked as she plated the éclairs.

"Your department's loss is my gain. Siobhan's very efficient, even when she's stuck at home with a sick baby. I adore my grandchildren, but I'm relieved those days are behind me." My mother might kvetch—a Jewish word April had taught me—about once being thirtyish and raising children, but her exceptionally youthful beauty and unparalleled attention to new products revealed her fear of aging.

"Are you two close? I know Siobhan had been relying on Bertha Crawford's help with babysitting, but after Bertha got sick and her son died last week, it hasn't been easy." I was curious whether my mother knew of any ill feelings between Quint and Siobhan, based on what Bertha had mentioned at the funeral parlor.

"That poor boy! I must admit, I never much cared for your brother's friend. Quint always seemed to find trouble, and I've seen him get too forward with women. He and Siobhan had a quarrel recently, and I didn't like the way he was behaving. Not very gentlemanly." My mother tut-tutted as we walked into the dining room and placed the tray on the table.

I asked my mother to give me an example, and she revealed what'd happened between Siobhan and Quint the previous month. When Siobhan had dropped the twins off at the Crawford house, Bertha asked her for a favor—to deliver Quint's lunch on the way back to campus. After Siobhan met Quint, chemistry sparked between the two of them. Quint must've convinced Siobhan to spend the night with him one evening while his mother watched the babies. "Siobhan thought he was genuinely interested in her. When she tried to get more serious with him, he backed away, claiming his heart belonged to another woman. She was terribly angry, and I don't blame her. I don't think Quint meant any harm, but it truly upset Siobhan. She wanted to teach him a lesson, but I kept telling her to let it go, that American boys can be foolish. That poor girl still gets bothered whenever I mention his name. Quint always thought he was God's gift to women, but unfortunately, he won't be able to redeem himself now that he's gone. It's positively disheartening when someone young dies from an accident like that." She fussed with a strand of auburn hair that wouldn't properly tuck behind her ear.

"Has he done things like that before? Or was it a one-time occurrence?" I asked, surprised at learning about this side of him. He could be persistent, but I thought he was a decent guy who knew how to treat a woman. Helena and Tiffany never mentioned anything negative that would lead me to believe otherwise. Imogene wouldn't have dated him if he'd been that callous. Could he have changed?

"I'm really not sure, but it'd gotten bad enough that Siobhan considered telling Bertha what her son had done. She didn't have the courage to break the woman's heart, especially during chemotherapy, with tales of her son's ill-mannered behavior. Instead, she searched for a new nanny."

"Do you think Siobhan tried to get revenge against Quint?" She was a strong woman and could strangle someone, especially if he'd been inebriated and unable to fight back. I needed Connor to confirm whether Quint had been drunk the day he died. I didn't recall smelling any alcohol in the cable car, yet Siobhan definitely had the right-sized hands based on the coroner's description.

"Siobhan has a temper, but she's a smart girl and wouldn't get into that kind of trouble." My mother shook her head and waggled her nose for emphasis on her point.

"Was she in the office the day Quint died?" I thought back to how Siobhan had acted in class the day before and the day after Quint's murder, but no alarms stood out.

"I'll have to check. I don't remember and will look at my calendar when I get to work tomorrow," my mother replied as Nana D entered the dining room.

"Let's get our meal out of the oven. Your dullard husband's getting crabby in the other room, Violet. I can't stand that man's voice sometimes," Nana D groused as she walked by us and then yelled back to the living room. "Get your butts in here, everyone. We've gotta eat before King Wesley bores us all to death with his oh-so-wonderful stories about himself."

"No need to shout, Your Honor, we all followed you into the dining room in case you accidentally tripped and fell over your ego. We wouldn't want you to break a hip, now would we?" my father announced while taking his seat at the head of the table. Even in Nana D's house, he assumed what he felt was his rightful place once Grandpop had passed away. Their battles for control had been epic over the years, and often I'd just sit back and listen to the wild accusations and hidden undertones flying by me.

Once the meal finished, Eleanor left for work. Timothy offered to wash dishes with Aunt Deirdre as part of their continued relationship growth exercises. "Those who clean together always shine together, right, Mom?" he said upon turning to Nana D. Calling her *that* wasn't going over well!

Nana D and I both turned away to make fake gagging sounds this round. Timothy's time in the recovery program had converted him into an overly sappy human being. I couldn't wait to see how things transpired once he returned to Paddington Enterprises, a corporation known for being as cutthroat as any of the major international companies it did business with. I grabbed two tumblers and the bottle of whiskey from Nana D's cupboard and nodded at my father to join me on the porch. Emma was playing fetch with Baxter while my mother discussed her sister's wedding plans with Nana D.

"Excellent idea, son. You know exactly how to turn the afternoon around," my father cheered while patting me on the back as we stepped outside. A gentle breeze carried the scent of fresh fruit from the orchard. I was tempted to take a walk but had urgent business with my father.

"Don't get too excited yet, Dad. I have an ulterior motive." I waited for him to sit on a wicker chair before pouring and handing him the whiskey. "We need to have a discussion about Gabriel."

"I see. Would you be buttering me up prior to dropping a bombshell on me? You definitely take after your mother more than me, son." He chugged half the tumbler and cleared his throat with a loud, raspy groan. "I'm ready. What are you two boys up to, and what do you need from me to get started?"

My father had once envisioned his three sons all going into business together to build a family empire. My oldest brother, Hampton, had joined a prestigious law firm years ago and would be relocating to Pennsylvania in the fall. When I'd left town to focus on the film and television industry, Dad's dream was crushed, but he often tried to redirect my interests.

It hadn't worked until he'd convinced me earlier this year to help him build an advanced communications program at Braxton. We'd been playing well together in the sandbox, but that was mostly because there were multiple people involved in the project.

"Gabriel might be in trouble, and I think you know a lot about it. He mentioned that you took care of something when he left town eight years ago." I paused to let the silence linger, hoping it made my father uncomfortable enough to be honest with me.

"That business is all in the past. There's no reason to dig it up again. Besides, I don't know for sure what happened, and sometimes things are better left unsaid. Why don't we talk about something else?" My father stood and looked out on the horizon, jangling coins in his pocket.

I listened to him breathing until I found the right words. "Whatever you did years ago didn't work. Gabriel might be arrested for his role in the jewelry thefts, and honestly, Dad, he looks guilty to me. I want to protect him, but I don't have the information to do so." I stood next to my father and stared across the farm, trying to understand what he focused on. "I suspect you do. We could work together to solicit him some help, the way families do all the time when one of their own is in need."

A few birds chirped and a lawnmower idled in the distance while he considered my request. "You do your best as a parent to protect your children when they're young. And you hope they learn their lessons and don't repeat your mistakes." My father leaned against the corner post, slightly worn down and hesitant to continue. "Hampton's done well, but he almost didn't make it through his last year at law school. He quit one day because he wasn't the best student in the class, then took off for a couple of weeks. I didn't find out until the school called us to check if he'd gotten ill."

"I didn't know. He's always seemed quite level-headed," I replied, feeling strangely saddened for my brother but glad to know he was actually human and had made mistakes.

My father told me how he tracked Hampton down and set him back on the right course to graduate on time. "Your sister, Penelope, pulled something similar, just as Eleanor and Gabriel made foolish mistakes at one point in the past. It seems to be part of this family's DNA."

I'd known about Penelope's elopement with her husband and how she'd confessed she'd done it just to spite my parents for trying to control her life. Eleanor had disappointed our parents when she didn't become a doctor and had taken a job as a waitress at the diner. Both my sisters had redeemed their actions years later, but it'd still been an awkward period for a while. "Maybe we get this rebellious strain from Nana D," I quipped, hoping to lighten the mood.

"Kellan, of all my children, you're the only one who's effectively stood up to me. You stop me from interfering in your decisions. You go out of your way to protect everyone in the family. I'm proud of you, son." My father leaned in to hug me, and for a moment, any proper response failed to rise to the surface. "I did something I shouldn't have eight years ago. Perhaps it's time you stepped in to fix it."

My father confessed a chilling secret that he and Gabriel had been hiding. After our father had accepted the offer to become Braxton's new president, Gabriel had decided not to transfer to Penn State. My brother's underground relationship had unexpectedly ended, and he knew he had to reveal the truth about his attraction to guys. Gabriel then moved to San Francisco to hide and buy himself time, but he'd stayed away longer than planned. We'd already discussed this piece the previous month when he'd returned to town; however, no one had known my father briefly decided to step down from his post as president to allow Gabriel the option of remaining at Braxton. Unfortunately, that's when Sheriff Crawford had approached our father with disturbing news that changed everything.

"The sheriff alleged that Gabriel was involved in at least one of the jewelry heists. He offered to cover it up, but he insisted both boys leave town to guarantee things would blow over for a while."

"What do you mean *both boys leave town*? Who else was involved?"

"Quint Crawford. Silas told me his nephew and Gabriel were involved together with the robberies. Didn't you just tell me you knew that already?" my father said with a cockeyed glance.

"No, I knew someone else had been involved, but I never had a name. When did Quint leave town?" No one had ever said that Quint lived outside of Braxton.

"About eight years ago around the same time as your brother. He only returned in April when he learned his mother was sick," my father replied, explaining that he'd initially refused to believe Gabriel was involved, but once he'd checked my brother's dorm room, he'd found pieces of the missing jewelry. My father then confronted Gabriel, who didn't deny the accusations nor admit to them. Instead, Gabriel focused on his struggle to accept he was gay and his frustration over our father's new job. My father made the decision to convince Gabriel to leave town not because he was ashamed of his son for being gay but because he wanted his son to have a better life and not be thrown in prison.

"I've felt awful all these years for being the reason he stayed away from everyone," my father said in a low and disheartened voice before explaining that Sheriff Crawford had later shared a copy of the pawn shop report with Gabriel's name on it. "I knew then your brother was guilty of something. Even if he didn't steal the jewelry himself, he'd stored it in his dorm room and hocked it in San Francisco. Maybe if I'd made Gabriel take responsibility for his actions, things would be different now."

I considered everything my father had just bared, including recognizing what his news confirmed: Tiffany had seen Gabriel with the jewels the day he'd skipped town. "Gabriel did this himself, Dad. Either he and Quint came back to Braxton to start stealing again, knowing that the sheriff had passed away last year, or Gabriel knows who's recreating the crimes now. Maybe there's an accomplice or a copycat."

We agreed to regroup the following day once Gabriel returned from the mountains. We assumed my brother hadn't disappeared again, but time would tell for sure. While my father went inside, I reflected on what I'd learned about his role and the story of the sorority's calla lilies. We were also missing records from eight years ago. The sheriff had been crooked. I wouldn't learn a lot from the past burglaries. I'd already spoken with Lydia and Tiffany Nutberry about the earrings that had been stolen from their place the previous month. Now, I needed to ascertain where Quint and Gabriel had been that night as well as the other three times more jewelry had been stolen.

Based on past occurrences, we had one day before the next theft would occur, if that nine-day pattern stayed consistent. If a theft happened, then Gabriel was probably responsible and needed help to turn himself in. If one didn't occur, maybe Quint had been the ringleader and Gabriel wasn't involved in the current round. I had to find out the truth to prevent my brother from making another mistake. More importantly, I had to accept that I'd failed to discover an important fact sooner—Quint had left town right after the original thefts too. While identifying the original accomplice and/or mastermind solved one problem for me, it created another more complicated one. If Quint and Gabriel had been the thieves, and they were back working together again, there was no longer a mystery accomplice to blame for Quint's death. I couldn't accept the killer was Gabriel, suggesting the only other logical solution was that Quint's death had nothing to do with the robberies. Now how would I solve his murder?

Chapter 12

After Aunt Deirdre told Emma about the newest flowers in the conservatory at the Paddington estate, my daughter begged to see them. Timothy offered to drive Emma back and forth, but I saw it as an opportunity to talk with Eustacia and Jennifer Paddington, his aunt and sister, to inquire what they knew about the robberies. We followed Aunt Deirdre and Timothy—I refused to call him Uncle Timothy this late in the game—to the estate. The three-story manor had been built in the early twentieth century and was approaching its one-hundredth anniversary. Timothy had mentioned throwing a soirée that summer for all their friends to celebrate his family's history and rise from the ashes of the year's tragedies. A small parking lot, a cedar-chipped path, and lush gardens with shrubbery and trees that'd been shaped into forest animals welcomed guests as they arrived at the mansion.

Bertha's replacement greeted us at the door. While Emma went with Aunt Deirdre and Timothy to check out the conservatory, I asked the new maid what she knew about the latest jewelry theft. Unfortunately, she'd started the week afterward, which meant she couldn't help me. "They didn't have anyone working the day of the burglary, sir. The Paddingtons were still interviewing for a replacement," she noted before leaving to locate Eustacia. When she did, the maid led me to a sitting room where Eustacia and Jennifer discussed wedding details.

"Kellan, what a surprise! What brings you by?" Eustacia sang from her baby-blue-tufted chenille chaise longue. Her cane, topped with a brass lion's head, rested by the side of the long chair, enabling her feet to stretch out comfortably. I didn't want to make her get up, so I leaned in for a perfunctory greeting. I'd known my nana's frenemy for years, and I was grateful the two of them had been on good terms ever since the election had been decided. "We missed you at Kirklands the other night, sleepy."

"You're quite funny." I updated them on Emma's botanical interests, then brought up Bertha Crawford. "I saw her at the funeral on Friday evening. She didn't look well."

Eustacia shook her head and sighed. The normal blue color of her frenzied hair had been toned down, but she would never relinquish the comfort of her classic 1980's pink tracksuits. When at home, despite demanding that others dress more sophisticatedly, she chose comfort over fashion. "Life should never end so early. I can't imagine what it must've been like to be electrocuted, that unfortunate soul."

At least the sheriff had been able to keep the truth about Quint's death from reaching as few people as possible. "I imagine you knew him as a boy since Bertha worked here."

"Yes, he used to visit when he was a small child. Bertha had been with us for almost twenty-five years before she retired," Eustacia added while staring innocuously around the room.

"Was Bertha working here the day the Paddington jewelry was stolen?" I asked, introducing the topic in a hopefully inconspicuous manner.

"Which time?" Jennifer placed knitting needles on her lap. She'd been creating what looked like a blanket for her baby, due that fall. Sporting less makeup than usual and kinky chestnut hair that had been trimmed an inch, Jennifer looked pretty and relaxed. Impending motherhood and marriage had softened rough edges and tendencies to act spoiled.

"I suppose both," I said, feeling a tad guilty about leading them directly where I needed them to go. "Eight years ago, Gwendolyn misplaced a brooch, right?"

Eustacia chortled. "Misplaced? It was stolen, my dear. She swore up and down for days she did not lose it at the Play House, but no one believed her. I know for a fact that she was telling the truth."

Interesting news. Helena had told me they'd taken it from her while attending the performance at the theater, but everyone else said they'd never seen it there. "What do you mean?"

"The show took place on a Friday evening. I'd been unable to go because my arthritis was flaring up and I couldn't get hold of Dr. Betscha that afternoon. I can't speak to what happened at the Play House, but the next day," she said, looking quite pleased with herself, "the brooch was sitting on Gwennie's dresser just where she said she'd left it, as plain as the wrinkles on her face."

"Then, you believe the thief stole it from here, not from the theater?" I was puzzled by the two different stories but knew there had to be a justifiable explanation. Helena positively said that Krissy had picked it up off the floor in the main lobby at the Paddington Play House. When Eustacia nodded, I said, "How do you explain several witnesses claiming they'd seen it while at the show?"

"They must have been confused. It was just a bunch of sorority girls, they probably saw someone else's brooch and thought it was Gwennie's," she replied with determination, turning to Jennifer. "You were there. Did you see it?"

"I hadn't been paying close attention, Aunt Eustacia. Bertha is the one who suggested the police should ask everyone who'd attended the show. Her son, Quint, had been here that day for her birthday, and he'd mentioned his friends had been on-site and might remember seeing something." Jennifer nibbled on a dry biscuit before presenting a fancy plate layered with others in my direction, another sign that her manners were improving since watching her mother pass away earlier that year.

I declined her offer, only able to focus on Quint's presence popping up everywhere. Why had he decided to steal all the jewelry? Did he rope my brother into it? Krissy Stanton claimed to have seen the brooch on the theater floor. How did it end up back at the Paddington estate after someone put it in the safe at the sorority house? It increasingly looked like I needed to pay a visit to Krissy, who might remember more than she realized. "What about you, Jennifer? What did you lose recently?"

Jennifer explained that she'd developed an unusual reaction to wearing silver jewelry upon entering her second trimester. She'd stopped using an antique watch her father had gifted her on her eighteenth birthday. It had crystals and diamonds on the faceplate and was worth a lot of money. "I decided to have it cleaned, hoping that maybe I'd be able to wear it again without getting a rash. It had been sitting on my nightstand the day it was stolen. Arthur picked me up for lunch, and I thought I'd set the security alarm before leaving the house. I might've forgotten... you know, baby brain and all."

Jennifer explained that no one else had been home that morning or evening due to the costume extravaganza occurring at Memorial Library. Millard had been at the office, Eustacia was with friends, and Ophelia and her daughters were on vacation; the school year had ended and they needed a break from a hectic schedule. When Jennifer returned to her bedroom that evening, the watch had been missing and a black calla lily sat in its place. "The watch was the only thing we didn't have locked in the safe that day. Bertha's last day had been that week too. The place was truly empty," she said, then turned to Eustacia. "Which reminds me, Bertha mentioned Quint would drop off the keys that weekend, but I never saw him. I don't suppose we should ask her about it now, should we?"

After Eustacia looked at me, synchronizing our newfound clarity and noting that she'd handle it, I said, "Don't you have cameras hooked up throughout the house?"

Eustacia laughed like a small child. "We did, but after the tragedy of Gwennie's murder, we had to order a new system. Timothy wanted to handle it, but he wasn't home from the recovery program. The new system is installed now." She also indicated there had been no signs of a break-in, which was why Jennifer originally worried she'd accidentally left the front door unlocked.

"Did you tell the police everything you've just told me?"

Jennifer nodded. "Except about Bertha failing to give us the keys. I'd forgotten that part. You don't think Quint had something to do with this, do you?"

"I really couldn't say, but that would be a strange coincidence with the keys and no sign of forced entry. Maybe he accidentally lost them." I needed to let April and Connor know what I'd learned. "I hope the police find the watch, it sounds very special to you,"

I suggested, wondering whether I should also pay a visit to Bertha to deliver an update on what I'd discovered. If she'd coughed up the keys to Quint, we might have found our explanation for how Jennifer's watch had been stolen.

Emma and Timothy joined us in the sitting room. They'd had a fantastic time looking at all the flowers and the pond in the middle of the Great Hall. "There's a mean plant that bites the goldfish, Daddy." Emma shuddered, hiding something in her hand behind her back. "I don't want one of those, and we're never bringing Baxter here."

"Good idea. What have you got there?" I turned her around and gasped.

"Aunt Deirdre says it's a cow lily," she giggled and handed me one that she'd been holding behind her back. "Someone cut a bunch and left this one near the pond. Aren't they pretty?"

"It's called a calla lily, and yes, they are very pretty. Especially these black ones." It was beginning to wither and droop, which suggested it hadn't been cut recently.

Timothy replied, "I called Uncle Millard to let him know that there were several missing in the Great Hall. He hasn't been by to clean the pond or monitor the flower gardens in a week. The last time he checked was the day of Nana D's birthday party when all was fine."

"Do you have any cameras that would show who might've been near the pond?"

Eustacia said, "Maybe, but it was probably that new maid. Don't worry, we'll take care of it, Kellan. If I didn't know better, I'd suspect it was our jewelry thief, but it's probably just a coincidence."

"Why do you say that?"

"All the flowers that were left as calling cards after the robberies were white calla lilies that someone spray-painted black. The ones missing from our gardens are legitimate black calla lilies. We only started to grow those two weeks ago, after Jennifer's necklace was stolen."

While Eustacia had a point, she didn't have the privilege of knowing that the ones left near Quint's dead body were also legitimate black calla lilies. No spray paint had been used for that bouquet. "Can I see the video recordings? I can't tell you why, but there might be something important on it."

Timothy said, "Of course, I trust you have a valid reason, but unfortunately, there are no cameras pointing near the pond in the Great Hall. We only installed cameras to secure the entrances, exits, hallways, main rooms, and exterior of the house."

That wasn't going to help me. If I knew who was inside the Great Hall, I might confirm who cut a bunch of flowers to leave near Quint's body after killing him. "Can you put together a list of people who had access between the time Millard tended the flowers last Sunday and Tuesday morning? Visitors, employees, anyone in the family, please. It's important."

Jennifer looked to her aunt and brother, then shook her head. "Isn't that when you found Quint Crawford's body?"

I nodded.

"Sure, I'll talk to everyone in the house and come up with a list," Eustacia firmly announced, then leaned on her cane to prop herself off the chair. "Come, Jennifer, we have work to accomplish and a new criminal to catch."

* * *

On the drive home, I convinced myself to disclose to Connor the news of the calla lilies being cut down at the Paddington estate. By informing him, I risked him intervening with Eustacia and insisting she turn over the list to him and not me. I'd address that if and when it happened.

Emma and I spent the rest of the afternoon together. While she read a few chapters from her favorite author, I prepared for my upcoming classes. We would have our first pop quiz that week, and I needed to design the questions to cover a wide variety of topics. By dinnertime, Emma had a craving for Chinese food. Confident that delivery would take too long, I ordered a few different options and drove to the restaurant to pick it up. Our order wasn't ready when I arrived, and the hostess let us wait in a corner booth with a bucket of free fortune cookies. A gold-painted, ceramic kitty—a traditional Chinese sign of luck—continually waved to us from a nearby shelf. Emma connected her earbuds and played a game on one of her devices. I scrolled through my phone to catch up on any work emails I'd missed since Friday. I had just opened the summary of Myriam's staff meeting when my name was called.

It wasn't from the hostess about my food. "Fancy seeing you here, Dr. Ayrwick," Krissy Stanton said as she sidled up to the booth. "This must be your lovely daughter."

"Yes, that's Emma." I poked my daughter's elbow and introduced them. Emma told me she was about to enter the next level, so I let her keep playing. "Are you coming or going?" I asked Krissy.

"Coming. I'm having dinner with my father tonight. He hasn't yet arrived," she said, sitting across from me. "Do you mind?"

"Not at all. I wanted to talk to you anyway." Luck was on my side this evening. I'd have to thank the Chinese kitty before I left. I couldn't have planned this impromptu meeting any better if I tried. "How's Marcus doing in his last two days before his position as town councilman ends?"

"Don't gloat too much. My father doesn't accept defeat easily. He's probably planning some sort of coup, so you should tell your nana to be on the lookout," Krissy warned. Her tone was mostly friendly, so I didn't take it as a threat. "To be honest, I'm getting tired of Dad's games and planning to tell him at dinner tonight."

"Relationships with our parents are often quite painful, I hear you." Had I just found my way to bring up Quint's death to Krissy? "I'll be sure to caution

Nana D. She spoke with him yesterday, at least he called her. By the way, I heard a strange rumor. I wonder if you'd know anything about it."

"What's that?" she asked, playing with a set of unwrapped chopsticks and tapping her foot against the side of the booth. When I asked her about the work Quint had done at her father's house, Krissy huffed. "It's not a rumor. Quint was my friend, and he did amazing work. I was home the entire time watching him rewire several rooms."

"Your dad's known to be a... piece of work. No offense intended to you, of course. Do you think he did anything to hurt him after Quint told people your father wouldn't pay up?"

Krissy's eyebrows arched high, and her mouth opened wide. "I... I... never thought about it. Dad's been angry ever since he lost the election. I haven't seen much of him. He can be vengeful, but Quint never mentioned anything." Her entire demeanor had changed in front of me once I suggested it.

"Well, I wouldn't worry too much then," I said, uncertain myself how far Marcus might go to stop someone from hurting his reputation. When the hostess told me that the food would be ready in five minutes, I leaned toward Krissy and quietly said, "Do you mind if I ask you another question that might be uncomfortable to answer?"

"Ummm... sure, is this about the incident with Imogene in class?" she asked, swallowing deeply.

"No, it's not." I clasped my hands together and cracked my knuckles. "I know what happened eight years ago when you were pledging the Alpha Iota Omega sorority. I was hoping you might fill in a few blanks for me."

Krissy recoiled quickly and looked in the lobby to see if her father had arrived. "I don't want to talk about that, and I should probably move to my own table."

"Krissy, wait," I said, holding up my hand. "I just want to know what occurred at the Paddington Play House the night Gwendolyn lost her brooch. The rest of her family swears she had it at the estate the following day, but you and the other girls had stolen it the previous night." I explained what I knew about the prank and how the brooch had disappeared from the safe, then suggested Quint might've been involved.

"If I tell you what I know, will you agree to drop it? This happened a long time ago, and I'd rather forget the whole thing," she begged. When I nodded, she continued. "I stole the brooch out of the safe at the sorority house and gave it to Quint to return to the Paddington estate. I felt guilty about what we'd done."

I'd suspected something like that had happened, but I wasn't sure which girl had been the Good Samaritan. "Does anyone else know?"

"No, just Quint. He helped me steal it in the first place. Quint spent a lot of time at the Paddington estate, and he'd seen the brooch a few times. He'd stopped by to visit his mother while she was working the day of the show and took it for me. I never told the other girls about that part."

"That's how you were able to tell everyone you saw it on the floor in the lobby of the theater?" Part of the story was beginning to make sense.

"Yes. Quint swiped it for me, so we could fulfill the sisterhood's request before we were permitted to become members of Alpha Iota Omega. He'd dropped it in Gwendolyn's purse right before she left for the show, then I grabbed it while no one was looking in the restroom and told the other girls I'd found it on the floor. Later that night, the sorority president put it in the safe. I saw the combination and retrieved it the next morning. I gave it to Quint, who snuck it back in when he went to visit his mother for her birthday. I'd felt too guilty about the whole thing and didn't want to go through with it."

"Do you know what happened afterward?"

"No, it really went missing because the Paddingtons reported it stolen afterward. I saw Quint put it back in her room. Eustacia Paddington wasn't lying. She must've noticed it the next morning after he'd returned it. I was there with him to say happy birthday to his mother."

If Quint and Krissy had returned it, then how did it disappear again? When I asked Krissy if she had any suggestions, she looked humiliated over her role in the past. "Are you sure no one else knew what you and Quint had done? Is there a chance my brother was aware?" I needed to discover whether Gabriel or

Quint had acted alone or if someone else had been involved.

"I don't know. That was a really bad month for everyone. Imogene and Quint had been dating, then she abandoned him for Paul Dodd. Your brother started distancing himself from us, but now I know it was because he didn't know how to tell us about being gay," Krissy said, indicating her father was walking through the front door. "I recall Gabriel had been acting suspiciously the day he disappeared."

"Were you aware of the other jewelry thefts at the time?" I asked, unsure who had been told what back then, especially considering the sheriff was Quint's uncle and had hidden facts from people.

"Minor details until it hit the papers days after the last one, and by then, your brother and Quint had left town. The group fell apart." Krissy tapped Emma's arm and waved goodbye when my daughter looked up from her game. "I need to go. I'm sure you'd rather not run into my father."

Marcus scoffed at me as his daughter joined him in the lobby, and they strolled to their table on the other side of the room. When the hostess brought over my food, I paid the check and walked to the parking lot with Emma.

At least I now understood the confusion about the brooch appearing at the theater, but why had Quint double-crossed Krissy by only pretending to return it to the Paddington estate? I called Nana D and asked her to arrange a get-together with Bertha Crawford, curious whether she'd been hiding any information about the jewelry thefts. Could she know more than she'd confessed about her son?

After dinner and a game of checkers, Emma went to sleep. I contacted Connor to schedule our next workout. As I climbed into bed, he responded that we could meet Tuesday at the Grey Sports Complex before work. Then I saw several dots on the message appear and disappear. Connor had more to discuss but kept changing his mind.

Me: *Dude, you're gonna give me a seizure. Something else you need to say?*
Connor: *Was gonna call earlier but got wrapped up in something. Are you free tomorrow?*
Me: *I have a meeting, interview, and class, otherwise available. What's up?*
Connor: *Gabriel returned my call. I'm questioning him at four o'clock. April wants me to chat with you beforehand. She thinks you know more than you've said.*
Me: *Sure. The Big Beanery at 8:15, okay?*
Connor: *Deal. BTW, is something going on between you two? You once teased me...*

I began several replies only to erase each of them and try again. I gave up after six attempts, removed my glasses, and pulled the covers over my head. It was Connor's turn to see several dots on the message appear and disappear. I pretended not to recognize the irony of the situation, keenly aware he ultimately responded to me and I was abandoning him without an explanation.

There was always tomorrow when the promise of a better answer could arrive. I began to doze off, recognizing that if the thief had stuck to his or her pattern, tomorrow was nine days since the burglary at Lara's house when Imogene had been attacked. If a final robbery targeting the Stantons was going to occur, exactly where and when would it take place?

Chapter 13

Once Emma was safely on the bus the next morning, I drove to South Campus and met Connor at The Big Beanery. I checked my watch to confirm I'd made it on time, as punctuality had been instilled in me by Nana D ever since I was old enough to read a clock. She wouldn't let me use anything digital until I knew the difference between the big and little hands, just as I couldn't get Velcro shoes until I could properly tie my own laces. That woman never gave up until she got her way!

Other than a few people in line and my boss and her wife sitting in a corner booth, the place was empty. I waved at Myriam and Ursula, then got in the queue. Only one waved back, of course. By the time I was next to order, Connor joined me and added in his items. "Make that two more black coffees, skip the bear claws he idiotically ordered, and give us three fruit bowls, please."

I cast a disapproving look. "Desserts motivate me. If you want me to talk, then put them back on the list." I stared back and forth between the cashier and Connor, wondering who would win our standoff before the full weight of what he'd said hit me. In that temporary confusion, he inserted his credit card into the chip-and-pin device to pay for the order, minus the bear claws. "Why three?"

"For me," April said, as she idled over to the other side of the counter where the barista placed our breakfast. "I realized three heads are better than two when it comes to piecing together this doozy of a conundrum."

Once the fruit bowls were placed on a tray, April directed me to collect napkins and forks and located a table. I followed her and Connor, then slumped into the empty chair across from them. "I'm more jumbled than my mother trying to find her way around the kitchen. First, you tell me to stay out of your investigations. Then, you tell me to work with Connor but leave you alone. Now, you're joining us before I've had enough coffee to process the tomfoolery happening around me."

"Is he always this chipper in the morning?" Yanking a fork and napkin from my hands, April ignored the frustration building on my face.

"You should see him try to lift his first set of weights. I stand pretty close by in case he falls and knocks himself unconscious," Connor replied as he handed out fruit bowls.

"Do I need to be here? I might have better luck not getting sideswiped if I stood in the middle of commuter traffic on the highway," I grunted as they sipped coffee.

"You are right, Kellan. I've been giving you mixed signals," April said, offering one of the rare concessions I'd usually witness only during full moons in a leap year once a millennium. "Connor and I had a lengthy conversation yesterday about your involvement in our jobs."

I briefly slid my gaze to Connor's stoic face, unable to read him. Was my name being called upon strictly for professional reasons or had a smattering of personal interests popped up? April began by explaining that it'd be better to share information, highlighting my familiarity with many of the people involved in the jewelry thefts and Quint's murder. She reiterated the inability for me to speak to anyone else about the case, stressing her reticence to reveal key details to a private citizen. "You're not an official deputy, and you haven't gained any special privileges, so don't let this go to your head."

"I promise I'll be worth it," I said in an unexpectedly confident and amorous voice, then winked at April. What was happening to my self-control around this woman? "I mean, you can completely trust me. Right, so...."

Connor must have noticed my startling tone because a crafty grin formed on his lips. "Did you want me to stick around, or would you rather talk to April alone, Kellan?"

"Let's just get on with our discussion," I replied and kicked him under the table. He and I would have an incredibly painful tête-à-tête the next time I was spotting *him* while *he* bench-pressed too much weight. "Shall we start with the jewelry heists or the electrocution-slash-strangulation death?"

"I assume they're connected, but let's start with the murder." Connor's revelation about Quint's death surprised me, especially when he clarified the order of the events. "The coroner worked with Dr. Betscha to confirm exactly what happened in the cable car. Quint was electrocuted before he was strangled to death." Based on the burn marks and the residual effects in Quint's system, he was electrocuted around midnight. He hadn't suffered a cardiac arrest, which meant the electric cables weren't what killed him. Quint must've grabbed a wire while installing a panel, thinking the power supply had been turned off, then passed out from his injuries. "It may or may not have been accidental. The autopsy showed little alcohol in his system."

April interjected, "What's odd is that the power was turned off when Connor checked it that morning. Someone, possibly the person who'd strangled him, tried to confuse us."

"Tell me what you know about the time of death." We'd seen the finger impressions on his neck. If Quint had been injured and weakened from the electrical surge, he wouldn't have been able to stop his attacker from choking him. Anyone involved could've killed him, pending the size of their hands.

"Between twelve thirty and one that morning, about seven hours before you found him," Connor replied, sharing the key details from his report. "There was major bruising on his larynx and windpipe, but it wouldn't have taken much force based on his condition from being electrocuted."

"Do you think the same person who tried to electrocute him stuck around and finished the job?" My stomach began to grind with disgust upon thinking about the cruelty Quint had suffered. What kind of person could do such a thing? Although he'd been a thief, his murder wasn't justified.

"It's definitely a possibility, but we can't be certain. We're checking alibis for everyone he'd been seen talking with the last few weeks," April said, finishing her coffee and signaling the waitress for a refill. "Which brings us to the jewelry thefts and the reason we want to speak with Gabriel."

"Before you say anything else, there's something I should've told you sooner. I only got confirmation this weekend, and it might change your approach." I hoped they weren't angry that I'd kept the details about the Alpha Iota Omega sorority's prank from them. I finished explaining everything I knew, including what my father had shared about the previous sheriff's blackmail and what Krissy had revealed about returning the brooch with Quint at the Paddington house.

Eyeing me intently, April snarled, "This changes everything!"

Connor said, "I'll contact Eustacia Paddington to directly submit to me the list of people with access to the flowers at the estate. I'll also have someone check for any fingerprints, but it's unlikely we'll find any at this point."

After we finished organizing the case, we devised a plan where Connor would interview all the girls who'd pledged the sorority, applying enough pressure to force someone to crack and share additional information. He'd also obtain their alibis covering the hours preceding and including Quint's death. April would follow up with Siobhan Walsh and Marcus Stanton to determine if either had been involved in the murder. I was tasked with convincing Gabriel to reveal everything he knew when they met later that afternoon. I let both Connor and April know that I planned to visit Bertha after my class, to see if she could remember anything else as well as inquire about the keys to the Paddington estate.

I tossed my glasses on the table to give my eyes a break from focusing on their livid expressions. "Look, I get that I screwed up by not contacting either of you immediately. I just talked to Krissy last night about that final part. I wanted to find out what Gabriel knew before I updated the Wharton County Sheriff's Office." I genuinely never intended to keep the information from them, but saving my brother was important to me. April grabbed the tray containing the remains of our breakfast from me when I attempted to pick it up. After a brief game of tug of war, I let it go, hoping something would accidentally fall onto her. Unfortunately, she was too careful and stepped away before anything spilled on her lap.

"I get it." Clearly frustrated and ready to wring someone's neck, April tossed out the garbage and hastily wiped the table with a napkin. "I'm not angry at you as much as I am at those who lied or hid information in the past. We could have prevented this second round of robberies and Quint's death."

Once they left The Big Beanery, I realized April had inadvertently thrown my glasses away with the trash. Unwilling to rifle through nasty garbage containers, I grabbed a spare pair from my satchel and made a mental note to read her the *Riot Act*. When I put them on, I noticed how crowded the café had become and scanned the room in search of my interviewee. Ten minutes later, a tall African American woman in her late forties, the candidate for the fall semester's assistant professor role, showed up. Dr. Lawson would be a strong addition to the department, but in the end, she disclosed a potentially complex connection to Wharton County, setting off a few glaring warning signs. I'd mention it to Myriam, who'd make the final decision whether to hire the esteemed historian.

Knowing I had a bit more time to kill, I verified with Bertha I would visit her at seven thirty that evening, then thanked Nana D for setting up the meeting. I also called my mother to see if she'd checked her calendar about the ideal day to hang out each week. I wanted to catch her before she got stuck in meetings. "Great, so we'll do lunch on Fridays at noon in the campus cafeteria."

"Perfect. While I have you on the phone, let me confirm that other thing you asked me," my mother added, clicking a few keys in the background from her office in Admissions Hall.

I'd forgotten she was going to verify if Siobhan had been working on Tuesday morning the day after Quint had been killed. "I appreciate it. I doubt she did anything, but at least we'll know for sure."

"I keep notes whenever my staff is late. I try to cut Siobhan a little slack because she has such tiny babies, but I want a record in case it ever gets out of hand." My mother was very observant, despite the disconnected glare and relaxed composure she'd outwardly display. "Ah, yes, she was late that day. Siobhan told me she had taken the twins to the downtown clinic for some emergency care the night before. Turned out they just had croup, I believe."

I thanked my mother for the information and considered how to prove Siobhan's alibi. With all the security around patient medical records, it wouldn't be easy. Then again, April was going to speak with Siobhan, so I should just let the sheriff do her job, right? As I stood to leave, I bumped into someone in my distracted state. "Pardon me," I apologized and stepped aside, so he could walk past.

"I was just looking for a table and thought you might be leaving," a familiar-looking man replied, glancing toward someone at the front counter. Then, the sandalwood scent filled the air around me.

"Nicholas Endicott?" I asked, noticing his father, Lindsey, was the person he'd been searching for in line. "I'm Kellan Ayrwick. I know your dad, and I think you might be friends with my brother, Gabriel."

"Oh, yes, I've heard your name in the past. It's great to finally meet you," he replied and thanked me when I offered him the table.

"No problem, I was just leaving. Listen, I'm sorry to hear about your friend, Quint."

"Thanks, man. He was definitely taken too quickly. Call me Nicky, everyone does." A firm handshake greeted me before he brushed a few crumbs from the table. They'd been in April's spot, not mine. Luckily, the interviewee had sat on the other side of me. April was such a hot mess! Nana D had always demanded that I clean up after myself. As he pulled away his hand, I saw a large scratch on his forearm and black paint on his chipped fingernails. Could he have gotten the scratch while attacking Imogene during the robbery? Were the black stains from spray-painting the calla lilies? Was Nicky the unknown accomplice? He noticed my stare and responded, "Construction work can be messy and painful. I was cutting and staining some beadboard at one of my sites."

I thanked fate for dropping this opportunity in my lap but wasn't sure whether to believe him about the cuts and black paint. "Quint once told me he was eager to buy into your company. It's great to hear friends can go into business together without any worries," I said, hoping to learn something of value during our exchange. I knew extraordinarily little

226

about Nicky, but since he was Lindsey's son, I'd start with the benefit of the doubt by assuming he wasn't involved in any crimes.

"Yeah, that wasn't the exact plan. Quint wanted to be part of the company, and we were friends, but I didn't plan to share ownership with anyone else." Nicky waved at his father to come over.

"Oh, I must have misunderstood. Was everything okay between you two?"

Nicky nodded. "I prefer not to mix business and pleasure. Endicott Construction is my baby." He looked startled by my questions and finished speaking abruptly as his father reached the table.

"Nana D is preparing for tomorrow's inauguration. Thanks for your help all along," I greeted.

"Good to see you, Kellan. Such a small town, eh? How's Seraphina?" Lindsey replied.

"Swell." I decided to dive in. "I heard you're a runner, Nicky. Maybe we should hit the Braxton campus trails together one day. There are some great ones on the hills near the cable car station."

Nicky looked as if I'd suggested we become best friends forever and was suddenly unnerved by my presence. "I like to go each morning before I head to my job sites. Sure, maybe I'll see you around."

When the conversation hadn't led anywhere, nor could I come up with an approach to learn where he'd been the day Quint died, I said goodbye and drove to North Campus for a meeting with the team working on the college expansion plans to offer a graduate curriculum and convert Braxton into a university the following year. After an hour of reviewing the up-coming deliverables, we were released to finish the rest of our day. I had a few hours before class but needed to organize the pop quiz details. When I got back to my office on South Campus, I realized I'd left my satchel under the table at The Big Beanery. While walking past the cable car station to retrieve it, I visited Cheney who was applying the finishing touches. He indicated he planned to do a test run the following morning to verify the repairs had been completed and the car was ready for the grand reopening that week. He said that Nicky had also offered him a full-time job at the construction company, so things were finally looking positive.

I took the pathway to The Big Beanery and approached its front door, the handle fabricated to resemble the portafilter on a classic espresso machine. Through the glass, I saw the table was still empty, which would make it easy for me to dash inside to grab my satchel and hasten right back out. I collected my belongings, then heard my brother's voice booming through an open window. I left via the side door, walked around the corner of the coffee-bean shaped building, and peered into the parking lot. Standing in the outdoor seating area, Gabriel was chatting with Nicky. I stepped closer to listen to their conversation before interrupting them. Well there you go, call me an *eavesdropper,* after all!

"Listen, I owe you the money, take it," Gabriel pleaded while handing an envelope to Nicky.

"If I needed it that desperately, I would've tracked you down." Nicky pushed the envelope away.

"I'd feel a lot better if I repaid my debt. You did me a huge favor the night I left Braxton."

I couldn't lose my chance to confront my brother before they finished conversing.

"Gabriel, just let it go. Use the money to buy yourself something and move on," Nicky said as I approached them. When he saw me, his head retracted quickly, and he looked stunned. "Kellan?"

Gabriel said, "Are you following me? I was clear the other day. I don't want to talk to you."

"I know about your four o'clock meeting this afternoon. What I don't know is why you're handing an envelope of cash to someone in the middle of a parking lot. Care to explain, brother?"

Nicky backed away. "Sounds like a family dispute. I hope you guys work it out. I'll call you later."

My troublemaking sibling turned to me and shook his head. "You're a pain in my—"

"Just don't. I'm tired of the half-truths and partial stories about why you left town and what led you to return. Stop being an immature child, and do the right thing for a change," I chastised.

"Fine," he spit out and began walking away. "You wanna talk? We'll do it my way this time."

"Where are you going?" I beckoned while running after him.

When he stopped, Gabriel stood in front of his motorcycle and unlocked two helmets. "Hop on. I want to have this discussion where no one else can interrupt us." Gabriel fastened his helmet, knocked the kickstand up, and started the bike. Over its powerful roar, he yelled, "Let's do this."

Chapter 14

A warm, gusty wind parted my lips and flushed my cheeks as Gabriel's motorcycle instinctively navigated the highway heading northbound through the Wharton Mountain range. When we were teenagers, he used to ride his two-speed bicycle to Crilly Lake to escape the monotony of family life. He always preferred to be alone when he needed to think, and I speculated that he was taking me to the place where he'd once made all the major decisions in his life. I wrapped my left arm around his chest to keep myself steady and let the other loosely grip the side of his waist. Somehow, it felt wrong for me to depend on my brother for support. It was supposed to be the other way around right now.

At the last exit in Wharton County, he slowed to take Dead Man's Curve at a reasonable speed. A kid I'd gone to high school with hadn't been so lucky the week we'd graduated and lost the future he deserved by racing around that curve too swiftly. The new Gabriel could be reckless, but he would never endanger our lives. I'd only been on a bike once before when some buddies of mine in Los Angeles had taken me to a rally for a race they'd entered. The thrill of driving down the California coast with them one afternoon had left quite an impression on me. No wonder April and Gabriel had purchased bikes of their own, not that I'd ever let Emma chance a ride while I was alive. I had my limits, as hypocritical as it might make me, and being a doting and semi-controlling father was the priority.

Gabriel stopped about twenty feet before reaching the lake and waited for me to disembark. By the time I removed my helmet, felt my heart slow its excessive pumping, and wiped a dead bug from my glasses, he'd tossed off his shoes, rolled up his pants legs to his knees, and sat on the edge of the dock.

I plopped down next to him and said, "Remember when the head cheerleader, Misty Donovan, told everyone you tried to steal her panties in gym class... and the captain of the football team tracked you down while we were playing Frisbee at the park?"

Gabriel nodded.

"You weren't afraid of anyone back then, and you're not afraid of anyone right now. Are you?" I shoved his head a few inches to the side in a playful older brother manner.

He smirked and ran his fingers through his hair to fix the mess I'd made. "Clearly, everyone must know by now that I was never interested in Misty's lace panties."

"I guess, maybe, you desired the captain of the football team's lace panties?" I busted out laughing at my joke-slash-insult, cradling my head against my lap with my arms covering my neck to try to contain the potential damage. I never should've let my guard down because the next thing I knew, my brother shoved me off the dock, and I landed in the cool water fully clothed and highly embarrassed.

Gabriel crossed his arms. "Hey, you were right. I'm not afraid of anyone right now." He stretched an arm in my direction and helped me climb back on the dock.

"I've got class to teach in a few hours, you jerk," I said and handed him my glasses. "Dry those, if you don't mind."

"We can swing by Danby Landing to get you a change of clothes. You're such a prima donna, Kellan. And people think I'm the one they need to worry about causing a scene in public."

We sat in silence for ten minutes watching a couple of fish swim past. A large white bird soared close by and attempted to snatch one unsuccessfully. "If you're not more careful, Gabriel, someone's gonna swoop down and catch you when you least expect it. Why won't you let me help?"

"Because I screwed up and deserve to be punished." Gabriel confessed the entire story to me, and I knew he wasn't leaving anything out. At one point, tears were even shed over the loss of a complicated friendship when Quint Crawford had been murdered in the cable car the previous week.

Within the group, Nicky and Paul had been best friends, and Gabriel and Quint had been best friends. Nicky was always after his next girl, yet Paul and Quint both had a thing for Imogene Grey. Imogene and Quint had dated for a few months, until Lara Bouvier confronted Quint and told him that he wasn't good enough for her daughter. She'd threatened to launch an investigation into his uncle's shady behavior. Although there'd been persistent rumors about his uncle, Sheriff Crawford, being shifty and on the take, nothing had ever been proven. Quint didn't want any bad press to hurt his mother, so he agreed to leave Imogene alone. It'd destroyed him because he'd always felt like the weakling in the group—everyone's family had money but his. Quint then began instigating trouble on campus which caused the group to break up. At the time, Gabriel had been dating his secret boyfriend and was trying to stay under the radar. Except one day, Quint had stumbled upon the truth.

"At first, he acted like everything was okay, and that it didn't bother him. But the more he pushed Imogene away to protect his mother, the more he became angry about anyone who'd fallen in love," Gabriel explained as fine worry lines formed along the sides of his mouth.

"That must have been tough on your friendship," I commiserated.

"Yep. It gradually got worse. One day, he told me he wanted to leave town, and he wanted me to go with him. I'd just broken up with that guy I told you about, and everything was falling apart for me. Dad wouldn't listen to me about not accepting the Braxton presidency, and I needed some space."

"What does this have to do with the jewelry thefts? I'm not sure I understand."

"Quint was the thief. He'd wanted to get back at everyone who'd angered him that semester. Krissy had asked him to steal something from the Paddington estate while he was visiting his mother. He helped her out, but then she ordered him to put it back. That was the last straw for him; he was tired of being treated like his mother—a maid or servant." Gabriel explained that Quint needed money to leave town and had attempted to blackmail a few folks, but when it hadn't worked, he'd turned to robbery.

"Quint would've been a good spy, based on what you're telling me."

Quint had originally thought if he stole a few pieces of jewelry, he could sell it in another state and start a new life. But then he was compelled to get even with the girls in the Alpha Iota Omega sorority. Imogene had told him the story about a girl's mother leaving a white calla lily on a boy's doorstep for nine days to reveal her daughter's crush, and how he would choose whether to return a black flower or a white bouquet, depending on his feelings. Since Quint wasn't interested in his friends anymore, he decided to punish them. When he couldn't find a black calla lily, he chose to spray-paint several white ones and left them at each robbery. "It was his attempt at a *screw you* to those who'd wronged him.

Quint didn't know a black calla lily was a dark-purple one, and I didn't want to make him feel stupid," Gabriel replied with a contrite smile.

"I can see why it'd make the situation worse." I shook my head at what I'd just learned, realizing that the person who'd killed Quint must not have known he'd been spray-painting white calla lilies. The killer used real ones because he or she didn't know any better.

Quint had hoped it would lead his uncle to investigate the sorority and their families, throwing the cops off any trail leading back to him as well as getting revenge on people like Lara Bouvier. It'd almost worked, but his uncle had discovered the truth. "Sheriff Crawford overheard Quint and me recounting what his nephew had done. He misunderstood, thinking Quint and I were in on it together."

"But you never stole anything, you just knew what he'd been up to."

Gabriel nodded. "Everything got crazy that day. I told Dad the truth about the guy who dumped me and that I was gay. He wanted me to tell everyone in the family and work through it together. I begged him to withdraw from the Braxton presidency, and he asked for a day to think about it. A few hours later, he stopped by the dorm room while I was in class and convinced the cleaning staff to let him inside, so he could leave a note for me. That's when he found the missing jewelry in my room."

"How is that possible if you weren't involved?"

"Quint had my spare key and planted the jewels. He'd set me up, even dressed like me to make it look like I was up to no good," Gabriel said, the frustration and pain evident on his face. "He was afraid that I'd turn him and his uncle in, to the mayor. He wanted something to hold over my head. Quint had planned the whole thing to ensure he didn't get hung out to dry by himself. He wasn't just opportunistic. He was crafty and cunning about protecting himself."

I pieced the rest of the story together. Tiffany had seen Quint in Gabriel's dorm room, not Gabriel, and thought my brother was responsible for the robberies. What a mess! "That's why Sheriff Crawford told Dad that you were involved and to check your dorm room. The sheriff had offered to cover it up as long as Dad pushed you to leave town. He was protecting his nephew."

"Yes, only I'd already gone to Nicky Endicott and begged him to loan me enough money to leave Braxton. That's what you saw me doing just now, repaying the money I'd never returned to him." Gabriel stood and unrolled his pants. "When Dad found me later that night, it was storming pretty badly. Quint was busy stealing from Marcus Stanton's alumni event during the power outage. I was fighting with Dad, who told me he knew what I'd done. He tried to give me money to leave, but I told him I never wanted to speak to him again. Our father thought I was the thief, and he never believed I could be innocent after I'd hidden everything else from him. When Quint finished his last robbery, he blackmailed me to leave town together that night and hock all the jewelry." Quint had threatened to tell everyone Gabriel was the thief if he didn't let him come on the trip. Nicky's money was only half as helpful as Gabriel had originally planned. They went to the pawn shop with the Roarke earrings as a test run. "I had no money left, and I did a stupid thing. Quint forced me to put my name on the paperwork. Then, we waited a few days to verify nothing happened once we'd received the money for the earrings."

"But what about all the money Quint stole from Marcus Stanton's office?" I asked, bemused.

Gabriel groaned. "I didn't know about it until the night I went looking for something in his bag. He was out getting food, and I found the cash. We had a huge argument when he returned to the hostel. Quint hadn't wanted to spend that money until he was sure the bills weren't traceable, and he wanted my name on any formal records to ensure nothing could fall back on him. His uncle had warned him. That night, Quint packed up his stuff, the cash, and the jewelry, and he disappeared. I never heard from him again. I panicked and entered crisis mode. I knew I could never come home again for a long time."

I could've killed Quint myself for what he'd done to my brother. "Is that why you called the pawn shop to tell them where to find the owners of the rubies?"

"Yes, I disguised my voice and left a message from a random pay phone in another part of San Francisco. Then, I got a job, went back to school, and you know the rest, I guess." Gabriel indicated we should head back if I needed to get to class on time.

"I know the rest in terms of your time away from Braxton, but what happened when you came back this year. Did you confront Quint again?" I asked as we reached his motorcycle.

"I didn't see him the first few weeks, but we ran into each other at lunch one day. He told me how bad he felt about the whole situation and that he hoped I could get past it. He promised me he'd changed." Gabriel explained that he told Quint he'd give it some thought, but they never found a chance to talk again. My brother had no information about the current jewelry thefts, nor did he know who might've been angry enough with Quint to kill him. "Imogene and Paul never knew what Quint had done, and now they're happily engaged in their own world. Tiffany, Imogene, and Helena don't know that Krissy had asked Quint to steal the original brooch, so they'd never suspect him of being the thief. Tiffany thinks it's me because I was with her at the funeral parlor the day her mother had been robbed, and she saw Quint dressed like me in my dorm room with the stolen jewelry. Nicky only hired Quint because he didn't know what the guy had done to me until I told him a few weeks ago."

Gabriel confirmed he had no alibi for the night Quint had been killed. He was at home sleeping and couldn't prove that he wasn't anywhere near the cable car. Nana D was sleeping too. Gabriel knocked the kickstand away and drove to Danby Landing, so

I could change clothes, then we headed back to campus. He went to work, promising to tell the whole truth to Connor later that afternoon.

As he left, I contacted Lucy Roarke to learn if she'd ever been told who'd stolen the rubies. She stated that Silas Crawford claimed he'd never discovered any names when the San Francisco police transferred the gems. He'd definitely been covering up his nephew's role and had chosen not to release any information he'd learned from the pawn shop to the Roarkes. I ended the conversation just as my father called to mention that he hadn't recollected anything else since our previous discussion. "But remember, bad blood runs through the Crawford men, so Quint's the true thief. I'm sure there won't be any more break-ins again, Kellan."

I wasn't so certain. Walking back to Diamond Hall, I contemplated everything I'd learned; new connections in the spiderweb of clues began to grow much clearer. Quint had been angry because he felt the girls in the sorority had taken advantage of him. Then, Lara forced her daughter, Imogene, to break up with him. Quint wanted revenge. He'd purposely chosen to steal from the families who'd founded Alpha Iota Omega, and he'd left the calla lily to implicate someone in the sorority for stealing all the jewelry. Except he'd gotten away with it and left town to cash in on his rewards.

When Quint returned to town, he'd begun repeating the crimes but in a slightly different manner. There was a more intricate pattern that no one else had figured out. In the first theft of each series, he stole from Gwendolyn Paddington and her daughter, Jennifer. In the second thefts, it was Agnes followed by her daughter-in-law, Lydia. In the third thefts, it was Lucy Roarke and her daughter, Maggie. In the fourth thefts, it was Lara and her daughter, Imogene Grey. When I considered the original fifth victim, Wendy Stanton, I found myself stumped. Wendy didn't have any daughters and her son was too young to be married. Then, I realized she had a stepdaughter, Krissy. If there was a new accomplice who'd killed Quint for an unknown reason, we might still have another burglary. Based on the pattern, it'd be happening very soon. Could we get ahead of the second thief and Quint's probable killer?

I needed to share my theory with Connor and April, but it would have to wait until after class. I made up an excuse, announcing that I needed to speak with Krissy and another student during the break about an issue with their transcripts. I wanted to ensure Krissy would be available to talk with me, in case she had any concerns about being targeted for a future jewelry heist. For ninety minutes, we discussed the pros and cons of changes in documentary-style reporting since the Internet had become available. While the first student came to see me during the break, Krissy did not. I told the first student that I was confused and had found what I needed for her files, so she could ignore everything. I searched the entire floor for Krissy, but she wasn't anywhere in sight.

Raquel saw me looking around. "Who are you looking for, Dr. Ayrwick?" After I told her, she said, "Krissy and Imogene went out the back door a few minutes ago."

I thanked Raquel and went to check for myself. Those exits were usually only for professors to get to our second-floor offices. The last time something unusual had sent me up that staircase, I'd found my first dead body. My stomach flipped at the thought of it happening all over again.

I ascended the first staircase, but they weren't there. Then, I heard a voice in the distance and realized someone had gone to the third-floor library space. I quietly climbed the steps, hoping not to make my presence known. When I reached the top of the platform, Krissy and Imogene were arguing. They couldn't see me through the small crack in the door-jamb, as far as I could tell.

"The police came by to see me today. They suggested Quint's death wasn't an accident. I know you were there." Imogene sounded nervous but determined to confront Krissy.

"I don't know what you're talking about. You really are a dumb little mouse. I don't understand what Paul sees in you," Krissy retorted with venomous anger in her tone, which I'd never heard before.

"Aren't you worried that I told them about you hanging around the cable car? I wonder if they're coming to interrogate you next, maybe arrest you for something, huh?" Imogene taunted, her normally calm demeanor holding firm.

What was Krissy doing in the cable car? Was Imogene referring to the day Quint was murdered?

"The cops called. I'm meeting them tomorrow. I have a lot to tell them about you too, you witch." Krissy took a few steps closer. "I was just visiting Quint that night. We were friends."

I reached for my phone to record the conversation, but I was afraid they'd hear me pressing buttons. I kept listening, curious as to what else they might say. My word would be good enough for the sheriff if anyone confessed that afternoon.

"At eleven o'clock the night Quint was electrocuted? I saw you before I went home to Paul's house that night." Imogene backed away and slipped behind a small chair.

I considered the layout of the room and wondered if there were any weapons around. Nothing came to mind, but I hadn't been up there in weeks. Even a book could hurt someone.

Krissy guffawed. "Yes, Quint and I had drinks that night. He mentioned needing to get something he'd left in the cable car earlier that day, so I went with him. That's all. You probably saw me leaving the parking lot while he remained behind working, before accidentally electrocuting himself."

"Odd time to be on campus, huh? Quint was very smart. I must agree with the police; I don't think he'd be foolish enough to leave the power on. I told them you'd been spending time there, that you tried to steal Quint from me back in college too. That detective was extremely interested in hearing what I had to say," Imogene replied.

I'd have to find a way to corroborate Imogene's story about going home to Paul that night. If Krissy had been there an hour before Quint died, did it mean she was guilty, or had she seen someone else skulking around the cable car? She'd known about the purpose of the calla lilies and asked Quint to steal the first item for her. Had I missed key clues when she revealed the story at the Chinese restaurant the other night? I tiptoed down a few steps, worried they might find me eavesdropping. I had to rethink my plan to talk to Krissy about the next potential robbery. Perhaps this girl was wound more tightly than I'd realized. Could she be Quint's accomplice, trying to cover her tracks?

* * *

After class finished, I wrote a few lesson plans and sent a text to Connor and April to inform them I had urgent information. When I checked the time, I realized they were still cross-examining Gabriel and I had to collect Emma from the bus stop. She'd taken the later bus home today. Once I did, we drove to Bertha Crawford's house to provide an update on what I'd discovered since Quint's funeral service.

Emma regaled me on the ride over by sharing stories about all her new friends at camp. I also learned that Miss Roarke, Helena to me, had gotten into an argument with someone who'd shown up that afternoon at the school. Emma recalled that the other woman kept saying, '*How could you not tell me he was a cheater?*' She then asked me, "What's a cheater, Daddy? Is that like when Nonno hides cards in his jacket pocket?"

I hadn't realized Vincenzo was that obvious in front of Emma. "Oh, sorta, honey. That's why I always say it's best to be honest and learn how to be a good loser. You can't win them all." I'd have a word with my father-in-law the next time I saw him, to suggest he stop doing foolish things when Emma was nearby. Would it be awful of me to wish he'd been kidnapped instead of Francesca? I still hadn't produced a reasonable plan on how I'd tell Emma that her mother was alive. Any day now, Francesca might be a free woman again. I should've been thrilled by the news, and perhaps six months ago, I might have been. Too much had happened this year, I supposed. Whom had Helena fought with at work?

Emma and I knocked on Bertha's door, and she yelled for us to come inside. She lived in a small three-bedroom home not too far from the Betscha mines where her husband used to work. Nana D had told me that her brother-in-law, Silas, the former sheriff, had moved in with her after his brother died, to help provide a male role model for his young nephew. Based on what I'd learned, he'd been successful. While the sheriff had been a corrupt law enforcer, Quint had grown up to be a thief.

"Have a seat. This must be Emma," she said. After quick introductions, Bertha told Emma she'd baked cupcakes that were cooling on the kitchen table. "You can put the icing on them if you'd like."

Once Emma raced to the kitchen, I said, "Thanks. I appreciate you giving me time this evening."

"Based on the darkness in those normally pretty blue eyes of yours and the hesitancy in your voice, I assume you've come bearing unwelcome news." Bertha removed the oxygen tube clipped to her nose and rested it on a nearby shaky table. "I needed to learn to breathe on my own again anyway."

"You're a smart woman, and I'm truly sorry to have to deliver this news." I sat on the couch next to her and rubbed her cold hand. Bertha had been putting up a good fight, but the chemo had taken a lot out of her. I worried she didn't have much longer to live.

"Out with it. My son did some foolish things, so don't worry about breaking an old woman's heart. I did the best I could to raise that boy, but when we lost his father, things never did improve. There were some bad influences hanging around." She sighed while glancing at a picture on a shelf across the room. It was a framed photo of her and her husband with Quint when he was a small boy.

"I know with certainty that Quint stole all the jewelry and cash from a few families eight years ago." I paused to let her take in the information. Unmoved, she continued to stare at me. "He roped someone else into hocking a few pieces, then he must've taken off and lived on the profits."

"It makes sense. I got a few expensive gifts in the mail from him shortly after he left last time. Did he

246

continue to steal once he left Braxton?" Her chest heaved up and down with great force.

After Bertha recovered, I said, "I'm not certain, but I suspect he had something to do with the recent string of burglaries. I also know your brother-in-law covered up the original ones."

Bertha expressed sorrow for the son she'd lost when he was a young boy and the one she'd lost once he'd grown up and followed in his devious uncle's footsteps. "Your classic family tragedy. A mother always knows when her son is up to no good even if she can't admit it to anyone else until too late."

"The other person involved years ago is currently talking to Sheriff Montague."

"Do you think this person killed my Quinton?" Bertha's eyes teared.

I handed her a tissue. "No, ma'am. I believe with every fiber of my being he didn't harm your son. But my good friend is the lead detective on this case. I'm confident he will find the real criminal."

"You've been honest with me, Kellan. I appreciate that. You can search Quint's room if you want, though I don't know if you'll unearth anything. One of his friends came by wanting to be close to him one last time," Bertha said, drying her cheeks and reattaching the oxygen tube to her nose. "He hardly kept anything in there. Doubt you'll find much."

I was curious to hear a friend had rummaged through the room. "Do you recall who?"

Bertha closed her eyes and pressed her fingertips together. "She came in right after I finished baking.

Mixing the cupcakes had knocked the wind out of me. I told her to just go ahead into his room. I didn't have my glasses with me, and I'd taken a painkiller. I was simply too out of it to remember much."

"Can you describe the girl?"

Bertha couldn't recall any specific features other than she had medium to dark hair. "About the same age as Quinton. I must've fallen asleep. Next thing I remember, you were knocking at the door."

It sounded like Imogene, but when I showed her a picture on my phone that I'd found online, it didn't help. Bertha was tired. It was time for us to leave. I checked Quint's room myself but only found a set of lock picks and other tools he'd used to break into various places. "Is there anything else you can tell me, before we head out?" I waved to Emma, who'd brought an iced cupcake to Bertha.

"Take a few home, sweetie. I don't have any grand-children. It makes an old woman feel useful to bake them for someone who loves them so much." Bertha reached out and tousled Emma's hair, then turned to me. "Quinton did have some money the last couple of months. He kept paying all the expenses to keep the house up. The Paddingtons offered to pay my medical bills, but I wouldn't let them. My pride stood a little too firm, I suppose. I feel awful that my son stole from them years ago."

"If you remember anything about the woman, please give me a call." Before we left, Bertha confirmed she'd given the Paddington estate keys to her son to return and assumed he'd followed through on the task. We both agreed he must've used them to steal Jennifer's watch. The keys had either gone missing again or Quint tossed them, so they couldn't be traced back to him.

Emma and I left Bertha's place and spent the evening with Nana D. I lacked the energy to update Connor and April on what I'd learned from Bertha. When they contacted the distraught and sick woman, they'd find out. Gabriel confirmed he'd survived the discussion with Connor and promised to call soon to explain how it had gone. Knowing tomorrow was Nana D's first day as the new mayor, I climbed into bed to get some sleep. Then, I noticed a new message arrive on my phone.

Connor: *The Paddingtons sent me the list. This is confidential information. Lots of visitors but only four could've had access. Imogene and Paul brought an engagement present and were left waiting in the Great Hall for a few minutes. Krissy Stanton got lost using the restroom after stopping by to collect a donation for a charity she was sponsoring. Nicky Endicott dropped off a quote for some construction work on the ceiling in the Great Hall, and he was alone while the maid went to get him a glass of water.*

Four people with access, but just because one had dropped a bouquet of black calla lilies near Quint, it didn't mean they'd also killed him. I needed to produce a plan to interrogate everyone myself. Hopefully by morning, the best approach would reveal itself. As I nodded off, I realized tonight had been nine days since the jewelry theft at Lara's place, yet nothing else had happened. Based on the pattern, it should be in progress right now or within the next twelve hours. Would anything happen overnight?

Chapter 15

Nana D held her press conference promptly at nine the next morning outside the county administrative building. Mother Nature cooperated by delivering a glorious day with bright sunshine and a soothing seventy-five-degree temperature. It was an almost near-perfect moment, short of Town Councilman Marcus Stanton's rants at the back of the crowd. All four towns in Wharton County had elected a new councilman, which meant there were five new leaders joining the ranks at the half-year mark. What a welcome July had brought in!

I committed to letting Emma attend the inauguration ceremony but planned to drop her off at Woodland Warriors Day Camp later that morning. Lara Bouvier agreed to meet for lunch to discuss the jewelry thefts as long as I promised a quote for her television segment covering Nana D's first day in office. A little quid pro quo never hurt anyone if it focused on sharing information to solve a crime, at least I kept assuring myself that while worrying about what kinds of questions Lara might throw at me.

"Where is she? I can't see her," Emma said as she jumped up and down to get a better view of the coverage. We stood on the sidewalk at the front of the crowd listening to the first speaker, but no one would see Nana D until she stepped through the black curtain and up to the platform. Being five-foot-tall had both advantages and disadvantages, and she kept herself well-hidden until it was her turn to speak.

"Nana D's campaign manager is almost done," I explained, lifting Emma on my shoulders. "She's backstage rehearsing her speech and waiting for a memorable introduction."

Based on the final agenda for her first day in office, Nana D was on a mission to prove she was the best woman for the job. The morning would kick off with a press conference to highlight and thank previous town leaders for their service, followed by a thirty-minute inauguration ceremony where my grandmother would unveil her three-month vision. She'd coordinated an outdoor street fair and lunch where she'd meet and greet all the local business owners, visit the town's homeless shelter, and hold a question-and-answer session for the general population to suggest ideas her office should consider as priority tasks. In lieu of a formal cocktail party—Nana D wasn't a fan of fancy affairs—she invited the local choirs from religious organizations and schools to entertain the crowd over a picnic dinner in Wellington Park. Paddington Enterprises was funding both meals, ensuring no town resources were used to pay for her opening day. To close out the evening, Nana D scheduled her first official meeting with the new town board members for nine o'clock, assuring all citizens that her team wasn't afraid of working late hours to better help Wharton County.

When the outgoing mayor and Nana D's campaign manager finished speaking, and Nana D sauntered to the podium, Emma was the first to squeal and initiate a flurry of applauses. "She looks beautiful!" Emma shouted and bounced jovially on my shoulders. Nana D had dressed for the occasion in a vintage black pantsuit and open-collared strawberry-colored silk blouse. Her long red hair was elegantly braided and wrapped in a small cone shape on the top of her head, covered in black netting, and topped with a magenta-colored rose. She'd even worn her new pink horn-rimmed glasses, and her very presence reminded me of a younger version of a supreme court justice I greatly admired.

"Good morning, Wharton County," Nana D projected into a pumped audience who were thrilled about the potential changes new blood would bring to their cherished towns. "It is officially time to take my oath, and I can think of no one I'd rather see standing beside me than this beloved group of people."

After Judge Grey swore Nana D into office, she thanked her predecessor and offered to share the spotlight with him for the day. Former Mayor Grosvalet declined, citing a need to let the future begin today. Nana D began her speech, covering a few minutes of her background and credentials, a glance at what it took to get her voted into office, and what she promised to deliver in ninety days.

"I am not the type of leader you've had in the last decade. You chose me because you wanted change. And change is what you're going to get...." Nana D gracefully shined a spotlight on the corruption and laziness she'd watched happening all around the county but quickly introduced a focus on eliminating any form of bribery during her term in office. She reminded everyone there would be conflict, but unlike it'd been in the past, it'd now be resolved for the benefit of all citizens.

The horde around us was wild with hope and admiration at my grandmother's stories of the past, as was I until Nana D specifically called me out in the crowd when she talked about the future. "Kellan is the next generation of leadership this county needs, and I plan to work closely with him to ensure folks like him come back home to make Wharton County the top county in Pennsylvania."

I noticed my parents and Eleanor huddled at the back of the animated crowd. Why wasn't Gabriel with them? I wanted to know what'd happened when Gabriel spoke with Connor, but of course, he'd gone into hiding again. When the major activities ended, Emma and I headed to the parking lot, noticing Nana D approaching.

"Eleven o'clock tomorrow morning. My new office, please," she mandated while sidling up and hugging me.

"You were amazing today, but what's this meeting about?" I asked, trepidation in my voice.

"Sheriff Montague will provide a report to me about the Quint Crawford murder investigation. You need to be there." She kissed Emma's forehead and tightened the clip in her hair.

"I'm not sure that's a good idea. I have lots to do, and that won't make April happy to see—"

"You may not be on my staff," she interrupted with a wave of the hand, "but I pay you with enough desserts and a rent-free cottage. You don't have a way out of it unless you'd rather me not bake anymore... besides, you'll just casually show up to see how my second day is going, and *surprise*, the sheriff happens to be there." Nana D gave a severe and shifty glance that said she wasn't joking.

"Doesn't this contradict what you said about bribery an hour ago?"

"Emma, your daddy is a sour grape. I'm promoting you as my new assistant mayor. I expect you to convince him to show up tomorrow," Nana D directed at my daughter as she traipsed away. "Kellan, this wasn't a suggestion. Be a good grandson and do what the mayor tells you to do, brilliant one."

I fought the urge to kick the curb, especially when Emma turned to me and said with a finger pointing in my direction, "Yeah, brilliant one. Mayor Nana D gave you an order. I'd do what she says, or she'll put you in jail." I relinquished, dropped Emma at camp, and met Lara for lunch. It had to be an improvement to my day thus far.

Lara and I huddled up in a corner booth at the Pick-Me-Up Diner. Though somewhere in her mid to late forties, the buxom brunette, also one of the most intelligent people I'd ever met, could easily pass as her daughter's sister. Born to French parents, she'd grown up in the United States and had once been a fashion model before getting entangled with the Grey family.

"An historic day," Lara said, activating a recording device and opening a screen on her tablet to take notes. "Seraphina Danby, first female mayor. Paul Dodd, youngest town councilman. We should be proud of our families."

"Oh, that's right. I forgot, Paul is engaged to your daughter, Imogene. She must be busy planning their wedding and deciding what her position should be as Braxton's First Lady." I laughed at the thought of Braxton having someone in that role. Marcus Stanton had conveniently flaunted his single lifestyle after his wife had passed away several years ago.

"Yes to the wedding. Doubtful to being in the public eye. Imogene is very shy. She must have gotten that particular personality trait from my ex-husband." When Lara laughed, a wrinkle-free face lit up the diner. She was a beautiful and cultured woman, and I could see why she'd garnered WCLN's lead investigative reporter and co-anchor position on the evening local news.

"I have enjoyed working with Imogene in class. She mentioned taking this course to better understand your job. It must feel great to have a daughter following in your footsteps."

Lara threw a hand up in the air. "Oh, I love her to pieces, but we are vastly different women and have very dissimilar taste in men. I'm just glad she finally accepted Paul's marriage proposal. Hopefully now that Quint Crawford is dead, she will kick the habit of trying to fix the men she dates."

I'd only met Lara a handful of times, but she was much more open than I'd expected. "I am aware Imogene and Quint dated years ago. Wasn't that over in college when he left town?"

"Yes, but she pined for him the whole time. She and Paul have been more off-and-on-again than a Hollywood power couple's rocky marriage. My daughter finally said yes to Paul this spring when she moved back home from France. A week later, she's having lunch with Quint and telling me how much she'd missed him." Lara waved over a waitress to order food.

I waited until the server walked away, then put forth, "Do you think something was going on between your daughter and Quint again?" I couldn't decide how it had fit in with what Emma had overheard at Woodland Warriors regarding someone yelling at Helena about a cheater.

"I'm not one to gossip, and that's not why we're here, is it? Let's stick to the key points today," Lara said, changing the topic to my grandmother. We spent the next thirty minutes discussing Nana D's plans over lunch.

When our plates were cleared and coffee ordered, I resumed the conversation. "You were going to tell me everything you knew about the jewelry thefts, right?"

She nodded. "Tell me why you care. I understand the journalistic need to find answers and seek the truth, but you left that life when you relocated from LA. I'm not entirely sure I understand why, but that's a story for a different day." Lara was direct but fair, an approach most people liked about her.

I took a moment to consider my answer. "Life is about balance. My daughter needed to be around her family, and I wasn't comfortable with some of the influences on the West Coast. In Braxton, I can teach her better values and provide a less stressful lifestyle."

"I assume you're referring to the Castiglianos?" she said, typing away on her tablet. "I'm not going to publicize any of this, so don't worry."

"Thanks. Yes, my in-laws are complex people. When I left the television show, I lost my analytical side. Teaching is fantastic and rewarding but cracking complex puzzles and holding people accountable for their actions is important to me." I'd been trying to find someone who understood my passion for solving crimes. Lara seemed to identify with this inner desire.

"You and I are a lot alike," she responded with a smile. "Maybe we should work together more often. Tell me what you know about the jewelry thefts. I'll fill in the blanks on anything I can clear up about Quint's death. I know they're related somehow."

Could I trust her? I provided a few quick points of interest without revealing anything the sheriff wouldn't want me to disclose nor mentioning Gabriel's role. "As near as I can tell, Quint had something to do with stealing the jewelry. His mother and I had a lengthy conversation about it. Someone visited her yesterday, but Bertha can't remember much about the girl."

"Imogene has always been fond of Bertha. I suppose she might have gone to see her. I'll see if I can find out, but I doubt she had anything to do with the jewelry thefts or Quint's death. The rumors circulating around the station are that Quint was murdered. That electrical issue wasn't an accident."

I shrugged. "I wouldn't know for sure. You'd have to ask the sheriff or Connor Hawkins, the lead detective on the case."

"And your best friend. I can see it on your face. The rumors are true. You wouldn't make a good criminal, Kellan. You can't lie to save your life, but I like that about you," Lara said, peeling the lid off a non-fat dairy creamer container and pouring it into her coffee. "I'll tell you what I've uncovered about the missing jewelry."

Lara explained everything that had happened at her house the previous week. Imogene admired a tiara her grandmother on the Grey side had given to her years ago. She wanted to incorporate it into her wedding ensemble and planned to bring it to the bridal salon for consideration. She'd been living at the Grey estate where she'd kept the family heirloom safely tucked away, but she'd planned to spend the night at Lara's place the night of Nana D's seventy-fifth birthday party. She'd also brought the tiara with her, so she could go directly to the wedding salon the next morning. Lara had been doing a news segment at Nana D's party, and Paul was at his house working on his plans as the new town councilman. A noise had woken Imogene while she was napping, and she thought it was her mother coming back home. When she got up to check, it was dusk, and she had trouble seeing from the glare of the setting sun. Someone knocked her over and tried to run out the door. She knew the layout of the room better than the thief, and when she was trying to escape, he tripped over her again. She struggled with him, scratched his arm, and he whacked her on the head with a bowl from a nearby table.

"Who do you think it is?"

Lara sat back and turned off the tape recorder, unwilling to say anything that might hurt her daughter while being recorded. "Imogene wouldn't inform the police, but she told me that very few people knew she'd kept the tiara that night. A couple of family members at the Grey estate, but they could've stolen it at any time in the past. She was afraid it was one of her friends."

"You think it was Quint, don't you?"

"She'd had lunch with him that day, and he'd asked her to give him another chance. He wanted her to

260

break up with Paul, but Imogene needed time to think about it. Paul made her feel safe and offered her a future without worrying about money or what people would think."

"Quint must have been angry. Could he have stolen the tiara to make her feel afraid, perhaps to sell it for money to support them? Does she have her own money from the Grey family?" Whoever confronted Helena at the camp must've been talking about Imogene cheating on Paul, at least it seemed the best explanation so far. Maybe Emma had gotten it backward. Was Krissy upset about Imogene and Quint hanging out? Perhaps she'd been interested in Quint herself just as she had been years ago.

Lara shook her head. "Not a lot. It's all in a trust for when she turns forty. In the Grey family, you must prove your worth before Hiram will let a penny go to the next generation. He's a tyrant, and that's ultimately why my marriage to his son never worked out."

I sipped coffee and processed Lara's news. "Do you think Imogene told Paul that Quint asked her to get back together?"

"Paul is focused on his new role in shaping the future of Wharton County. He's loved her for a decade, but Quint coming back made him nervous. I asked Imogene if she confessed to her fiancé what Quint had requested of her, but she wouldn't tell me. Ever since Quint died, she's been a shell of her former self. As much as I didn't want him with my daughter, I could see how much she loved Quint. He made her feel like a queen among women." Lara's phone began to vibrate, and she took the call.

While she spoke to her boss at the station, I paid the bill. Could Lara have been worried about Quint hurting her daughter and taken matters into her own hands?

After she ended her call, she stood. "I need to go. My boss moved up a deadline, and I must interview someone today. Don't worry, it has nothing to do with what we spoke about."

"Lara, when did Imogene tell you that Quint asked her to break up with Paul?" If Lara had known before Quint died, it might give me cause to worry about her honesty.

"Ha! If you're angling to find a way if I killed the loser, you can stop right there. I didn't like Quint Crawford, and I sure as heck didn't want the man anywhere near Imogene. But I have my limits. I would've hired someone to beat the crap out of him if I'd been able to prove he was the one who'd attacked her in my home. I'm not gonna call people like your in-laws to permanently whack him, though." Lara leaned in to kiss my cheek, then smiled when she pulled away. "I leave that kinda stuff to your family, darling."

"You're a riot, Lara. Hold up, before you go," I said, preparing to leave with her. "Since we both believe Quint was the current thief, and it looks like someone might have intentionally electrocuted or killed him, who's at the top of your list?"

"I don't believe for a minute it was Paul. As I said, he's all about his life in politics now. Krissy Stanton has always been a thorn in my daughter's side, and her father was incredibly angry about Quint telling people he'd been stiffed by the Stantons for work he'd done. If I didn't have this other story, I'd be focusing on the Stantons and Nicky Endicott. Nicky only hired Quint because they were old friends, but Imogene said they fought all the time about the construction business."

After Lara left, I made some notes on my phone while waiting for the hostess to check if Eleanor was available. Her office door had been closed, and I didn't want to interrupt if she was meeting with someone. The waitress returned to the front counter and said, "She had to pick up a few things at the supply store that didn't come in on time this week. Eleanor won't be back until later this afternoon."

"Got it, thanks. I saw the door shut and thought she was on the phone."

"No, Chef Manny is on a break. He's inside with his wife," she noted and left to clear a table.

Wife? Had Eleanor spoken with him about the conversation I'd overheard? She never updated me, but knowing my sister, she'd endlessly berated him. I was curious myself about what was going on and decided to poke my head in to say hello. Emma adored Chef Manny, and if he was leaving town, I wanted to know.

"Who's there?" Manny said after I knocked on the door.

"It's Kellan. Just wanted to say hello."

When the door opened, I did a double take at the person standing next to Manny. "Raquel?" What was one of my students doing with Eleanor's chef?

Raquel stepped forward and draped her arm around Manny's waist. "Hi, Dr. Ayrwick. Have you met my husband, Manny Salvado?"

I stood stunned for a moment, then realized my mouth had hung open a few too many seconds. "I never expected to see you two together. I'm sorry. Just a brief state of confusion." He'd recently gotten married to someone from out of town. Raquel indicated she was new in town and waiting for her husband to figure out some things with his job. The conclusion made complete sense now. Except, was I about to lose a student and Eleanor a chef? "Congratulations to you both. I confess, Manny, I overheard you the other day talk about getting married and potentially moving to Las Vegas." I inhaled deeply and leaned against the doorjamb when they backed into the office. Could I ask about their future plans?

Raquel looked as if she realized she might have given too much away when we'd spoken. "Maybe I should leave you two alone. I have some errands to run." Raquel kissed Manny's cheek and told her husband she'd see him at home that evening.

Once she was gone, I turned to Manny. "So, has Eleanor confronted you? I mean... you have to do what's best for you, but she'd really miss you."

Manny waved me in and shut the door. "This marriage thing is new to me, Kellan. I really like her, but

I might be in over my head. I don't know what to do." A few lines around the corner of Manny's mouth offered significant concern over the situation he'd found himself in. Earlier that spring, he and his buddies had taken a trip to Las Vegas after the previous owners of the diner had sold it to Eleanor. He was certain she would fire him and hire her own staff. He and his friends had hung out with a few girls at a club all night. Raquel was one of the girls, and they'd gotten together several times that week. On his last night, they hit the strip to party before returning home, and his friends had dared him to do shots most of the night. The next morning, he and Raquel woke up in bed with matching wedding rings.

"My friends were a little hazy on how it happened, but they were at the all-night chapel with us when we went through with the ceremony," he spit out, slapping his hand to his forehead with a pervasive thud I could feel across the room.

Wow! I thought what happened in Vegas was supposed to stay in Vegas. I guess not. "Do you love her?" His mixed nod and shrug told me he had no clue. "I assume if she's here, that means she's moved in with you. Is Raquel pressuring you to leave town?"

"Not exactly. She has bigger ideas about what she wants to accomplish in life. Raquel's been staying here for a few weeks, then heads home to visit her family and friends." He cracked his knuckles and looked at the ceiling in silent prayer. Then, he admitted that Eleanor still didn't know the truth.

"What do you plan to do?"

"For now, I guess, we're bicoastal until we decide the best solution. Raquel is trying to hook me up with some folks back home where I could get a job in one of the big restaurants. My family would kill me if I got a divorce. They're deeply religious." Manny explained that they've been chilly toward his wife because of the lack of a traditional wedding. "Can you talk to your sister?"

It wasn't my job, but the guy looked desperate. "I'll think about it. For now, don't say anything. If she asks you, though, you have to tell her the truth."

Once Manny acknowledged my advice and gave me a huge bear hug that almost cracked my ribs, I left Eleanor's office and grabbed my phone. I'd felt it buzzing in my pocket earlier but couldn't check while learning Manny's news.

When I listened to the voicemail, I felt the weight of doom lurking on my doorstep. Marcus had left me a message "Kellan, we need to discuss these jewelry thefts. I have proof that your brother has just stolen something from my family, and I am giving you the courtesy of a heads-up call before I turn this matter over to the police. I have a proposal to make, and if you're smart, you'll accept it without any questions. You have until five o'clock to return my call, or I'm contacting Sheriff Montague."

Chapter 16

"I completely forgot, thank you so much," I replied to the mother of one of Emma's friends. The girls had gymnastics practice at seven this evening, and we'd agreed to share transportation responsibilities. I called Woodland Warriors to let them know who would meet Emma at camp this afternoon since I'd be picking up the girls when they finished at eight thirty. As always, I was grateful when the school requested the secret codeword to prove who I was before they would agree to let Emma leave with someone else. Next, I texted Helena Roarke and her teacher to confirm release authorization. This day and age, one could never be *too* careful.

I agreed to meet Marcus at his house, which was next door to Nana D's farm, Danby Landing. Although his siblings lived in the family estate on Millionaire's Mile, he'd bought his own place years ago. I had no idea what the man wanted, but undoubtedly, it would be a dangerous meeting. He was on the warpath after his loss to Nana D in the election, and if he had something on Gabriel, it would be difficult to talk Marcus out of whatever cunning plan he'd concocted.

I pulled up to his house just as the cell phone Cristiano had given me began to ring. I couldn't ignore it, so I pressed accept and greeted him.

"It's Francesca," my wife said in a calm voice. "Cristiano thought you'd want to hear from me."

"Hi," I said with dire hesitancy in my voice as I stepped outside the SUV. "Is everything okay?"

"I'm fine. Cristiano set a time for the meeting. He'll release me unharmed, if my parents deliver everything he asks for in his next request: All the evidence of any past wrongdoing on the part of Las Vargas, a signed agreement officially turning over fifty-one percent of Castigliano International to his family, and a videotaped promise they will not seek any retribution or revenge." Francesca sounded as if she were negotiating a business deal and not the terms of her own release.

"Will your parents actually do that?" The volume of the concessions was astronomical. Of course, Francesca would be worth it to them, but something didn't feel right about this deal.

"They have no choice. Cristiano's father has made it clear that he expects his son to get rid of me permanently if my parents do not acquiesce." Francesca paused to speak with Cristiano, then returned to our call. "I haven't spoken with them in three months, Kellan. I need you to tell them how important it is

that they do this. I don't want to suffer the consequences."

"I understand. Tell me where and when, and I'll
make sure they show up." I couldn't let them harm
my wife. I knew things had changed between us, but
she didn't deserve to die because of what her parents had done over the years. "I'll protect you." Stress
and fear plummeted inside me until they knocked my
body out of balance and sent me careening against
the stone pillar in the Stanton driveway.

"Cristiano wants to speak with you now,"
Francesca said, abandoning the call.

"I told you we were close to a solution, Kellan. If
you listen carefully and obey every instruction I give
you, this will all be done tomorrow night." Cristiano's
smooth voice was not a comfort, despite his inten-
tions. He told me that Francesca had left the room,
so we could speak openly.

"Just tell me what to do, okay?" I refrained from
letting my voice expose apprehension. The perspi-
ration forming under my arms was enough of a re-
minder. "I'll drag the Castiglianos at gunpoint to your
meeting spot, if I have to."

"That's just it, you won't need to worry about
that. I've got a much simpler solution in mind." Cristiano explained that he wanted me to collect the evidence from the Castiglianos ahead of time. Most of
it would be saved electronically on a storage device.
Any physical copies, other than the agreement signing over their business, were to be destroyed.

"Then what?"

"Tomorrow evening at nine o'clock, you will meet me at a specific location for the exchange," Cristiano replied.

"Fine. That gives me just over twenty-four hours. Where do you want to meet?" I checked my calendar to confirm tomorrow's schedule and decided I'd ask my parents to watch Emma for the evening.

"I'll let you know thirty minutes before the meeting. I can't have you sharing that location with anyone in advance. I've seen how much time you've been spending with the sheriff lately. I wonder what your wife would think about that budding relationship." Cristiano must have smirked because a sinister sound emanated through the phone.

"It's not what you think. We're working on something else together—"

"I don't care to know the details. If you tell April Montague anything about this conversation, or any cops or FBI agents show up near the drop-off point, the deal is over. You, your wife, and your daughter will discover what it's like to swim in the middle of Crilly Lake with your feet and hands shackled together in iron cuffs and a plastic bag tied around each of your heads." Cristiano said nothing else and waited for me to respond.

"Your instructions are crystal clear, Cristiano. You're also the scum of the earth." I couldn't control my temper and pounded my fist against the stone pillar. "But I will do what you ask."

"I'm really not like my family. I've told you before that we could be friends in another life. I'm carrying out orders from my father, just as you're carrying them out for me. I'm the middleman in this predicament." Cristiano verified the timing of his plan and hung up the phone.

I stood at the end of the driveway absorbing the severity of the situation while blood trickled down my hands. My life had suddenly turned into one of the *Godfather* movies, but there was no character I could conjure in my mind that would assure me things would end up okay. I called the Castiglianos to relay the instructions. Vincenzo indicated he and Cecilia would have what I needed the following morning. We agreed to meet at noon for the first exchange.

I stared at my personal cell phone feeling desperate to call April with the details of the plan, but if I told her anything, Cristiano would kill Francesca. I wasn't sure which risk was the bigger one to take, but I had little time to decide. Marcus Stanton barreled down his driveway, anger in his voice.

"What took you so long? I have important things to do. Are you prepared to protect your little brother, Kellan?" Marcus, an early-sixty-something louse with a penchant for much younger women, had two features people ruthlessly gossiped about—eternally sweaty hands and a thinning pompadour that had seen better days. Neither short nor tall, thin nor fat, he was the preeminent plain and dull man except for those notable exceptions. Unfortunately, he thought much more highly of himself.

"Listen, Stanton. I've had a heck of a day already, and let me assure you," I blasted while stomping directly up to his face. "You are the least of my concerns right now. My brother hasn't done anything wrong, and if you've got any evidence, I'd bet my last dollar it's been manufactured by one of your lackeys. I'm getting close to throttling the next idiot that threatens me. You want to test my patience? Bring. It. On." The fury inside me must have been percolating for months. I knew better than to release it in a physical manner, but I could unleash a nasty verbal tirade on him if necessary.

Marcus stepped back with a genuine look of fear formulating in his demeanor. "I'm certain we can work out a mutually acceptable deal. There's no need to get agitated."

Noticing his retreat, I willed myself to calm down so that we could have a productive conversation. "What is this so-called evidence you have?" Yanking a tissue from my pocket, I pressed it to my bloody hand.

Marcus handed me a photograph of Gabriel from the Stanton home security system. "Look at the timestamp."

"It was taken at eight forty-seven this morning," I replied, studying the photo to understand what was transpiring in the scene. "It looks like my brother is standing on your front doorstep. What about it?" I'd been wondering why Gabriel hadn't shown up for Nana D's inauguration ceremony, but I figured I could've missed him if he'd hung out somewhere else. I reminded myself to call my mother when I was done with Stanton to ask her to watch Emma the next night. My memory was shot lately.

"I left the house this morning at eight fifteen to attend Seraphina's little press conference. My daughter was with me, and Krissy can verify what I'm about to tell you." His face was reddening like a tomato as he spoke. Whether it was his temper, anxiety, or the warmer weather, I couldn't be sure. Nor did I care.

"Out with it, please. I don't have all day." I tapped my foot impatiently, waiting for him to get the point.

"Krissy got home at ten o'clock. She had a headache and couldn't be out in the sun. When she arrived, she found the safe unlocked and its door wide open. I'd kept cash and several pieces of my late wife's jewelry inside. It was all missing!" He threw his hands to his hips and glared at me.

"What does that prove? Gabriel must've stopped by to see Krissy, but she was with you downtown." My tolerance level was at its peak, and if he kept pushing me, he wouldn't like the results.

Marcus handed me a second picture. "Look at this one. It's from a side camera just three minutes later. Your brother was peering through my kitchen window."

"Okay, so he was persistent. How did he supposedly get inside?"

"When I got home to check for myself, I found a whole bunch of glass underneath the window in the mudroom around back. I don't have a camera there, so I can't show you another picture. But there are several footprints. Someone broke in during the two hours Krissy and I were gone."

"And you think it was my brother? This isn't proof. Let me see this glass," I said, marching past him up the driveway. His information didn't make sense unless the thief was breaking the nine-day pattern. The theft was supposed to have occurred yesterday. Gabriel may not have been with us at the inauguration, but I wasn't going to jump to any conclusions about his guilt. After our last conversation, he'd convinced me he was innocent.

Marcus came running after me. "I called you because we can work this out privately. If you get Gabriel to return what he stole, I won't press charges. But there's one more condition."

I walked around his house, ignoring his words. When I arrived at the broken window, I noticed all the glass was on the outside. Four large shards would fill ninety percent of the hole in the window. A few small pieces were scattered in the flowerbeds, but from what I could tell, the window had been broken by someone standing on the inside. Most of the glass wouldn't be on the ground outside. Either Marcus was trying to con me, or someone else with a key had stolen the items from his house, then broken the window to make it look like a robbery. Could Marcus have done it himself? Or was Krissy involved? Based on what I'd overheard, and what Lara had told me, either scenario was entirely possible.

Although I'd eventually call his bluff, I decided to play ball for a few more minutes. "Sure, we can keep this between us. What is it you want?"

"Convince your grandmother to step down from the mayor's office. She can recommend me as the replacement. I was the other candidate, and people won't want to wait for another election." Marcus smiled like a kid in a candy shop, only this kid wasn't one anybody should ever trust.

"How do you expect me to do that? No one will believe Nana D decided to quit after all the effort she put in to get this position. Seriously?" Was the man losing his mind?

Marcus kept urging me to consider his deal, threatening to call the cops without delay if I didn't agree. "It happens more than you think. Seraphina could claim she had a health scare, or maybe she has to leave town to visit one of your uncles wherever they're living these days."

Nana D's two sons, my interesting yet peculiar uncles, traveled for work. Zachary, a big-game and wildlife veterinarian, currently studied African elephant migration for the summer, and Campbell was on a covert humanitarian mission in the Amazon jungle. We hadn't heard from either in months, but that wasn't unusual due to their intense work and frequent isolation from society.

"I'm calling your bluff, Marcus. For one thing, you haven't mentioned anything about a calla lily. One had been left at all the previous crimes, so something doesn't feel right here. For another...." I explained the inaccuracy of the position of the glass, then told him I had a better deal to make.

His eyes darkened, and he kicked a pile of nearby dirt. "Don't try to mess with me, Kellan. I've still got pull in this town, and just because she's the mayor doesn't mean Sheriff Montague will listen to your nana. The sheriff follows the law, and if she thinks Gabriel is responsible, she'll arrest him. Especially since the last time we talked, the jewelry thefts were connected to the Crawford murder."

"That ship has sailed already. What I find most interesting is your family's potential role in Quint's death. How about you tell me where you were the night Quint electrocuted himself? Or how about Krissy? I overheard a conversation that leads me to believe she knows more than she's said." I shoved my sticky hands in my pocket and began to walk to the front of the house, knowing the rat would follow and beg for more information.

"I was in a late-night meeting with our former mayor. You can check with his assistant about it. I had nothing to do with Crawford's death," Marcus growled, chasing quickly behind me but unable to maintain my pace.

When I got to the SUV, I turned around and calmly asked, "Then, you weren't trying to get revenge for Quint telling people you never paid for his construction services? If that's the case, maybe April Montague will summon your daughter to the sheriff's office for a discussion."

"Nicholas Endicott was paid in full two days before the election. If I wanted to kill Quint, don't you think I would have done it sooner to stop him from spreading any negativity about me?" Marcus clamped a beefy hand on the SUV door so that I couldn't open it.

"It's time for me to leave. Get your hands off—"

"Krissy assuredly has an alibi for that night. Maybe she saw a calla lily today too. I'll discuss it with her, and we can close this matter. Don't you go thinking we're done with this negotiation. As soon as I confirm Krissy is in the clear, even though I know my daughter is innocent, I'll take these photos to the police. You have until tomorrow at noon to accept my terms, Kellan." Marcus waggled his finger inches from my nose and reiterated his point before plodding back up his driveway and pulling out his cell phone.

April was supposed to follow up on the feud between Quint, Nicky, and Marcus on the unpaid construction work, but I was certain Stanton wouldn't have lied to me. He had to know I could easily check his alibi, so I temporarily believed him when he said he had nothing to do with Quint's murder. I wasn't as convinced about his daughter's innocence and had to find a way to get her to talk to me in a public setting. Why had the thief waited an extra day to execute the last robbery?

I checked with Gabriel to understand what he'd been doing at the Stanton house that morning. When he answered on the first ring, I could hear shouting in the background. "Where are you? Some sports game?"

Gabriel asked me to hold on for a second, then reconnected twenty seconds later. "Sorry, I was just leaving Kirklands. I met Nicky for a drink after work."

My watch indicated it was already six o'clock. The day was going by way too quickly. Gabriel explained that Krissy had texted him the night before to ask for a ride to the inauguration ceremony because she had lent her car to Tiffany, who had sent hers to the shop for a seatbelt recall. "Did you notice any broken glass around one of the windows?"

Gabriel said he didn't, but he also had only looked at the front and side windows. "I thought it was strange that she asked me to pick her up at eight forty-five and wasn't around this morning. I waited in my car for a few minutes, but I didn't want to be late to Nana D's ceremony. Krissy never answered the doorbell or my calls, so I left."

"Okay, thanks. Listen, Marcus Stanton might be making trouble for you, so just be careful. How'd it go with the sheriff and Connor?" Why did Krissy ask Gabriel to pick her up, then go with her father instead? What was she up to?

"Fine. They haven't decided what to do about my involvement in the jewelry thefts from eight years ago, but the sheriff promised she wouldn't be letting it go easily. I'm not allowed to leave town or discuss it with anyone else except for you. What's up with that?"

"Another time, brother. I can't get into it." And I couldn't because even I didn't know anymore. "I'll call you tomorrow. I've got a lot of crazy stuff going on, and I need to find Krissy."

"Hold up. Krissy might still be here with Tiffany. They were drinking a few tables away from me. I was gonna confront her on my way out to ask why she blew me off this morning, but then you called. Want me to interrupt her?" Gabriel asked.

"No, I'll head over there. I don't need to pick up Emma for another couple of hours. Thanks." After I hung up, I drove to the bar. On the way, I called my mother to beg her to watch Emma the following night. She had just gotten home from work and was waiting for my father to get back with a pizza he'd gone to pick up. My mother hated waiting for the delivery folks to show up, as the food was always cold. Of course, she was excited to watch Emma. "I appreciate it, Mom. You're the best."

"I'll collect Emma at the bus stop at seven o'clock, but I have a late meeting with a prospective student at eight. Emma could hang out in the conference room for a bit. I don't expect it to go too long."

It would be better if Emma was concealed on campus with my mother while I was somewhere else meeting Cristiano and Francesca for the exchange. After we disconnected, I informed Woodland Warriors that Emma would take the late bus home tomorrow from day camp. By the time I reached Kirklands, I was starving. I walked into the bar and found Tiffany sitting by herself.

"Hey, I haven't seen you in a few days." I gestured a harried-looking bartender to order a burger with everything on it and a large ginger ale, then turned back to Tiffany. "Can I get you anything?"

She declined. "You just missed your brother. He was here with Nicky and some work colleagues, but they all took off. How's everything?"

"Not so good," I said, sipping from my glass and dropping a napkin on my lap. "I was told Krissy Stanton was here, and I need to speak with her."

"Good luck. She snuck out the back when your brother stepped outside. I think she's avoiding him. Besides, she's on her way out of town," Tiffany said with a hint of annoyance in her voice.

"Wait, what do you mean?"

"I met her for a drink and to return her car. She was going to let me borrow it for a few days, but something urgent popped up and she needed it back right away," Tiffany said, then hopped off the barstool and collected her purse from the undercounter hook. "Gotta head out. Take care."

"Before you go, do you know why she's leaving town?" I had my suspicions but wanted confirmation before taking any action. Things were starting to fall into place based on what had happened at the Stanton household today.

"I guess it doesn't matter if she's leaving town. I can tell you what she told me." Tiffany signaled the bartender for another drink and mentioned that it should go on my tab. "Krissy wanted to say good-bye before she hightailed it out of Braxton. She was worried about something, but I don't know exactly what it's all about. She dumped a lot of drama on me tonight."

"Did she give you any names or details you can share?"

"Krissy confessed that she'd been trying to snare Quint ever since he returned to Braxton a few months ago. His death had been a lot harder on her than she'd admitted last week."

If my assumptions were correct, Krissy must have figured out Quint had stolen all the jewelry and had taken it harshly. Could she have killed him in a struggle at the cable car trying to convince him to turn himself in? "Did she say anything about why she had to leave so quickly?"

"Just that no one understood her. I guess she was angry with Imogene too. Apparently, Quint was still in love with Imogene and wouldn't commit to Krissy. My guess is Krissy's tired of all the chaos in her life and needed a break." Tiffany explained that Krissy had a crush on Quint back in college, but he had been dating Imogene, so she'd backed away sophomore year. When Imogene had split up with Quint and chosen Paul, Krissy thought she had a chance. Then, Quint left town without telling anyone why. Krissy had always blamed Imogene for driving Quint away from Braxton. She didn't know that he'd been stealing all the jewelry and needed to escape based on his uncle's shenanigans and blackmail.

"It must have been hard on her. Do you think she's already skipped town, or can I catch her?"

Tiffany threw her hands in the air, extricating herself from the conversation. "Who knows? My Uber is outside. You might be able to catch her tomorrow. She mentioned something about a quick trip to the bank in the afternoon before she could head out of town."

As Tiffany left, my burger arrived. While I ate dinner, I ran through a number of theories. Bertha had said a girl showed up at the house and was in Quint's room. It was either Krissy or Imogene, but I couldn't be sure which one. Imogene could've wanted to say a permanent goodbye before she fully committed to Paul. Maybe Krissy found the jewels Quint had stolen and took them with her to the bank for safe keeping. What I wasn't certain about was whether she planned to turn them over to the police or to get rid of them, so Quint's memory wasn't further sullied with proof of his crimes. I just couldn't figure out how the latest situation with Marcus that morning fit in. Was he lying to me, or had something changed Krissy's plans to attend the inauguration with Gabriel? Either way, who'd broken into the Stanton house and taken the cash and jewelry from the safe?

I was flipping through my phone to call Krissy when Siobhan Walsh and Nicky Endicott gallivanted into the bar and grabbed a corner table. He pulled out her chair and kissed her on the lips before taking his own seat. Gabriel had said Nicky was always out with a new girl but seeing him with Siobhan was startling. What kind of scheme were those two cooking up together?

Chapter 17

I paid for my meal and sauntered over to Nicky and Siobhan's table, curious to find out for myself whether it had anything to do with Quint's death or the missing jewelry. I still didn't have confirmation about Siobhan's supposed visit to the doctor at the same time Quint was being murdered.

"What a surprise to see you two together. I stopped in for a drink and was just about to leave when you both sat down." I tucked the credit card receipt in my pocket and waited for their reply.

"Hey, Dr. Ayrwick," Siobhan began with a minute fluster and flash of panic. "We're on a date. I met Nicky when he came to stain some beadboard in my living room last week, and we hit it off."

"That dark stain you picked was perfect for the room." Nicky had a sneer forming on his face. "She's a delightful woman. I'm excited to spend more time with her," he said, reaching for her hand.

"As long as you don't cut yourself and bleed on my floor again," Siobhan quipped.

If what he'd just revealed was true, Nicky's fingers might not have been stained black from spray-painting a calla lily, and he hadn't gotten his injury from attacking Imogene and stealing the tiara at Lara's place. He might not be the secret accomplice. "I won't keep you guys, just wanted to ask a couple of questions." I turned to Siobhan and said, "My mother mentioned the twins have been sick a lot. She was worried when you had to go to the hospital last week. Everything okay?"

Siobhan nodded. "Yes, my son was fine, but my daughter had croup. It's common, but I couldn't get in to see the pediatrician. I was so glad the clinic remained open at that hour."

"Really? Which one did you go to? I'd love to have a back-up in case Emma is ever sick, and I don't want to go to the emergency room." It sounded like a logical statement, and in truth, I should have a better back-up than Nana D's old-fashioned remedies.

"Downtown, near the Pick-Me-Up Diner," Siobhan said, pulling her hand away from Nicky's.

"Kids. Always a worry, huh?" He seemed disinterested as he gazed around the room for a server.

"True, they get sick often. Does the clinic always stay open late? I guess it was busy, huh?"

Siobhan looked at Nicky and offered an apology for the interruption to their date, then grabbed her purse. "I think I still have the invoice. It wasn't that crowded," she said, then retrieved an envelope and pulled out the bill. "Says that I paid at twelve-thirty in the morning, and the hours of operation are... hold on, let me check... they closed for new patients by midnight. I was the last person to leave there."

Based on her timing, she was at the clinic and couldn't have been at the cable car confronting Quint. I supposed someone else could have taken the twins to the hospital and was covering for her, but I couldn't see Siobhan murdering a man for potentially leading her on. When I asked her about it, she acknowledged she'd been angry, but a few days later, she and Nicky had gone on their first date. "Aye, I got over Quint pretty quickly. I am not the kind of woman to go around killing men for being cads!"

After Nicky confirmed he had been near the cable car station and had dropped his running gloves the morning I'd found Quint's body, I realized he probably hadn't been the one to kill the man. I needed to be certain, so I asked about the unpaid bill with Marcus. "Do you think Quint's decision to go public had anything to do with Stanton losing the race? Was Marcus angry enough to seek revenge on Quint?"

He looked surprised at my inquiry but recuperated quickly. "Paul Dodd and I were talking about that earlier. Stanton was neck and neck with your grandmother for a while, but when Quint began telling people, Marcus did experience a shift in his numbers." While Nicky ordered drinks for him and Siobhan, I planned my next questions.

"Marcus was yelling about it this afternoon. Told me he paid the bill to you right away, that the confusion was on Quint's part because he didn't know you'd already taken care of it."

Nicky nodded. "Quint never was good with the accounting side of the business. He thought because he'd gotten Krissy to convince her father to use him as the contractor that he'd get the full amount from Stanton. It was through my company, and it took a few days to sort that all out."

"I guess once that was fixed, everything turned out okay, huh?" I wasn't sure what else to ask but felt like something obvious was at my fingertips.

"Yeah, Marcus tried to get a discount, as usual. Claimed that his daughter was helping Quint with all the work. Krissy was just interested in learning about the business, even followed me on a couple of jobs to understand how to do basic electrical work. She found the whole thing enthralling for some reason. We good, man?" Nicky clearly wanted me to leave, so he could proceed with his date.

I wished them goodnight and headed back to my SUV. Everything was pointing to Krissy now. If she'd been knowledgeable about electrical work, was she savvy enough to cause a power issue in the cable car that knocked out Quint? When he didn't die from the initial injury, did she then decide to strangle him? It was looking more like I'd found the culprit, prompting me to chat with April as soon as possible to discuss our next steps.

After leaving Kirklands, I picked up Emma and her friend at the gymnastics facility, then dropped her friend off at home. Emma and I took the puppy for a walk and played with him for a few minutes. I was grateful one of Nana D's farmhands would stop by twice each day to walk Baxter while Emma and I were at work or camp. Once we were finished tiring out the adorable little beast, Emma complained that she was so exhausted, she could sleep for an eternity. My daughter climbed into bed and passed on our normal story time. It was okay to skip it occasionally, and I had an urgent call to make. April needed to know what had happened with Marcus and Cristiano earlier that day. And I deserved to talk to someone who was on my side for a change.

* * *

"Are you okay, Daddy? You look funny," Emma said while we waited for the bus to pick her up Wednesday morning. I'd considered driving her to camp but didn't want her to think there was anything out of the ordinary about today.

"Of course, sweetheart. It's just a really big day at work for me. You know how much I love you, right?" I cradled her warm cheek and kissed her forehead, silently willing the universe to protect her. "I'll do anything necessary to keep this amazing smile on your face."

"I know. You're the best. Sometimes I think about Mommy and get sad that she went to Heaven. I'll see her again one day." Emma gripped the back of my neck and held on tightly. "Way in the future because I'm gonna live forever."

"That's true. You're gonna be as old as Nana D one day, and promise me, you'll never forget that I tried to do the best things possible for you, okay?" I let Emma pull away from me as the bus arrived, then grabbed her for one final hug to give me the strength to do what needed to be done. If everything went according to plan that night, Francesca might be back in our lives. "Remember, Grandma will pick you up on the late bus today. She's gonna take you to her office at Admissions Hall."

Emma waved as she boarded the bus, then turned around giggling. "See ya tonight! Tell Baxter I love him."

Sixty seconds later, the yellow school bus was just a trailing vision in the distance. My eyes were brimming with the desire to cry, but I forced the tears back into their hidden state. Desperation clung to my soul for one of my grandmother's trademark hugs.

After finishing some work for an upcoming class, I arrived at the downtown administrative offices to update Nana D with Cristiano's plan.

"It'll work out, Kellan. God is looking out for this family, and you've been through the wringer more than enough for the Castigliano family. If there were ever someone who could negotiate terms to fix past mistakes, I believe it's you." Nana D had more strength in her arms than she had in her words that morning, and her message had been super loud, utterly clear, and difficult to top. "Don't do anything foolish. Trust your instincts."

"Scout's Honor," I said, as an aide knocked on the door to Nana D's new mayoral office to let us know that April had arrived.

As she entered the room, April jerked her head. "What are you doing here?"

When I'd called April the night before to strategize about the meeting with the Castiglianos and Las Vargas, I neglected to reveal my plan to attend her conference with Nana D. We'd focused on how to communicate today to ensure my safety and offer the best chances of Francesca's imminent return. I'd saved all the news I'd been collecting about Quint's death, including Krissy's potential guilt, for today's encounter. "I sent Emma to camp this morning and needed someone to tell me tonight would turn out fine," I replied, feeling guilty about the small lie. I had no strength to fight with April about anything else.

"I understand." April rubbed my shoulder. "Your family has your back, and that's a good thing."

Nana D narrowed her eyes at the discussion with April but wisely kept her thoughts to herself. "I'd like Kellan to stay while we discuss the jewelry thefts and Quint Crawford's murder. He's been instrumental in past investigations and knows the players. Any concerns, Sheriff Montague?"

April pursed her lips ready to disagree, then pulled up a chair and sat near the desk. "Not at all, Mayor Danby. I'm confident Kellan will keep anything we discuss in this room to himself. His intuitions have been helpful to date."

April wasn't backing down because she was afraid of Nana D. As two primary leaders protecting Wharton County, the women had a certain respect for each other. April was biding time to present objections at the right time. This conversation would do little harm regarding the open cases we were investigating.

Nana D asked April to summarize what she'd done to date. Once finished, we decided the scratches that the coroner had identified on Quint's body had come from Imogene's attack when he'd burglarized her mother's place. Based on the timing the coroner had specified, it was a perfect match. I'd been hoping they'd come from an accomplice, someone who might've then turned around and killed Quint two days later. I wasn't that lucky. Nana D then asked me to provide any working theories or new information I'd obtained since my last conversation with the sheriff. I said, "Based on everything we've heard to date, we know Quint stole the jewelry eight years ago. Gabriel might've helped him leave Braxton and hock some of the items at the San Francisco pawn shop, but he doesn't appear to have profited from it. Quint took all the money when they parted ways."

April nodded and folded her hands in her lap. "I believe Quint returned to town to take care of his sick mother and saw an opportunity to steal more jewelry. Based on his anger over mothers interfering in their daughters' lives, he recreated the crimes with the same families. I suspect there was an accomplice this time too, as security was more heightened and complicated to avoid."

"Krissy Stanton is probably that accomplice, and she seems resolute to leave town. Marcus might be involved too." I told Nana D and April about the blackmail attempt over Gabriel's visit to the Stanton house. "He gave me roughly twenty hours, and the deadline is coming up shortly. I expect him to contact the Wharton County Sheriff's Office by early afternoon."

"I don't have enough to do anything other than bring in Krissy for questions at this point. Yes, she has knowledge of electrical construction. Yes, she might've visited Quint's bedroom and taken something from it. Yes, you overheard that Imogene can place her near the cable car that night," April explained, the frustration in her voice clear and deep.

"Can you put a tail on her?" Nana D suggested, pacing the room. "Stop her from leaving town?"

"We have to do things in the right order, Mayor Danby. As soon as we're done here, I will speak with Detective Connor Hawkins about his previous interviews with Imogene and Krissy." April explained verification of Tiffany and Helena's attendance at a midnight movie while Quint was being killed.

With alibis for the time of Quint's murder confirmed for Siobhan, Nicky, Helena, and Tiffany, we were left with Gabriel, Krissy, Paul, and Imogene as the only other potential suspects. "We know Gabriel didn't do it even if no one can verify his whereabouts when Quint had been strangled. Paul and Imogene are a possibility even though it's not likely based on Lara Bouvier's input. I suppose if Paul had found out

Quint was the one who accosted his fiancée, he might have sought revenge."

Nana D agreed to be more patient and wait until the following day before asking for an update. She knew April and I had to focus on the nine o'clock Castigliano trade-off. Once she left to meet with her staff, April and I finished chatting about the evening's approach.

"Cristiano will call at eight thirty to tell me where to meet him. He's watching, so you can't be anywhere near me," I said, worried that a slip could cause monumental failure in the plan.

"You're going to carry this tracking device." April handed me a new pair of glasses. "My FBI contact had a chip embedded in the frame."

"Wait! How did you get the details of my prescription? Oh… how clever, you stole my glasses the other day at The Big Beanery." My mouth dropped open in shock.

"Never underestimate me, Kellan. I'm a determined woman." April stood and removed my current pair of glasses. I could smell the new lavender body wash on her skin as her fingers brushed against my ears. "They're an identical match."

As April leaned back, I gently cradled her wrist. "I don't know how to thank you for doing this my way. You're not whom I expected, based on the day we first met."

"Neither are you," April replied, her hand quivering against mine. "You can be arrogant and stubborn sometimes, but there's also this incredibly ador—"

"Excuse me, are you two going to be leaving soon? I've got to clean up in here for Mayor Danby," a deep voice boomed from the doorway.

April turned around and told the assistant with inordinately bad timing that we were finished. While she was looking away, I closed my eyes and accepted the truth. I was developing feelings for the woman even with everything we'd been through together in the last few months. This was not a complication I could focus on until everything else calmed down in my life. I bolted from my chair and hurried to the other side of the room. "Sorry, we were working on a case together."

April and I left the office, pretending the moment never happened. An awkward and distant dance followed us from the silent office to the elevator, where we listened to light music and ignored each other. When we reached the lobby, she said, "I can track you wherever you are as long as you're wearing those glasses. Cristiano won't suspect we've done anything to them."

"I hope so," I mumbled, looking around the front entrance, certain a Vargas henchman followed me. "That's why we couldn't get the FBI involved or wire me. He'll check as soon as I show up. He's quite clever."

April opened an app on her phone and showed how she was able to track me via GPS. "It's extremely sensitive, so we'll be able to get to the address or building, but not specifically where inside. You'll need to drop breadcrumbs if you can, but don't be obvious."

"What about the fake storage device? You were creating false documents and files in case he checked the size of content." I waited for April to scan the lobby.

She slipped a large thumb drive into my coat pocket. "That's what you'll give them if they ask for something before I show up."

Our plan was straightforward, but there was little room for chance or error. There never was in a situation like this. Neither party trusted the other, and someone would always do something unpredictable. If I stayed the course, we had a solid chance of escaping unharmed.

I'd finish teaching my class tonight, then head home and wait for instructions from Cristiano. Once he told me where to meet them, I'd repeat it aloud on a recording device she'd already concealed in my living room. Someone from April's team would dial in to listen to the location as a fallback in case the GPS device in my new glasses failed to work. I'd drive to the meeting point and try to delay the handoff, assuming I could demand to see proof that Francesca was alive before handing over the storage device. Hopefully, it would give April's team enough time to surround the building and ensure a safe rescue. It could turn into a hostage situation if Cristiano checked specific files, but we expected that he would trust us once I handed over the signed agreement turning over fifty-one percent of Castigliano International to him. As he walked out of the building, April would nab him. If he sent Francesca and me out first, then the cops would enter the building for the capture.

"Call me after you get everything from the Castiglianos. I'm going to apprise Connor of what he needs to follow up on with the Quint Crawford case." April left me standing in the building with a dark cloud hanging over my future, and maybe the beginnings of a much brighter one down the line.

I headed to campus where the Castiglianos would be waiting. When I arrived at Diamond Hall, I found them sitting on a bench just outside the back entrance.

"You better not mess this up," Cecilia warned, a scathing look of judgment cast in my direction. "You've abandoned my daughter before, and I promise you, if that happens again tonight, you will suffer the consequences."

Vincenzo hushed his wife and suggested we recommence the conversation in my office behind a closed door. I let them sit first, then asked, "Why are you willing to hand over your company so easily? I've got a sneaky suspicion you're keeping information from me."

"You've got strong instincts, Kellan," Vincenzo said as he handed me the storage device and the folder with the signed agreement. "Some of the contents of this drive could get my company and family into trouble, but it's nothing my lawyers can't make go away. As for this so-called agreement—"

"It's not valid, and any court will throw it out the window. We've been coerced into signing the contract," Cecilia scowled in repugnance. "We're doing what we have to do to get our daughter back. Rest assured, we are not simply complying without our own equally injurious plan in place."

"You can't do anything to hurt her," I shouted, then soothed my voice so no one overheard us. All I needed was Myriam listening in and getting herself involved. "What kind of game are you playing?"

"Silence, Kellan," Cecilia replied, narrowing her gaze in my direction and forming an ominous smile I wouldn't soon forget. "Tonight will go as planned. You will turn over what Las Vargas has demanded. Meanwhile, Vincenzo and I have evidence of our own that we plan to disclose this evening. It might just convince Cristiano Vargas to release Francesca and return the storage device back to you."

"But he specifically said you cannot show up," I reminded them, thinking about his vicious threats and direction on how the evening would proceed. "How will you know where to find them?"

"We have our ways, Kellan. My wife will not do anything foolish, but I promise you that we will win this war." Vincenzo grabbed Cecilia's hand and led her through the hallway.

As they walked down the front staircase, Myriam poked her head out of her office. "Didn't we recently have a conversation about the type of visitors you've been having lately, Dr. Ayrwick?"

I wanted to rip into her, but I knew misplaced anger only exacerbated a problematic relationship. She'd also addressed me for the first time with a full title, something I hadn't expected. "You're one-hundred-percent right, Dr. Castle. This will be the last time you ever see those two again. I am done with this circus family and the self-absorbed drama they bring with it."

* * *

The end of my lecture arrived quickly. I spent most of it analyzing every decision I'd ever made since Francesca disappeared from my life over two-and-a-half years ago. In the first half of class, the students completed the pop quiz I'd designed. In the second half, they worked in pairs to compare and contrast distinctive styles of documentaries. Krissy Stanton never showed up, and Raquel was a little standoff-ish when I attempted to talk to her on break. Eventually, she admitted that she thought I was angry with her over Manny's potential relocation to Las Vegas. I assured her that I understood married couples needed to do what was best for their future and that I harbored no ill feelings. I cautioned her to be gentle when telling Eleanor of their final plan.

I collected my satchel and headed toward my office to drop off the quizzes. Before I reached the hallway, Imogene called out. When I looked back, she stood near the doorway with her fiancé.

"Dr. Ayrwick, I've been asked to introduce you to Paul. He was waiting for me outside Diamond Hall and wanted to meet you," Imogene said, holding his hand and resting her head against his shoulder. She stood several inches shorter than her fiancé, clutching her purse and tablet with reddened knuckles, embodying someone who'd rather be anywhere but right there.

Although I needed to check if April had located Krissy, a minor delay wouldn't impact my plans. I walked toward them with my hand stretched out to greet Town Councilman Dodd. "Good to make your acquaintance, Paul. I believe you and my brother, Gabriel, have been friends for a number of years."

"Yes, unless you count those eight years where we lost touch," he added with a brief but hearty laugh. Paul had jet black hair, broad shoulders, and a shiny complexion, one more polished than Nana D's silver collection. His duds must've cost more than my first car, and that was saying a lot since I'd saved up for three summers to buy a five-year-old Honda in prime condition.

"Congratulations on your new role. I'm confident you will be a stronger and more effective leader than your predecessor," I pointed out, throwing the strap of my satchel over my shoulder. "I'm also very sorry for the death of your friend, Quint Crawford."

"I'm still shocked we've lost him." Paul sighed and dipped his head toward Imogene. "Life must go on. Thank you for the praise. I'm excited to work with your grandmother for the benefit of Braxton."

While I had them both, I asked a few more questions. "From what I understand through Krissy,

Quint's tirade against Marcus might've sunk his run for mayor. Have you heard anything like that?"

Paul leaned back on the heels of his feet and rocked back and forth. "Quint was a good guy, once upon a time. Ever since he returned to Braxton, he was a changed man. Darker. More troubled. I'm afraid to say, there's a rumor he might be the thief who attacked my poor Imogene."

Imogene made a small guttural sound. "Let's not speak ill of the deceased, Paul."

"You might want to be careful what you say, Councilman. The sheriff might ask where you were the night Quint died," I quipped, ensuring I laughed at my own statement to keep the conversation light.

"I'd like to see them try. I was at home with my fiancée. Besides, didn't Quint accidentally electrocute himself?" Paul asked, retrieving his phone and opening a new app. "In case you don't believe me, look through my photos from that day. I'm not even sure exactly what time he died."

"About midnight," I said, recalling Imogene claimed to be near the cable car an hour before then. If she'd been at the cable car, why would Paul say she was with him at home? Who was lying?

Imogene grabbed for the phone but missed. "Dr. Ayrwick doesn't need to. He trusts us, right?"

"Let him decide for himself. I'm working with his grandmother, so there can't be any doubt in his mind. I've heard how much of a snoop he can be," Paul replied, then turned to me. "I'm selling my house to find something bigger and better for Imogene. We took these for the real estate listing that night before we both went to bed. Imogene got home about eleven fifteen that evening, I believe."

I nodded hesitantly, took the phone from Paul, and shuffled through the photos, focusing on the timestamp as each one flew by my eyes. He had various shots of rooms in his house, starting shortly after eleven and ending at twelve fifty right about when Quint had been killed. Imogene was in many of the pictures too. While Paul or Imogene could've had something to do with the earlier electrocution attempt, neither could've gotten to the cable car station to strangle Quint and returned home to take those photos. Imogene had probably seen Krissy there at eleven, then gone home to Paul. I supposed the photos could've been a doctored alibi, but Lara was certain they were both innocent.

"Good luck with the sale, it's a beautiful home," I replied, hoping to keep the conversation flowing. "Have there been any updates on the burglary? I assume no one's returned your tiara."

Imogene shook her head. "It's missing, and I'm probably never going to get it back. Paul wants the sheriff to search the Crawford house, but they haven't gotten a warrant."

I convinced myself I could push harder, even prompt Imogene to reveal if she was the woman who'd gone to see Bertha earlier that week. "Why don't you visit Mrs. Crawford and see if you can find anything in his room? She'd love the company, I'm sure."

"We'll give it some thought. Thanks, Kellan." Paul wrapped his arm around Imogene's shoulder. "We should be going, honey. You have to prepare for that dinner. Don't want to be late, do we?"

Imogene smiled sheepishly. "Krissy won't be there. I could use the break from that woman."

My ears perked up. "I notice she skipped class this evening. Are you two still not getting along?"

Paul replied, "They are not. Krissy was at the bank earlier today. I saw her in the room with the safety deposit boxes. I had to get added to the town's account to authorize future spending, so I stopped in after lunch but before Imogene's class started. Krissy must've skipped the lecture, and she's probably about to skip town. I say she should get a failing grade if nothing else, right?" He led his fiancée to the door with a sycophantic grin while wishing me a good evening.

Chapter 18

If Krissy had been in town earlier, she might not have left Braxton. I checked my watch to confirm I had more than enough time before Cristiano's call. I could stop at Marcus Stanton's house to convince Krissy to tell me what she knew about the jewelry thefts. If she was Quint's accomplice, I would appeal to her sense of friendship to protect Gabriel from any blowback. By the time I reached the parking lot, my cell phone rang. I jumped, thinking it was Cristiano calling earlier than he'd indicated. It wasn't the phone he'd assigned to me that was ringing. "This is Kellan."

"It's Connor. Sheriff Montague is here with me, and she asked me to give you a call."

"Everything on track for tonight?" I asked, uncertain if she'd told Connor anything about Francesca's return. We'd agreed to keep it between us, but if she needed help to coordinate, she might have enlisted him."

"What's tonight?" he asked.

"Never mind, I had my dates mixed up. What can I do for you?"

"Marcus Stanton showed up at the sheriff's office a few hours ago claiming Gabriel had broken into his house and stolen jewelry and cash. Your brother is in custody. We thought you'd want to know." Connor's voice was flat. I knew he hadn't wanted to deliver the news but figured I'd prefer to hear the unsettling information from him.

"He didn't do it. You can't believe that scoundrel Stanton," I shouted, feeling an increasing desire to drive to the man's house and harangue both him and his daughter.

"That's what we believe too. Only one problem, though."

"What now?" If my life didn't calm down, I'd be a prime candidate for an early heart attack.

"I visited your brother just over an hour ago to ask him some questions. We met in the parking lot at Braxton before he was heading out for the day. I'm not sure how to tell you this, Kellan," Connor began in a hesitant voice. There was something strange about how calm he was before finishing his statement. "Gabriel had some of the missing jewelry with him. Not everything, but a few pieces that had been stolen in the last month were in a backpack on the passenger seat of his car."

"You've got to be kidding me. This is a setup. Gabriel wouldn't be stupid enough to leave stolen jewelry in his car," I exclaimed. Paul saw Krissy at the bank; she must've been storing it there for safekeeping but realized we were closing in on her. How could I convince Connor?

"April and I talked about it. Unfortunately, she's busy on another case but told me to work directly with you on this one. She wants me to put your brother in jail for the night."

This nightmare was withering my last nerve. "Have you found Krissy? I'm driving to the Stanton's place to confront her. I'll make her admit what she's done." It had to be Krissy. There was no one else in the group who was still close with Quint and had been to his room to get the stolen items.

"Kellan, I need you to trust me. We have reasonable cause to put your brother in prison for twenty-four hours. April agrees, someone is setting him up to take a fall," Connor pleaded. He explained that the jewelry Marcus claimed Gabriel had stolen from him wasn't in the backpack. If Gabriel was trying to sneak out of town, he would have had all of it together.

"What are you going to do to stop it? He's my brother, Connor."

"Listen to me for a minute. If Krissy is the thief, she's trying to implicate Gabriel tonight. Then, she'll skip town with the jewelry she stole from her father's safe. I have no idea what's going through her head, but I'm convinced we've found Quint's killer." Connor begged me not to interfere with their plan. "If your brother is in jail, and we catch Krissy leaving with her father's money and jewelry, then we can prove Gabriel is innocent. I won't let anything bad happen to him." Connor paused to speak to someone else in the room. When he returned to the call, he said, "Gabriel says he's okay and to let me do what I have to do."

"Fine, but for the record, you're all gonna pay in spades for doing this to me!"

Connor laughed. "Why are you going to the Stanton house? I really think you should stay away."

I was stressed enough. I knew I should focus on one problem at a time. Waiting for Cristiano's call to meet him that night was my priority. "You've got a point. Okay, I'll let it go for tonight."

Connor assured me he'd update me as soon as they were able to get a warrant to search the Stanton house. Marcus had stopped them from getting inside earlier that afternoon without one, even though it was supposedly to obtain fingerprints from the break-in. Connor was already suspicious and had begun putting his case together for the judge. When we hung up, I drove to Danby Landing to prepare for Francesca's return.

After checking that my mother had picked up Emma at the bus stop, I quickly showered and attempted to relax. I had no desire to eat dinner, and I was unwilling to have a drink in case it clouded my judgment. I grabbed my shoes and tossed them on the floor next to the couch. It was too early to put them on. I sat in silence worrying over how things would go that night.

At precisely eight thirty, Cristiano called. "Do you have a package for me from the Castiglianos?"

"Yes, it's ready to go," I confirmed, patting the right pocket in my jeans. I'd hidden the real one in my shoe just in case I encountered any trouble with the fake one. While I didn't want to lose the only evidence we had against my in-laws, protecting Francesca came first. Would they find a way to show up tonight?

"Good, you follow instructions well. I like that about you." He paused to relay the news to someone nearby, probably my missing wife. "We'll convene at home plate on the Grey baseball field at Braxton. I thought it was a fitting location for Francesca's return home."

Outdoors might be a safe place. April could more easily track me with the GPS device without any interruption from walls or other barriers. It might also provide easier access for her team. As I thought about the plan, it worried me. Cristiano was smart, and this would open him up for potential danger. "Are you sure meeting on the baseball field near the Grey Sports Complex is the best place?"

"I hope that's not doubt in your voice, Kellan. Francesca assured me that you knew how to accept explicit directions," Cristiano replied.

"Okay, just checking. Don't lose your cool over it!" I repeated the location to be sure the recording device in my living room captured it, then stepped outside the front door of the cottage to check if anyone was watching from elsewhere on the property.

"We'll see you in thirty minutes. And please remember, Kellan, we know everything you are doing. Are you enjoying that lovely breeze across the front porch of your little cottage? It can be dangerous to walk around barefoot on a wooden surface. You might get splinters." Cristiano had someone scouting my every move. Where was this person? "You know the rules. No cops. No Castiglianos. No weapons. No funny business. We will be checking everything. Do not show until precisely nine o'clock."

When I confirmed his demands would be met, he hung up the phone. I had fifteen minutes before it made sense to leave Danby Landing. I desperately wanted to call April to verify everything was in place and that she'd heard the location. I paced the front porch with my ears intently focused on every strange noise. The recording machine beeped, and I knew April's team had dialed in to pick up the location. My confidence jumped one small notch higher on the already beaten-down scale.

Then I heard Krissy Stanton talking on her cell phone across the yard. I stepped closer to the fence and peered through a hole near one of the knots in the wooden gate. She was feverishly loading suitcases in the trunk of her car. I ran inside the cottage and stepped into my shoes. If I acted quickly, I could confront her before she took off. I sent a text message to Connor, letting him know I'd seen Krissy at the Stanton house.

I tiptoed down the gravel driveway and cut across the side lawn to the gate between our two properties. Within two minutes, I'd unlatched the lock and raced to her open front door. I stepped into the foyer and looked all around.

Krissy clomped around the corner almost crashing into me. "What are you doing here?" She backed up a few steps and dropped a bag to the floor. Her eyes were dark and distant.

"I know what you've done, Krissy. How could you do something so awful to one of your friends?" I put up an arm to stop her when she tried to barrel past. "We need to talk."

"I know trying to leave town is stupid, but I have to get away from my family. Gabriel will be fine, my father doesn't have a case against him," she said, tears forming in her eyes.

"You've got that right. Gabriel will survive, but you'll wind up in prison. You won't get the death penalty, but I'm confident you'll spend decades in prison for strangling Quint." I should've been more careful with my accusations, especially knowing she'd killed one person already and I could be next. Then what would happen to Francesca and the Castiglianos? I couldn't control my actions anymore. I suddenly understood how similar Nana D and I were. My body seethed with anger over reckless people who called themselves friends, people who would steal from you just as soon as murder you.

Krissy froze in place with tears streaming down her cheeks. "What are you talking about? Quint was electrocuted, not strangled. I never intended to kill him, just to scare him. It was an accident. I feel guilty enough already for what I've done. Don't make it any worse."

I paused to digest what she'd told me. The look of panic and shock on her face seemed genuine. "Didn't you strangle your boyfriend when your plan to electrocute him failed?"

"No, I didn't even know he'd been strangled. And according to him, he wasn't even my boyfriend." Krissy cocked her head and squinted. "Something doesn't make sense to me."

"Maybe you should start at the beginning. Tell me exactly what you did," I said, encouraging her to divulge her secrets as quickly as possible. "I have somewhere important to be soon, but I can give you ten more minutes."

"If you're telling me the truth, and someone strangled Quint, then I need to get out of here even quicker than I thought." Krissy tried to run past me, but I snatched her arm and pushed her toward the foyer wall.

"No, I want to understand what you know, what you did to him," I shouted, wanting to shake her until she agreed to talk. Even in my fury, I knew restraint was the optimal approach.

Krissy wiped her face dry and sat on the stairs opposite me. "Quint was the jewel thief. I didn't realize it at first. I told you that he helped me steal the brooch from the Paddingtons eight years ago, but evidently, he took the prank even further back then and was recreating the crimes again this year. He'd been secretly collecting information from everyone to identify the best times and places to rob them."

Krissy explained what she knew about the jewelry thefts. Shortly after Quint had stolen the brooch for her eight years ago, he'd seen Imogene and Paul kissing in Memorial Library. When Quint confronted Imogene, she told him that her family didn't approve of him and wanted her to marry someone better. Then, Lara tried to blackmail Quint with evidence of the bribes his uncle had taken. Imogene's mother had been trying to force Quint to leave town. He was enraged about not being accepted by the upper crust of Wharton County, so he planned revenge. Using the details from the story Imogene had told him about the sorority's calla lilies, Quint decided to target all the founding families in Alpha Iota Omega. She'd always suspected Gabriel was the thief because he'd been keeping secrets back then. Krissy had thought Quint was acting odd because Imogene had ended their relationship, so she tried to comfort him. Quint rejected her when she asked him on a date because he'd been angry and focused on getting revenge before leaving town.

Krissy had never known this until a few weeks ago when Quint returned to town. Krissy admitted to him she'd never stopped loving him. She tried to convince him to give her a chance, but Imogene flirted with Quint at Kirklands one night. When Quint was drunk, he revealed to Krissy he'd thought Imogene still loved him and that he still loved her. "I was so angry at Quint for hurting me again. I confronted Imogene and threatened to tell Paul if she didn't stay away. Imogene finally agreed to tell Quint she only loved Paul. Then, I had to deal with Siobhan."

"Huh?" I was perplexed at the change in direction.

"Siobhan and Quint slept together. He was devastated by Imogene's recent rejection. Instead of throwing himself at me, he hooked up with Siobhan. When Quint realized that he'd given her the wrong impression, he broke it off, but it was too late by then. I was angry about him always ignoring me, so I told Paul about Imogene secretly meeting Quint at Kirklands. I also told Quint that Imogene had taken the tiara to her mother's place that night. She'd bragged about it when I saw her on campus that day."

"Get to how Quint died." I was anxious to hear all the details but unable to stay much longer.

"Fine. When Imogene wouldn't end her engagement, Quint assumed she'd just been using him to make Paul jealous. He broke into her mother's house to steal the tiara, only he didn't know Imogene was sleeping there. He tried to escape, but she recognized him." Imogene never told Paul, and she didn't want to press charges because she was afraid the truth would come out about her feelings for Quint resurfacing. "When I confronted Quint, he confessed that he could never love me and that I was just a good friend. I was so livid with Quint, I wanted to hurt him in a monumental way."

"What did you do to the electrical panels inside the cable car?"

Krissy closed her eyes. "It was foolish. I just wanted to shock him. I'd been learning a lot by hanging around him, and Nicky had taught me basic electrical work, so I felt assured that I'd only scare Quint and teach him a lesson. Something went horribly wrong, and now I think I know why."

"Please hurry up, Krissy. Tell me what happened in the cable car." I wish I had that recording device now, but I could always update Connor and April after the meeting with Cristiano Vargas.

"Quint and I were meeting for a drink late that night. I'd already gone over to strip a few of the wires and turn on the main power supply at the station. We met up, then I begged him to show me the renovations." They'd stopped on campus to visit the cable car where Quint proceeded to boast about the work he'd been accomplishing. He thought the power had been off and flipped on his cell phone for some light. When he surveyed the panel, his hand had touched the wires, severely stunning him. "I wasn't thinking straight and turned off the power with my bare hands. I'd forgotten to wear gloves that time because I was nervous. Quint had been electrocuted, but he was still alive even though the shock had left him weak and hardly able to move. I'd gotten my revenge, but I also knew he would be fine. When I'd been at the Paddington estate earlier that day, I'd seen a bunch of black calla lilies and thought it'd be a perfect way to throw the entire disaster in his face. I'd retrieved them from my car after turning the power off, then tossed them near his unconscious body, so he'd know someone wanted revenge on him for what he'd done.

I left him to sleep it off and went home. He never knew what I'd done to him."

"You're saying when you left, he was still alive?"

"He was. I swear," Krissy cried out. "When I learned he'd died the next day, I couldn't tell anyone. I was scared the cops would put me in jail for what was supposed to be evening the score." Krissy explained that she was the woman who'd confronted Helena at Woodland Warriors because Helena had known Quint was still interested in Imogene and only leading Krissy on. Krissy thought her supposed friend would've tried to protect her rather than let Quint hurt her.

While she had a point, I had five minutes to arrive at the baseball field. "Did you find the jewelry Quint had stolen and hide it in Gabriel's car today? He's been arrested, but he's not guilty."

"Quint was the thief, not me. I have no idea how it got in Gabriel's car." Krissy promised that she didn't try to set up Gabriel and had never known where Quint hid the jewelry. "But now, I'm scared someone else saw the whole thing happen at the cable car. I got a call earlier today from a disguised voice. This creep threatened me," Krissy said, beginning to hyperventilate.

"How?" I was getting more confused as she explained the situation.

"The caller taunted me about witnessing what I'd done to Quint. I thought it was Imogene because she'd threatened to tell the cops that she'd seen me near the cable car too."

"So, you no longer think it was Imogene calling you?" If Krissy hadn't gone into Quint's bedroom the other day, Imogene was the only other girl who could've visited Bertha's house. Who else would've taken the jewels from Quint's bedroom and put them in Gabriel's car?

"It was at two o'clock today when I got the call. Wasn't Imogene in class with you?" Krissy paced the foyer as if she wanted to stomp holes through the ceramic tiles.

Imogene had been with me at two o'clock today, but I had no time to linger right now. Hearing the rest would have to wait until after the Vargas meeting. "I have to go, but you need to speak with Detective Connor Hawkins. Maybe Paul Dodd was your blackmail caller. Could he and Imogene be conspiring together?"

"No, Kellan. Now that I'm piecing everything together, I know who it is. I saw someone following me the other day. When I confronted her, she had a valid explanation. I let it go at the time, but after today, I'm not sure anymore." Krissy froze in the foyer and faced the front of the house. My back was to the door. I couldn't see what was going on behind me. She gasped and pointed in my direction.

"What? Who do you think it was?" I implored, wondering what she was staring at and why she'd raised her finger at me.

A familiar voice answered, "Krissy must be dumbfounded to find me here. She's much smarter than I gave her credit for, and I'm guessing she's started to figure out a few things."

I turned around slowly as the trigger of a revolver cocked into place. When I came face to face with the woman holding the weapon, my mind had a meltdown in confusion and panic. Was I going to miss the meeting with Cristiano now? "What the hell is going on?"

"You might recognize me as Raquel Salvado, Chef Manny's new wife, but you'd probably know me a little better if I shared my maiden name. Allow me to properly introduce myself. Before I got married, my friends, family, business associates, and the government referred to me as Raquel Vargas. I believe you know my brother, Cristiano." Raquel waved the gun and instructed me to step backward, next to Krissy. "Maybe it's time I shared a little story about how well you all knew your friend, or shall I say foe, Quint Crawford."

Chapter 19

With a gun pointed at my chest, I had little time or focus to assemble what I was missing. Krissy clung to my arm as if it were a lifejacket. The color drained from her face like someone had wrathfully shaken an Etch-A-Sketch. My heart raced and breath quickened. "What about the meeting with Cristiano to exchange the storage device for Francesca?"

Krissy swallowed deeply. "Your wife? I thought she was dead."

Raquel laughed wildly. "Amateurs. Do you really think I'd let them meet in an open field where anyone could see them wandering around and call the police?" She glanced into the nearby living room to survey her surroundings. "The two of you need to sit on that sofa in front of the window. Pull the shade down first. The sun hasn't fully set."

While we complied, Raquel reached her hand toward me. "Give me the device now. Then we'll talk. I've sent Marcus Stanton on a wild goose chase about his missing jewelry, so he won't be home for at least an hour."

I clumsily patted down my pockets, uncertain which one I'd left it in earlier. When I found it, I second-guessed the decision to deliver a fake copy of the evidence that the Castiglianos had compiled, but it would look far worse if I admitted what I'd done earlier. I took a step forward before sitting on the couch, cautious not to move too quickly and risk having my arm shot off by a crazed mafia woman. "Here, this is what Cristiano is expecting. The signed contract is back at my house."

"We'll deal with that later. Let's talk about poor stupid Quint," Raquel began, leaning against a sideboard opposite us in the Stanton living room. She held the gun in her hand aimed directly at me, but her eyes occasionally darted back and forth to Krissy.

"You killed my boyfriend," Krissy snarled, her knees vibrating like the strings of an exquisite violin being stroked by a fine French bow. "You won't get away with this."

The irony of the situation seemed to have been lost on Krissy. She's the one who tried to electrocute him. My guess was if she hadn't stripped and loosened the wires to teach him a lesson, Quint would've been strong enough to fight off Raquel. "Let her talk, don't make things worse."

"Smart man, Kellan," she replied, then turned to Krissy. "Listen, girlfriend to girlfriend .. Quint was a con artist. No woman should put up with a liar who doesn't treat her properly. I saved you from a life of

317

misery." Raquel was proud of herself for ridding the world of a man who'd taken more from it than he'd given.

Krissy squirmed but refrained from opening her mouth. A clock on the far wall read nine-oh-seven. We were officially late, but April must have been able to track my location with the GPS tracking device embedded in my glasses. Would she send a patrol car to check on me?

"What's going on with the meeting at Grey Field? I'm not trying to distract you, but what happens next with Francesca?" I asked, hoping to divert her attention, in reality. As much as I worried for my safety, as well as Krissy's, my instincts told me to delay Raquel as long as possible.

"I spoke with my brother a few minutes ago. We've moved the meeting location. I don't trust you, and he's blinded by that vixen wife of yours." Raquel approached the sofa opposite us and sat with her elbows on her knees and the gun aimed at a very precious part of my body. "We'll be seeing our loved ones in a little while. Don't worry, everything's been taken care of."

Raquel was eager to share the story of how she'd easily integrated herself into the life of several people I knew. In animated fashion, she covered her arrival in Braxton four months earlier right before Francesca had been kidnapped. "My family knew the Castiglianos had faked your wife's death, but we could never prove it. They kept her well-hidden and paid their employees top dollar to keep it secret.

When Francesca flew here to stop you from trying to relocate, we had undeniable proof. A security worker at the airport had taken a photo of her and sent it to us. We know how to take care of people on our payroll too."

"I get it. Vincenzo and Cecilia are awful people. I agree with you, but I had nothing to do with whatever vendetta your families have against each other. You have the documents from the Castiglianos; just let Francesca go, and everything can move forward," I said, hoping to find the rational side of Raquel. How had I missed picking up any clues while she'd been a student in my class?

"It's not that easy anymore, Kellan. Let me finish telling my story. You have a habit of talking too much, and I feel it's my duty to advise you that you'll do better in life if you shut up sometimes." Raquel told us that while Cristiano had focused on a plan to kidnap Francesca, she was responsible for collecting information and discovering secrets about the Ayrwicks and to blackmail people to do their bidding.

On an early stop at the Pick-Me-Up Diner, Raquel had overheard that Manny, Eleanor's chef, was planning to visit Las Vegas. She followed him out there and got him drunk one night, then convinced him to get married. It gave her an excuse to hang around the diner without people being suspicious. She'd begged Manny not to tell too many people that they were married until she could work out a few personal things with her family. He was happy to comply and openly talked about Eleanor, me, and any of our friends that visited the diner. "Honestly, Manny is a good husband. Except, of course, we're not legally married. We never filed with the state of Nevada, and the guy who married us never had a proper license. He owed a favor to the Vargas family, and well, now it's been repaid."

"You've collected all this data about us, that's brilliant. How does Quint Crawford fit in?" I hadn't brought my phone with me and had no way to notify anyone what was going on. I glanced sideward at Krissy who seemed frozen in a trance. Fear had taken over her ability to do anything or work with me on an escape plan.

"Quint liked to talk. I overheard him in the diner chatting to your brother, Gabriel. They were discussing all the jewelry Quint had stolen years ago, and Quint needed help to pay his mother's bills."

Raquel had offered money to Quint if he would spy on me and handle a few important tasks for her. Quint had watched Emma and me at the pet store, then purchased and delivered the puppy to the cottage the previous month. Apparently, Quint's slippery tentacles had invaded my entire life, and I'd been completely clueless for weeks. I had to hand it to Raquel; she was devious and cunning. I never realized Quint was pumping me for information the entire time I'd visited with him at the cable car. "Why did you kill him?"

"Quint started to get too big for his britches. When I'd gotten everything I needed from him, I gave him a nice bonus and told him to forget we'd ever met. He tried to blackmail me, but unfortunately he learned a lesson the hard way." Raquel tapped the gun against the coffee table when Krissy stirred and looked ready to bolt. "Stay where you are, sister. I'd prefer not to shoot you, but if I must, I must."

Raquel had known Quint was stealing jewelry again. She'd also discovered he was misleading Krissy and pining away for Imogene. Another of her goons had been following Quint to keep tabs on him. Raquel's henchman had seen Krissy sabotage the cable car renovation project and told his boss that someone might be trying to kill Quint. "When I went to the cable car station, Krissy had been running across the parking lot. I checked inside and saw Quint had passed out but was still alive. Krissy had placed a bouquet of black calla lilies she'd stolen while visiting the Paddington estate earlier that day near his unconscious body. After stealing one of the rubies from Quint, days earlier when he accidentally dropped one during our many secret meetings, I left it there in the cable car to implicate him and tie his death to all the robberies. I took immense pleasure in strangling my former snitch, watching the life and energy extinguish from a once supposedly clever and charming man. To hold something precious in your grip and be responsible for eliminating it from existence... there's nothing more I could ask for, to make my day complete. And voilà, my potential blackmail problem went away." Raquel grinned maniacally, watching Krissy's expression change from fear to shock and anger.

Krissy jumped across the table and punched Raquel. In the struggle, I tried to run, not because I didn't want to protect Krissy, but if I could escape, I might get to the phone to call 9-1-1. I didn't have enough time. Raquel swung the gun at Krissy and collided with her temple. Krissy flew to the floor and hit her head against the coffee table.

Raquel aimed the gun at me as I reached the hallway. "Stop, or I'll blow your ass to pieces, even if it's quite a fine—"

I backed into the room, turned around, and sheepishly said, "Okay. I think I'll stay put for now." Something dawned on me as I walked closer to her. "You complained to Myriam about me. Why?"

"Just causing trouble for you. I wanted you to feel attacked from all angles. It was my way to keep you off balance... unable to figure out what I was up to." A menacing smile formed on her lips.

"It almost worked." I hadn't trusted her but also wasn't able to pinpoint the exact reason.

Raquel instructed me to tie up Krissy with the wires from a piece of art that had been hanging on the wall—thick, coarse metal that was pliable but strong enough to hold someone at bay. I lifted Krissy, whispering in her ear that I'd do everything I could to save us. Raquel pointed to a nearby chair in the corner where I tied Krissy's hands to the back wooden rails and her ankles against its feet.

While I was directed to stand in the corner, Raquel inspected my work. "It'll do for now. Krissy looks like she's about to pass out anyway."

As I stood there, it hit me. Raquel had been the woman who went to Bertha Crawford's house under the deceptive guise of wanting to spend one last moment in Quint's bedroom before saying goodbye. "You took the jewelry Quint had stolen and implicated my brother earlier today."

"Guilty. Quint had sold a bunch to pay for his mother's expenses, so he only had a few pieces remaining in his bedroom. I worried you were getting too suspicious, so I decided to keep your meddlesome mind focused elsewhere," she confirmed, then waved the gun at me to march toward the front door. "Let's go. Someone else will come by soon to take care of Miss Stanton. We're due at the new meeting point in fifteen minutes."

"Wait," I stalled, noticing it was nine thirty. April had to be worried that I hadn't shown up at the baseball field. She'd come looking for me soon, finding the cottage empty and my SUV still onsite. "What made you think I was getting close? I had no clue you were involved."

"You had a crime show. You asked too many questions. I was sure you'd figure out the connections in no time at all. Besides, Krissy was catching on and might have discovered it herself. She knew I'd been following her the last few days. I had someone call earlier to try and get her off the scent, but she told you about it anyway. She'll suffer later tonight when she takes a nice, long swim."

"Where are we going?" I demanded as she pushed me out the door with one hand and jammed the gun into my shoulder with the other. While it was possible I could overpower her, I couldn't take a chance that—given her diabolical mindset—she'd shoot me.

"I found a lovely place that should be relatively quiet this evening. In fact, Cristiano is there with Francesca and a couple of our bodyguards," Raquel replied, directing me to shut the door. We walked across the lawn and through the gate as I had done earlier. Raquel truly had been watching my every move. "Oh, that's right," she said, stopping me once we reached my front door. "You're probably familiar with the location. Tell me, Kellan, have you visited your mother's office at Braxton recently?"

Emma! "No, please, we can't meet there." My stomach plummeted to the floor in anticipation of disastrous consequences.

"Go inside and get the signed contract. We can discuss it while you drive us there," Raquel insisted. The sun had set, but the front porch light shined across her face. It was then I knew only one of us would survive that night. No one threatened my daughter and got away with it.

I snatched the keys to my SUV and the agreement from the couch where I'd left it prior to rushing out of the cottage. I wanted to repeat the changed location aloud in case April's team had continued to listen in. "Does the new drop off point have to be Braxton's Admissions Hall? What about Diamond Hall in my office? No one's there, and it's even quieter."

"Aren't you cute? You should know my team destroyed that recording device Sheriff Montague planted earlier. Let me guess, when you heard that strange noise, you thought your little friend was obtaining the details?" Raquel took the key from me, shoved me out the front door, and followed closely behind.

I finally understood the far-reaching tentacles of Las Vargas. I had little hope left other than to believe they would keep their word and not harm my daughter, mother, or Francesca. At this point, I'd give my own life to ensure Emma's safety. "Please, I'll do anything."

"Good, then as soon as we park the car, you will remove your glasses. Unfortunately, you need them to drive, otherwise I would've smashed them by now." She waited, while I hopped into the SUV, before boarding and handing me the keys. "Yes, I know about the GPS device too. Drive."

Raquel ignored everything I said and held me at gunpoint while we drove to Braxton. I considered quickly jerking the steering wheel to throw her off balance, but the insane woman wouldn't think twice about taking control of the car and shooting me as soon as I made a sudden movement. I complied with her demands and parked in a nearby empty lot.

"Give me those," she said, thrusting my glasses to the street and crunching them with the heel of her red stilettos. "I'll be your eyes and navigate you to the building."

I thought I'd seen a dark car following us, but if I had, it was probably one of Raquel's bodyguards. Maybe campus security would drive by and wonder who was working late that night. Connor's replacement still hadn't been hired, and the college's security crew was lighter during summers, but I had hope someone would find us before long.

After we walked to Admissions Hall, Raquel called Cristiano. We stood outside the front entrance until he verified it wasn't a trap and checked me for wires or bugs. As I entered, I focused on remembering the layout of the office. It was eerily quiet. Where was everyone?

Raquel handed me over to Cristiano. "Kellan's been cooperating, but he's got quite an outlandish mouth on him. Are you sure I can't have a little fun teaching him a lesson tonight?"

"No, *hermana*. We only hurt those who hurt us. For all intents and purposes, Kellan is an innocent bystander." With his usual calm and collected tone, Cristiano addressed me next. "My sister tells me the only negative experience she's had these last few months on this mission was listening to you teach class. Raquel never was one for the movies; she much prefers being part of the action."

Without my glasses, my confidence was diminished. I felt disoriented from not knowing my surroundings, but I experienced adrenaline and fear coursing through my veins. "Where is my family?"

"I'm very sorry it's come to this, Kellan," Cristiano empathetically replied, then whispered something to Raquel, who quickly disappeared from the room. "Emma and your mother are currently sitting

326

in an office with one of my employees. They're both fine, but I'll send him back for Krissy soon."

"And Francesca?"

Footsteps shuffled behind me. "I'm right here, Kellan."

I turned around and reached my hands in the direction of her voice. My vision was so impaired, I could only see something if it were a foot from my eyes. Everything around me was a blur, amorphous shapes and colors, no facial distinction or depth perception. "Are you okay? Have you seen Emma?"

"I'm fine. I saw them bring juice and cookies to her. Emma thinks it's a game. Your mother is with her, but they haven't seen me. I promise you," Francesca said, grabbing my hands, "I won't let them hurt her."

"I'd give you two a moment alone, but I'm afraid we might not have a lot of time," Cristiano said. His shadow crossed to the side of me, and he spoke to someone else. "Do you have the items he was supposed to deliver?"

Raquel replied, "Yes. The agreement has been signed, and it's in my back pocket. I haven't checked the storage device. He and the sheriff were fiddling with it earlier. Do you have a computer?"

"I'm sure Kellan's mother can help us with that," Cristiano replied and directed someone else in the room to bring her out of the office.

"I'm going to step away for a minute, Kellan. I don't want Emma to see me until we can talk to her together," Francesca whispered in my ear.

The room was beginning to feel hot, stealing the little oxygen I had remaining in my lungs. The air conditioning was always lowered at night, and there were too many of us standing in a small area without open windows and breezes. I felt grateful that Francesca was in a position to focus on protecting Emma, but what would occur when they checked the storage device? April was supposed to be here before that happened, but now, she had no idea where we were.

Cristiano said, "Violet, darling, I'm going to need your assistance. Can you please log on to a computer, so that I can read the contents of this drive?"

My mother managed to squeak out a yes before noticing me. "Kellan, Emma... Emma is okay. I can't believe Francesca—"

"It's okay, Mom. Just do what they want, and everything will work out." I wasn't sure whom I was convincing at that moment.

While my mother assisted Cristiano with the files, and Raquel shoved the gun against my back, I heard a sound coming from a nearby office.

"No, wait, you can't go out there," a raspy voice shouted.

Then, I heard Emma. "But I want to see Grandma. I don't understand this game anymore."

My panic intensified. I willed myself not to do anything rash. Emma must have seen me.

"Daddy's here." I heard tiny footsteps racing across the floor, but I couldn't do anything.

"Emma, I thought you were going to be a good girl and listen to me," Cristiano said.

I couldn't tell for sure, but it looked like he'd grabbed her arm as she ran by to stop her from reaching me.

"Who's that?" she asked, probably pointing at Raquel, given I didn't know everyone in the room.

At that moment, everything happened so fast, I could barely understand what was going on. Francesca stepped back into the room and walked toward us. She bent down in front of me, no more than ten feet away, saying, "My precious, Emma. It's—"

The door busted open, and two people rushed inside. I couldn't identify them at first, but I recognized their voices.

The fury behind Vincenzo's words was alarming. "Your lookout guard has been disarmed and knocked out. We've had enough drama for tonight, Cristiano. It's about time we had a little discussion."

Raquel grabbed me and aimed the gun at my forehead.

Emma and my mother both screamed. I saw a quick flurry of action in front of me and assumed either Cristiano or Francesca had picked up Emma.

"Listen, old man, your family started this game when you invaded our territory and killed several of our finest employees," Cristiano replied in a suave yet chilling voice. "You were not supposed to arrive here tonight. How did you find us?"

"We followed your sister and Kellan. We've been watching all night trying to figure out where the meetup was going to happen," Cecilia announced. She must've also held a gun because I could hear her racking the slide into position.

"Please, let me take Emma away from here," my mother begged.

"I'm frightened. I don't understand what's going on. Is that my mommy?" Emma's voice was strained. I knew my daughter. Her eyes were scrunched together as she clung to whoever held her, fighting to get free. Whenever she was scared, she ran and hid until I could protect her.

I'd always blamed it on the shock she'd gone through upon learning her mother had died. No one else could comfort my baby when she felt abandoned, except for me. "She's only seven years old. Please, don't hurt her."

Francesca whimpered, helpless while her worlds collided in one giant mixing bowl of miscalculated rage. She wanted to comfort our daughter but must not have thought she could do anything to safely break the tension.

"Kellan, nothing will happen to Emma. I'm holding and protecting her," Cristiano advised. He sounded sincere, but the room was a powder keg, and I could do nothing to stop the potential explosion. He addressed the Castiglianos. "You've handed over the evidence and your company. It's time for you to leave, and I'll let Francesca go."

"Not so fast," Cecilia sputtered, her words filled with an intense charge. She stood inches away from us. "There's one more piece of evidence we need to discuss."

"What's this all about?" Raquel's voice echoed in my ears, exponentially irritating me.

Vincenzo tossed something to my mother. "Would you mind bringing up this video on the monitor? As always, it's lovely to see you, Violet. You haven't aged a bit."

Her hands still trembling, my mother managed to insert the drive into the USB slot on the laptop. A window popped up on the screen with a single file available to select. She double-clicked it, and a new window came to the forefront. I couldn't make out the words, but I knew the shapes.

"Maximize it and raise the volume, will you, Violet?" Vincenzo requested with his gun still aimed at Cristiano. He'd never take a shot with his granddaughter in Cristiano's arms.

"I'm scared, Daddy," Emma cried and reached for me.

I'd lost track of where Francesca stood at that point. My heart broke into pieces at what was unfolding before me. Not being able to visualize any details made it even more tragic and haunting. "It's okay, baby, just a few more minutes."

Cristiano tried to comfort my daughter. "It's all a fun game, Emma. Just keep your eyes closed, and you'll be back to your daddy soon."

My mother must have enlarged the video. Someone began to speak on it, but I wasn't sure of his or her identity. I couldn't see details, given the loss of my glasses and not being close enough. By squinting and straining, I could make out only the bare minimum of actions.

"*Ah, Quint Crawford. You were once a valuable asset to my family. Now, you're nothing but an almost dead man,*" a cold and virulent voice from the video cautioned.

"*What are you planning to do, Raquel?*" another voice said on the recording.

"*We don't want his last moments to be a struggle. Life shouldn't be this difficult for anyone. Turn that camera off and ensure no one's watching.*" It was Raquel's sadistic tone I clearly heard this time.

"*What are you doing to him, boss?*" the guy operating the camera questioned. A few moments of silence followed. "*You're gonna strangle him?*"

"*It was necessary. One more problem solved. As I told my brother, a woman will always save the day,*" Raquel replied on the video.

While my mother gasped across the room, Raquel screeched. "That's impossible. How did—"

"Perhaps you'd like to strike up a new deal," Cecilia suggested, then explained that the goon Raquel had following Quint had double-crossed the Vargas family and recorded Raquel while she strangled Quint to death. "It took me a while to track him down, but when I did, he was more than willing to sell me the video in exchange for a small sum of money to start a new life somewhere else."

Raquel released me and inched toward Cecilia. "He disappeared this afternoon. Now, I understand why. That arrogant son-of-a—"

"I'd rather not hear any foul language from you, young lady," Vincenzo replied, squaring off with her, still at least ten feet away. "You've done enough. About our deal, it's renegotiation time."

The next few minutes were a blur, and not just because I couldn't see what was happening. Raquel pushed past me and lunged for Vincenzo. I careened into a desk. After regaining my footing, I scanned the room to locate Cristiano and my daughter, trying to decipher their voices in the cacophony. My mother screamed bloody murder, and a burst of footsteps rushed by me from the front. I heard April yell, "This is the Wharton County Sheriff's Office. Drop your weapons and put your hands up!"

A few seconds later, several gunshots reverberated in the room, followed by an intense screech from my daughter. I covered my head and dived to the ground toward where I thought she was being held captive. I had no idea who'd been hit and cared little about protecting myself at that moment, only my daughter. "Emma," I cried out, begging for mercy from anyone who'd listen and promising my own life in return for her absolute safety.

Chapter 20

"I'm so sorry, Kellan. I can't imagine how you're feeling," April comforted me. We sat in my mother's office with the door closed. The gunshots from an hour ago still echoed in my head. I'd seen shoot-outs in the movies and through recreations for my former crime show, but to live through one in person was a whole different situation. To essentially watch someone be shot to death directly in front of you was something I'd never want to experience again.

"Have you ever killed someone before, April?" My weakened state of mind barely allowed me to respond, but I was beginning to come around.

"Unfortunately, tonight wasn't my first time. It's only happened on a handful of occasions, but it never gets any easier." April grabbed both my hands and covered them with hers. "In a situation like that, instincts kick in. I saw her raise the gun, but I didn't know who she was going to shoot."

"Raquel is definitely dead?"

April nodded. "They've loaded Vincenzo Castigliano into the ambulance. Raquel was able to get two shots in before *Old Betsy* took her down. He was hit in the chest. I'm not sure how it'll turn out." She brushed my hair out of my eyes and placed a pair of glasses on my face for the second time that day. "It's a good thing I kept your original ones from our breakfast this morning."

It felt good to be able to see again. "Thank you," I said, staring directly at the woman who'd just saved my entire family's life. My vision of April was now undeniably clear. "Where is everyone else?"

Once the earlier shots had been fired and April assumed control over Admissions Hall, I'd run to my daughter and grabbed her from Cristiano's arms. I'd lost all sense of what was happening in the room around me. I'd carried her to the closest office, shut and locked the door, only opening it again when my mother finished speaking to the cops and beseeched me to see her granddaughter. We'd comforted Emma for fifteen minutes before Connor let us know that it was safe to come out again.

"I'm allowing Cecilia and Francesca to go to the hospital with Vincenzo. They're both in handcuffs, and we'll deal with booking them later. If there's any chance Vincenzo won't make it, I wouldn't want to deprive his family of a last goodbye. There are several police officers with them, and both will be under scrutiny for the time being." April handed me a cup of water and urged me to drink some slowly.

"Emma is still with my mother?" I hadn't wanted to leave them alone but needed a few minutes by myself to process everything that had happened. I was ready to see them both again.

"Yes, she's asleep in your mother's arms. She'll be okay, you know. Kids are more resilient than we think," April assured with a knowing glance. "Let's talk for a few minutes about how this all happened. I want to be sure I understand everything while it's still fresh in your mind. I promise, just a brief summary, and then tomorrow or the next day, we can go through the details."

I stood and crossed to the other side of the office and updated April with everything that had happened after I'd returned home from class. "I hung up with Cristiano and heard Krissy's voice once I'd stepped outside again." When I said her name, I remembered that she'd been tied up in the Stanton house. "Oh, Krissy, she's—"

"Krissy's fine. At some point after you and Raquel had left, Marcus returned home early and found his daughter. She'd only passed out, and the head injury was minor. Krissy helped us track you down," April explained. Before losing consciousness, Krissy had heard me repeat the location of where Raquel planned to take me. "Marcus called the police. Connor heard the call details on dispatch, and he rushed over to the house. Krissy was worried about you, Kellan. She felt awful about everything that had happened, especially what her father had tried to pin on Gabriel. We also matched Krissy's fingerprints to the ones found on the electric supply box under the cable car platform. She claims she just wanted to hurt him, and knowing she hadn't wiped her prints from it, that's probably the truth. She's a smart girl. I doubt she'd intentionally attempt to kill him and purposely leave evidence behind."

"You're right. Did Marcus admit he lied about the stolen jewelry from his safe?"

"Not exactly. Krissy was the one who'd planned to flee with it. She broke the window to make it look like a regular burglary, assuming everyone would think it was the fifth robbery aligning with the previous string of jewelry thefts. When Marcus reported it to us a day after he spoke to you, he genuinely believed your brother was responsible." April explained that Marcus had confronted Krissy sometime after reporting it, and she confessed that she'd stolen the jewelry and cash, hidden it at the bank, and planned to leave Braxton. Her father had cut her off financially after losing the election because she'd been involved with Quint, the guy whom Marcus believed had cost him the win. Krissy and her father had fought for an hour earlier that afternoon after she arrived from the bank and began packing the car to leave. Marcus disappeared to find a way to stop her, but when he returned home, he'd found his daughter tied up in the living room.

"They're down at the sheriff's office with Connor sorting out that situation. As soon as Connor knew what had happened to you, he called me, and that's how I was able to track you guys down to Admissions

Hall." April had proved tonight why she was the best person for the sheriff's role in Wharton County. Not only did her staff respect and trust her, but she was able to catch the criminal in the end.

"What about Cristiano? What will happen to him?" Through everything, as ruthless as his family had been, he kept promising that he never wanted to harm Emma. I'd believed him, but he was still partially responsible for everything that had transpired this evening.

"That's going to be tough. You knew I was investigating the Vargas and Castigliano families. Cristiano has managed to keep himself squeaky clean. Until I speak with your wife, I do not know what happened. He's outside with his sister." April opened the door to the office and let me peer into the main part of the room. Cristiano sat on the floor, cupping Raquel's hand.

"Can I speak to him?"

"I don't think that's a good idea, Kellan."

"Just for a minute. I want to thank him for something."

April agreed and walked over to them with me.

Cristiano looked at me, his expression unreadable. I could sense the devastation that surrounded him. He peered at Raquel, who lay peacefully at his side, and closed her eyelids. With a lengthy sigh, he rose. "Is Emma okay?"

I nodded. "I'm sure we'll have more to say to one another in the coming days, but there are two things I feel compelled to tell you before leaving."

"Yes?" He breathed deeply, likely waiting for me to rip him apart.

"Thank you for protecting Emma, and I'm truly sorry about what happened to your sister. I have little idea who she was outside of this event, but the woman I grew to know in class always felt like someone she'd wanted to be on the inside." I turned and began to step away.

Cristiano grabbed my arm. "Raquel was once a good person. As a child, she had a passion for the changing the world for the better. Our father is a tyrant, and he insisted she be part of the family business. It is his fault that she died tonight, not yours or anyone else's."

"Does that mean you won't seek revenge against the Castigliano family?" I asked, hoping the war would end so that we could all move on with our lives.

"Your friend, the sheriff here, will do her best to convict me of several crimes. None of them will stick. I've done many wrong things in my lifetime, Kellan, but after tonight, I'm a changed man." Cristiano released my arm and let an officer place a pair of handcuffs on him. "I didn't kidnap Francesca, and I'm confident she will tell you the truth soon."

Stunned by his response, I could barely move. As Officer Flatman led him away, I called out and asked them to stop. "Wait! If you didn't kidnap her, who did?"

"No one. Francesca came of her own volition. She knew the only way to end this war was to turn in her family. She blamed them for losing you and her daughter for all these years. Francesca insisted on working the negotiations through you, so that she wouldn't have to deal directly with her parents. Neither you nor Emma were ever at risk until Vincenzo and Cecilia showed up here tonight. They should've listened to us, and none of this would've occurred." Cristiano closed his eyes and mumbled a silent prayer. When he opened them, much of the pain that had been plastered across his face had disappeared. "I'm in love with your wife, Kellan. I believe she is in love with me too. I hope that's going to be okay because I plan to fight for her. No hard feelings, *mi amigo*?"

"Take him away, Officer Flatman," April demanded, gripping my shoulder and dragging me in the opposite direction. "There is another time and a place for you to address all that nonsense. Let's bring you back to Emma and your mother."

I watched Cristiano's snarky grin as he was led away. What he'd said hadn't bothered me at all. Too much had transpired since the last time Francesca and I had been happy together, perhaps we'd all find a win at the end of this conflict.

When the door to Admissions Hall opened, I saw my wife standing outside near the ambulance before it drove away. She and her mother were directed into the backseat of a squad car headed to the hospital to check on Vincenzo. "May I have one more favor, April? I need to speak with her."

"Yes, of course," she said as we walked to the car. "Keep it brief for now. Let her focus on her father, then you can deal with explaining her return to Emma."

April stayed behind while I approached Francesca. Cecilia was already in the squad car.

"Did you really let me think you'd been kidnapped this entire time?" I asked.

Francesca's face was red and blotchy. She wiped a few tears against her shoulder and sniffled. "I did what was necessary to protect Emma's future. When I left Braxton, I went to Vancouver to be somewhere that reminded me of you and our past together. You hurt me, Kellan, when you told me I couldn't see Emma anymore."

"That doesn't answer my question." I firmly held my ground.

"When Cristiano found me, I had no intention of doing anything harmful. We spent a few days together talking about our families. Although we'd known who each other was, even met as kids a few times, he was different than I expected. Cristiano understood what it was like to grow up in a house where people's lives were carelessly played with as if they were meaningless." She sighed and lifted her handcuffed hands to her heart. "Our life together was different. You helped me escape from that type of crazy, and I never wanted to go back to it. My parents forced me to live in hiding, and when Cristiano presented an opportunity to escape, I went for it."

"So, that's a *yes*. You knowingly let me worry a second time. First, I think you're killed in a drunk driving car accident. Then, I think you're kidnapped by a rival family. What's next?" I said, feeling only contempt for my wife at that moment.

"What's next is that I'm going to visit my father at the hospital and pray that he survives his injuries." She shook her head at me, and for the first time, I saw an entirely different side of the woman I'd once been deeply in love with. "And then, I'm going to work with Cristiano to ensure neither of us goes to prison over what has happened. We started out only wanting to end the war between our families, but we ended up falling in love."

"Does that mean we're over?" I asked, knowing in my heart it was true but needing to hear the words from Francesca. "What about Emma?"

"I think we've been through too much to fix anything between you and me. I'd like to be friends, but it depends on what you do next." Francesca nodded at the officer to open the door to the squad car.

"What does that mean?" My heart began to race again.

"Emma needs to know I'm alive, that I love her. Are you going to keep me from my daughter?"

I hadn't formulated a plan. All I knew was that I had to be honest with Emma. "I won't keep you from her, but I'll do anything necessary to protect her from something like this ever happening again."

"As I said, maybe you and I can be friends. Once Cristiano's lawyers ensure he and I are released from custody, I intend to find a compromise. I know you won't let me have custody of Emma, and no court in the world would grant it to me after today."

"I'm angry with you right now. Let's have that discussion when we have a better sense of the future." I needed time to think. Hopefully, Emma didn't ask too many questions when she woke up. I was certain she'd seen Francesca for at least a minute inside the building. "I'm sorry about your father."

"You'll hear from me soon." After Francesca stepped inside the car, the officer shut the door and jumped in the front passenger seat.

As they took off, April sidled up. "You okay?"

"Not right now, but I will be."

"What can I do to help you?"

When April stopped speaking, I turned toward her, smiling for the first time that evening. Despite the darkness surrounding us in the sky, there was a floodlight shining from behind her that gave her an unusual glow. I saw the softened lime-green eyes of a woman who genuinely worried about me. I felt the consuming energy radiating from a huge heart that comforted me. "I have a wedding to attend on Friday. It's for my aunt and her fiancé, but it's a double wedding because two other people we know are getting married. After everything we've been through these last few months, I feel like I owe you something fun in return. How would you like to attend it with me?"

"Little Ayrwick," she teased with a curious voice. "Are you asking me on a date?"

"That all depends," I replied, shoving my hands in my pockets and lifting my chest. "Didn't you agree to stop calling me that awful, mean, absurd, rude name?"

"I suppose I did."

"Then I suppose I did too." I looked toward the sky and watched a few stars blazing down on us. "I'll call you tomorrow with all the details. For now, I need to take my daughter home."

April smiled merrily before slowly wandering away in search of an officer.

I felt a sudden change in the atmosphere and knew things were finally starting to move in a positive direction. As I stepped forward, I felt a pain shoot up my foot. "April, hold up," I called, jogging awkwardly to catch her. "I have a gift for you." I removed a shoe to retrieve the storage device containing the evidence the Castiglianos had originally provided.

Tilting her head, April looked at me with a peculiar expression. "Did you seriously just pull that out of your sweaty shoe and try to hand it to me as if it were a gift?"

"I don't know to give someone on a first date anymore. It's been a long time since I went on one of those. Besides, I showered three hours ago." I shrugged and rolled my eyes. "Should I just shut up?"

April leaned in really close, so that our lips were barely two inches apart. "If we weren't standing at a crime scene, and you hadn't just said what you said, I would have kissed you by now."

"That doesn't sound like a legitimate excuse to me. Go ahead, make my night," I replied, reducing the gap to only one inch and closing my eyes. We were breathing the same air at that very moment, and it felt like one shared breath could carry us through the whole night.

"I think I'll save that notion for our first legitimate date after the wedding. Or after you get divorced. I don't usually date married men." April stepped backward a few feet, and a charming and wicked smile formed on her lips when I opened my eyes again. "I have grand expectations of any man I date. You should know I'm hardly the type to be wooed easily."

I let her walk away claiming the final word this time. I never minded losing a small battle when I was absolutely certain I would win the entire war. I reflected on my interaction with Raquel earlier that evening when I promised myself only one of us would make it out alive tonight. At the time, I'd been scared it wouldn't be me. While I valued life way too much to feel good about what had ended up happening, I permitted myself to feel blessed that the good guys had won for a change. I returned to the Admissions Hall to be with my daughter and mother, uncertain what the next few days would bring but strong enough to handle it. When I walked through the main room, I saw a man kneeling beside Raquel's body. The forensics team was still addressing the scene, but they'd allowed Manny to visit before she was enclosed in a body bag.

Manny heard me approach. "I don't know what to say. How could I have been so foolish?"

I told Manny that we'd both been taken advantage of, so I knew how he felt. "Raquel didn't deserve to die, but we can't change the past. We can only focus on your future. I understand what's on your mind and how you're feeling. Please know that I'm here to support you however you need."

"The police told me everything she did. Is it true, Kellan? Did my wife really kill your brother's friend, Quint? And maybe your father-in-law?" The grief over everything he'd potentially done by giving his wife information about my family had finally impacted Manny.

"Yes, but there's something else you should know," I said, hesitant to burden the weakened man on top of everything he'd just learned. "Raquel told me earlier that your wedding wasn't real. She never filed the papers with the state, and the guy who married you didn't have a license."

Manny let the news settle for a minute, then hugged me. "I have mixed feelings about what you've just told me, but you are right. I am sorry for the loss and the pain impacting Raquel's family, but it means I have my life back, and I don't need to leave your sister alone with the diner."

Manny and I chatted for a few more minutes, and when he left campus, I had an inkling that the reason he'd been acting so weird around my sister wasn't just because he was afraid of deserting the diner once he thought Raquel would force him to leave Braxton.

He'd unexpectedly developed romantic feelings for my sister and wasn't sure how to tell her the truth.

The office door opened, and my mother waved me over. "Emma is awake."

I rushed into the room to check on my daughter. "Hey, baby girl. We can go home now. You need to get some sleep. Baxter will be so excited to see you, and I'll be home all day tomorrow with you. No camp until next week. How does that sound?"

Emma jumped into my arms and hugged me with more power than a seven-year-old girl should have. "That's awesome, but I have a question, Daddy."

I knew what it was, and I had no way of avoiding it. "What's that, sweet girl?" I said, looking toward my mother, who shuffled closer and kissed Emma's forehead.

"Was that Mommy I saw earlier, or was it just a dream?"

"Tell her the truth, Kellan. She's a strong little girl because of you. I have faith you will find the proper words," my mother whispered in my ear, shedding her own tears over the night's traumatic events. In an instant, my mother and I had grown closer once again. "You're both brilliant ones."

I replied to Emma, "Let's go home and have that discussion. I'll make you a cup of cocoa, we can climb into bed with Baxter, and Daddy will explain everything that happened to us tonight. Okay?"

Chapter 21

Thursday was the kind of bittersweet day that highlighted why I should be proud of my daughter and thrilled with the positive swing my life had taken upon returning home to Braxton. After a lengthy and difficult conversation the previous night, Emma understood that her mother had been taken by bad guys who'd wanted to hurt our family. We talked about the dangers of lies and secrets, remembered tons of precious moments she'd shared with her mother years earlier, and discussed how to move forward as a family once we sorted out the proper steps.

It was bittersweet because I had to tell Emma that her mother and I wouldn't be together in the future. I compared it to a divorce, which she understood, citing how her friend Shalini's parents had gotten divorced recently too. I realized that I'd need to think about filing formal separation papers in the future to officially announce my intent to divorce Francesca. Before we could do that, she'd have to be declared

348

legally alive again, at least as far as I understood from my brief Internet search. I decided to focus on Emma for the long holiday weekend and deal with the repercussions of everything else the following Monday.

Fern postponed the cable car ribbon-cutting ceremony until the subsequent week, so I spent Thursday with my family. Nana D had mayoral responsibilities to assure the citizens of Wharton County that the drama unfolding that week was fully under control. Nana D had even partnered with April to show a united front against crime in our towns, discussing how it happened and what everyone could do to prevent it from occurring again in the future. Limited details were released to the public for now. The county's official position was that the Castigliano and Las Vargas families ignited a turf war that had begun in Los Angeles and worked its way to Braxton the last few years. Nana D explained that the erstwhile sheriff had done little to hold the jewel thief accountable for his actions eight years ago, and we continued to suffer because of his dubious and unethical actions.

She lobbied hard to tell the truth to the citizens, but the county's attorney and new town council members felt it would be better to collect all the facts before distributing inaccurate information. Ultimately, Nana D yielded, not because she wasn't holding up her campaign promises to be honest but to ensure she didn't misspeak. She also threatened her staff with vague notions of torture if they didn't assemble a press release with all the details by the middle of the next week at the cable car reopening.

Nana D stopped by to chat before checking on Bertha, who was nearing the end of her battle with cancer. "The news about her brother-in-law's secrets and Quint's death has taken its toll on the woman. I'm afraid she won't make it until the end of the month, Kellan."

Nana D and I exchanged sorrowful glances over peppermint tea. I sliced the banana bread she'd brought and handed her a hearty piece. "Bertha didn't deserve a family like those two, but she had a good life. Everyone loves her in spite of all the trouble those two men caused."

We agreed to visit her together that weekend before she was too sick to recognize us as well as to take responsibility for her funeral plans. "Is Emma doing okay today?" Nana D asked, looking down the hall as my daughter rolled a tennis ball away from Baxter, trying to teach him to fetch.

"She slept in fairly late, then Mom and Dad came by to eat lunch with her. Gabriel was here, even Eleanor and Aunt Deirdre brought a few toys and games. Emma's tough, she'll be okay."

"When are you going to let her talk to Francesca?" Nana D had never really liked my wife, but she knew not to say anything disparaging, even if I'd agree with the words.

"Her father passed away at the hospital early this morning. Vincenzo's injuries were too invasive. She wants to see Emma as soon as possible, but we have an agreement that I'm hoping she'll stick to." We'd spoken for a few minutes when Francesca called to tell me what had happened to her father and promised to fairly co-parent for the sake of our daughter.

I hadn't told Emma that her nonno had passed away, but once we had details of his funeral service, I'd have another difficult conversation with my daughter that weekend. Francesca was allowed to remain at the hospital overnight with her father. Two cops, hand-selected by Connor and April, had been assigned guard duty outside the room to ensure nothing shady occurred. Francesca was distraught over her father's death, but she had a meeting with her family lawyer, Cristiano and his lawyer, and Wharton County's district attorney that afternoon to discuss next steps. The state of California would ask for extradition for crimes related to faking her death, which meant anything illegal she'd done in Pennsylvania would follow suit. It was too early to tell what would happen, but until any decisions were made, we didn't want to connect her and Emma. For one thing, it was a holiday weekend and no judge would change his schedule to accommodate the situation. For another, Francesca and Cecilia had a funeral to prepare, which might occur while they spent the weekend in prison.

"When does Emma think she'll see her mother again?" Nana D asked while stirring her tea.

"I told her that Nonno was hurt and in the hospital for a few days and that her mommy was taking care of him. I felt bad lying, but I will tell her the truth. Is it wrong to want her to have one happy moment at tomorrow's wedding before crushing her again?"

Nana D wrapped her arms around me and refused to let go. "It's not, brilliant one. You are the only one who knows what's best for her. I'll sit with you two when we get home from the wedding tomorrow night, and we can tell her together."

"Thanks, Nana D. She loves you so much, it'll be easier if she knows you're doing okay."

"I'm never gonna die. You've heard me say that ever since you were a small boy. I'm not letting my family get away with an easy life, not while I can live to a hundred-and-twenty and torture them every day," she replied with a waggish smile, then pulled out her phone to read an incoming text message.

"Urgent mayoral business?"

"Not exactly. It's your Uncle Zachary. He needs to speak with me as soon as possible," Nana D said, sitting back in the chair.

"Isn't he on a safari in Africa saving the elephants?" My uncle was an amazing veterinarian, but he'd taken off the previous summer while I'd still lived in Los Angeles. He'd been granted a one-year contract to save a rare breed from extinction and had jumped on the opportunity.

"Yep, hold on, let me call him quick," she replied, pulling up his number and dialing him. "Maybe he's getting married too!"

Uncle Zach had once been married. His wife died during childbirth many years ago. She'd been pregnant with twins, but unfortunately, only one of the babies had survived. My cousin, Ulan, was the boy who lived, and he'd been given that name because it meant *first born of twins* in Africa. Ulan was currently fifteen years old and had moved with his father to Africa for the school year.

"Zach, is that you? I can barely hear you," Nana said, then reprimanded him for not returning home for his sister's wedding.

While Nana D released a bunch of monotonous *uh huhs* and *ah hahs*, I checked on Emma. She and Baxter had cuddled up on her bed as she read a story about a little dog who'd gotten lost but found a new home. She looked at me and smiled when I poked my head further into her room. My own phone chimed as I shuffled down the hallway. It was a Los Angeles number, but I couldn't be sure who was calling. I hoped it wasn't a news outlet who'd gotten wind of Vincenzo's death and wanted an interview.

"Hello, this is Kellan Ayrwick."

"Hi, it's Gary Hill from the television network that owns the rights to your show, *Dark Reality*. I want to have a conversation with you about a few things."

Dark Reality technically wasn't my show. I'd been an assistant director on the last two episodes of the first season, but once it had been put on hold and the main director was fired, I was out of a job earlier that year. "Good to meet you. I guess you're the new executive producer who assumed control."

"Yes, that would be me. Do you have a minute to speak?"

"To be honest, it's not really a good time. I have a family emergency and a funeral to attend, but I could catch up in a few days." If I was about to be let go formally, I'd rather deal with more shocking news at a future date.

"I understand. That's not a problem. Listen, maybe you could fly out to see me next week. I've been doing some research on the show and your background. I've got a proposal for you to consider."

I guessed I wasn't being fired. "I thought that decision was on hold until early next year?"

"It was, but I move faster than my sluggish predecessors. I've read your files and the proposal you made to that former nimrod director who got canned. I want you back in Hollywood, and if you're up for it, we want to televise your idea to...."

I stopped listening to him at that point. I couldn't believe my ears. I'd just finished saying how being home in Braxton might've been the best decision I'd made all year long. Now, this happened. I agreed to a follow-up call next week and hung up with Gary to let the news settle.

I strolled into the kitchen in a daze, catching the very end of Nana D's phone call with my uncle.

"I'm not able to do that, Zach. If I could, I'd help you out, but I'm hardly at home anymore," she said to him as she looked up at me. A huge smile overtook her face before she responded again. "Actually, I have another idea in mind. Go ahead, book the flight. We'll make this work."

Nana D and my uncle talked for a few more minutes while I cleaned up the saucers and cups from our afternoon tea. What had she done to herself now? Nana D slammed her phone on the table and guffawed. "That boy of mine is absentminded and never plans ahead."

"What did he do now?" I shouted over the running water.

"He accepted an extension on that elephant project, and now he's gonna be in Africa for another year. I love my children to death, but they might actually stop me from reaching my goal of living another fifty years." Nana D grabbed her shawl from the back of the chair and tapped me on the shoulder.

I didn't like the wicked expression on her face. "I heard you tell him you couldn't do something, then you changed your mind. Spill it. You look like a cat who swallowed a canary."

"Now that the idea has sunk in, it's actually quite spectacular, brilliant one." She yanked my arm so I would bend down for her to kiss my cheek. "You won't be able to live here anymore, but we'll find you a new place."

"Huh?" I'd come to love living in the cottage. Why was she kicking me out? As Nana D walked toward the front door, I turned off the faucet, dried my hands, and raced to the living room. "What did you do?"

"Zach is gonna be too busy to pay attention to his son. He wants Ulan to stay with me for the next year. The schools are fine where he's working, but it's ostensibly not the same." Nana D pushed open the front door and sauntered onto the porch.

"What does that have to do with me moving out of the cottage?" If someone could lock my nana in a closet for the rest of her life, it would be the biggest blessing I'd ever receive.

"With my duties as the new mayor, I certainly won't have time to babysit Ulan. I'm done with raising kids, especially a hormonal teenager entering manhood. Your Uncle Campbell's still in the Amazon. Deirdre and Timothy will be newlyweds hopping back and forth across the Atlantic. That simply won't do." She stepped onto the main pathway and walked toward the driveway.

"Yeah, so?" I knew what was coming, but I didn't want to say it.

"Your parents have the room, but honestly, with the way some of your siblings turned out...." She swung open the car door, then spun, her hand cupping her chin and one finger tapping the side of her cheek.

"You. Did. Not."

"I did. Ulan will live with you for the next year while his father is trying to do something positive for the precious elephants. Emma will love having her cousin around. It'll be like an older brother." Nana D sat in her car, started the engine, and rolled down her window. "I guess you better start looking for a new place. With only two bedrooms, the three of you can't live here comfortably. Maybe Gabriel can take over the cottage now." Nana D waved at me and sped down the driveway to her next meeting.

I grunted. Twice. And then a third time because I realized I'd stepped in dog poop. "Emma, Baxter is not supposed to be out front unsupervised...."

* * *

On Friday, also Independence Day, we attended the much-anticipated double wedding. Aunt Deirdre asked me to escort her down the aisle since her father had passed away years ago, and her two brothers were out of town. She'd considered asking my father but quickly abandoned the idea. Nana D would be on one side of my aunt, and there was no way she'd share the role with Wesley Ayrwick.

Aunt Deirdre looked stunning in her vintage wedding gown when I met her in the dressing room. In just a few minutes, we'd walk down the path to a covered gazebo at Crilly Lake where she'd marry Timothy Paddington. Meanwhile, Timothy's sister, Jennifer Paddington, wore a beautiful but modern wedding gown that practically disguised her growing belly. Her Uncle Millard would escort her down the same aisle to marry Arthur Terry, Fern's son.

Friends and family of both couples were in attendance. Even my siblings, Penelope and Hampton, had returned for the weekend. Gabriel and his boyfriend, Sam Taft—Jennifer and Timothy's nephew—sat in the front row cheering them on. I saw them holding hands as I accompanied my aunt to the gazebo. On the opposite side of the seating area, Fern waved to me with tears flowing from her eyes. She'd never been so proud of her son and couldn't hold back her excitement about becoming a grandmother soon.

Eleanor had left the diner behind for the day, promoting Manny as her new manager, at least once Maggie, her mostly silent partner in the business, agreed with the change. He'd hold double duty as her chef in the meantime, but I was certain new things would blossom for them in the future. My sister might fight it at first, just as she struggled to deny everything until ultimately yielding to the truth. Perhaps she'd finally give up on my best friend, Connor, who was seated with Maggie in the far back making googly eyes at his date. Honestly, those two were meant for each other all along.

Emma was the flower girl, and she walked down the aisle leading Baxter at her side. She'd practiced with him several times, but no matter how hard she'd begged, he kept eating the cushion and swallowing the fake plastic rings that we'd strapped to his back. We weren't taking a chance that he'd eat the real ones on the wedding day, so Emma kept them safe in a small pocket in her dress. She told everyone how pretty she felt and that she couldn't wait until her wedding day in a few years. I explained that she would never be allowed to get married as long as I was alive. I won't share the inappropriate gesture Nana D taught her as an apt response—and at a wedding, no doubt!

Nana D shed another tear when the priest asked her who was giving away Aunt Deirdre. I handed her my handkerchief, but she brushed it aside, claiming her allergies were acting up from being outside near the lake. Grandpop Michael was with us in spirit; I could feel him at my side. I stepped off the gazebo and rushed to my seat, where April waited for me. I hadn't yet seen her that day. My attention had been occupied, keeping us on schedule and stopping others from bawling their eyes out.

When she came into view, my eyes bulged and my lips curled. She'd had her hair professionally styled into a chignon secured at the nape of her neck. A gorgeous green dress clung to her body, accentuating the shimmering lime pools that were her eyes. The perfect amount of cleavage peeked from the top of her dress, tempting me more than I desired, and a slit in the dress revealed two exquisite, shapely legs finished off with a pair of strappy heels. This was not the same sheriff I'd frequently seen wearing a tweed blazer, plain jeans, and boring boots.

"Who are you, and what have you done with April Montague?" I asked, sitting next to her and feeling my body react to the sudden hotness of my date.

"I assure you, Kellan… what you see is what you get with me. Everything is real, and there are many sides to me you've not been exposed to before." April grabbed my hand and shushed me. "There's a wedding going on here. Don't make me do something to shut you up." She opened her purse and showed me that *Old Betsy* was waiting inside, in case the need to make its appearance arose again.

When the ceremony ended, two new couples had become husband and wife. I reflected on my own wedding day—both the positives and the negatives that had since materialized. Despite a rough week, we had found our compromise, but my heart still panged for my wife's recent loss. I would visit her the next day to do whatever I could to help plan her father's funeral. She knew already, but I wanted to ensure they played a *Billy Joel* song to give Vincenzo a proper send-off.

The wedding reception was held at the country club not too far from Crilly Lake. After all the toasts, I turned to April. "This is probably an odd question, but have you ever been married before?" I knew she'd been engaged at one point, before her fiancé had been killed in a drive-by shooting.

"I feel like I know everything about your life. I guess I haven't shared much about mine other than what happened to my brother and my fiancé," she replied with a devilish gleam in her eyes.

"You didn't answer the question," I said, curious why she was avoiding the topic.

"No, I didn't answer it. Would you consider this our first date?" April countered, clinking our champagne glasses together. "Even though you are still married."

"Yes, I believe I would." I saw Nana D approaching and felt an urge to run for my life.

"We probably shouldn't cover all our history on a first date, right?" April said before swallowing half the contents of the glass. "Let's enjoy the process of getting to know one another."

What was she trying to tell me? Had she been married prior to the last fiancé? "Um, that's not fair. You know about Francesca. Shouldn't you be equally forthcoming about—"

"Your grandmother is almost here. We have time to discuss all that stuff, Kellan."

"Is it true?" Nana D asked, shifting her gaze from me to April, then back again a few times. "You understand my grandson is still a married man. And that I'm your boss based on our current jobs."

"Am I here with Kellan in an official capacity, you mean?" April offered as a response to Nana D.

Nana D crossed her arms. "Hmmm... I need a minute alone with my grandson, Sheriff. Would you mind refilling my glass?"

April took Nana D's flute. "Rest assured, Mayor Danby, I'm not the kind of woman to pry in another couple's marital woes. For the moment, I'm enjoying the company of a handsome guy who helped me solve a few investigations. What the future holds, I suppose we'll all find out." She winked at me, then seductively glided toward the bar on the other side of the room. Was that sashay for me?

My mouth hung agape until Nana D shut it with two fingers. "Maybe I misjudged that woman. You could do worse. You have done worse, actually, now that I think—"

"Please stay out of it. I have no idea what's going on, and my life is a mess, but I'm happy to be here with our family." I scanned the room to verify Emma still stood on my father's toes as he led her around the dance floor.

"That's fine. We have plenty of time to talk about it this weekend after we figure out how to welcome Ulan when he arrives next month," she complied, resting her head on my shoulder.

"Next month? I thought I had a few months before he flew here. How am I gonna find a new place to live?" I didn't dare bring up the phone call I'd gotten from Hollywood. Nana D might strangle me in front of everyone if I told her I had an offer to leave town again.

"Can it, or I'll slap your bottom silly in front of your new girlfriend." She tapped her foot against the floor, deep in thought. "You know, the old Grey place was on the market. I'm not sure it is anymore, at least if you believe the rumors."

Eleanor strode up just as Nana D mentioned the dilapidated house on the corner of Main Street near Millionaire's Mile that no one would buy. "The place that's been haunted for fifty years?"

Nana D smiled and slapped her thigh. "Yep, that one. The plumbing is leaking. The walls are falling. Just yesterday, a ceiling tile smashed into my shoulder and an angry spirit floated by me."

"I thought that place was ready to be demolished," I suggested meekly as my nerves prickled.

"It is," Eleanor said, tossing her head back and forth to the beat of the music. "Too many people claim they hear noises and voices emanating from it all the time."

"Ever since that woman vanished, there have been rumors about ghosts visiting the place. I blame it all on Hiram Grey," Nana D replied.

"What's he got to do with the woman's disappearance?" I asked.

"Don't you know anything about our town's history, big brother? His first wife went missing the day of that big fire in the old library. No one ever heard from her again." Eleanor shook her head repeatedly, reminding me of all the times she, Gabriel, and Nana D had ganged up on me in the past.

"That woman put a curse on their house before she skipped town. People always claim they see a spook haunting the place on the anniversary of the fire every year since it happened," Nana D said.

"Are you two pulling my leg?" My stomach sunk and my throat began to close.

Nana D was never one to tell ghost stories or believe in that sort of nonsense. Even though Eleanor claimed she was in touch with her psychic abilities, it was only something we joked about. "I don't know, Kellan. All I know is that's an historical home, and it would be a shame to let it go to waste."

"Are you proposing that I should buy the old Grey house, fix it up, and move into it?" I rolled my eyes at Nana D's foolish suggestion. "Nope, not happening. I will not deal with the paranormal or supernatural. I draw a line at the types of things I investigate when it comes to evaporating spooks!"

"You don't have to buy it. I already made an offer to the cantankerous old judge this morning. That restless tomcat couldn't wait to unload the place. You'll be able to afford it, trust me, brilliant one." Nana D accepted her refilled champagne flute from April, who'd returned in time to hear the news and toast my potential new home.

"I can handle dead people, but I'm not ready to live among a tribe of vengeful ghosts." Then, I hung my head and accepted Nana D would always run my life. What kind of adventure were we in store for next? It couldn't be worse than all the chaos and drama I'd stumbled upon so far this year. Could it?

Dear Reader,

Thank you for taking time to read *Mistaken Identity Crisis*. Word of mouth is an author's best friend and much appreciated. If you enjoyed it, please consider supporting this author:

- Leave a book review on Amazon US, Amazon (also your own country if different), Goodreads, BookBub, and any other book site you follow to help market and promote this book

- Tell your friends, family, and colleagues all about this author and his books

- Share brief posts on your social media platforms and tag the book (#MistakenIdentityCrisis or #BraxtonMysteries) or author (#JamesJCudney) on Twitter, Facebook, Instagram, Pinterest, LinkedIn, WordPress, Tumblr, YouTube, Bloglovin, and SnapChat

- Suggest the book for book clubs, to bookstores, or to any libraries you know

* * *

Sneak Peek at Haunted House Ghost (#5)

It's Halloween, and excitement is brewing in Braxton to carve jack-o'-lanterns, go on haunted hayrides, and race through the spooky corn maze at the Fall Festival. Despite a former occupant's fervent warnings, Kellan renovates and moves into a mysterious old house. When a ruthless ghost promises retribution, our fearless professor turns to the eccentric town historian and an eerie psychic known for her explosive predictions, to communicate with the apparition.

Construction workers discover a fifty-year-old skeleton after breaking ground on the new Memorial Library wing. Could it be Prudence, Judge Hiram Grey's first wife, who disappeared during a fiery

Vietnam War protest that destroyed parts of the campus? While Kellan and April dance around the chemistry sparking between them, a suspicious accident at the Fall Festival leaves Hiram in a coma and another dead body to investigate. Kellan's research digs up a tale of horror and pain about the true history and dastardly connections of the Grey family, forcing April to accelerate her plan to capture the elusive killer and placate the revenge-seeking ghost.

If you haven't read the first three books in the series...

Academic Curveball (#1)

Who killed professor Abby Monroe? When Kellan Ayrwick returns home for his father's retirement, he finds a dead body in Diamond Hall's stairwell. Unfortunately, Kellan has a connection to the victim, and so do several members of his family. Soon after, the college's athletic program receives mysterious donations, a nasty blog denounces his father, and a trickster attempts to change student grades. Someone is playing games on campus, but none of the facts add up. With the help of his eccentric and trouble-making nana, Kellan tries to stay out of the sheriff's way. But who is behind the murder?

Broken Heart Attack (#2)

Who killed Gwendolyn Paddington? When an extra ticket becomes available to see the dress rehearsal of King Lear, Kellan tags along with Nana D and her buddies. But once one of them dies of an apparent heart attack in the middle of the second act, Nana D asks Kellan to investigate. With family members suddenly in debt and a secret rendezvous between an unlikely pair, Kellan learns that the Paddingtons might not be as clean-cut as everyone thinks. But can Kellan find the killer, or will he get caught up his own stage fright?

Flower Power Trip (#3)

At a masquerade ball to raise money for renovations to Memorial Library, Kellan finds a dead body dressed in a Dr. Evil costume. Did Maggie's sister kill an annoying guest staying at the Roarke and Daughters Inn, or does the victim have a closer connection to someone else at Braxton College? As Kellan helps school president Ursula bury a secret from her past and discover the identity of her stalker, he unexpectedly encounters a missing family member. Everything seems to trace back to the Stoddards: a new family who recently moved in. Between the murder, a special flower exhibit, and strange postcards arriving weekly, Kellan can't decide which mystery in his life should take priority. Unfortunately, the biggest one of all hasn't been exposed. When it is, Kellan won't know what hit him.

About the Author

James is my given name, but most folks call me Jay. I live in New York City, grew up on Long Island, and graduated from Moravian College. I spent fifteen years building a technology career in the retail, sports, media, and entertainment industries. I enjoyed my job, but a passion for books and stories had been missing for far too long. I'm a voracious reader in my favorite genres (thriller, suspense, contemporary, mystery, and historical fiction). as books transport me to a different world where I can immerse myself in so many fantastic cultures and places. I'm an avid genealogist who hopes to visit all the German, Scottish, Irish, and British villages my ancestors emigrated from in the 18th and 19th centuries.

Writing has been a part of my life as much as my heart, my mind, and my body. I decided to pursue my passion by dusting off the creativity inside my head and drafting outlines for several novels. I quickly realized I was back in my element growing happier and more excited with life each day. My goal in writing is to connect with readers who want to be part of great stories and who enjoy interacting with authors. To get a strong picture of who I am, check out my author website or my blog. It's full of humor and eccentricity, sharing connections with everyone I follow—all in the hope of building a network of friends across the world.

When I completed the first book, *Watching Glass Shatter*, I knew I'd stumbled upon my passion again, suddenly dreaming up characters, plots, and settings all day long. I chose my second novel, *Father Figure*, through a poll on my blog where I let everyone vote for their favorite plot and character summaries. It is with my third book, *Academic Curveball*, the first in the Braxton Campus Mysteries, where I immersed myself in a college campus full of so much activity, I could hardly stop thinking about new murder scenes or character relationships to finish writing the current story. Come join in the fun!

List of Books

Watching Glass Shatter (October 2017)
Father Figure (April 2018)
Braxton Campus Mysteries
    Academic Curveball - #1 (October 2018)
    Broken Heart Attack - #2 (November 2018)
    Flower Power Trip - #3 (March 2019)
    Mistaken Identity Crisis - #4 (June 2019)
    Haunted House Ghost - #5 (September 2019)

Websites & Blog

Website: https://jamesjcudney.com/
Blog: https://thisismytruthnow.com/
Next Chapter author page:
https://www.nextchapter.pub/authors/james-j-cudney

Social Media Links

Amazon:
https://www.amazon.com/James-J.-Cudney/e/B076B6PB3M/
Twitter: https://twitter.com/jamescudney4
Facebook:
https://www.facebook.com/JamesJCudneyIVAuthor/
Facebook:
https://www.facebook.com/BraxtonCampusMysteries/
Pinterest:
https://www.pinterest.com/jamescudney4/
Instagram:
https://www.instagram.com/jamescudney4/
Goodreads:
https://www.goodreads.com/jamescudney4
LinkedIn:
https://www.linkedin.com/in/jamescudney4

You might also like:

Murder on Tyneside by Eileen Thornton

To read the first chapter for free, please head to:
https://www.nextchapter.pub/books/murder-on-
tyneside-cozy-crime-mystery

Mistaken Identity Crisis
ISBN: 978-4-86745-280-6 (Mass Market)

Published by
Next Chapter
1-60-20 Minami-Otsuka
170-0005 Toshima-Ku, Tokyo
+818035793528
27th April 2021

Lightning Source UK Ltd.
Milton Keynes UK
UKHW041305060223
416419UK00006B/188

9 784867 452806